VALLEY OF DEATH

ELITE RESPONSE FORCE BOOK TWO

P R ADAMS

PROMETHEAN TALES

This is a work of fiction. Names, characters, places and incidents are used fictitiously. Any resemblance to actual events, or persons, living or dead, is coincidental. All rights reserved. No part of this publication may be reproduced, or transmitted in any form or by any means, electronic or otherwise, without written permission from the author.

VALLEY OF DEATH

Copyright © 2017 P R Adams

All rights reserved, including the right to reproduce this book, or portions thereof, in any form.

Illustration © Tom Edwards
TomEdwardsDesign.com

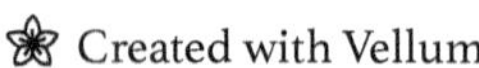 Created with Vellum

ALSO BY P R ADAMS

For updates on new releases and news on other series, visit my website and sign up for my mailing list at:

http://www.p-r-adams.com

Books in the On The Brink Universe

The Stefan Mendoza Trilogy

Into Twilight

Gone Dark

End State

The Rimes Trilogy

Momentary Stasis

Transition of Order

Awakening to Judgment

The ERF Series

Turning Point

Valley of Death

Jungle Dark

Chariot Bright

Dawn Fire (2018)

<u>**The Burning Sands Trilogy**</u>

Beneath Burning Sands

Across Burning Sands

Beyond Burning Sands

∾

<u>**Books in The Chain Series**</u>

The Chain: Shattered

The Journey Home

Rock of Salvation

From the Depths

Ever Shining

DEDICATION

For the service members who served in Afghanistan in 2002.

1

8 September 2175. 50 LY from Plymouth Colony.

IN THE VOID OF SPACE, a silver-blue glow appeared a nanometer slice through nothingness. The glow brightened and traced the edges of an opening as it widened into a circle fifty meters across. A roughly cylindrical vessel passed through, and the glow tore free of the rift edges to attach to the vessel's gray hull. That hull ran nearly six meters in diameter and fifty meters in length. Milliseconds passed as the vessel burst through the hole, which closed. After a moment, the silver-blue glow faded, and the vessel fired maneuvering rockets to decelerate. Panels slid open midway across the hull's surface, each ninety-degrees apart, and thick, metallic arms telescoped out. At the end of each arm, missiles tipped with blinking, red lights shifted on gimbals, as if seeking a target. Each missile was less than a meter long and carried little fuel. Before the vessel came to a complete stop, the missiles launched.

After several seconds, the missiles stopped firing their rockets, and the tips burst open, ejecting hundreds of tiny sensors in multiple directions. Instantly, the sensors started sending data back to the missiles, which relayed the data back to the vessel. It analyzed the data flow for several minutes, then it fired the maneuvering rockets again, and the silver-blue glow covered the gray surface once more. The vessel accelerated, and another rift opened.

The vessel passed through the rift, and the silver-blue glow disappeared. The missiles tumbled for a short while longer before detonating in bright flashes, scrambling the sensors.

Not even ten minutes passed from the vessel's arrival to its departure.

MEYERS SAT in Conference Room 3 of the *Valdez*, the smallest of the ship's meeting areas. He rocked side to side in his chair, his lean body too light to make the chair squeak much. The room was dark except for the display screens suspended from the ceiling. His eyes seemed even bluer in the cyan glow of the displays, and his blond hair seemed gray. He was seated at the long, black table that dominated the center of the room. That table, a gift from the Intelligence Bureau, amounted to a concentrator for the ship's processing, a recent redundancy system added to counteract systems attacks the Elite Response Force had suffered on Bellar Colony. As he drummed the plastic tabletop with shaking fingers, Meyers glanced up at the displays, trying to imagine what it would show when the message buoy returned.

If it returned, he corrected himself.

But it had to return. Taylor had always been reliable.

Meyers twisted slightly at the chime from the hatch. "Enter."

The hatch unlocked and opened, revealing Master Sergeant Carl Paxton, the ERF's most senior NCO. His skin could have been cut from old leather. It would be generous to say he was a plain man. Standing straight, he was maybe 175 centimeters, and Paxton rarely stood straight. He had brown hair going gray, thinning, and trimmed close to his scalp. Silhouetted by the passageway lights, his crooked nose was almost comical. He could have had the nose fixed but it was a point of pride, originally broken in his final fight with his father.

Paxton glanced up at the display, then settled into a chair at Meyers's left as the hatch closed. "Water don't boil any faster from watching, Colonel."

Meyers glanced down at his drumming fingers. "I know. I'm just worried."

"Worried about whether she'll show or worried what she has to say?"

"Yeah."

Paxton chuckled softly. "Maybe worried someone'll tell you no if she has what you're looking for?"

Meyers stopped drumming the tabletop. "You know, I've never been good with people telling me no."

"I noticed."

"When you have people telling you from as far back as you can remember that you can't be more than what the system allows, it eats at you."

"I'd imagine so. Family, too?"

Meyers nodded and turned his attention back to the displays. "My parents fought it in their own way—teachers, artists, theater...they did it all. Just enough to get by in an old Pennsylvania mining town. But they thought that was as high as we could shoot. Me? I wanted that big money, living out there in the metacorporate orbitals. Show them all, right? No genetic modification, the first non-Jimmy hired for an engineering position, move up to head a division."

"Dream big."

"Yeah." Meyers winced and looked down at his feet. "I ever tell you I got frostbite? Walking eight kilometers in a blizzard to make a couple hundred bucks. Tuition savings. Because I was told I couldn't."

Paxton snorted and said something, but it was lost in the chime of the hatch.

"Enter," Meyers said. "Leave the hatch open for now."

The hatch opened, admitting Intelligence Bureau Agent Ladell Barlowe and Private Becky Starling. Barlowe settled opposite Paxton; Starling settled to Barlowe's right. Barlowe was Paxton's height but slim, like Meyers. Starling was a little taller and broader than Barlowe, with shoulders nearly as wide as Paxton's. She matched Barlowe's prim and proper mannerisms—tapping at a shiny black, palm-sized device secured to the back of her hand and then looking up at the display before staring off into space at her own earpiece display. A small, black spider rested beneath her collar.

"That an approved ADPAX, Private?" Paxton leaned across the conference room table to get a better look at the device but ended up staring at the spider.

Starling's brown eyes focused on the real world, meeting Paxton's for a second before dropping to the tabletop. She bit her full upper lip, and the spider-bot shifted deeper beneath the cover of her collar. "Well, Sergeant, I—"

Barlowe blinked rapidly, as if trying to clear dust from his eyes, then he looked at Meyers. "It's issued by IB. I figure she works with me all the time—"

Meyers raised a hand. "It's good. Private Starling, make sure you register that with the *Valdez's* security officer. Same with that spider-bot. I don't need anyone getting upset that we're encroaching on their domain."

"Lonny, it'll show up as an IB asset on their Grid." Barlowe sighed dramatically and pursed his lips. "No one's going to say anything."

Steps echoed in the passageway outside, and Meyers turned to see Captain Brigston and Lieutenant Commander Cooper approaching the conference room from the lift. Brigston seemed to be moving with a purposeful slowness; Cooper—hunched over and red in the face— seemed to be uncomfortable with the pace. He was tall, with broad shoulders and a burliness that combined with a heavy brow, deep-set eyes, and slow manner to give the impression of a gentle giant. Brigston fiddled with the buttons of his white shirt where it bunched over the slightest beginnings of a paunch. He was a few months shy of forty, and as if on cue, his stringy, brown hair had started to thin enough that his pale scalp showed. He adjusted his belt and stepped into the conference room.

Meyers stood, as did Paxton and Starling. A second later, Barlowe stood as well.

"Sorry for keeping you waiting," Brigston said as he settled into the chair at the far end of the table opposite Meyers. "We've been checking systems again in case your lead comes through and we have to jump."

"I think that's a great idea." Meyers settled into his chair and tapped the tabletop. "So, you'll be taking this offline?"

"Before we jump," Cooper said. He was still standing, his pale face washed blue by the displays. He looked at Brigston, who nodded once. "We can create a new Grid and run every system from this platform. Instant failover, negligible performance impact to critical systems. Hey, are those ADPAX systems? I don't think I've seen them before."

Meyers flinched and wished he'd simply told Barlowe and Starling to put the devices away.

Barlowe's eyes narrowed. "IB Advanced Personal Computing Systems III."

"IB? Are they hooked into the Grid?" Cooper looked at Meyers.

Meyers choked back a sigh. "Private Starling was planning to register hers after the meeting. Who's the security officer?"

"I can handle that." Cooper pointed at Starling's device. "But they shouldn't be on the Grid without authorization."

"They're IB assets," Barlowe said. "You understand we have—"

"Can we table this for the moment?" Meyers looked at Brigston, pleading.

Brigston waved at the seat to his right, and Cooper settled in, blushing.

Meyers looked back up at the display. "Barring disaster, the probe is five minutes, twenty-two seconds into its search by now. I thought we should all be here in case it returns on schedule. Or doesn't."

Brigston turned toward Barlowe. "Still nothing back from IB on this Taylor?"

"There's no way the message could reach Earth and return to Plymouth in the time I had to get a query off." Barlowe's coppery brown skin almost glistened in the blue glow of the overhead display. "Everything I have on her in the Plymouth database is too old to be useful. She left the Rangers during the drawdowns before the Metacorporate War, started up her mercenary outfit, and three years ago Taylor's Rangers— her company—purchased a refurbished yacht, an old EEC research vessel."

"What about her Army records?" Brigston leaned back in his seat and looked from Meyers to Paxton and then Starling. The look was almost imperious, as was the tone.

Meyers found himself having to bite back a response. On one level, he could understand Brigston's behavior but on another, it was unbecoming. "I can vouch for Cassidy. I knew her in the Rangers. She was a good soldier."

Paxton jerked his head toward Meyers. "My assessment matches the colonel's, sir."

Brigston smiled at Starling but it seemed to Meyers forced, strained. "Private?"

Starling jumped in her seat. "Sir?"

"Do you have anything to add?" Brigston shot Meyers a questioning look, as if challenging the decision to include Starling in the meeting.

Don't start something, Jeremy, Meyers thought. Not now.

"Well, I can only tell you what Captain Taylor's records showed, Captain." Starling stared off into space. "Uh, she was decorated: Purple Heart, Meritorious Service, campaign ribbons—"

Brigston leaned forward. "But what's your *assessment*, Private? You *are* here to provide intelligence analysis, aren't you?"

Meyers caught a glare from Barlowe, but there wasn't much to be done.

Starling looked down at the black tabletop. "Well, based off what we know, I think this sounds like a worthwhile lead to check out, sir." She cleared her throat, possibly to deal with the quiver in her voice. "Honorable discharge, decorated, no challenges to her request for her personnel to be registered as Class IV Lancers, and she has a good history with the colonel and master sergeant. The message sender matches the registration of the Taylor's Rangers vessel of record, and the Universal Grid ID matches hers. I agree with Colonel Meyers that the numbers she used in the data look like code. It didn't take much to correlate those numbers to SunCorps' operations during the Metacorporate War once Colonel Meyers provided the context. So, yes, sir, I think she's trying to contact us about Waverley."

Brigston nodded. "Thank you."

"So, what's the worst case scenario?" Meyers asked. "We jump to the coordinates, we lose systems off the jump and flip to the backup concentrator, and some SunCorps vessel rigged with explosives or missiles comes at us. We can handle this threat, right? That's why we spent so much on this." He patted the black tabletop.

"Worst case—" Brigston looked up as the display glowed brighter.

A rift appeared in space, widening, then closing after a ten-meter-long cylindrical vessel shot through and began decelerating.

"That's our buoy vessel," Cooper said, each word drawn out slow and soft.

"Confirmation of a vessel waiting at the coordinates," Barlowe said to Meyers. "Single vessel within sensor range. Matches the profile of her ship."

Meyers locked eyes with Brigston. There was a mixture of understandable caution and ridiculous resentment in Brigston's stare, but Meyers hoped it wouldn't come to anything. He lifted his hands about shoulder width, palms showing toward the *Valdez's* captain. "If that's her, and she's got a lead on Waverley, we can't pass on this opportunity."

Brigston shook his head. "Why not just come to Plymouth?"

"For the same reason she wouldn't just transmit the data. She's got something big. She's worried. That's why she gave us this narrow window of time to meet her in the middle of nowhere."

"It's the perfect place for an ambush."

"Everywhere is the perfect place for an ambush." Meyers felt his blood pressure rising. "We barely have time to get the systems online and make the jump to the rendezvous point."

Brigston adjusted his collar. "I have a ship and crew to worry about."

A ship and crew that were placed at the ERF's disposal, Meyers thought to himself.

Brigston craned his neck to look fully at Cooper. "Lieutenant Commander Cooper?"

"It's what we're here for, sir." Cooper's cheeks darkened, and he squinted so that his small eyes were barely visible. Those were familiar signs of discomfort when he was forced to counter his captain.

"All right." Brigston stood.

Meyers stood as well. He sighed with relief when Barlowe stood nearly as quickly as the rest.

Brigston smiled, but it looked more like a grimace. "Let's see what Captain Taylor has to offer—information or an ambush. Commander Cooper."

Meyers waited until Brigston and Cooper—now moving at a normal pace—were gone, then said, "Please close the conference room hatch and lock it."

The hatch closed and clicked.

"I'm sorry about that." Meyers felt his shoulders slumping as he spoke. There was a pressure building in his chest, a tension that had only gotten worse over the last few months. "We're all feeling the stress."

The corner of Paxton's mouth curled up in a snarl. "Some're handling it a lot better than others."

"Perhaps. What matters right now is we've got to be ready in case this turns out to be some sort of deception. Agent Barlowe, Private Starling, that means the two of you providing whatever support you can to the *Valdez's* crew. Can you get with Commander Cooper?"

Starling nodded despite Barlowe's sour face.

"Thanks. And thank you for providing your assessment for the captain. That was good work under pressure." Meyers smiled, drawing an embarrassed smile from her; she quickly looked away.

"I think we better get with the commander now, Colonel," Starling said.

"Open the hatch, please," Meyers said. The conference room hatch unlocked and opened. He watched Barlowe and Starling until they reached the lift, feeling the tension in his chest increase at the noticeable limp both exhibited. "Close and lock."

Paxton arched an eyebrow and his eyes flicked from the hatch to Meyers. "She's a soldier, Colonel."

"So now I'm coddling her?"

"Not yet."

Meyers sighed and plopped back into his seat. "She's pushing herself hard. Dr. LaRoque said she should go another two months with physical therapy or she could be facing long-term spinal injury. Same with Ladell."

"She'll be fine. Her femur's fully healed. That was the bigger problem. Everyone knows about the deadline. Millions of soldiers out there unemployed. No one wants to add to those numbers."

And that was the ultimatum facing them all: They had less than a year to find Chad Milton Waverley, former CEO of SunCorps, the most powerful metacorporation known to humans. If he wasn't dead or jailed in that time, the United Nations would shut the ERF down, and they would all be out of a job. It was a terrible thing to hold over their heads, but there was nothing Meyers could do about it.

"Looks like the captain's got a burr up his ass," Paxton said.

"The restructuring." Meyers couldn't believe the pace the UN was moving at. They could drag their feet over the most trivial request for munitions, personnel, and tech upgrades but when it came to cost-cutting, they were like lightning. Budget cuts and drawdowns were one thing; going after the Navy was something entirely different. "I think he's giving serious thought to resigning his commission rather than taking on Army rank."

"Combined Forces rank. Everyone's going through the same thing, Colonel."

Meyers shrugged. The Army was getting another uniform change, more ranks were being combined, and everyone was becoming a soldier in the Combined Forces. Hardly the sort of system shock the Navy folks were facing. On top of that, Brigston's date of rank would be adjusted to make him officially subordinate to Meyers. It was messy.

The intercom announced the countdown to acceleration and activating the gravitic systems, which amounted to entering into a wormhole. Meyers debated just staying in the conference room. Normally, Brigston would expect senior officers on the bridge. Meyers figured his presence would be too galling at the moment.

"I guess I'll head to my quarters until we know whether I've led us into a trap." Meyers stood.

Paxton shook his head. "Taylor was a good soldier."

"I know. I'm more worried about what could rattle her this much."

2

____

THEY CAME out of the gravitic drive jump without any more trouble than a few lights flickering. Meyers had just settled into the chair built into his cabin's desk, lost in thought in the cool quiet of his cabin when their arrival was announced. He looked around the cabin in appreciation: a comfortable bunk, a sink, a closet, the desk, warm and textured floor tiles, access to a bathroom—head, he reminded himself—shared between senior officers. It was a good life.

Space travel had been part of Meyers's job since his selection for Captain Jack Rimes's crazy ERF concept eight years before. Meyers was getting used to it. The alien gravitic drive technology continued to amaze him. More amazing was the way refinements were constantly fielded by researchers, including the ability to make longer jumps through the wormholes the drives created. Going from Earth to Plymouth Colony was getting closer to two weeks now. Unfortunately, simple jumps like they were taking to meet with Taylor's ship weren't getting any faster and only a little safer.

Incremental steps, he reminded himself.

He brought up Taylor's military file from his earpiece's storage and connected to the display terminal attached to the desk. Taylor's piercing blue eyes and angular, masculine face glared back at him. Pronounced brows, heavy jaw, thick neck—she exhibited all the hallmarks of a Kimmy. If not one of the chemically enhanced, she had been at the very least a heavy steroid user at some point.

But she had always been solid. Reliable.

He pulled up the specs on the yacht she'd purchased for her mercenary—*Lancer*—group. The yacht wasn't so different from the *Tesla*, the ADMP yacht discovered on Sahara during the Genie Wars.

Big enough to hold a mercenary company, he thought. Not comfortably but...

He drilled down into the deck plans. When General Quarters sounded, he jumped.

"All hands, all hands! Battle stations!"

Meyers connected to the bridge communications system and monitored. Alarms blared loud enough to make it hard to pick out the quieter exchanges. The crew was calmly working through the problem, which seemed to be...nothing. Sensors showed Taylor's ship on a slow approach. No weapons locks, no sensor sweeps.

Where's the threat? Meyers wondered. He tapped a beat on the desk surface. Finally, he disconnected and tried to open an audio channel to Brigston, who didn't respond for several seconds. When he finally did, Meyers asked, "Jeremy, what's up?"

Brigston was silent at first. "I'm not sure yet," he finally said. "It seems your contact Taylor is closing. Something about that ship's approach seems to have set off our defense profile."

"General Quarters? I was just looking her ship over again. It doesn't have any—"

"Would you like me to cancel the General Quarters, Colonel?"

Meyers rolled his eyes in disbelief. Brigston had never been so petty before. "I was asking about the defense profile. A ship like that has a couple railguns—"

"It could be stuffed full of explosives and programmed to ram us."

"Jeremy, could we—"

"I've asked Commander Cooper to give the profile a good look. For now, my recommendation is to stay on General Quarters and be alert. What would you suggest?"

A part of Meyers wanted to shout into his earpiece. He had to remind himself Brigston wanted a confrontation. He wanted proof he was going to be shunted aside, bullied, rendered irrelevant. "I'm taking Paxton, Barlowe, and Starling down to the Hangar Bay Observation Room. If Captain Taylor's ship proves not to be packed full of explosives, could you ask her to meet us there?"

"Of course." Brigston ended the connection.

Meyers pushed his chair back and stood. Technically, he was supposed to be in an environment suit with the ship on alert. It was an annoyance, another way to slow everything down. Like showing up late to the meeting in the conference room.

What's up with you, Jeremy? Meyers wondered. He couldn't recall Brigston ever being so...fragile.

After a few seconds, Meyers realized he would only be feeding into Brigston's behavior by not following protocols. Meyers took his environment suit out of the locker and pulled it on over his uniform. He set the helmet on, checked integrity, then opened a channel to Barlowe, Paxton, and Starling. "I'm heading down to the Hangar Bay Observation Room. If you could meet me there, I'd appreciate it. In environment suits, please."

Paxton nodded. "On our way, Colonel."

As simple as that, he answered for the others. And Barlowe didn't object.

Meyers made his way down the stairs, barely acknowledging the crew moving around him. He imagined the same hostility radiating off them that Brigston was giving off. In reality, though, they simply muttered, "Excuse me, sir," or bowed their heads in acknowledgment if they did anything at all. It was General Quarters, after all.

He stepped into the Observation Room, the same room where he'd once dissected a proxy body that was ultimately determined to be a human. The military had quietly swept the sticky little conundrum of whether killing an artificial body that was technically human amounted to murder or a war crime. There were a lot of uncomfortable questions left unanswered from the Metacorporate War. The UN was still trying to figure out other-than-human rights. Were genies humans? At what point did augmentation—genetic manipulation, cybernetic replacements, proxies—take away someone's humanity?

Meyers chuckled to himself. Philosophers and religious scholars had spent centuries theorizing about what constituted being human. Religion might have largely faded away in the face of human advancements and space travel, but the question was still unanswered: What makes us who we are? What makes us human?

The hatch off the passageway opened, and Paxton stepped into the room. He adjusted the collar of his environment suit before joining Meyers at the wall that looked in on the hangar bay.

"General Quarters, Colonel?" Paxton placed a hand against the clear shield running from about one meter above the floor to the ceiling.

Meyers shook his head. "Something about the way the ship approached set off the automated alarm."

"Don't sound much like Cassidy."

Meyers glanced at Paxton, surprised by his sudden informality. "I had a friend who was pretty close to Taylor. He said she could be a hard-ass but never unfair or unreliable. She had a good reputation among the Rangers."

"So why the alarm?" Paxton cocked an eyebrow at Meyers. "Right?"

"Yeah."

The hatch opened again, and Barlowe entered. He had his environment suit draped over an arm, his helmet cradled in the crook of his other arm. A few steps behind him, Starling entered, struggling with the helmet seal.

"Sorry, Colonel." She tried and failed to set the helmet back on the rim around her neck. Her arms moved with more stiffness than the suit should have caused.

As if sensing Meyers's concern, Paxton stepped over to Starling and adjusted the helmet seal. Neither he nor Starling said anything. She set the helmet into place and joined Meyers at the window just as the alarm went silent.

Paxton smirked. "Looks like Captain Taylor decided not to attack."

Meyers watched the hangar bay, saying nothing until the lights powered off and the belly door fell away. There were three open spaces that could hold most shuttles in common use. A golden glow framed one of those spaces on the hangar bay floor and ceiling, and a few minutes later, a shuttle raised up through the opening and settled onto the indicated space. More time passed in silence as the belly door sealed, and the hangar bay filled with atmosphere.

When the shuttle's rear hatch slid open, and the ramp slid down to the floor, Meyers moved back to the passageway hatch. "I think it's time we met Captain Taylor."

They waited at the hangar bay hatch until atmospheric pressure was stable. Meyers led them in, stopping a few meters shy of the shuttle ramp. Cassidy Taylor stood there in a dark gray-green camouflage uniform reinforced with environment suit fixtures. She was taller than Meyers remembered. And older. She was half a head taller than him, and her wispy, blond hair was cut down to a high-and-tight. She sported a scar along her right jawline that extended up to her ear.

"Lonny?" She stepped toward him, gloved hand extended. "Colonel, huh?"

They shook, and he turned to the others. "You must remember Master Sergeant Paxton?"

"How could I forget? Carl." She shook Paxton's hand and smiled; it softened her features considerably.

"This is Agent Ladell Barlowe from the Intelligence Bureau and Private Starling from the ERF. She's been working closely with Agent Barlowe for the last several months, trying to learn all she can. We lost a lot of good people the first time we—" He saw the scowl on Taylor's face. "What?"

Taylor nodded at Barlowe. "There was a Ladell Barlowe involved in that X-17 situation, wasn't there?"

Meyers's eyes went wide. He had no idea how Taylor could have known about that. "Of course. Long story. Maybe we can talk about that some other time." He turned toward the door. "If you'd like to accompany us—"

"No fucking way." Taylor took a step back toward the shuttle ramp. "I'm taking a helluva chance here, Lonny. I gotta know who I'm dealing with."

Meyers turned back and held up a hand. "He's one of us. These are the people I selected for this meeting. I'd trust them with my life." He saw Starling smile and look away.

"No offense, but I gotta know about them for *my* life." Taylor glared at Barlowe.

"You're safe." Meyers turned back toward the door. "I know your time is valuable."

Taylor stared at Barlowe for a moment longer, then relaxed. "Damn right it's valuable. I see the funds in my account, or I say nothing more."

"I wouldn't expect anything else. Can we..." He took a step toward the door.

A long silence passed before she pulled her eyes from Barlowe and followed.

Meyers's stomach turned. Taylor wasn't easy to spook. Whatever was going on had to be big. Really big.

Like the location of Chad Waverley big.

THEY FILTERED into Conference Room 3 and settled at the table without a word—Meyers at the near end, Taylor to his right. The room was warm and dark except for soft track lighting. Meyers caught the slightest hint of body odor or something sour coming off of Taylor's uniform. The moment felt awkward, like an interrogation instead of a meeting with an old comrade. The skepticism and anxiousness in Taylor's eyes were unmistakable, and Barlowe's delicate features were now strained.

"Is Cassidy okay, or would you prefer a title?" Meyers asked, hoping to break the tension.

Taylor's nostrils flared, then she turned to Meyers. "Sure, it's fine."

"Is this about Waverley?"

Taylor flinched. "Lemme check my account." She stared off into space.

"The message buoy downloaded account data before we left Plymouth."

"All right. I see it." She seemed to relax; the payment must have been a relief. "Yeah, it's about the bounty."

"Then I can authorize a direct transfer to your account for the tip." Meyers turned to his left as Paxton leaned forward and held up a finger. "Before you say it, Carl, I know. We'll validate the quality of the tip before we pay, but I have every expectation this is what we've been looking for. Cassidy?"

Taylor nodded, once again looking anxious. "Has to be. This—what I saw—was fucked up. All kinds of fucked up."

"Tell us," Paxton said.

"Six months ago, when we was officially getting transferred over to Lancer status, I got wind through this clearinghouse—an old acquaintance—that something big was up. Big money. Fucking market's flooded right now—you know that, right? Anybody with a gun can register as a Lancer, and some of the frontier colonies, they don't care if you're a walking body bag with a Class I license or a combat vet with a Class IV."

Meyers remembered the way everyone had talked about Savoy and the other Lancers on Bellar Colony. "There's a lot of trouble out on the frontier."

"Shit's growing too fast; nobody wants law and order, least not if they have to pay. All kinds of bullshit." Taylor shook her head. "Anyways, we was looking at a few offers. I'm running with three platoons right now, technically company strength. No one's paying for that big a force. Or that qualified. Except for this tip I hear about. They're looking for platoons and up. Top dollar. Bonuses. Sounds too good, right? But I got to know. I got bills to pay, mouths to feed."

Meyers tried to look sympathetic. He wondered how close he'd come to stumbling into mercenary—Lancer—work. Surviving the Metacorporate War and its fallout hadn't guaranteed a future with the ERF, and he'd burned his bridges with the metacorporations.

"Wh-what's the problem taking the contract?" Starling asked. Her wide eyes had been glued to Taylor since she'd come aboard.

Taylor seemed to size Starling up. "If it's legal? Nothing. It sounded perfect. Fuck that. It sounded desperate. Or maybe some sort of setup."

Paxton cocked his head. "Setup? Like jerking you around?"

"Nah. The offer was pay up front, or I wouldn't have bothered. Still, I've heard talk about ambushes. Usually it's squads, maybe a platoon. You offer a job, tell them where to meet, maybe get them drunk, maybe just gun them down. Whatever. Then you take their gear and dump their bodies. And if they could do that with a ship like I got?" Taylor shrugged.

"Oh." Starling blinked, and her mouth stayed open.

Taylor smirked. "Yeah, ain't an easy life but it's what we got. Anyways, I took the payment to cover travel, flew out to the coordinates, and met with the guys doing the hiring."

Meyers found himself leaning in. "And?"

Taylor's right cheek ticked up in a sneer, stretching the scar along that side of her face. "It stank. All kinds of vague bullshit and lies. You negotiate enough contracts, you know when someone's lying to you. I mean, shit, they all lie to you—am I right, Carl?"

Paxton smirked and nodded.

"But this?" Taylor shook her head. "Serious lying. But I got a chance to talk to some of the other people there for the negotiations. This force, it's approaching battalion strength. People were signing on because of the money but also because they liked the idea of a force that big."

"Battalion?" Barlowe looked around the table. "That's illegal. The articles around Lancer operations are clear. Hiring a couple companies is the upper end, and you have to register with the Special Security Council. No one's going to approve that."

Taylor crossed her arms over her broad chest. "Like I said, it stank."

Meyers considered the numbers Taylor was talking about and what a force of that size could be used for. He caught himself drumming his fingers on the tabletop and looked up, curling his fingers in embarrassment. "How long was the contract for?"

"A year. Signing bonuses, material bonuses, retention bonuses. It's a lot of money. A lot."

"I can't think of any reason for something that size other than an aggressor force." Meyers looked at Paxton. "Carl?"

Paxton shook his head. "Who could afford it except for a few of the biggest colonies?"

Meyers looked to Barlowe and Starling; she was still staring at Taylor. "Ladell? Private Starling?"

"Uh..." Starling's eyes dropped to the tabletop. "Nothing, sir."

Barlowe frowned. "They're breaking the law and not just a little."

"But does it sound like Waverley?" Meyers couldn't quite make the connection. Waverley would have had to set the process into motion before the attack on Bellar. He certainly had the money but did he have the reach?

"Waverley or the metacorporations," Paxton said. "And why the hell wouldn't they just use him as their proxy for something like that?"

Starling glanced at Paxton, embarrassed. "Something like what, Master Sergeant?"

Barlowe blew out a frustrated-sounding sigh. "Finishing up what they started."

"What they—?" Starling's eyes lit up. "Another Metacorporate War?"

"Smaller scale," Meyers said. "Maybe enough to pull off a coup on a major colony. Or on Earth. Or to take us out before we get back to full strength."

Paxton tapped his nose in agreement. "I think this falls under our directives for preemptive strikes, Colonel."

"Waverley or not." Meyers couldn't see any way there would be blowback. Either Taylor was selling them legitimate data and the ERF had to act to prevent an illegal Lancer unit from forming, or Taylor was luring them into a trap, and the only thing that could trap them would be a larger military force. "You have any idea where they're hiding these forces?"

Taylor pulled a sliver of data film from her right breast pocket. "There was a couple former Rangers who were sure I was going to sign on." She considered the data film for a few seconds before sliding it across to Meyers. "Never heard of the place."

Meyers slid the data film into his earpiece. "Rangers, huh?"

"Terry's got a company. Best one I saw there." Taylor watched his reaction.

"Terry?" Meyers's stomach flipped.

"Yeah. Look, we was all bitter about the way things went down, especially after the war. The Rangers was used in some pretty hopeless situations, and then they just booted people out when they didn't need them anymore. I lost a lot of good friends, and it still hurts when I think about it, but I'll be goddamned if I ever sign on with the metacorporations. Not after all they did."

Suddenly, the idea of going after the Lancer force was unpleasant. There had been a time when Terry Lewis had been Meyers's best friend. And now he was signed on with an illegal operation that had to be taken down.

"Colonel?" Paxton's thick eyebrows were arched.

Meyers grunted. "Thanks, Cassidy. This definitely qualifies as a tip."

Taylor stood. "You gonna transfer the funds?"

"Already done." Meyers stood and led her to the door, suddenly feeling small and weak in her presence. "I'll escort you back to your shuttle."

They walked back to the hangar bay without another word. Meyers's thoughts were a maelstrom of confusion and anxiety. A battalion-strength Lancer force, an old friend, former Rangers, and a mysterious team behind the hiring. It couldn't get much worse.

As Taylor's shuttle exited the hangar bay, Meyers wondered if his depleted ERF was ready for the challenge.

They have to be, he realized. There was no one else.

3

11 September 2175. Plymouth Colony.

MEYERS STEPPED off the shuttle and into Plymouth's hot, thick air. After a week aboard the *Valdez*, the earthy, almost sweet musk of the surrounding jungle hit him hard. A fine sheen of sweat beaded his brow by the time he was halfway to the Operations Center, pale gray in the intense morning light. He exhaled loudly, trying to clear the faint metallic taste from his mouth, the last residue of the *Valdez's* recycled atmosphere.

"What's got you so wound up, Colonel?" Paxton's dry growl sounded barely labored.

Meyers glanced over his shoulder. Paxton was keeping pace far too easily just a few steps back. "That ship in orbit." Meyers jerked his head skyward. "Coop—Commander Cooper—said it had a UN designation but refused to provide him anything more than that it was here on official business." That was never a good sign, as far as Meyers was concerned.

"Why not just call down to Ops and check for official updates?"

"Because this can only be the sort of thing I prefer to see myself."

"Up close and personal?" Paxton chuckled.

Paxton already knew the answer to that, which annoyed Meyers. Normally, Paxton's enjoyment of confrontation and other people's discomfort with it didn't bother Meyers. In the face of what could potentially be yet another UN intrusion into ERF operations, it was hard not to be at least a little bothered.

Someone exited the Operations Center building—uniformed, dark-skinned, thick, and tall. The form put on a beret and hurried toward them.

"Looks like Captain Singh's got something for you, sir," Paxton said.

Sure enough, as the form drew closer, Meyers could see it was Singh. His dark eyes and close-shaved beard made him seem even darker. He broke into a strained smile as he came to a stop and saluted, stretching the pale scar over his lip enough for it to be noticeable. "Colonel Meyers, you did not call down." Singh's low voice sounded even raspier than normal, as if he had been shouting.

Meyers returned the salute, then glared over his shoulder at Paxton's chuckle. "I thought it'd be best to check on things firsthand. What's going on? Did we get our weapons resupply?"

"No, Colonel, no resupply." Singh looked uncomfortable, fidgety.

"No resupply? That means I'll need to make adjustments to the manifest. I'll have to sneak that through without Brigston's approval. Wonderful. So, what is it then? What has you so worked up?"

"It is the United Nations, Colonel." Singh glanced back toward the Operations Center. "They have assigned us a liaison."

"Son of a bitch."

"There is more." Singh rested his hands on his hips just as the door he'd exited opened. "Reinforcements. An entire platoon."

"Commandos?" Meyers tried to pick out details of the person standing outside the building, apparently watching them. The form was slim and dressed in a sleeveless cream blouse with deep coral skirt. Feminine, he thought. Thanks to a large pair of sunglasses, dark hair and pale skin was all he could make out.

"No, sir, not Commandos."

"I see. Is that the liaison?" Meyers nodded at the languidly approaching form.

"Miss Timkul, yes. The colonel will find her interesting."

The name rang a bell. Meyers glanced at Paxton. "Where have I heard that name before?"

"Timkul? Wasn't that the woman that McNutt's squad tried to rescue?" Paxton's eye never left the woman.

"Shit. Yes. Prime minister of Thailand. Did she have a daughter? Niece?"

The woman was close enough that Meyers could see that her hair was pulled back and tied up in a bun. She had a round face with wide cheeks and bright red lipstick on a narrow, pouting mouth. Her outfit seemed like something that would be purchased from a boutique, especially the glittering rose gold open-toed shoes. The stiletto heels seemed to sink into the moist earth with each step, possibly explaining her pace. Her stylish sunglasses rested on a button nose.

"Colonel Meyers?" Raised almost to shouting, her voice was cool and hard.

"What's her title?" Meyers spoke out of the corner of his mouth.

"She is special envoy, Colonel," Singh said. "She likes the title."

"Special Envoy Timkul." Meyers stepped toward her, hand extended for a shake. "Captain Singh was just telling us about your appointment."

Timkul shook his hand but didn't smile. She was nearly his height and narrow at the shoulders, although not frail looking. "The *Wollongong* sent word that the *Valdez* had hailed it, but there was no mention of you coming down."

Meyers glanced skyward, squinted against the blinding light of the sun, and looked back down. "Once I was sure it was a friendly ship, I wanted to get down here as soon as possible."

"Is that normal protocol, Colonel?"

He took in a deep breath and caught a whiff of her flowery perfume. Although it smelled wonderful, it was impractical and even dangerous on a primordial planet like Plymouth. "I'm not really sure what the protocol is when a civilian ship arrives from the UN carrying military reinforcements."

Timkul pulled her sunglasses off and glared at Singh. "I had planned to introduce you to Sergeant Domnikov and Chief Pivovarova myself."

"Sergeant?" Meyers turned to Singh. "I thought you said they were platoon—"

"They are a platoon, Colonel." Timkul crossed her arms. "Their officers were disqualified shortly before shipping off."

Meyers bit back the urge to say he wasn't surprised. The Russian military was a mess thanks to its close ties with corporate interests, especially EEC. And after EEC had followed the other metacorporations off Earth, the nepotism and cronyism that had afflicted the officer corps since Russia's economic collapse only became worse. "I'm sure they'll fit in well enough. We have exceptional officers in place already. Captain Singh, what would you think of putting them under Lieutenant Spinoza?"

Before Singh could respond, Timkul said, "They will need to be integrated under a more senior officer. Secretary-General Peng suggested perhaps Captain Singh himself."

Meyers recoiled. "Captain Singh's my XO. He doesn't have any direct—"

Timkul crossed her arms over her chest and twirled her sunglasses in her right hand. "This was the secretary-general's suggestion, Colonel."

Singh bowed his head, as if embarrassed.

Meyers fought back an exasperated gasp as Timkul's brown eyes squinted. They were distractingly pretty eyes, large and shapely. "Miss Timkul, don't you think the military should be left to managing something as intimate as personnel assignment?"

Timkul's brow creased. "Intimate, Colonel?"

Paxton and Singh both looked away, and Meyers felt himself blush. "Intricate," he said, waving his hand as if she should move on from the gaffe. "Detailed. The minutia. My point being that things don't usually go well when you have civilians getting into the gritty details of military operations."

"Certainly it works better than the military getting involved in politics."

"Right. Like Turkey after its military failed to remove a religious radical. How many decades did it take for them to crawl back to sanity?" Meyers immediately regretted saying that when he saw Timkul's lips pull back.

"I will be sure to pass that knowledge on to the secretary-general."

"Fine." Meyers hadn't wanted an argument, not with so much to do and with so little time. "When I get back, we'll take this up." He tried to step to her right, but she stepped in front of him.

"When you get back? What is that supposed to mean?"

Meyers looked back to Paxton and Singh for support. Paxton had his helmet off and was slicking sweat from his scalp, and Singh's mouth was open in surprise. Meyers tried to calm himself. "It means we have a very credible tip we need to check into."

"A 'tip'? About what?" Her mouth pursed.

"Waverley."

Timkul stiffened. "You must tell the secretary-general."

"No, we mustn't. If I wait for approval from the UN, I'll miss the window of opportunity. We're already weeks behind whoever's putting this group together for Waverley."

"Group?"

Sweat trickled down Meyers's cheek. "Mercenaries. A Lancer force."

"I don't think I can allow something—"

Meyers held up a hand. "Madam Envoy, I believe your assignment was to liaise with me, not to tell me how to run my battalion."

Timkul spun her sunglasses slowly. Sweat darkened the coral blouse above her crossed arms.

"Ah, Colonel?" Singh stepped forward. "Perhaps there is a compromise?"

Timkul arched her eyebrows and turned on Singh. "And what would that be, Captain?"

"The Russians could serve under Captain Hecker." Singh turned to Meyers. "It will be months before we see the replacement platoons come in for C Company, Colonel."

Meyers rubbed his thumbs against the palms of his hands. "I had planned to take C Company with me."

Timkul smiled. "Then that is an excellent compromise. The Russians should accompany you." She twirled her sunglasses again, this time slowly.

Meyers closed his eyes and wished he'd followed his original plan to stay aboard the *Valdez* and transmit orders for A and C Company to mobilize. As soon as Cooper sent word of detecting the *Wollongong* in orbit, Meyers allowed his worry about the safety of the installation to override even basic tactical thinking. Now he was being outmaneuvered by a woman too young to be a serious politician.

"We're heading into what is very likely going to be a combat situation." Meyers spoke slowly and—he hoped—calmly. "After what happened on Bellar Colony, these companies are barely at half strength. If my tip is correct, we're going against a battalion-strength force. We'll need properly trained soldiers who know how to operate as a unit."

"Then the Russians are perfect for you." Timkul placed the sunglasses back over her eyes. "They're 2nd Spetsnaz Brigade." She turned and headed for the building, stopping and turning to look back. "Also, Colonel, I do believe I will accompany you."

Meyers waited until she was back inside, then he pulled his helmet off and slicked sweat out of his hair. "Thanks for the support, you two."

"She is a witch, sir. Bedeviling," Singh said. He slapped at his pants leg, as if brushing away dust.

"Certainly has all the leverage right now," Paxton said. "Quite a fine looking woman, don't you think, sir?"

"I was too busy being pushed around to notice." Meyers slipped his helmet back on.

Paxton tapped his helmet camera and grinned. "I sneaked a few pictures if you want a look later. I was mostly going for that strange look on your face but I caught her, too."

Meyers squinted. "Strange look?"

"Sort of like..." Paxton squinted in exaggerated concentration. "Desperation, sir?"

Meyers shook out his shoulders and straightened. "Master Sergeant Paxton, why don't you work with Captain Singh to get designated personnel and gear aboard the *Valdez*, please."

"Of course, Colonel."

As Meyers walked away, he heard Singh say again, "She is a witch."

The idea stuck in Meyers's head. He should have been able to stand up to someone so young. She wasn't even his age, and politicians took decades to hone their skills. He had some time to figure out how to keep her from coming along on the mission, at least. That victory alone would be worth losing his first engagement with her.

EVERY SQUARE CENTIMETER of the *Valdez's* hangar deck was maximized to hold Darts and shuttles. At the far end of the hangar, a single Javelin and Arrow were parked next to each other. Ships and equipment were secured, all panels shut, all cables stored, yet the area felt cluttered. It felt dangerous. Meyers walked between the wings of two Darts, twisting to keep the tips from brushing his shoulders. The hangar bay air was stale and warm, and the mineral smell of fuel and lubricant clung to everything. At the far end of the hangar, Cooper squatted beneath the Javelin, a beefy hand running over the fuselage, which reflected the pale amber lights.

They were the only personnel in the hangar bay.

"Chief Merriman says he doesn't like these," Cooper said. "All the battery problems we saw when we took them apart...I don't care for them at all."

"Barlowe doesn't trust them, either." Meyers squatted until he was at eye level with Cooper. "But I'd imagine Merriman has his own reason for not liking things right now."

"Have you seen her?"

"Chief Pivovarova? I checked her file." Meyers thought back to Pivovarova's personnel packet. She had top marks and several commendations. "I certainly trust her more than the Spetsnaz troops. They used to be elite, exactly what we'd want. Now?"

Cooper shook his head. "She just doesn't understand."

"Pivovarova? Do I need to have Hecker talk to her?"

"She's like a bull in a china shop. She just came in and took control. Regulations are pretty clear about how you configure a hangar bay like this." Cooper looked around and threw up a hand, exasperated. "She damn near clipped this Javelin's wing against the Arrow. How're we supposed to launch these?"

"She didn't explain how we could launch from this configuration, and you let her make the change?"

"Well, yeah, she explained."

"Did it make sense?"

Cooper squeezed his small eyes shut. "Yeah, I guess. But it's not regulation."

"Coop, they do things differently, that's all. They're used to making things work with even more limited resources."

Cooper duckwalked out from under the Javelin before standing and moving to the nearest Dart. He ran a hand along the back end. "You think these can really handle space flight?"

"We'll be in environment suits."

"Wish we had more Arrows back from depot. These Darts have negligible weapons loads, and they're not really meant for sustained combat."

"I don't see us using any of these ships for anything more than shuttling us down. Any ship-to-ship engagements are going to be between the *Valdez* and whatever these Lancers have left in orbit. These Darts are probably the most resilient craft we have, all things considered. We'll be okay."

"We'll do some more system checks. Just to be safe."

Meyers stood. He reminded himself he needed to be patient, to give Cooper a chance, but all the patience slipped away at the sight of Cooper's pinched face. "You going to talk to me about this or not?"

Cooper sighed. "I talked to him. You know how Jeremy is. I don't know that I've ever served under someone so laid back. It's not just about the demotion or the change to Army rank. The more senior officers are really pissed about this. I've heard a couple say they're considering resigning when we get back. It's really tearing him apart."

"I need you to be my ears, Coop. If we're going to lose people, I need to tell the UN to reconsider. But if you can get everyone to just give this a chance, it changes things. We've all gone through change—"

The hangar bay hatch opened, and the sound of booted steps echoed off the deck. Meyers signaled for Cooper to hold his position. When he nodded acknowledgment, Meyers crept around the Dart until he could see who had entered. Chief Pivovarova was near the hatch, hunched over a toolbox, which she opened by tapping her earpiece. It was barely visible beneath pinned-up blond curls. She wore a maintenance bunny suit, cinched at her waist by the arms. Her torso was covered by a dark green T-shirt, the neck of which was pinched between wide, full lips. As he approached, she reached into the toolbox and pulled out a screwdriver and examined it. She turned suddenly and jumped at the sight of him. The T-shirt fell from her mouth, and her eyes flew wide. He couldn't help noticing they were an even richer green in the bright lights than in her file images. She raised the screwdriver like a knife, then blew out a sigh of relief, puffing out soft cheeks.

"Colonel, I am sorry! You surprised me." She placed her empty hand on her chest, pushing the material against her skin, highlighting the swell of her breasts. It was the sort of thing that some women might do as a calculated maneuver; Pivovarova didn't seem to even think about it. There was a small streak of grease over her right cheek and at the tip of a nose just a slight bit too large for her face. She smiled, and every aspect of that face suddenly seemed to fit perfectly. "It is good I am slow with this screwdriver, I think."

"It is." Meyers smiled in return. He suddenly felt uncomfortably aware of the form beneath the loose T-shirt and bunny suit. "Um, if you don't mind my asking, what are you doing down here?"

Her face screwed up, and she tilted her head and then nodded. "Ah, it is because of the sleep schedule? I switch with Chief Merriman. There is too much to check to sleep." She unsealed her left leg pocket and pulled a slim device out. "I am eating dinner and see report. You see?" She tapped through the device's interface and held it out to him. "Electrical system problem on Javelins. Lieutenant Commander Cooper and Chief Merriman made note? See?" She pulled the device back and tapped to another screen. "And Arrow? Several notes about systems software? I will see for myself."

Meyers looked over the Arrow report, although he already knew what it said. "We'll have almost three weeks for you to look things over more closely, Chief."

"Yes, I understand, Colonel." She bounced up and down. "It is only that I am excited to see such nice ships and to know them. I cannot sleep. Is that why you are here?"

"Yes. Commander Cooper and I were discussing how you planned to launch these ships from this floor configuration." Meyers raised his voice when he said Cooper's name.

Pivovarova craned her neck to see past Meyers. "The commander, he is here?"

Cooper stepped into sight.

"If you like, I can come back later?" Pivovarova asked.

"Actually, we're done here." Meyers looked toward the hatch, and Cooper started toward it. "I don't know that I like you being down here alone, though. We have a pretty strict policy about folks pairing up."

"I have someone coming to help me. He is just getting settled in with his squad. He likes to talk while I work. I pretend to listen." She smiled again.

"All right. But don't push yourself too hard. We launch in eight hours."

"A few hours doing this and other assigned tasks, Colonel."

Meyers followed Cooper out of the hangar bay and turned right, nearly bumping into a man as he stepped out of the lift. The man was taller than Meyers and gangly, with a bulbous nose and red lips.

"Ah!" The man staggered backward, laughing. His curly, red hair glowed like a halo of fire in the passageway light. "So sorry, Colonel!"

Meyers recognized the young man as one of the Spetsnaz soldiers. He wore a baggy ERF uniform and sported a sloppy-looking day or more of whiskers. Even over the man's body odor, Meyers could detect the slightest hint of alcohol, which annoyed him. He realized this was Pivovarova's talkative assistant, and that the man was off-duty but alcohol was tightly controlled. The young man hardly seemed a threat, but something about his laughter and behavior made Meyers want to launch into a quick reminder about uniform, appearance, and hygiene. He let it go, even though he could feel Cooper's glare. "Carry on."

When they were in the lift, Meyers turned back to Cooper. "Can you do this for me, Coop? The ERF can't function without this fleet, and the fleet relies on a strong officer corps."

Cooper bowed his head and sighed. "I'll do what I can."

Meyers clapped Cooper on the shoulder. Having someone like him on the inside at least gave the ERF a chance. Meyers didn't even want to think of losing such experienced crew, but he knew things could easily be bad enough that folks could walk away.

Without a fleet, Meyers thought, they couldn't operate. The ERF couldn't exist.

MEYERS STEPPED off the lift and froze. Special Envoy Timkul stood at the end of the passageway, staring at the hatch to his room, one hand raised as if to activate the hatch chime. She wore a coat and pants now, another outfit that—even from a distance—seemed extravagant and out of place. Her perfume was in the air: subtle, sweet, flowery. It was as out of place as the outfit.

He stood in the shadows near the lift, hoping the night-lighting and the lift's quiet operation would be enough for him to go unnoticed.

It wasn't.

She turned and stared into the shadows where he stood, and then she took a hesitant step toward him. "Colonel Meyers? Is that you?"

He sighed and drummed his fingers on his thigh. "Miss Timkul. Can I help you?"

She came closer, moving quicker when she entered an unlit section of the passageway. "I was hoping we might spend a few minutes going over the particulars of this operation. I haven't seen or heard anything, and my access to the ship's Grid is limited."

"Everything's locked down right now. Once we launch, we can discuss the mission. That's just operational security."

She was less than a meter away, close enough for him to see the frown on her face and the lines that produced. It made her look older than he was sure she was. "I have full clearance, Colonel."

"Operational security has nothing to do with clearance in this case."

Timkul drew back and crossed one arm over her chest. "Don't patronize me, Colonel."

"Patronize?" Meyers looked past her to his hatch. "Miss Timkul, it's late. I have to be up in six hours to oversee our launch alongside Captain Brigston. Really, you should be getting to bed as well."

Timkul stiffened, and her eyes narrowed. "Are you propositioning me, Captain?"

"Propo—" The exasperated sigh he'd been fighting back slipped free. He rubbed his forehead. "No, I am not trying to proposition you. I am trying to get you to leave me alone so I can get some sleep. We can discuss the mission in detail tomorrow after we've launched, and there's no chance of anyone or anything transmitting compromising data to the message buoy. And, no, I'm not implying you were contemplating putting the mission at risk, Madam Envoy. I'm trying to answer your questions before you can ask them. Now, can we please go to bed?" Meyers closed his eyes in disbelief. He was too tired, and Timkul's combativeness was pissing him off. "That came out wrong. Can you please go to your cabin and let me go to mine?"

Timkul said nothing for a second, and when he opened his eyes, he saw her nostrils flaring. He prepared himself for a scream and accusations, but she just turned and walked down the passageway, arms still crossed. When she hooked left and disappeared down the other passageway, he finally let himself relax.

At his hatch, he hesitated and glanced up the passageway. Timkul was in the guest cabin opposite Brigston's. They would all three be sharing the bathroom—the head. He didn't want to risk running into her again, but he desperately needed a shower. After a few seconds of uncertainty, he settled on grabbing his towel, a change of underwear, a robe, and his hygiene kit. If she wanted to make a scene, she was going to. Better to get it out of the way now.

Already, the mission was taking on too many complications for his liking. As he locked the bathroom hatch, he reminded himself that all missions had complications. He just needed to start stripping away what he could now, before things got out of hand.

He undressed and stepped into the shower, annoyed that he couldn't get Timkul off his mind. She was just a politician, he told himself, just another reminder that the United Nations would never be content to let the ERF run without meddling. The hot water blasted him in the chest, for a moment driving Timkul and the Russians and the idea they were potentially going up against a battalion with little more than a company from his thoughts.

But the reality of the situation came back soon enough, and he eventually found himself tossing and turning in his bunk, second-guessing the mission and allowing Timkul to come along. And then he finally fell asleep.

4

———————

12 September 2175. Orbit around Plymouth Colony. CFN *Valdez*.

MEYERS YAWNED as he stepped off the bridge. He was sleepy. His eyes were itchy, and his stomach burned from the stress of being so close to Brigston during the final launch preparations. Every little decision had involved a questioning glance from Brigston, an implied, "Does the colonel agree?" And it hadn't just been Brigston. His staff seemed sullen, resentful, and angry. All the way up to the point where they accelerated away from Plymouth and engaged the gravitic drives, Meyers felt like a prison guard being sized up by the inmates.

I need breakfast and some sleep, he thought.

He forced himself down the passageway, promising his tired brain a stim and a steaming cup of coffee. The real stuff. That seemed to get cooperation from his legs long enough to get to the lift. The galley was one level down, just a handful of steps across the way.

The lift door opened, and a puffy-eyed Timkul stared at him from the center of the car. She straightened and moved closer to the wall to her left. "I assume we've launched?"

Meyers considered taking the stairs, but that would only delay the inevitable. He stepped inside and pressed against the back wall. "We did. I'm going to the galley if you're up for breakfast?" He hoped she'd already eaten. Her perfume was giving him a headache and making his heartburn worse.

"Would you be willing to talk about the mission?"

He avoided her glare. "We've launched, so we can discuss it, yes."

When the door closed, she crossed her arms and backed away from him. "That was inappropriate, what you did last night."

Meyers felt the pressure building between his temples. He'd been tired, had a slip of the tongue. There had been no contact, no threat. He wasn't even attracted to her. "I'm sorry. I was very tired. I didn't—"

The door opened, and she slipped out. "I talked to Captain Brigston this morning." Her voice filled the passageway. She turned and adjusted the coat she was wearing: black, shiny like silk, with indigo vine patterns. "You could have waived the operational security limits. He said he could have before things changed."

He breathed easier at the realization she was talking about declining to discuss the mission rather than his slip-up about going to bed. "Eight hours matters that much?"

She responded with another frosty glare.

Meyers walked past her to the galley entry. There were very few people in sight, mostly staff. The crew would be busy for a while yet now that they were launched. A young, scrawny sailor in oversized culinary whites straightened and stepped closer to a grill visible through a glass display. To the cook's right, a stack of trays rose a half-meter high from a stainless steel shelf.

Meyers headed to the line, grabbed a pair of trays, and set them on the tray counter, then he ordered a protein paste and cheese omelet. Blue text flickered on the glass separating him from the cook—the omelet order. Meyers tried to focus on the bacon-like scent rising from the grill but kept going back to Timkul's irritating claims that he'd been betrayed by Brigston. Meyers realized that he needed to talk to Brigston. Soon.

Timkul came closer. "Why were you resistant?"

Meyers turned at her voice. She stared at the cook while she brushed back a dark strand of hair, tucking it behind an ear that was slightly over-sized. It was the only imperfection he had noticed in her appearance, the first hint she was human rather than a political robot. It actually managed to make her more attractive. "Resistant?"

"To the Russians, to sharing mission information, to engaging with me as my role dictates." Blue text appeared on the glass next to his order: egg whites omelet with vegetable paste. "Are you resentful of having a woman in my position, Colonel?"

"No."

"But you had problems with Colonel Ramawat. I've seen the report."

Meyers squeezed the edges of his tray. "I don't know which report you've seen or what it said, but my problems with Colonel Ramawat started and ended with his competence."

"You had a history of problems with authority, did you not?" She looked at him, one eye squinted slightly. "With Colonel Rimes, and with the Commandos before that."

Meyers took his plate from the cook, who seemed entranced by Timkul, then moved down to the bread dispenser, which produced two thin, lightly toasted multigrain slices. Although normally not inclined to seal himself off from the rest of the crew, Meyers crossed to the raised, enclosed area set aside for senior officers. He hurried to the coffee urn, poured himself a large cup, then returned to the table and waited. When Timkul arrived, he pulled a chair out for her. She seemed uncertain how to react at first but a few seconds later, she set her tray down and seated herself.

"Thank you." It came out cool and distant, and she turned her attention to her napkin, unfolding it and setting it in her lap.

"Would you like coffee?"

"A small cup, with cream. A teaspoon."

No "thank you" that time, he noted. He didn't have the heart to tell her they didn't have real cream aboard but doubted she would be able to tell the difference. She was almost certainly used to the real thing, but the coffee would probably be enough to put her off noticing anything else.

When he was finally seated, he took a drink from his cup and let the hot fluid sit on his tongue for a little while before swallowing. The pressure behind his eyes faded. "Miss Timkul, before we go over the mission, could I ask you a question?"

She chewed a forkful of egg for a few seconds, prim and proper, then dabbed at her lips with the napkin. "Of course."

"Is there something personal behind this? The way you've treated me?"

She leaned back in her chair and cocked her head curiously.

Meyers tried not to let that irritate him. "Your mother, perhaps?"

Timkul folded the napkin again. "My mother was a career politician. She survived two assassination attempts, but she always knew she would die in service. We all did."

It was a dead-end angle, he realized. "That's very brave. It must have been challenging for you growing up."

"My family feels strongly about our duty to our people."

Meyers's stomach growled. He cut a chunk out of the omelet and stuffed it into his mouth. That was followed by a big bite of toast. Timkul bowed her head as she ate and watched him from beneath her perfectly arched eyebrows. When he was done, she looked up, once again dabbing her lips. She was wearing a different shade of lipstick than the day before, he realized.

"Tell me about the mission, Colonel."

Meyers leaned back in his chair. People were filtering into the galley now—ERF, a few sailors. They would all be "soldiers" soon enough. "The planet's known informally as Siberia. It's not a nice place—a bit of an odd axial tilt, big arctic regions, rugged, not the best atmosphere for long-term exposure. It's way down the priority list as potential colony planets go. We have intelligence indicating mercenary forces—Class IV Lancers—are being hired and transported there. Contracts running several months, Earth-time. Numbers are expected to exceed battalion level."

Timkul almost smiled. "Do you make a habit of pursuing Lancers around the galaxy?"

"If the estimates that they're gathering a battalion are correct, the people hiring these Lancers are breaking the law. And if it's a battalion, who do you think would be hiring them in the first place? Who could afford it?"

"That's how many, exactly?" she asked nonchalantly.

"Let's say a thousand. That's the upper end."

Her eyes widened slightly, the first sign she could be caught off-guard. "And you're taking how many soldiers with you?"

"We'll be able to field about 150." Meyers found her surprise delicious. "We faced worse odds during the Metacorporate War. We had superior training, leadership, and gear during that war, and we'll have the same here. Of course, if the UN had seen fit to provide the requested weapons upgrades, munitions, vehicles, and personnel, the advantage would be more significant. Plus there's the element of surprise—"

"Your operational security."

"Yes. But we need to move now, before there's any chance word could reach them and Waverley can slip away."

She looked down at her lap and idly played with her napkin. "What makes you so sure this is Waverley?"

"Like I said, who could afford this? Metacorporations. And Waverley."

"I see. Are you familiar with the story of *Moby Dick*, Colonel?" She straightened and looked into his eyes, openly smiling.

Meyers worried he was walking into a trap. "No. Should I be?"

"It was an American novel from centuries ago. It was about the perils of obsession."

"People read old American novels in Thailand?"

Timkul seemed caught between mirth and anger at that. "I was educated abroad, mostly on the American east coast, but my people aren't illiterate savages."

"I didn't mean to imply they were. I should have known there was a reason for your lack of any meaningful accent."

Once again, she seemed about to smile at the same time her brow wrinkled. "Accents are a matter of perception, aren't they? Anyway, in this story I mentioned, the captain of a ship pursues a white whale called Moby Dick across the world seeking vengeance, and it ultimately costs him his ship and his life."

"So, what, I'm this captain and Waverley is Moby Dick?"

Timkul shrugged. "You're not concerned about being so outnumbered?"

"I'm not expecting to actually fight a full battalion. These are Lancers. A lot of them are former military. They're not going to fight to the last soldier. We need to hit them hard, make it clear that resistance isn't going to work, and everything will wrap up quickly."

"It sounds easy."

It sounded far more hopeful than he'd intended; it sounded naive. He looked around the galley, taking note of the segregation of sailor and soldier. "We'll work up a plan. We have mortars and explosives. We can choose where to attack them. The intelligence we have indicates there's a valley they pass through to get from one base of operations to another, and they move between those bases about once every six weeks. There's a good spot in the valley where things narrow, cutting into the numerical advantage. And we'll have air superiority, and like I said before, surprise. They won't have anything approaching the firepower of the *Valdez* and our missile frigates."

"But you consider the risk things could go wrong worth it?" She seemed to be playing with him.

"Everything the ERF does comes with risk."

Her smile brightened. "That sounds like an easy excuse to cover for obsessive behavior. Are you so sure of your motivations, Colonel?"

"I'm not motivated by vengeance, if that's what you mean." Meyers felt flustered.

"Then what does motivate you?" Her smile seemed to turn hostile, teasing.

"Duty."

"To the United Nations or to something else?" She looked around the galley. "Your people?"

"My people are you and the Special Security Council. They're the citizens of Plymouth and Earth and every colony." He didn't appreciate the way she seemed to be questioning his loyalty.

"What about the metacorporations? Are they your people?"

And there it was, the heart of her questioning. "Are you asking me if I've forgiven them for what they did during the war? Millions dead or missing. War crimes. Billions and billions of dollars in damage across every planet."

"Forgiveness seems a stretch." She sipped at her coffee and set her cup down. "Have you accepted that the war is over?"

"Of course." His palms itched; sweat moistened his T-shirt along his spine.

"And so you see the metacorporations the same way you see your ERF?"

Once again, he sensed a teasing tone in her voice. "You ever serve in the military, Miss Timkul?"

She stiffened slightly. "I've had security training." Her tone was defensive.

"One thing you may not understand about the military without serving..." He emphasized *serving*. It felt good, like landing a solid point during a debate. It drew a barely perceptible wince from her. "There are sacrifices. Constant. Daily. You're asked to do things no one else is asked to do. Killing is only part of it. So, if you're asking me do I see the people who work for the metacorporations in the same light I see my fellow soldier in, the answer is simple. No, I don't. When they make the same sacrifices for the common good, when they live in the same conditions and face the same threats, when they watch their friends get disfigured or turned into something that can't even be scooped into a bag for burial, then I might see them as equals. I don't care what the UN says; you can't grant a corporation the same status as a human. In addition to all that, there's what my people do in service for our brothers and sisters, and there's everyone else."

"It sounds like you believe the military is special, Colonel." Timkul fidgeted with her napkin again, then looked up at him. "Is that a matter of faith?"

"I'm not much for faith."

"I see." She crossed her arms. "Would you say this mission is an exception?"

Meyers flinched. "What? No. We have the data we need to justify acting."

"You do? I searched for data on this Siberia just now, while we were talking. There's hardly anything on it. Higher gravity, terrible storm systems, a somewhat erratic orbit, magnetic field shifting. That's about it."

"I told you, it's not high on anyone's list for settlement or research."

"But didn't you blame the Security Council for sending you to Bellar Colony without enough intelligence, Colonel? Now, here you are doing the same thing."

Meyers looked away. He saw Captain Hecker approaching from the food line, tray held low enough to reveal a plate with fruit slices and vegetable paste. Already a half head taller than Meyers, Hecker's erect posture made that difference more pronounced. With dark-brown hair and light-brown eyes, Hecker could have mixed in anywhere easily enough, but a noticeable overbite combined with bright, white teeth to jump out against the almost gold tone of his skin.

"Good morning, Colonel." Hecker's "good" sounded more like "goot," but his ready smile and pleasant nature made such little things easy to overlook.

Meyers stood. "Morning. How have your new troops settled in?"

Hecker's eyes darted to Timkul, and when he looked back, one eye was squinted. "Indoctrinations will go on for some time, Colonel."

In other words, Meyers realized, the Russians weren't doing well. "Have you met UN Special Envoy Timkul?"

"No, Colonel, I have not had the pleasure." Hecker turned to Timkul and extended a long, bony hand. "Captain Theodor Hecker, Madam Envoy, C Company Commander."

Timkul shook Hecker's hand and stood. She seemed dainty and small compared to him. "It's so good to have the chance to meet you, Captain Hecker. I'm sure we will be working together closely. I have an interest in seeing the Russians succeed. The ERF cannot afford another debacle like it saw on Bellar Colony."

Meyers clutched at the napkin sitting in front of him. "If you two will excuse me?"

He didn't wait for them to reply, rushing down the few steps to the main floor and heading toward the exit, arms swinging at his side. Outside the door, he nearly ran into Sergeant Banh. The smaller man stumbled backward, his wiry arms thrown out for balance. He caught himself on the far side of the passageway.

"Sergeant Banh, I'm so sorry." Meyers held a hand out, but Banh was already recovered.

"It was me, Colonel. I did not watch where I was going." Banh stood straight, and his dark eyes darted up and down the passageway.

"I could've done better myself. How're you feeling? You up for the mission?"

"My injuries have healed, Colonel. I am fine."

"When we nearly lost you on Bellar, it really affected me and Sergeant Paxton...all of us."

Banh squinted his right eye—already slightly smaller than his left—and moved closer, heavy eyebrows knit. "Colonel, would it be possible that you would have a moment?"

"Of course." Meyers waved toward the stairwell. As they approached the hatch, he looked around to be sure they were alone, then said, "What is it?"

Banh closed his eyes and bowed his head, and his lips moved as if he were rehearsing. A few seconds later, he nodded slightly and opened his eyes again. "We have talked before about this, Colonel, but my duty is to my soldiers to speak out." His golden skin darkened slightly as he blushed.

"This is about the request for a chaplain?"

"It is, Colonel." Banh blinked rapidly. "Many of us are Christians, and there is concern among us many that we are not being understood."

Meyers felt his own cheeks flush. "No one is being mistreated or misunderstood in this, Sergeant Banh. Everyone has access to automated chaplains, counselors, or whatever else they need."

"But, Colonel, this means more to us than others." Banh shook his head. "We have not left our beliefs behind."

"No one's asking you to." Meyers glanced back toward the galley. He heard the dull thump of boots from beyond the hatch; someone was coming up the stairs. He waited until several sailors noisily exited the stairwell and headed toward the galley, then turned back to Banh. "Sergeant, there's no room in the budget for something like this. You're going to have to deal with it like anyone else."

"But it is how we speak to God, Colonel."

"If the military were to make an exception for you, they would have to make exceptions for others. Before long, we'd be back to carting around noncombatant personnel, and with the budget constraints we face, that would mean releasing combat personnel to make room. You understand? The UN has hard limits on us. Very hard limits."

Bahn bowed his head. "I understand, Colonel."

"I'll tell you what, if you can get someone in your squad to pursue a minister's degree or certification or..." Meyers winced. He had no idea of the educational requirements of the ministers or priests or whatever it was Bahn's particular religion called for. "Find someone who wants to be your chaplain, and we'll see to it that training's paid for. Deal?"

Bahn closed his eyes and seemed to consider the idea. His eyes opened again, and he seemed calm. "It is not my place to know what God has chosen for us. I hope it is this. Private Lamh has spoken of an interest before. His fiancée, her father is a preacher."

"Why not you? You're in a leadership position. It might be good for you."

Bahn stiffened, then nodded but he seemed anxious. "I will think on this, Colonel."

"Good." Meyers patted Bahn on the shoulder. "See Captain Singh when we get back. Tell him what we talked about."

"Thank you, Colonel." Bahn spun and almost ran to the galley entry.

Meyers wondered if he might benefit from talking to a counselor himself. He knew their scripts and understood the logic behind the automated sessions but that wasn't enough. When he was being honest with himself, he could admit that he was still having problems dealing with Camille and Kara's deaths. He still wasn't sure he wanted to be ERF battalion commander. He couldn't help wondering what sort of life he'd given up by fighting in the Metacorporate War.

He laughed at the thought a metacorporation would have taken him on, war or not. He had excellent grades and had completed demanding programs but the schools he'd attended weren't prestigious. He was just another overeducated nobody.

The hatch clanged open, and he waved a sailor out before entering the stairwell. Dealing with Timkul and Banh had driven the fatigue away. Now Meyers wanted something to drive away the frustration and annoyance. And the pounding headache. He needed a good workout.

His earpiece chirped. It was Cooper. Meyers hurried down the steps. "What's up?"

"We need to talk."

Brigston and his officers, Meyers realized. "Hangar Bay, five minutes?"

Cooper seemed to mull that over. "I'll be there."

Meyers disconnected with a curse and wondered if bringing Waverley to justice was really worth it all. He remembered Timkul's white whale comparison and chuckled bitterly. It was going to be a long trip to Siberia.

5

———————

30 September 2175. Siberia.

TURBULENCE SHOOK the Dart until it reached the point Meyers could no longer pretend he was getting anything done. Nausea was a frozen ball deep in his gut. He could taste vomit at the back of his throat from earlier, and he shook from intermittent sweats and chills. His breath was a foul steam in the cold. Across the aisle, Paxton was still sealed up, apparently unaffected. He seemed to be caught up in something being displayed on the inside of his helmet visor, which glowed slightly. Timkul was to Meyers's immediate right, and like him, she'd raised her visor. Sweat trickled down her forehead, and she breathed through her open mouth. She even managed to make that seem dignified.

Meyers leaned as close to her as his harness would allow. "You can turn your environment suit temperature down if you're hot."

Timkul put on a brave face, but there was no way she was feeling hot. The Dart wasn't designed for the sort of cold outside any more than it was designed for the vacuum of space. Meyers wouldn't allow himself to take satisfaction from Timkul's suffering. He had minimized contact with her after her implication that he was somehow at fault for what had happened on Bellar Colony. When contact had been unavoidable, she had only made it worse, acting as if nothing had happened and she wanted to keep up their professional relationship.

But she was still the special envoy, he reminded himself. He had to be bigger than her.

He glanced past her at Hecker, who'd brought down two of the Spetsnaz: Domnikov, the senior Russian sergeant, and the skinny drunk from outside the hangar bay, Private Repin. Across from them, two of Hecker's better soldiers sat stiffly in their harnesses, helmets sealed. Meyers knew the two men well. Sergeant Klinsmann was reliable, the sort of soldier Meyers would love to model the ERF off of. To Klinsmann's left was the extremely capable Corporal Strauss, an efficient and resourceful soldier who would be wearing sergeant stripes soon enough. Strauss was a little pudgy, but that was something that would come off with more time on Plymouth.

Squeezed into what amounted to a crew chief's seat to Meyers's left was Chief Pivovarova. Her harness hugged her curves tightly. Her helmet was angled as if she were staring at the mound of gear centered between the two rows of seats.

Meyers leaned toward Pivovarova, and her helmet came up. "Something wrong with the gear, Chief?"

She smiled, transforming her face into something whose whole was greater than its parts. "I do not wish to question your Chief Merriman's work but that—" She pointed at the gear. "It is not quite right."

The gear—quick-erect structures, perimeter sensors, a communications array, and heaters—didn't seem to have any more play or rattle to it than normal.

"You don't like the look of it?"

She shook her head. "Looks, it is fine. It is the sensors. Here. Is all right?"

Meyers realized she wanted to send him something. "Please." An invitation to share her workspace popped up. He accepted.

Pivovarova had set up one of the most intricate and personalized earpiece environments Meyers had ever seen. Pictures slowly swirled around a brilliant yellow wireframe that defined a large, domed virtual chamber or office. Meyers saw snowy fields with scrawny trees; what looked like a farmhouse with lush green crops; an ugly tractor driven by a homely, wrinkled man with a larger version of her nose; two dogs that could have been wolves running above a stream bed where Pivovarova and another young woman laughed and splashed and wore far too little clothing. He forced himself to concentrate on the yellow wireframe center, where a table held what looked like several old television sets. One of the televisions contained a copy of the entire workspace, which held another television and so on until there was nothing but a yellow dot. It reminded him of Russian nesting dolls.

"This one," Pivovarova said. An avatar of her dressed in a simple overall and wearing a broad-brimmed hat appeared and pointed to one of the televisions. The display showed a series of amber-colored symbols floating in the air. "Is easier with enhancement." Wires connected the amber symbols, taking on the vague shape of cargo straps. Another animation ran, and the wires became straps covering a crude representation of the gear.

"Is this a problem?" He highlighted the amber symbols.

"No, Colonel." Turbulence shook the Dart again, and her avatar pointed at three symbols gone red. "This is problem."

Meyers looked at the gear pile. There was more play and wobble than he'd noticed.

Pivovarova tapped his arm. "Is not yet problem. How much turbulence we have left. That is where problem is."

Meyers couldn't imagine the turbulence improving. Ensign Hassan's last communication was a series of growls and yelps interrupted by warnings that there was really rough weather between them and the LZ. They'd had the luxury of a video channel at the time, and the color had been blanched from her olive skin. Her brown eyes had jumped from one area of her display to another, never once looking into the camera, and her wide mouth had been stretched to the sides of her helmet.

He considered Pivovarova for a second, then said, "I hate to ask, Chief, but is there something you could do?"

Pivovarova's eyes lit up. "I am afraid to ask permission. Is not Chief Merriman's fault."

She pushed her harness up and stood. After finding her balance, she reached up to secure a cable from the semi-rigid chest plate of her environment suit to an eyehole along the ceiling. As she tried to connect a second cable to another eyehole, the Dart plunged. She threw her arms up as she rose toward the ceiling. Meyers reached out to grab her, but his harness held him in place. She cracked into the ceiling with a loud *thunk*, and at the same moment, the Dart leveled off. Pivovarova dropped toward the floor but the cable she'd secured to the eyehole held, twisting and suspending her half a meter shy.

Meyers heard something snap and realized it was the top cable securing the gear. A meter-long plastic tube-like canister—the perimeter sensors—tore free and bounced toward Strauss and Klinsmann. Strauss twisted enough to avoid the impact but Klinsmann couldn't. The canister caught him in the shoulder and helmet before bouncing away. Klinsmann twisted in his harness, then slumped.

The Dart plunged again, sending the canister and Pivovarova back up to the ceiling, where the canister slowly rolled toward Domnikov and Repin.

Meyers opened a channel to Hassan. "We've got gear loose and two injured!"

"I'm sorry, Colonel." Her voice—normally soft—was strained from shouting. "Things are very unpredictable at the moment."

"Make them predictable, Ensign! Level off!"

Pivovarova somehow managed to attach another line from her suit to a second eyehole just before the Dart leveled off and the canister dropped to the floor, missing Domnikov's feet by millimeters.

Pivovarova came to a rest above the floor and played out enough line to kick forward and snatch the rolling canister. "I will control this, Colonel."

"Do that." Meyers checked everyone's vitals; they were elevated because of the turbulence but no one seemed in danger. Corporal Strauss was twisted in his harness, checking Sergeant Klinsmann's external readout, but Meyers could see Klinsmann wasn't in danger. Pivovarova was twisting and hopping around the gear like a gymnast ballerina, running new straps from other anchor points. "Ensign, we have things under control back here. ETA?"

"A few more minutes, Colonel." Hassan's voice was even now, with only a hint of the earlier strain. "Infrared imagery is all I have in this storm, and it shows the clearing less than one hundred klicks out."

Meyers glanced back at Pivovarova, who had her hands balled into fists resting on hips; she was satisfied. "Chief, we're landing in a few minutes."

Pivovarova saluted. "I am tied down, Colonel."

Meyers blushed, hoping she had made an innocent mistake.

She edged around the gear, unhooking lines as she went. The Dart rattled and hopped a couple more times, but she kept her legs wide and braced an arm against the wall above Meyers to compensate. The whole time, the smile never left her face. Meyers caught himself staring and had to hold himself back from offering a helping hand. His cheeks burned when he realized Timkul was watching him, one eyebrow arched.

Not long after Pivovarova was secured, the Dart decelerated. It banked, dropped again, then leveled off. Meyers gritted his teeth as the vehicle shimmied and twisted during its final descent. That gritting intensified when they slammed into the ground and the landing gear and fuselage groaned.

"Sorry about that, Colonel." Hassan's voice was a shameful whisper. "I have good data to share with the other pilots now. These winds..."

He could imagine her shaking her head the way she did when something got under her skin, lips twisted to one side. She was a good pilot, and he reminded himself he needed to acknowledge that. "Thanks for getting us down here in one piece. Go ahead and get a briefing up to the *Valdez* while we unload."

"Roger, Colonel."

Meyers undid his harness, taking enough time that Hecker was able to get to Klinsmann first. It was tough not knowing how a wounded soldier was doing but Hecker was Klinsmann's commander. Meyers forced himself to hover only long enough for Hecker to sense there was someone watching, then headed out through the airlock. Instinctively,

Meyers wanted to grab gear and help with the unloading but that wasn't his role, either. It was just one of the things that he was still coming to grips with.

The outer airlock door opened, and the cold hit him like a slap. He sealed his visor, signaled for the soles of his boots to widen out to deal with the snow, and headed down the ramp, noting in the Dart's floodlights the slickness of the snow that had already collected. It took a moment for the suit to cycle out the air, which had been surprisingly fresh and pleasant. The floodlights reached to the edge of the clearing they'd chosen for their Operations Center. Thick, brutish trees dark as pitch circled the clearing about fifteen meters out. Where there were no trees, man-sized boulders jutted up from the ground. Beneath the white blanket of snow, the ground was relatively flat and hard.

Meyers heard a chime, a private channel request from Hecker. "Go ahead."

"Sergeant Klinsmann is fine, Colonel. A bruised shoulder and some wooziness."

Meyers relaxed slightly. "He can sit out this unloading. Let's see how our new soldiers handle the task."

"Chief Pivovarova already has everything ready for unload. She is good."

"Let's see if the same applies to Domnikov and Repin." Meyers turned to watch how the team handled everything. He wanted to warn them about the ramp, but that was part of the challenge: situational awareness.

Strauss was the first down the ramp, the canister of sensors held against his chest. He had no problem dealing with the snow. Domnikov and Repin followed immediately behind, hauling the habitat pieces between them. Repin—already struggling with the weight of the load— lost his footing for a second, then adjusted. Pivovarova seemed to handle the slick ramp the easiest, sliding a couple smaller cases ahead of her before jumping into the snow. She opened her helmet and turned her face to the sky, snapping at the puffy snowflakes.

"Is like winter at home!" Her laughter was captivating—deep and warm. It froze Meyers just as he thought about scolding the team to hurry.

And then he saw Timkul at the top of the ramp, struggling to get her footing while helping Klinsmann down; Hecker watched from behind, hands raised to catch either. She was small and frail next to the two men but that didn't seem to stop her. Meyers could barely make out Paxton behind them all, visor up, mouth twisted.

Meyers clapped his gloved hands together. "All right, let's get this gear into place. Chief, if you could help Sergeant Domnikov get the Operations Center up?"

Pivovarova's smile disappeared, and she shot a disgusted look at Domnikov. "Yes, Colonel."

Klinsmann opened his visor and stepped clear of Timkul. There was a red welt on his heavy brow, almost centered over the thick gold of his eyebrows. He took the canister from Strauss and dragged it over to Meyers, coming to a stop with a salute. Klinsmann's crooked grin pressed his lantern jaw tight against the helmet's insulation. "I can put the perimeter sensors up, Colonel."

"If you're up to it."

"Thank you, sir." Klinsmann sealed his helmet and headed for the tree line.

Timkul watched the others for a bit, then she made her way over to Meyers, arms crossed. Her visor was up and her eyes were watering. "Colonel...?"

Meyers held a finger up and accepted a call from Hassan. "Go ahead, Genevieve."

"Colonel, we're not going to be able to use the drones to run reconnaissance on the valley. They don't have the flight systems to handle turbulence like what we encountered, and it's going to be worse in the valley."

"We can't go in there blind." Meyers's stomach clenched up. Bellar had been a mess because the UN had rushed them into action. This mission was all on his own timetable. He looked west, toward the valley, one hundred klicks out, across a nasty, jagged range of cliffs. "Can we get a Dart rigged up for recon, send it in there?"

"Commander Cooper is looking into that already. Chief Merriman thinks so."

Meyers felt a stab of guilt at the thought that Pivovarova should be involved. "Keep me informed." He turned back to Timkul, whose arms were still crossed. He opened his own visor. "I'm sorry; I just had an important update."

Timkul squinted. "Something I should be apprised of?"

"No." Meyers heard the ice in his voice, felt the heat in his cheeks. He was being unprofessional. "It's an operational matter. We can't use our drones for reconnaissance. The turbulence we encountered..." He shook his head.

"The weather report I saw this morning seems to have been inaccurate." She brushed snow from the strands of dark hair bunched against her cheeks. "Several degrees Celsius off."

"They'll get better once they've had time to gather more data." Meyers trusted weather analysis about as much as he did intelligence analysis, which wasn't much but he needed both.

Timkul looked around the clearing. Her hands were now rubbing the arms of her suit, as if that could help through the armor. "Colonel, isn't it possible you moved too quickly?"

"Of course it's possible. I don't think I did, though."

She pointed at the black shapes—trees and rock—surrounding the clearing. "Waverley is probably the richest person alive, and he's lived a life of luxury. If this is one of the nicer areas of this hemisphere, do you really think he would be here?"

"Miss Timkul, Chad Waverley lives in a yacht. We saw it on Bellar Colony. It's probably a toasty twenty-one Celsius right now, wherever he is."

"But without your reconnaissance, how will you know if he's here?"

"We're sending a Dart down."

She shivered. "But Captain Brigston said there were no ships in orbit. How would they even have gotten people down here? It seems like a lot of risk to be taking for so little likely reward."

Meyers rubbed his gloves against the material covering his armored thighs and turned to watch Domnikov's progress. Repin, the smaller of the two, seemed to be having trouble dealing with the wind but Pivovarova was helping him. They had the floor down and two walls nearly in place.

Meyers turned back to Timkul. "I believe I mentioned before that risk-taking is part of our charter."

Her face bunched up, and he readied himself for a showdown. If she tried to assert her authority and cancel the mission, he would fight her. It was overreach.

"Captain Hecker seems very confident this will be quite easy." Timkul seemed to tense up, then just as quickly seemed to relax. "This is your mission, Colonel."

He felt the implied *But I will be watching.* "Thank you, Madam Envoy."

Meyers stomped over to the where Paxton stood watching the Russians. Without turning, Paxton opened a private channel. Meyers accepted the invitation.

"You having a little trouble with Madam Envoy, Colonel?" Paxton's voice was feisty, teasing.

"I guess I don't take an outside authority trying to intrude very well."

"More authority problems." Paxton didn't say anything else for a few heartbeats. "Sounded to me like she was asking about the wisdom of risking so much without proof."

Meyers edged parallel to Paxton and shifted to consider him. "You agree with her?"

With his visor down, Paxton was inscrutable, a statue. "She don't know Cassidy."

A gust of wind nearly bowled Repin over and took the walls down, but Pivovarova caught the anchoring lines and dug in. Domnikov came in behind her and grabbed hold—a little too intimately, Meyers thought. Strauss ran over from where he'd been unpacking other gear. Despite the lack of experience working together, they quickly had the structure standing and properly anchored.

It was a reassuring sight for Meyers. "I don't think we have a choice, Carl. Someone's gathering an army. Waverley or not, we can't let that happen."

"No, sir, we can't."

"You think Hecker's right? You think this is going to be a quick show of force and they fold?"

Now it was Paxton's turn to shift and look at Meyers. "Captain Brigston seems to think air superiority makes it a foregone conclusion, and I would normally defer to the expertise of officers, sir."

"However?"

"However, I have yet to see a mission go to plan, and it ain't in my nature to believe one ever will. And after what we ran into trying to put down in the most promising LZ, well, I feel I'm within my rights to say not a goddamn thing we do will ever be easy, sir."

Meyers let out a breath, reassured now that someone he respected had expressed the same unease that was eating at his gut. "But you're still onboard with the mission?"

"Can't see a way we can avoid it."

Meyers closed the channel and walked several meters out, feeling his way over the unpredictable ground. There was so much hidden beneath the snow and ice that each step felt like it might send him flying. When he came to a stop, he glanced skyward, admiring the swirl of snow and the sheet of dark clouds. Light peeked through those clouds here and there, and between the stars and his position, the *Valdez* waited.

He opened a video channel to Hassan. "Genevieve? Put us through to the *Valdez*. It's time we got that Dart airborne and committed to this mission."

"One moment, Colonel."

Meyers glanced over his shoulder at Timkul. Her visor was closed, but she seemed to be watching him. Of course she was, he realized. He was about to commit the ERF to another crazy mission, and this time, there was no one to blame but him. He wondered if that's what she wanted, what the UN wanted.

"Colonel?" Hassan's voice was soft, reassuring. "We are connected to the *Valdez*."

"Thank you, Ensign."

A video conference opened, with Brigston and Hassan looking into their cameras. Brigston was in the small cabin off the bridge, the captain's private space. His face was tight, tense. The color had returned to

Hassan's face. Frizzy strands of black hair bunched at the edges of her forehead.

Brigston glanced around. "Is the special envoy going to join us, Colonel?"

"No." Meyers couldn't believe Brigston even brought Timkul up.

Brigston leaned back, as if Meyers was making threats. "I thought she had something of a consulting role?"

"Not for this. It's a military matter."

"Aren't you risking antagonizing her?"

Meyers glanced at Hassan. Her eyes were wide, and she seemed uncomfortable. "Let's move on to the matter at hand. We had some real surprises with the weather, and we had a piece of gear tear free. It could have been a lot worse, but Chief Pivovarova managed to get another strap into place, and Ensign Hassan got the Dart back under control."

Brigston sucked in his lips. "I've seen Ensign Hassan's data."

"We'll need to be sure to reinforce the securing straps." Meyers did his best to keep his tone even. He didn't want to make things worse with Brigston.

"I'm not comfortable proceeding without reviewing the data from—"

"We're proceeding forward as planned." Meyers cursed himself for snapping. The tone hadn't been so bad, and his voice hadn't raised but Brigston's eyes said it all: open wide, eyebrows arched, a stinging sense of rebuke. "It's the timetable and all the unknowns. Where's their fleet? Where are they? That place where they've holed up, they must have chosen it because of the cover this weather provides. Can we even find them?"

"Well." Brigston blinked and seemed to gather his composure. "We can't recon with the UAVs."

Why? What's the need for a fight? "We'll use a Dart."

"I saw the recommendation. I can't say I agree with it."

"We don't have a choice. Task Ensign Nunoz. Load Two-Seven-Three up with Ensign Hassan's data. Kit it out for reconnaissance and nothing else."

"I checked that gear myself." Brigston leaned back into the camera.

And that was the problem, Meyers guessed. Brigston was taking personal offense at everything, starting with the gear coming undone. "The strap broke," Meyers said. It was all matter-of-fact—nothing personal. "It's just the turbulence, the way things are on this world."

"Merriman did a good job loading that Dart."

"Jeremy, I saw the strap break with my own eyes. The straps were stressed."

Brigston's cheeks flushed. "Someone could have sabotaged them."

"Who? Why?" Meyers wished he could dismiss Hassan from the video channel, but that would only make things worse. She seemed as uncomfortable as when they'd been in the worst of the turbulence. "Are you accusing the Russians?"

"Chief Pivovarova had full access to the Dart." That seemed to be reason enough for Brigston. He plucked something from his shirt and tossed it away.

"Fine. Have Cooper review the security videos. If he finds something, we act on it. Otherwise, let it go." Meyers turned to watch Pivovarova and the others as he spoke. They nearly had the Operations Center complete. "In the meantime, let's get the ships prepared and have that recon Dart launched."

"I don't feel that's safe," Brigston said.

"Put that in the record then."

"I will."

Meyers could feel his opportunity to salvage his relationship with Brigston slipping away. "I want Nunoz launched in fifteen minutes. Operation Shadow Valley is a go."

"You're taking unnecessary risks, Colonel. I'll be noting my concerns."

"I appreciate that." Meyers tried to even out his breathing. "Ensign, I believe we're done with the call. Thank you."

"Yes, sir." Hassan's eyes darted back and forth between them. "Thank you, sirs."

The video connection died, and Meyers swallowed. He fought back a sense of dread. He trusted his instincts, and they told him this was the right thing to do. He trusted Cassidy Taylor, and he trusted his team. He just wasn't sure he could trust anything else.

6

1 October 2175. Siberia.

THE OPERATIONS CENTER felt like a walk-in freezer. Meyers paced the interior, helmet sealed, shivering, occasionally glancing at the video displays lining the east wall. Against the gray of the material, the displays were a blinding white: fields and skies of snow, ice-caked cliffs and boulders. It only made the sense of cold worse.

He was alone except for the displays, cargo cases stacked nearby, and a handful of space heaters. A small room with a cot occupied the northwestern corner.

A chime brought his attention back to his suit's status display. He was already below fifty percent power. The suit was burning through its reserves quicker than he could recharge with his pacing and jumping. He dropped the target temperature by a full degree.

It was going to be worse down in the valley, he realized.

The building's entry flap opened, and Paxton's stout frame filled the space. He stepped aside, letting in the gray sunlight before Barlowe and Starling filed in. Paxton followed them inside and sealed the flap again.

The space heaters in the corners kicked on, and Meyers opened his visor; the others followed suit. The air took on a smell like burning plastic. It was that or keep the helmets sealed up.

"I'll try to keep this short," Meyers said. "Captain Hecker should be joining us."

Paxton's screwed-up face asked the unspoken question: *No Brigston or Timkul?*

"I wanted to hash out things for the ERF and IB before engaging anyone else." Meyers stopped short of saying, *in case you were wondering.* They all were, obviously.

One of the snow-white displays turned to a slightly darker static, and then Hecker's face appeared. Snow coated his helmet, and ice frosted his suit. The warm, gold tone was gone from his skin, leaving it a bright, irritated pink. He stood inside a smaller structure that Meyers recognized as the Tactical Operations Center or TOC, a forward analog to the one they were standing in. The TOC's walls shivered and bowed behind Hecker.

"Colonel, I am sorry for being late. We are experiencing problems with the signal—" Hecker's face froze in a smile for a second before the screen switched back to static and then to the snowy display. It couldn't have been planned better.

Meyers stared at the screen for a second, wondering if they had discovered yet another challenge to mission viability. "All right, so we'll have Hecker intermittently." He looked at the others. "While we wait for his connection to return, let's get started with the updates. Agent Barlowe, Private Starling?"

Starling looked to Barlowe, her wide eyes clearly stating her deference.

Barlowe settled onto a cargo case and twisted to get a better look at the wall of displays. "Hecker has this data already. Probably doesn't need it, since he's already living the experience." Several displays switched to different angles taken from an aerial view. Cliff walls swept by, intermittently switching from three-dimensional wireframe to breathtakingly clear imagery. The mountains gave way to jagged, icy hills, and then to a gentler sloping that leveled off into a winding, white valley broken by the occasional boulder or outcropping. The general shape of the valley containing the chokepoint they were interested in was a winding run of maybe twenty kilometers. It mostly angled northwest to southeast.

"Ensign Nunoz's flyover was helpful." Barlow frowned. "If we were penguins. Or reindeer."

Paxton scratched the bridge of his nose. "Maybe we should consider recruiting some. Load 'em up with RPGs and machine guns."

"We'd have better luck finding these guys if we did."

Meyers studied the displays. "Nothing from infrared or other imagery?"

The video began again, this time keeping the wireframe and filling in textures of what must have been beneath all the snow and ice. The cliffs had little soil covering them, as far as Meyers could see, and there was no sign of significant flora. At the base and down into the valley, it didn't get much better until things truly leveled off. Even there, the soil appeared to be fairly shallow, and the only thing that seemed to be growing was some sort of hardy fungus clumped atop stone here and there.

Barlowe paused the video to point to a few spots where the valley's soil looked disturbed and the clumps seemed to have been torn free of the stone. "We know they've been through the valley and in something heavy enough to get through the snowpack."

"But they're not there now?" Meyers squinted as he examined the image.

Barlowe and Starling shook their heads. Barlowe pointed at one area where the video blurred out. "We need to get one of your analysts to check that area. Put some of my imagery equipment down in the valley, and we'll be able to do better work."

"Soon." Meyers advanced the video and drilled down on the apparent course of destruction left by the Lancers. "Private Starling, what do you make of this?"

Starling looked from Paxton to Barlowe, possibly seeking approval to respond or just reassurances it was okay to screw up. "It'd have to be tracked, Colonel. Maybe with skis or skids to supplement but it sank deep, and that snow is frozen solid a few centimeters down. If they're really changing bases every six weeks, they can't have been down there too long. That's the only real evidence."

"Tank? APC? Mobile gun?" Meyers noted how quickly her eyes dropped to the floor. Her skin, normally a slightly bronzed shade of hot cocoa, darkened slightly around her cheeks. She still wasn't confident in her own analysis.

"Armored vehicles make sense, I guess. Sir." She hunched and shifted her weight slightly, making her seem smaller than she was. Maybe after realizing what she had done, she straightened again and brought her eyes up to look at Meyers. Standing nearly at attention, she could almost look him straight in the eyes. "It wouldn't make sense to waste resources on a mobile gun platform or a tank, Colonel. Not tracked. Not unless they were lightly armored and had small guns."

"Why's that?" Meyers tried to keep his tone neutral, but he was encouraged by her confidence.

"Well..." She looked around at the others again, then seemed to steel herself with a sigh. "You're not getting a heavy tracked vehicle into the valley driving through those mountains, so you're landing them from space, or you're driving them into the valley from somewhere that can be traversed."

"Like their northwestern base of operations."

"Yes, sir. The data we have indicates two places they could enter the valley—their base about sixty klicks northwest of Captain Hecker's position, and another area about two hundred klicks southeast of his position." She puffed her cheeks out and exhaled. "I just can't see that. Why bother bringing a heavy vehicle into the valley and then out again?"

"So, leave them at one of your bases?"

She nodded. "Or don't use any at all, sir. You risk breakdowns and accidents otherwise. I mean, unless you're picking people up. But a battalion? That's a lot to move with self-propelled guns or tanks, so it means we're back to APCs."

Meyers suppressed a smile. It was a solid analysis based on the limited data they had. "So, they have heavy APCs. We can assume anti-personnel weapons."

"Yes, sir. General purpose rounds from the mortars could probably tear up the—"

Hecker reappeared on the display. "—nel? Test, tes—" His eyes lit up. "Ah, good!"

"Just in time for the intelligence brief, Captain," Paxton said.

Hecker chuckled. Droplets of water trailed down his armor from the melting snow and ice. "We are going to need extra batteries and charging stations, Colonel. The cold is pushing everything to consume much more power."

"We'll see what we can do." Meyers forwarded the video file of the briefing to Hecker. "Review the file I just sent you when you get a moment."

"Of course, Colonel." Hecker glanced off into space.

Meyers brought up the forward operating station's profile. "What's the status on the defensive barriers and weapons system integration with the fleet?"

Hecker's eyes instantly locked back onto the camera, and a frown tugged the corner of his lips down. "Yes, we are nearly done with the barriers. The weapons integration..." His lips peeled back, revealing bright teeth. He looked around, clearly uncomfortable with everyone being on the call. "I was hoping to speak to you about that, Colonel."

Panic gnawed at Meyers's gut. "Agent Barlowe, could you and Private Starling work up some guesses about what sort of vehicles we might be looking at based off the tracks? Models, capabilities, vulnerabilities?"

Barlowe made a sour face as he stood. "Of course. Becky."

Starling almost jumped, although it didn't seem like she was upset about being dismissed. She followed Barlowe to the door, both of them visibly limping.

Meyers took a step toward them, suddenly hating himself for pushing them both so hard. "That was some solid work, Private."

Starling turned just far enough for him to see her eyes widen and a smile cross her face. She looked down. "Thank you, sir."

Once the entry flap was sealed again, Meyers turned back to Hecker. "What is it?"

"The Russians, Colonel." Hecker shook his head. "Their work on the buildings, it was sloppy. And on the equipment, it is even worse. Sergeant

Klinsmann is trying to get a connection to the *Valdez* for the weapons systems, but it would seem unlikely to succeed."

"Sabotage?" Meyers asked, gut clenching.

Paxton turned slowly to regard Meyers, head tilting curiously.

They're his soldiers, too, Meyers realized.

Hecker seemed to consider the idea for a few seconds, then he shook his head. "I think incompetence is the more likely reason. And dereliction of duty. The scrawny one, Sergeant Klinsmann reported smelling alcohol on his breath."

"Private Repin." Meyers could have kicked himself. "Make a note of it."

Paxton wrapped fingers around his mouth but his eyes challenged the idea.

"Not a reprimand," Meyers clarified. "Something to discuss with him."

Paxton seemed to relax.

"Of course, Colonel." Hecker stared off into space for a bit. "About the weapons system integration?"

"I'll see if I can get Commander Cooper to come down and assist." Meyers could've sworn he'd heard Paxton snort. "What about the rest of it? Are all the buildings up? Is the LZ clear? Navigation instrumentation working?"

Hecker straightened even more than normal. "Yes, Colonel. We have created an incline of snow up to the LZ, then a meter drop-off and leveling. We are ready for deployment."

"Good. We'll bring the rest of C Company down first. I'll be holding half of A Company here in reserve."

"An excellent idea, Colonel."

"I'll keep you updated on the request for Cooper's assistance. Meyers out." He disconnected as Hecker saluted, then resumed pacing.

"You seriously thinking of asking for the commander's help, Colonel?" Paxton's skepticism leaked into his voice. "And mind if I ask why the hell you're talking about reprimanding someone who was just attached to our unit without a day of training, sir?"

"No reprimand, Master Sergeant. But Repin was drunk onboard the

Valdez. We need to nip this in the bud. As for Cooper, I don't think we have a choice."

"I hope you don't mind if I watch?" Paxton chewed on his bottom lip.

"Of course not." Why let my pain go to waste, Meyers thought. He connected to Brigston privately and sent the video feed to one of the displays. It wasn't fair to Brigston, of course, but there was no need for him to know he was being watched. He'd already decided on whatever path he was going to take.

After what felt like a stretched-out period, Brigston accepted the connection request. His head was slanted back, as if offended by the sight of Meyers. "Colonel. Everything going to plan on-planet?"

"We're facing some complications. Connections to the *Valdez's* weapons systems, mostly. I was thinking it would be a good idea to have a weapons officer come down."

Brigston recoiled even further. "I think we'd be better served having the *Valdez* control the weapons. You could coordinate fire over comms."

"The *Valdez* would control fire. This is just an override to prevent firing on friendly positions and emergency control in case comms break down."

"How would you manage control without comms?" Muscles bulged along Brigston's jaw.

"Jeremy, let's not..." Meyers locked his hands behind his back.

Brigston leaned forward. "It's my ship, Lonny. Goddammit, leave me something."

"I'm not taking command of the task force."

"You might as well. You treat it as if it's nothing more than troop transport and support."

Meyers wondered what else Brigston thought the task force was. After the Metacorporate War, there weren't any other fleets to engage, and since controlling land was the key to enforcing the government's will, supporting and transporting troops seemed an excellent way to ensure a career. Why Brigston had such a problem with that was beyond Meyers's understanding. "This is just a way to ensure the people on the ground have control when the shit gets hot."

"So now you think things are going to get hot?"

"Always assume the worst and hope for the best." Meyers reminded himself that Brigston had years more experience and was a good officer. Solid. Proven.

Brigston relaxed slightly. "I could send Lieutenant Gaeta down—"

Out of the corner of his eye, Meyers saw Paxton shake his head slightly, clearly perplexed. "I was hoping Commander Cooper could help out," Meyers said.

"Lieutenant Commander Cooper's my security officer now, Colonel."

"And he's still your best weapons officer. He knows the controls—"

"Lieutenant Gaeta can handle—"

"I'm not asking for Gaeta—I'm asking for Cooper."

Brigston jerked forward and shouted, "And I'm telling you no, Colonel. No! I can send down Lieutenant Gaeta, or you can do without support from the *Valdez*." His head shook, and his cheeks almost glowed. He sucked in a breath and leaned back, brushing the front of his shirt. After a few strokes, he cleared his throat. "Or you can *order* me to send Lieutenant Commander Cooper down."

Meyers stared at the screen. He wondered if Brigston would behave the same way if they were in a private conference room, maybe sharing a drink. Could they find common ground without all the kilometers separating them?

It didn't matter, Meyers realized. The distance was there. This was Brigston's call.

Paxton watched Meyers, arms crossed, waiting for the inevitable.

"Send Lieutenant Commander Cooper down to assist Captain Hecker with the weapons system integration, Captain."

Brigston flinched. "Aye, sir."

The connection died.

Paxton whistled. "Well, you've lost him."

"Yeah." Meyers had dreaded the moment, but he'd been sure it was coming.

"Nothing you could've done about it. Just a bad mix of bureaucratic idiocy and pigheaded pride."

"That doesn't make it feel any better, Carl."

"Wasn't meant to." Paxton walked to the exit, where he stood with his back to Meyers. "He's not the only thing eating at you."

Meyers brought the flyover data up on the displays. "No, he's not."

Paxton turned to consider the images. "Not convinced it's Waverley?"

"Where would he hide his yacht? One of those bases? Why bring a battalion into a snowy shit hole like this and then move them through the valley on a fixed schedule? There's nowhere for them to go once they're in there. Even if they have APCs, there's a limit to what they can do with ground vehicles."

Paxton stepped closer and watched the video play through but offered nothing more than a harrumph.

"You don't hire out a battalion of Lancers by accident," Meyers said.

"Most folks wouldn't." Paxton's head tracked along the path of the valley.

Meyers turned to consider Paxton. He was squinting, staring at the enhanced imagery. Meyers could feel an idea forming, but it was taking its time. "Would you let someone leave after they found out what you were doing and turned you down, Carl?"

Paxton looked at Meyers. "That bugged me, too."

"So, if this isn't Waverley, who is it? What's their game?"

"Can't say, Colonel." Paxton examined the images for a while longer, then strolled to the flap and let himself out.

Meyers left the flyover on loop while he tried to tease out the idea that had been forming in his mind. Finally, he gave up. He sealed his visor, powered down the space heaters, and settled onto the cot in the small room. The walls were nothing more than thick fiber kept rigid by a modest current. They could stop small arms fire but couldn't keep the cold out. Not completely. And they definitely couldn't keep the distracting thoughts out.

We came out here on a wild goose chase, he thought to himself. We're going to lose most of the *Valdez* officers when we return home.

His thoughts turned to Timkul and her accusations that he was obsessed.

He closed his eyes and tried to catch some sleep but couldn't stop wondering if he'd let his emotions push him into a deadly decision.

7

2 October 2175. Siberia.

SNOW CRUNCHED beneath Meyers's boots as he walked the perimeter of the forward operating site. What passed for morning sunlight cast the trees in a gray shroud. Twenty meters away, the closest building was an almost indistinguishable white, cloaked in snow. He sucked in the air—crisp, clean, and thicker than what he had expected at such an altitude. The air was also cold enough that he couldn't leave his visor up for too long without his skin stinging. He pressed against the thick, dark trunk of what passed for a tree on the planet and scanned the sky and the camp. Dark clouds were visible to the northwest; they were moving in.

The site was situated in a protected clearing, hard to spot and hard to get access to without aircraft but he still felt vulnerable. He brought his visor down and caught the faintest trace of heat overhead, a streak of white across the surprisingly clear sky.

A connection request came in from Dart One-Zero-One; it was Ensign Hassan. He accepted and watched the white streak split into two.

"This is Colonel Meyers. Go ahead, Ensign."

"Colonel, we are en route, ETA five minutes." Hassan's voice had taken on its usual calm after several flights in Siberia's atmosphere.

"I'm seeing another contrail, or I was."

"Arrow Two-Two-Seven, sir. Commander Cooper heading into the valley."

"Looks like we've got another storm blowing in." Meyers headed back toward the Operations Center as quickly as the snow allowed and quieted the warning chime that told him the Dart was inbound for landing.

"We're getting chop up here." She sounded like a child bouncing on a lap.

"What're you bringing me, Santa?"

"A Company, Colonel." He could hear a smile in her voice. "Two squads at a time."

Meyers looked toward the valley where Hecker was gathering the main force, but the storm was already hanging over the distant peaks. The wind began shaking the trees around the perimeter, and the gray morning light faded. His Battlefield Awareness System indicated three people were approaching from the habitat buildings: Barlowe, Starling, and Timkul. He turned and waved them into the Operations Center.

"Don't try anything crazy, Ensign." Meyers unlatched the entry flap and waited for the others.

"We'll stick to conventional landing, sir. Hassan out."

The connection died just as Barlowe arrived, decked out in the lighter armor he had taken to since the Dart crash on Bellar. His visor was up, assumedly to make the display of distaste and frustration on his face easier to see.

"Good morning, Ladell!" Meyers tried to smile as intensely as Barlowe was frowning. "I hope your protein paste was as tasty as mine."

"Can't taste anything in this cold," Barlowe muttered.

Starling saluted as she approached, then followed Barlowe inside. Timkul looked skyward before she entered. Meyers followed them inside and sealed the flap, then made his way to the nearest space heater, which was already giving off an angry, orange glow. He set his helmet down on the floor a short distance away.

"So, what has everyone up so early today?" Meyers flexed his fingers as he spoke.

Barlowe squatted in front of the opposite heater. "I want to know when you're going to get an intelligence analysis team into the valley. You'll have to ask the envoy what brought her here."

Timkul was struggling with her helmet; Starling stepped closer to help. "I wanted to get an update on the situation, thank you, Agent Barlowe. Since you haven't seen fit to invite me to your meetings, Colonel."

Meyers breathed as deeply as he could. "Well, there hasn't been much to update."

"You've had three meetings since our arrival." Timkul didn't seem angry, but that was probably her diplomatic training. "Do you always discuss nothing?"

"We've discussed the lack of progress, actually."

Timkul joined Starling at the heater on the other side of the entry flap. "I thought I saw you watching the sky. That warning chime indicated a ship incoming?"

"Dart One-Zero-One. Ensign Hassan. She's bringing down personnel from A Company."

"And how are Sergeant Domnikov and his men doing?" Timkul twisted around, probably to show him she was smiling, being pleasant; it felt intrusive.

"Sergeant Paxton's going to visit with Domnikov today."

"That sounds good." Timkul rubbed her gloved hands together.

"It's all part of the integration and training they would normally receive on Plymouth." Meyers hoped that came out as pleasant as Timkul's words had. He turned toward Barlowe. "We had to push the intelligence team back in the queue, Ladell. We're having problems with the gear. Coop's...um, Lieutenant Commander Cooper is bringing down some more equipment to see if he can effect a workaround. We need to get weapons system integration going with the *Valdez*."

"What's the problem, sir?" Starling had looked comfortable when asking the question but that comfort rapidly transformed into embarrassment. "I mean, if I can ask, Colonel."

Meyers chuckled and hoped Timkul didn't end up asking the same question. "Sounds like a few things, but they don't seem to have the weapons online yet."

"They were reporting power issues yesterday is why I ask, sir." The familiar quiver was back in Starling's voice.

"That's one of the problems, yes."

"There's a pretty easy way we could reroute power among the control systems. I mean, if we wanted to. Sir."

Barlowe raised his eyebrows and tilted his head, saying *I told you she was good* without a word.

Meyers wasn't worried about Starling being good; he wanted to drop the conversation before Timkul figured out what was up. "Well—"

"If it's the guns not being synced up, that's not really that big a deal. You just run substations, maybe in pairs. A couple linked mortars, a linked pair of railguns, some machine guns...you just sustain fire long enough and targeted precisely enough, it's pretty devastating." Starling's eyes grew wide with excitement as she described the potential of the systems.

"Probably best if you talked with the commander about it. You can accompany us."

Timkul's eyes jumped from Meyers to Starling. "You're going into the valley?"

"I wanted to get a look at it. We don't have good video feeds running yet."

"Perhaps I should go along." Timkul sounded pleasant but she wasn't making a request.

"There's not much to see there yet." Meyers wasn't sure how hard to fight.

"Good. Better I see it before you frighten these Lancers into surrender."

Let it go, Meyers told himself. "We'll be making a couple flights out. Maybe you could come with the second group?"

"Is that when you're going, Colonel?" Steam curled from Timkul's nostrils.

"I was just concerned about how packed the Dart's going to be. And the storm."

Timkul turned back to the heater. "I'm sure we'll have enough room. Perhaps I could sit in that crew chief's chair if we're short of seats."

The hum of the Dart's fans filled the space outside the Operations Center, and the flap shuddered. Meyers waited until the engines died down before opening a channel to Hassan and inviting her into the Operations Center. A few minutes later, the flap opened, and she stepped through. She pulled her helmet off and shook out her shoulder-length hair, black and wiry. She joined Starling and Timkul at the space heater, noticeably shorter and wider at the hips than either of them.

Hassan laughed as she looked around the interior. "I was expecting champagne and caviar, Colonel."

"We'll serve it when you deliver it." Meyers hooked his thumbs inside his belt. "How was the flight down?"

"Good, sir." Hassan sounded calm, confident. "We're getting the hang of it."

"Ready for another run? Into the valley?" Meyers nodded toward the others. "Give us a chance to inspect things and talk to Commander Cooper."

"Y-yeah. No problem, Colonel." She didn't sound as confident.

Meyers could see the anxiety in the way she turned to look at him. "You've been flying a lot?"

She nodded. "Eight sorties, counting this one. One late last night. In a storm."

"We'll make it as quick as possible. Who'd you bring down this morning?"

"Uh, Sergeants McNutt and Banh, Colonel." She was trying to put on a brave face.

"Okay. Two hops over—McNutt's squad and us first." Meyers made a circle with his finger to indicate the others. "Then you bring Banh over and bring us back. After that, you're done for the day. Deal?"

She pulled her helmet back on. "Guess I'll get the engines prepped."

Meyers opened the flap for her and tried to avoid making eye contact with Timkul.

Timkul joined him at the entry. "Do you always push your people so hard, Colonel?"

"We operate with very limited resources. Missions are never easy. We work hard; we play hard. She'll get some time to rest soon. She's one of our best pilots. They're going to count on her early. That's the way it is."

"You should have more reliable people." Timkul crossed her arms.

He fought back a smirk. "I've been saying that since the war ended, Miss Timkul."

Timkul quit trying to pretend like they were sharing a pleasant moment and grabbed her helmet from the floor near the heater. He did the same, sealing the visor and holding the flap aside for the others to head out. Outside, what little sunlight there had been was gone. It was nearly like he remembered early winter evenings near Pittsburgh, with bruised and swollen clouds stretching out to the northwestern horizon. Hassan brought the engines online, kicking up a fog of battered snow that hung over the clearing. McNutt and his squad hauled the last of the cargo down the ramp and set it into the storage structure, where Banh's squad began breaking things out and sorting them.

Meyers headed for the structure, pausing in the entryway. Snow wheeled around his boots as he opened his visor. "Sergeant Banh, Sergeant McNutt, a minute?" He headed toward the nearer of the personnel structures.

McNutt arrived first, visor raised, dark blue eyes popping out against his faintly copper-brown skin. His broad shoulders were thrown back, as if he were ready to fight. A few seconds later, Banh arrived—shorter, slender, shivering, the deep gold skin of his face twitching against the cold. There was no sense of hostility in his posture, despite the earlier confrontation over a chaplain for his unit.

"I hate to do this, but we're going to need to change the schedule around." Meyers saw McNutt's cheek tick up. He was always ready to challenge decisions. "We're having problems in the valley, so I want to get A Company down in there until we get things turned around. We'll still use you as reserve forces, but we need to get our systems deployed quickly, or we won't be ready if the Lancers show."

McNutt sneered. "The Russians, right?" His New Zealand accent was thick, usually a sign he was angry. "They're a mess. Captain Hecker had his unit tight before now. How's Gerhardt liking that, watching his pale-skinned heroes stumbling around like idiots?"

"Let's stow that, Sergeant. We'll get them trained up." Meyers looked at Banh. "Sergeant Banh, get the gear sorted and check the systems out. Ensign Hassan will be back in a couple hours to pick your squad up. Get the fire base ready; your team will be back here by morning."

Banh saluted. "We will be ready, Colonel."

Meyers saw Paxton making his way out of the farther structure and waved him over. "Master Sergeant, I was just updating Banh and McNutt on the change of plan."

"Change of plan, sir?" Paxton cocked his head. "Can't say I recall one."

"We're heading into the valley."

"The Russians." McNutt shook his head.

Meyers let it go. He'd promised A Company airborne operations once the engagement began, a chance to truly test their training, but now they were being tasked to cover for someone else's mistakes. They needed to see it as a team-building opportunity, but that would only come with time, not him beating them over the head about it.

"I want to get a look at things personally, and I know you wanted to talk with—" Meyers glanced at McNutt. "To brief everyone on battalion policy."

Paxton's head rocked back; he understood. "Let's get it going, Colonel."

Meyers shuffled through the snow, leaving Paxton to deal with McNutt. He was a deadly soldier, but his hard-nosed attitude made it hard to bring a diverse team together. For McNutt, you were one of his people, or you were a problem.

More learning, Meyers told himself. More growth. We all need it.

He kicked the snow off his boots at the top of the slick ramp, narrowed the soles back to normal width, then shook snow free from his arms and chest. When he was sure he'd done all he could, he crossed to his seat and pulled his harness down. Timkul sat to his right, staring straight ahead, visor down. She didn't seem up to antagonizing him anymore, which was good. They would be in the valley in thirty minutes or less, which would fly by without her attacks. He looked forward to some peace. A minute later, Paxton entered the Dart, followed by McNutt and his squad. The ramp retracted, and the airlock closed.

"All right," Hassan said over the intercom, "we are cleared to enter the valley airspace. This shouldn't take long, but you'll need to secure yourselves."

The engines grew louder, and the Dart lifted off. Meyers felt a tension slip from his body that he hadn't recognized before. After thinking about it, he realized it was the sense of helplessness he'd felt on Bellar when he'd lost command to Ramawat. Meyers glanced at Timkul and reminded himself she was just there as a liaison.

If violence broke out with the Lancers, this would be his battle.

HASSAN SET the Dart down in a broad, relatively flat area clear of larger rocks. The landing was about as rough as her first one on Siberia. A snow-covered Dart rested six meters away, where a squad of Hecker's soldiers were embedding equipment under the snowpack. More instrument landing and other navigational aids, Meyers realized. That should have been one of the first things finished. It made Hassan's reluctance to fly into the valley more understandable.

Meyers was the first out of the airlock. It was colder and windier in the valley, and visibility was limited to twenty meters at best. As he descended the ramp, he switched to thermographic imaging and let his BAS search out any existing private networks. He found Hecker's command network and requested access; Hecker accepted.

"Captain Hecker, sorry for the short notice. I was hoping to get a look at things firsthand." Meyers twisted around in time to see Paxton assisting Timkul down the ramp. "And the special envoy wanted to be sure...we had things under control."

Hecker's ID appeared forty meters out and closing. "Good to have you down here, Colonel. The commander has been looking the controls over."

Cooper's ID appeared a few meters behind Hecker's. "Colonel? We need to talk." Cooper sounded close to panic. "I brought some concentrators and amplifiers down, but it's not going to be enough."

Meyers trudged across the snow, shifting his eyes from the thermographic image to a small screen showing him simple, enhanced imagery. "What's up?"

"Those cliffs, this weather, the damaged antenna." Cooper and Hecker were yellow splotches against the deep blue snow. "We need to get something up there."

Meyers followed the direction of Cooper's right hand, which seemed to be pointing at a distant, hazy outline of a huge mountain to the south. Meyers hurried forward until Cooper and Hecker were almost orange shapes, each saluting. He returned the salutes and switched back to the enhanced imagery. "You want to get something up on that mountain?"

Cooper opened a direct video connection using his internal helmet camera. His face was flush, and his eyes were puffy. "They bent the shit out of the antenna. We can get a smaller one up there and make up for it. I got a signal amplifier running down in the TOC. Shit, Tactical Operations Center."

Meyers smiled. "It's just us on the line."

"Okay. Well, we should finally have full BAS capabilities here in the valley, at least."

"And that antenna will be enough for the weapons integration?"

"If you keep the Russians' clumsy paws off it, yeah." Cooper sighed.

Hecker joined the channel. He had a bashful, shamed look about him —eyes down, forehead wrinkled. "If you two are talking about the Russians, it is my fault, Colonel."

"No. Master Sergeant Paxton's going to talk with them. We brought Sergeant McNutt's squad to help get things where we need them."

"Shit." Cooper shook his head. "We don't need the antenna banged up more."

Meyers fought back an angry retort. "So, have him take up a patrol. He's solid. We can count on him."

Hecker looked past Meyers. "He is still down a sniper?"

"And Starling's still helping Agent Barlowe out." Meyers considered bringing Timkul into the conversation. Providing reinforcements—

quality reinforcements—was apparently harder for the UN than setting arbitrary deadlines to prove the ERF's worth or sending along liaisons with personal agendas. "McNutt's squad can handle whatever you throw at them."

"I will detail them out to check the western perimeter," Hecker said. "There have been some problems with the sensors there."

"Wait." Meyers invited Barlowe to the channel. "Ladell, Captain Hecker's getting ready to send McNutt's squad out to the western perimeter. Where was that spot you wanted to get some of your imagery gear?"

"Northwest." Barlowe sounded testy, and he was grunting from exertion. "I'll send you the coordinates."

Meyers looked at Hecker when the coordinates came in. "Maybe send them along with Agent Barlowe, get some imagery systems running deeper in the valley?"

Hecker seemed to chew on that. "Yes, Colonel." He marched off stiffly.

Cooper dropped back to a private channel with Meyers. "I think I might have gone a little too far with him," Cooper said. "But it's…"

"I know. Not his fault, though. By the way, Starling was asking what sort of problems you were running into. She had some ideas that seemed to have potential. She's sharp as hell. Maybe you could take her up there with you?"

Cooper grimaced, as if he'd been gut-punched. "This is really specialized work."

"Barlowe says she's got a way with systems. It's almost intuitive with her."

That seemed to make things worse for Cooper. His brow furrowed, and his eyes squinted to tiny, beady glints. "The captain's already upset about me being down here. Giving one of your people any sort of access to our systems, especially with those IB systems…you know that's going to push him over the edge."

"So, just have her haul stuff around if you don't trust her."

Cooper sighed. "It's not trust."

"Then take her along. Give her some training. She's a demolitions expert."

Cooper's eyes lit up. "Seriously?"

"Probably knows ordnance better than systems. And if you don't take her up with you, I'm going to get an earful from McNutt. He resents the hell out of her being tasked to—"

"Okay, okay. I'll take her up." Cooper's shoulders slumped, defeated. "Any chance I could get Hassan to fly us up there?"

Meyers recalled the look of dread on Hassan's face when he'd asked her to fly them out to the valley. "She's pretty fried. I told her she was done for the day when she brought—" He turned at the sound of a Dart launching. "And there she goes. She's bringing Bahn's squad out to help."

Cooper pointed back the way Meyers had come. "I've got the gear loaded up in Dart Three-Zero-Eight. That's Lieutenant Kumar's but if I had my choice, I'd rather Hassan or Nunez handle this. I don't get the sense Kumar's as experienced with this sort of flying."

"He flew with the MARCOS," Meyers said. "He can handle it."

"Yeah." Cooper turned to consider the valley to the west. "At least the Lancers haven't shown up yet. Shit, Lonny, this could really go bad if they showed up before we got everything set up. We still need more batteries and charging stations with as cold as it is. Even the suits can't keep up with the heating requirements."

"I know." Meyers bristled at the reminder that things were already going off plan. "We still have time to pull this together."

It finally seemed to dawn on Cooper that he was making matters worse. He straightened. "You know, I think I'll go get Private Starling and talk to her about her weapons systems ideas." He saluted.

Meyers returned the salute. "Thanks, Coop. I'll send Banh's squad up with you when you're ready to go."

He waited until Cooper was gone, then began surveying the complex. Like Cooper said, it was only a matter of time before the Lancers showed up, and if that time was soon, things were going to get ugly.

8

———

2 October 2175. Siberia.

THE TOC WAS a mirror of the main Operations Center they'd set up in the clearing. Gephardt was hunched over in the far right corner, pale golden hair and pink skin almost white in the snow reflected from the wall of displays. His eyes—a bluish gray—were locked onto a piece of equipment that Meyers assumed was part of the gear damaged by Domnikov and his men. The system's glossy black case reflected the angry red of an overworked space heater. Meyers pulled his helmet off and sealed the flap behind him. Even with the space heaters cranked to full, the building was cool enough that his breath misted. He'd spent too long outside, but he wanted to see Banh's squad aboard Three-Zero-Eight and Ensign Hassan on her way back to the *Valdez* for a little rest before warming up.

Meyers sniffed at the air. "Smells like that system's fried."

Gerhardt snorted. "Nah, that's just the fucking space heaters. This thing's got a crack in the main circuit, right at the power feed." He looked up and blinked, then stood. "Shit, Colonel. I didn't know it was you."

Meyers waved for Gerhardt to take his seat. "I didn't know you were a systems expert."

"No expert." He crouched over the system again, pulling away flex cards and wiring. "I worked around my grandfather's place when I was a kid. He and my dad were engineers, systems designers. Y'know, power and infrastructure management. Not really my kind of thing. I don't trust machines."

"Strange to hear from someone whose life depends on the BAS."

Gerhardt shrugged. "I guess."

Meyers made his way over to examine the system. It looked like a command module, probably from the weapons systems. He pointed to a crack that ran along the corner near the power receptacle. "That's some pretty serious damage."

"Fucking gorilla would've had a hard time doing that much damage. And there was water inside the case. These things are waterproof."

Meyers considered that for a moment.

"You should see the antenna." Gerhardt snorted. "I thought Commander Cooper was gonna shit himself. 'Who fucking did this?'" His voice was high-pitched, like Cooper's when he became angry. "Goddamn Repin."

"You think it was deliberate?"

Gerhardt looked up suddenly, the humor gone from his face. "Sabotage? Shit, Colonel. That's a pretty big accusation."

"I'm asking for your opinion, not making an accusation."

"Well." Gerhardt's brow wrinkled. "Shit. I wouldn't want to make that call, Colonel. They could just be first-class fuck-ups."

Meyers ran a hand along the cracked case. "It's possible." He turned to the displays and began flipping through imagery of the mountains. "Commander Cooper's talking about taking his gear up to one of the mountaintops. Did you happen to catch which one? It looked pretty big."

Gerhardt joined Meyers in front of the displays. "That one." Gerhardt stepped closer to the display and brought up a control interface on the screen. He moved along the steep cliff face until it leveled off, then followed the ledge into a broad, open, flat area. "Here. Like a little plateau, up at the peak. Don't need an ace pilot to put down there. Could probably put one of the heavy mortars up there and hit damn near anywhere in the middle of the valley."

"Not with any accuracy, not with this storm sitting on us."

Gerhardt glanced at the ruined control system. "With the right controller..."

It was awfully convenient that the critical parts of their gear had been damaged. The sort of convenience that could lose battles.

Meyers's earpiece chimed; Barlowe was requesting a private channel. Meyers stepped to the corner opposite where Gerhardt had been working. "What's up, Ladell?"

"We're en route to the position, about five klicks out." Barlowe was breathing hard. "It just occurred to me that I'll need some help with the cameras and systems setup. McNutt's not going to be any good. Maybe you could send Becky?"

"She's going out on a mission with Cooper." Meyers tensed, waiting for the blow-up.

"A mission with Cooper? Is that why McNutt's in such a mood?"

"Probably." As far as Meyers was concerned, McNutt only had one mood, but others might be able to pick up subtle variations in *intense*.

The only sound on the connection for several seconds was Barlowe's labored breathing. Meyers imagined each step in the cold and snow with Barlowe's injured back. "You need to push your intelligence assets up the queue and get them down here, Lonny. I'm not supposed to be doing this sort of thing. I'm a fucking liaison, not a soldier."

Meyers muted and looked back at Gerhardt. "Sergeant Gerhardt, what's your squad doing in the rotation?"

"We've got the western perimeter next shift."

"When's that?"

Gerhardt stared off into space for a moment. "Four hours and change."

"Lonny, you hear me?" Barlowe sounded agitated.

Meyers came off mute. "One second." He muted again. "How would you like a chance to get off patrol for today?"

"Fuck yeah." Gerhardt stood. "Sir."

"Get your squad together. I want you to take one of those small shack assemblies and a generator out to where Agent Barlowe's setting up surveillance gear. His back's still a mess, and he needs help with some of the systems work."

The enthusiasm drained from Gerhardt's face at the mention of Barlowe. "I'm not sure it's fair for us not to pull our fair share walking the perimeter, sir."

Meyers gritted his teeth. "Sergeant Gerhardt, you remember our discussion when we promoted you? Our expectations were very clear: maturity, tolerance, and professionalism."

Gerhardt cast his eyes down. "Yes, sir."

"All right, get moving."

Gerhardt grabbed his helmet and headed for the exit.

Meyers held out a hand. "I know this sounds boring, but this mission could turn bad in an instant. Stay alert."

"They're just Lancers." Gerhardt shrugged, petulant. "If they're even out there."

Meyers bit back a comment. He un-muted. "Ladell, I've got Gerhardt's squad heading out to assist. When they get there, they'll relieve McNutt's squad."

"Why are you sending *him*?" Barlowe's voice dripped with disgust.

"I think he can help with the systems work. Plus, I'm having them bring a generator and shack out to your position. You'll be able to stay warm while you set the surveillance system up."

"The only thing Gerhardt knows how to do is spew racist and homo-phobic crap, Lonny."

"If he does, you let me know."

"He doesn't have to say anything. You can feel it coming off him."

"We're trying to rehabilitate him. It's not easy finding people as skilled as he is. He's worked around IB for years. Show him why he should respect you. Give him a chance."

Barlowe sighed dramatically. "Fine. But if he screws up, I want—"

"If he screws up, I'll take care of it. Personally."

Once again, the connection was silent other than Barlowe's breathing. Suddenly, he chuckled. "That's pretty good, Lonny. I can't believe you made me appreciate McNutt but you did."

Meyers smiled and disconnected. He sat in front of the displays, alternately examining the broken control system and the landing area Cooper had identified. Something about the two unrelated items was annoying, and Meyers couldn't figure what it was.

The flap opened, and Hecker stepped through, followed by Timkul. Hecker secured the flap, then removed his helmet. Timkul finally seemed to have the hang of removing hers.

Hecker looked around, frowning. "Have you seen Sergeant Gerhardt, Colonel?"

Meyers cursed himself. "I'm sorry, Captain. I was going to contact you, then I got distracted." He pointed at the broken case. "Gerhardt was working on that. When I saw he had experience with systems, I asked him to relieve Sergeant McNutt. Agent Barlowe needed someone to help him set up his surveillance equipment, and that's not McNutt's strength."

"Ah. I see. Thank you, sir." The frown didn't leave Hecker's face.

"I, uh. I also promised to shift Gerhardt's perimeter duty out a day." Meyers could see the tension in Hecker's face. "I'm sorry. I should have consulted with you."

"Not at all, Colonel. The battalion is yours, after all."

Meyers could see Timkul in his peripheral vision. She initially watched the interaction without showing any reaction, but it was clear she was picking up on Hecker's frustration. She turned to the space heater, not saying a thing. Meyers took a step toward her, ready to explain the situation; he stopped when a connection request came in from Cooper.

"Go ahead, Coop." Meyers grabbed his helmet and considered stepping out even though he could feel Timkul watching. Listening.

"We're approaching the peak," Cooper said. Video suddenly kicked in, revealing the white mountainside, steep and unclimbable except for a couple challenging spots near the top. "You getting the belly camera? This place, if we can land on it, would be pretty safe. Maybe leave a squad up here. You wouldn't need anything more than that. Anyone coming up out of the valley, you'll see them. They'd have to know what they're doing. There's no easy path up, not without insertion."

"Is that ledge where you wanted to land?" Meyers recognized the broad, flat area from the flyover imagery.

"Yeah. Lieutenant Kumar seems pretty confident, but we're going to give it a test run first." Cooper's tone was disapproving. "Sergeant Banh wants to take his squad down before we land, secure the LZ, all that. I don't think it's necessary. I thought I'd check with you."

"If Kumar can hover a few meters up, I think it'd be a good idea."

"Nothing's up here but us."

Meyers considered the imagery on the displays. The hairs on his neck stood up, but he couldn't see anything out of the ordinary. It was just a flat area that led to a peak to the east. That peak rose another hundred meters or so, but it narrowed quickly and offered no real flat areas like the one Cooper had chosen. A ripple of snow at the peak's base indicated some sort of gradual step up, maybe two meters high, possibly a sign of an avalanche or rockfall. There were boulders and outcroppings between the outer extreme of the ledge and the base of the peak, but they couldn't hide anything significant.

"Lonny?" Cooper sounded impatient.

"I'd rather we have eyes on, Coop."

Hecker's curious gaze caught Meyers's attention; he held up a finger to ask for a moment but Hecker was already looking away. Meyers recognized the signs of an important call: pacing, leaning forward, staring into space.

"All right, we're circling around now," Cooper said. "Looks clear."

"I'll stay on until you're down safe." Meyers watched Hecker, who seemed even deeper into his call than before.

"Oh!" Cooper suddenly sounded excited. "Private Starling explained her idea—"

Hecker turned and waved a hand to get Meyers's attention, then pointed at the displays, which now showed two soldiers standing in the snow. What looked like a defensive barrier was barely visible in the video.

"Coop, we've got some sort of incident down here." Meyers walked toward the display, trying to make sense of what the soldiers were doing. "Can I put you on hold for a second?"

"Sure." Cooper's excitement instantly transformed into annoyance.

Meyers muted the connection to Cooper and moved closer to the display. "What's this?"

The soldiers stood in front of a meter-and-a-half-high post of some sort, covered in snow. One of the soldiers seemed to be staring off into space while the other scraped snow and ice from the top of the post. Their IDs popped up: Klinsmann and Strauss.

Meyers finally realized the post was one of the perimeter sensors. The uneasy feeling returned. "Are we having problems?"

Hecker pointed to another display, and the perimeter came to life. It stretched roughly north to south across the valley floor, a string of green lines indicating there was no movement, thermographic variation, signal traffic, noise, or reflection for one hundred meters out. In weather like they were facing, the sensors were operating at the outer edge of tolerances but everything showed green.

Audio, shared by Hecker, came over Meyers's earpiece. "Captain, you see now, *ja?*"

Hecker leaned in closer to the display; Meyers did the same. Nothing changed. They were green.

"You show green, Sergeant Klinsmann." Hecker straightened. "What is that you did there?"

"Resetting, Captain." Klinsmann, the soldier who had been squatting and scraping snow and ice from the post, stood and slowly turned in a circle.

A section of the green lines disappeared from the perimeter display, creating a gap at least five meters wide that ran all the way out into the valley.

"Now the signal is gone," Hecker said.

"It will return, Captain." Klinsmann was looking toward the camp, not the valley.

Meyers's mind told him something was wrong. He squinted at the displays, trying to spot the error but all he saw was snow. "Why'd he reset the sensor?"

Hecker shrugged his shoulder. "Sergeant Klinsmann, there was—"

The sensor came back online, and the network of green lines turned into a mixture of amber and sickly green. One turned red for a second, then amber.

"What the hell?" Meyers connected to the security command console and pulled the view of the perimeter back so that he could see the entire compound.

Klinsmann waved toward the compound, and two forms separated from the nearby snow. They began hop-running, focusing on speed instead of stealth. "Colonel Meyers?"

"Yes. What's going on, Sergeant?"

"The sensor, it was not responding." Klinsmann pulled his CAWS-5 from its brace and turned back to the valley. "I could not get past the initial control interface."

Meyers's breath caught. "Have we been compromised?"

Klinsmann sighted down the barrel of the gun, and then Meyers saw Klinsmann's weapon register inside the perimeter sensor, riding the array of data. One of the amber threads stretched into tendrils extending out into the valley. Something moved in the snow out there, and Klinsmann shifted his sights.

He fired, filling the valley with the roar of his gun. Whatever had been moving dropped.

Klinsmann lowered his weapon, and the perimeter sensor lines returned to various shades of green. "Are their indigenous life forms on this planet, Colonel?"

"Nothing substantial logged in the survey records. Not this far north." Meyers saw that Timkul was watching now. He remembered that Klinsmann had sent two of his soldiers back into the compound at speed. "Miss Timkul, please put your helmet on." Meyers put his own helmet on.

"Permission to go beyond the perimeter, Colonel?" Klinsmann had the CAWS-5 back in its brace.

Meyers looked at Hecker. "Your call."

"Permission granted, Sergeant," Hecker said. "Corporal Strauss, have the rest of the squad fan out, if you would please."

Klinsmann moved past the sensors, quickly hunching down to present a lower profile.

Meyers un-muted his line to Cooper. The belly camera showed that they were hovering over what looked like an ideal LZ. "Coop, look, we may have a situation here."

"What's going on?"

"Maybe nothing, but it looks like we had a perimeter sensor problem." Meyers felt his heart racing as Klinsmann moved over the snow. He was less than twenty meters from the fallen form. His lights revealed something slightly darker than the surrounding white blanket. "I'm thinking we might need to abort your landing."

"Lieutenant Kumar's got us in position right now. He said he's got this." Cooper switched from the belly camera to his helmet internal camera. "We need to get this gear set up, Lonny. No gear, no support from the task force."

"Just…just hold position. Okay?" Meyers wanted to reexamine the imagery. Something felt *wrong*. He willed Klinsmann to hurry up.

The form in the snow resolved more. It was covered in white and gray. A trunk and arms stood out in the snow. Legs. Blood.

An assault rifle.

"We have a Lancer, Colonel." Klinsmann pulled the body so that it laid flat on the snow. Wind whipped a fringe of white fur surrounding the head. "Stealth gear." He pulled a device from a front pouch of the body and tucked it away into a pouch of his own, then examined the assault rifle. "WS-A88 assault rifle. Pacific Armaments, post-HuCorp acquisition. These are solid weapons." He searched around the front of the suit, found a zipper, and undid the top, revealing another layer of clothing, a light uniform jacket, pale gray. Pockets in the jacket provided more items that Klinsmann shoved into his pouch. He took a moment to examine the bullet hole in the outer garment and jacket, then unzipped the jacket. Inside, there was a nondescript green uniform top, and inside that were thermals. "No armor to speak of. Reconnaissance."

Or saboteurs, Meyers thought to himself.

Klinsmann pulled the corpse's helmet back, and long, dark hair spilled out. Blood trickled from shapely, dark lips, and lifeless, brown eyes stared at the dark sky. Klinsmann gasped. "South Asian—Pakistan, maybe Afghanistan. Young. I would guess under thirty."

More shots rang out inside the compound.

Hecker turned toward the flap, hand reaching for his CAWS-5. "Squad leaders, status report!"

Voices—frantic, confused—flooded the open channel.

Klinsmann's voice overrode the others. "It was another reconnaissance person, Captain. We are clear now."

"This is Captain Hecker. Squad leaders, I want the camp searched. Assignments by grid sent...now. Status every minute. Everyone stay sealed up. *Schnell!* Hurry!"

Meyers relaxed slightly at the realization Hecker was on the same page—there could be bombs or gas weapons inside the perimeter. For the moment, the compound was clear but they had been compromised. The enemy knew someone else was in the valley.

The ERF had lost the critical element of surprise.

9

2 October 2175. Siberia.

Meyers was already getting tired of the sound of snow crunching beneath his boots. No matter how fast he moved, he couldn't lose Timkul. When she had asked to accompany him out to the perimeter, he couldn't say no. She glared at him from the top right corner of his visor but said nothing. He had hoped that stopping to see the corpse of the reconnaissance Lancer killed inside the perimeter would put her off; it hadn't. She had stared at the gore, and he thought she might have been sick for a moment when one of the soldiers flipped the dead woman's corpse over, revealing blood and brains dark in the white snow. That hadn't been enough to turn Timkul back but her face was pale, and her lips quivered. Regardless, she stuck with him.

Meyers continued forward, leaning into the wind and the blur of snow, hoping her voice might finally come over the communication channel. Let her beg off and return to the TOC, he thought to himself; she didn't.

With no need to worry about concealing their location anymore, lights had turned the camp bright as...well, a winter day in Pittsburgh. In the BAS display, the gray walls of the structures were pale blue wireframes. The augmented reality feed didn't capture the way the walls shuddered in the hammering wind. Klinsmann and his squad were green outlines beyond the outer edge of the buildings, surrounding the first corpse. Meyers stopped a meter short of the corpse, scanned the perimeter sensor line, then pushed forward.

Klinsmann had laid the body out on the snow inside the perimeter, dark hair fanned out around her head. A dark red smear across the white traced where she'd been dragged. Her outer garment was spread wide beside her like a canvas, and her gear was stacked on it: assault rifle, backpack, bags, and electronic devices. Klinsmann had put her mask back on to cover her face.

Meyers picked up the nearest of the electronic devices and twisted it around in his hand. He'd seen similar devices, like an ADPAX—hackers kits, essentially.

"It was that device," Klinsmann said as he pointed toward the perimeter sensor. "Took out the sensor."

"Overloaded it." Meyers triggered the device but a security interface popped up, prompting him for credentials. It seemed a simple enough system that he could probably overcome the interface with some time but they didn't have time. "This isn't high-end gear."

Klinsmann looked toward Strauss and shrugged. "It defeated our security."

Meyers examined the other devices. One was an optical enhancement system, the other some sort of signal detector. "There's nothing here powerful enough to overcome our security." He left unsaid the obvious: The spies would have needed inside help.

Out of the corner of his eye, Meyers spotted Timkul leaning over the corpse. She pulled the mask away with a shaking hand and touched the dead face.

"She doesn't even look old enough..." Timkul's voice was a whisper.

"Old enough to pull a trigger?" Meyers took the mask from Timkul and gently set it down on the dead woman's face again. "She comes from a region where people have been fighting each other for as far back as recorded history. It's all they know."

Timkul brushed her hands against each other, as if to get the death off them. "Why send in women?"

"Why not? They're smaller than most men, and they're probably familiar with this sort of terrain. A woman can pull a trigger or set a bomb as good as any man. Seems like an ideal scout or insurgency resource."

Timkul just stared at the black hair sprayed out on the snow. "She seems..."

"She was a Lancer, Miss Timkul. She killed for a living. It was a choice she made, probably to escape the poverty and backward ways of her people. She wasn't kidnapped and forced into this." Meyers felt his temper rising. It really annoyed him that Timkul seemed to identify with someone who had come to the camp to spy, maybe even to sabotage things. "These are the people we came to shut down. They're the enemy."

"I know." Timkul looked away from the corpse toward the camp. "Did they find anything yet? From the other one?"

"Nothing yet."

Meyers examined the outer garment, noting the way its fabric shifted in color slightly as he twisted and turned it. It had a basic chameleon-like functionality to it, something that could probably fool the naked eye and simple optics. He wouldn't be surprised to find temperature-damping circuitry inside the fibers. It wasn't a high-end chameleon suit like the ERF had in the pipeline, but it was perfect for a place like Siberia.

He muted his connection to Timkul and reopened his channel to Cooper. "Coop, what do you see up there?"

"We're hovering about fifteen meters out. All clear."

The video from the belly camera filled the display, revealing the ledge from a different angle, showing the outer edge that looked out over the valley. Meyers realized just how exposed and possibly fragile that position would be. He wasn't even sure the rock could handle the Dart's weight. He closed his eyes and thought back to the image Gerhardt had put up on the display in the TOC. If the ledge held, Cooper was right: It would be perfect to set a squad there and put equipment into place.

There was cover, no easy access from the ground, a quality landing spot. *If Cooper doesn't see anything, there's no justification for delaying the landing. I'm just being irrational and jumpy because of the perimeter breach.*

"Tell Kumar to go ahead, Coop. I'll let Captain Hecker know."

"Thanks." Cooper shifted his view to Starling. "By the way, I think Private Starling's ideas on deploying your munitions in the valley are solid. If we can get a couple robot platforms down here, you could probably get some improvised mines in place before it's too late."

"Good. We'll see if we still have time to try some of her ideas."

"You're going to need something against those numbers." Cooper sounded anxious.

"I know." Meyers brought Hecker onto the channel. "Captain, I've given the go-ahead for Lieutenant Kumar to land Cooper and Bahn's squad on the mountain. Any updates?"

"We found three devices, Colonel." Hecker's connection hummed and hissed, then his face appeared. The video switched to an external camera, revealing three black, smooth, palm-sized plastic cases laid out on packed snow. "I think they were planning to connect into and possibly take out our communications systems."

"Are those disabled?" Meyers wasn't familiar with the devices, and that made him uncomfortable. He realized Timkul was watching him, arms crossed over her chest. "One second. I'm bringing the special envoy into the channel. Miss Timkul? I have Captain Hecker and Lieutenant Commander Cooper on the channel with us. Commander Cooper is setting down on the mountain over there." Meyers pointed to the mountain to the south. "We'll be able to get a better signal to the *Valdez* from up there. Captain Hecker was just showing me the devices the other scout had planted inside the camp. They were probably meant to hack our C4I systems—communications, command and control, computers, intelligence. It would leave us deaf, dumb, and blind." He watched Timkul's face for a reaction.

She turned to him, and her face frowned from the corner of his helmet display. "Colonel Meyers, are your defenses often so easily overcome?"

"No." He didn't want to share his own concerns about that with her.

"Banh's in position," Cooper said. He had switched from the belly camera to his own helmet camera, and in that video, Banh and his squad stood inside the airlock. Banh raised a thumb. Behind him, wind-whipped snow from the landing area atop the peak, dropping visibility to twenty meters at best.

"Let him jump." Meyers watched until Banh and his men were gone, disappearing for several seconds before reappearing in the snow haze, spreading out as they trudged toward the boulders.

"Colonel?" Timkul's face was wrinkled as a prune. "If they can break into your security—"

"I know, Madam Envoy. We have a problem." Meyers gritted his teeth. He couldn't allow her to get inside his head. She should have just been a diplomat, all vacuous stares and platitudes, he thought. "If you'll excuse me, I need to alert some people we have operating outside the perimeter." Meyers shrank Cooper's display to the corner opposite Timkul's display and switched to a new channel with Barlowe. "Ladell? We've got trouble. Can you add McNutt and Gerhardt onto the connection?"

"McNutt said he heard a shot." Barlowe had his external helmet camera on, feeding the same thing he was seeing to Meyers. The BAS indicated there were three forms moving ahead of Barlowe: McNutt, Chavez, and Calderon. Cho's fire team trailed.

"A few shots, yeah. Spies inside the perimeter."

Barlowe came to a stop. "Inside the perimeter?"

"One of them, yeah. They've been eliminated, and we found the devices they'd planted. We think they were trying to cripple command and control—"

"We're heading back." Barlowe spun around, and Cho's team dropped into a crouch.

"Ladell, stop. Put McNutt and Gerhardt on the channel, please."

Barlowe switched the feed to his internal camera. He had the same sort of furious, incredulous look as Timkul. "Lonny, listen to me: We are heading back. If the Lancers already got inside your camp, they have to know we're here."

"I'm well aware of that. And I know they had to have help. Think about it. They got through the perimeter undetected. So, we have a problem. But that doesn't mean we can just abort the mission. There's too much at stake. We already spent too much to just pull up stakes and go. If we let these Lancers get away, the next time we see them could be in an ambush where we have no chance."

"You ever think that might be what this is?"

Meyers rubbed his gloved fingertips along the bottom of his palm; he could feel the pressure through the gloves but no other sensation. "Yes. Now, please put McNutt and Gerhardt on."

Barlowe rolled his eyes but a few seconds later, McNutt and Gerhardt were on the channel. McNutt's feed showed Barlowe and Cho's fire team; Gerhardt's feed showed his own face.

"Strange time for a chat, Colonel," McNutt said. His video indicated he was sweeping his surroundings in a way that would catch movement.

Gerhardt's breathing was hard, and his face glowed from exertion. "Colonel?"

"You may have heard shots fired," Meyers said. "We've dealt with a perimeter breach. The camp's safe for the moment. However, we've obviously been identified."

"We bugging out?" Gerhardt asked.

"Not yet." Meyers wished that someone would show a little faith in the mission. He felt isolated, without even a hint of support. "I still think we can get these Lancers to surrender if we do this right. I want those cameras up and running ASAP. We know where they'll have to come from. Those imagery systems of yours should give us what we need to maximize our weapons systems."

"This position's going to be awfully exposed," McNutt said. He was looking ahead. His feed showed they were still ninety meters out from their destination.

"So, keep it camouflaged. I'm counting on you to do your job." Meyers's eyes drifted to Timkul's face—still sour and disapproving—and then to Cooper's. Meyers filled his display with Cooper's feed and listened in.

Cooper stood in the airlock as the Dart settled to the icy ledge. His helmet reception sensitivity was cranked high enough to pick out every possible detail. Even in the gray light, the snow was bright. It spun around the Dart's landing gear, which disappeared into the white blanket and crunched against ice. Something groaned, and the Dart shifted, and Meyers was sure the ledge was going to give way beneath the craft. Before he could say anything, though, the groaning stopped.

"Cooper, this is Meyers. What was that? Did the ledge give?"

Cooper looked down into the snow. "I think it was ice cracking. It's a pretty thick shelf of rock. The Dart's not that heavy."

Heavy enough, Meyers thought.

The ramp extended, and Cooper stepped out of the Dart's airlock, head angled slightly, as if he were leaning against a significant weight. It's the gear he brought down, Meyers realized. He's carrying some out. Banh's squad had taken up positions behind the boulders and in lower areas overlooking the valley. One of Banh's soldiers—Luong—ran toward Cooper, who was waving the other man away.

Meyers shook his head. "Cooper, let him help—"

A flash, barely perceptible against the white snow, caught Meyers's attention an instant before the roar of heavy weapons fire reached him. He flinched, even though he knew it was Cooper and the others who were under attack.

"Get down! Cooper, get down!"

A round caught Luong in the right shoulder and spun him around. Dark blood trailed behind him and settled onto the snow where he lay. Cooper dropped a cargo carrying case and dove, and for a second, all Meyers could see was snow—red and wet—then Cooper rolled and looked back at the Dart, where Starling and the crew chief were wrestling another case down the ramp.

"Starling!" Cooper's hand reached out as bullets raked the Dart's side, punching through the light armor of the fuselage.

Starling seemed to understand what was going on before the crew chief. She shoved the case toward him, knocking him off the ramp as rounds whizzed through the air. A bullet cracked against the case, and then Starling, the case, and the crew chief were in the snow and out of sight.

Meyers fumbled through the BAS interface, desperately trying to find the Dart on the network. When he found it, he cycled through its cameras. He tagged the belly camera before switching to the cockpit crew camera. He stopped there, cursing as Kumar stumbled out of the cockpit and fell to the ground. Blood spilled out of his gut and pooled on the Dart's floor. Meyers switched back to the belly camera and tried to bring the Dart's belly railgun online, but he couldn't even access it through the ship's systems.

Meyers added Hecker to the channel. "Captain Hecker, we've got a problem up on the mountain." He merged the belly camera feed with Cooper's, which showed him crawling through the snow toward Starling and the crew chief. "There's a machine gun emplacement." Meyers cursed himself for missing what was now obvious. "This humped area of snow at the base of the peak...there, you see the muzzle flash?"

"I do, Colonel." Hecker sounded stressed. "What do we do?"

"We need to take that emplacement out. The Dart's shot up. We have casualties. I think Lieutenant Kumar's dead."

Hecker seemed to think for a second, then said, "We have no one to send up there."

"I know." Meyers blinked. Barlowe and the others would have to wait. They had their orders. "Try to get through to the *Valdez*. We need another Dart. A Javelin. An Arrow. Something. That emplacement needs to be taken out. At the very least, we need to evac the wounded."

Hecker sucked in air. "I will call them, Colonel."

"Lonny!" Cooper was shouting.

"I'm here. I can hear you."

"There's a fucking gun up here!"

"I see it. We're trying to raise the *Valdez*."

Cooper twisted around and his camera locked onto the pile of gear he'd dropped. He searched around until he spotted the case Starling and the crew chief had been carrying. "I'll call Brigston. I just need to check on the others."

"Get a Dart down here in the valley. Hassan. Have him send Hassan." Meyers hated pushing her so hard but she was his best option. "See who else he thinks could handle landing on that mountainside."

"Probably Nunoz." Cooper looked up at the Dart.

"Kumar's bad. I think he's dead. Looks like he took a couple rounds in the gut."

"Fuck." Cooper slowed. The snow was dark ahead of him. The machine gun roared again, and the sound of bullets punching through the Dart's skin came through Cooper's helmet loud and clear. He plunged his face into the snow. When he looked up again, snow dripped across the camera lens. "Private Starling! Petty Officer Hollins!"

A helmet rose from the snow a meter away. It was Starling. Cooper connected her to the channel.

"Hollins passed out," Starling said. "He's bleeding pretty bad." She stood enough to haul Hollins toward Cooper.

"Get to the boulders. I'll get the case." Cooper crawled past her, shifting his course to avoid the blood. He reached for the case's handle, which was mostly buried in the snow. For a second, it looked like the handle came away, and then Cooper raised something out of the snow: Hollins's hand. Cooper stuffed it into a pouch and grabbed the handle again. He dragged the case back toward the gear he'd dropped.

Meyers licked his lips. "Cooper, keep everyone down. Wait for rescue."

"Yeah, that was the plan."

"I need to check on the others. I'll get back to you." Meyers glanced at the other video feeds. Things were coming apart, moving too fast again. He needed to regain command of the situation. Now. Before everything spun out of control like it had on Bellar Colony.

10

2 October 2175. Siberia.

WIND-WHIPPED SNOW TURNED EVERYTHING A BLURRY, indistinct white. That same wind was a constant hum in Meyers's ears as he paced the perimeter, always keeping inside the sensors. He reduced the BAS's external microphone sensitivity until the wind was barely noticeable. A quick glance back confirmed Timkul was still there, fighting through the snow, apparently driven by her insatiable desire to foul up his command. He shivered, but his display showed he was close to twenty degrees Celsius. Anxiety, he told himself. He could almost taste it on his tongue, a troubling bitterness in his saliva.

He had to prioritize things. If Cooper got through to the *Valdez*, two Darts would be on their way down. Meyers tried to work out an optimistic and pessimistic schedule. Forty-five to ninety minutes seemed about right. He needed to put a plan into action.

Meyers connected to Hecker. "Captain Hecker, we've got two Darts inbound. Hopefully. I want a team headed up that mountainside."

"O-of course, Colonel." Hecker sounded skeptical.

"Not on foot. We'll have one of the Darts drop them. I saw a decent way up, not even two hundred meters down from the LZ. Do you have any people with alpine training?"

"Everyone, Colonel."

"Who's our best option?"

Hecker squinted an eye. "Klinsmann's squad. But..."

"Yes? What?"

"The Spetsnaz. Domnikov and Repin were mountain infantry. They were decorated, Colonel. Miss Timkul emphasized that during her briefing about the Russians."

"Shit." Meyers could feel Timkul nearby, trying to listen in, trying to influence his mind. "Find out who else was in that operation. Put Klinsmann in charge. Wait. Does he have rank on Domnikov?"

"The Russians had their date of rank reset to when they were assigned and given their ERF ranks. They are junior to everyone in their same rank." Hecker sounded like he approved of the idea. His unit had undergone the same thing.

"All right. Get them prepared. Rope, first aid kits. It's a rescue operation."

"Of course, Colonel."

"Thanks, Theodor." Meyers disconnected, ignoring the look of disapproval. Hecker was hardcore military, like Paxton, but for completely different reasons. The military was Paxton's religion, his belief system. Hecker was from a long line of German military officers. It was more than duty and honor for him; it was almost entitlement. And Meyers was sure he didn't represent the ideal of a superior officer for someone like Hecker.

"Colonel Meyers?" There was tension in Timkul's voice.

Meyers turned, imagining Timkul the way he'd seen her that first day on Plymouth. Armor made it almost impossible to read her body language. Her face scowled at him from the corner of his helmet display but the scowl could mean anything. He was sure it meant disapproval, though. Of everything. "Miss Timkul?"

Her head tilted up, and her face relaxed slightly. "I would appreciate an update."

"Well, if you can give me a second, I'll have one for you."

The tension immediately returned to her face and intensified. "Perhaps if you simply let me listen in to your channel? The BAS can do that, at least according to the training I went through. Piggybacking, I believe?"

"Yes."

"I would appreciate it if you would let me do that, please, Colonel."

Meyers tried to think of a way out of her request but realized he was being petty again. There was nothing to hide, and her request was reasonable. He enabled a channel between them that would keep her riding on his system the whole time. "Can you hear me?"

"I can. And I can see your systems as well. You have channels on hold to several people. Is there something the matter?"

"Commander Cooper was taking a team to the mountaintop to set up equipment that would let us stay in better communication with the *Valdez*."

Timkul nodded.

"But they were fired upon by a gun emplacement while landing. We're trying to get more Darts down here to effect a rescue." Meyers saw her eyebrows arch and realized she probably didn't understand what had happened and what he was thinking. "There's only one squad up there, and two wounded. Their pilot's probably dead, and the Dart was shot up. We need to get the people off that mountaintop, and we need to silence the gun."

"Should that be a higher priority than preparation for the enemy? I thought our presence here being discovered was a serious concern."

Meyers considered sharing his thoughts on just how long their presence had been known about but decided against it. For all he knew, she could be the source of the suspected leak. "We're capable of running multiple operations."

Her head reared back, and her eyes narrowed, then she looked away. She seemed offended by the idea he thought she didn't know what they were capable of. "Proceed, Colonel."

Proceed. It sounded dismissive. He connected to Paxton. "Master Sergeant Paxton, Captain Hecker's going to be putting a team together to get up to the mountaintop where Cooper and Banh are."

"He already contacted me, sir." Paxton's brow was knotted. "Might want to consider Sergeant McNutt, too."

"For the mountain climb?"

"He's one of the best we have, and Private Starling's in his squad."

It suddenly dawned on Meyers: He'd been making decisions without consulting Paxton. "That's a good point, but McNutt's squad is providing Agent Barlowe with security while he sets up imagery systems in the valley."

Paxton's thick eyebrows arched. "That's funny, sir. Captain Hecker said you'd assigned Sergeant Gerhardt to assist Agent Barlowe."

They're conspiring, Meyers thought. Pouting and commiserating about me not bringing them into the decision-making process. He exhaled. Timkul watched him, waiting, judging. "Okay. So. Here's the deal. We've been stretched thin. I've been making too many decisions without consulting my staff."

"That sounds harsh, sir." Paxton didn't sound like he meant it—not at all.

"Head to the TOC. You and Captain Hecker start handling things from there. As Miss Timkul has pointed out, we're probably going to have company sooner rather than later. We need to prep for that. I'll restrict myself to the rescue operation. Sound fair?"

"If I can speak frankly, Colonel, I'd say it sounds more reasonable than fair." Paxton's head rocked; he was moving. "Delegation, sir."

"I know. If you think McNutt should go, let him know. I need his squad to stay out there, though."

"Understood, Colonel."

Meyers closed his eyes. He didn't need to see Timkul's reaction to his being dressed down by Paxton. After muting long enough to fully exhale and draw in another breath, Meyers said, "Um, just to be clear, Sergeant Klinsmann's the lead on this."

The corners of Paxton's lips seemed to quirk up. "Training the new soldiers on ERF alpine operations—yes, sir."

"Thank you, Master Sergeant Paxton." Meyers let out the slightest breath of relief. He'd been sure Paxton would make some sort of comment about the Russians. He could see in Timkul's glare that she had expected the same.

Her mouth opened but before she could say anything, a connection request came in from the *Valdez*.

Meyers accepted. The video filled the top center of his helmet.

"Colonel, this is Captain Brigston. I would like to bring Commander Cooper and Chief Pivovarova into this call." Brigston's cheeks were flush but he seemed calm.

"Please do, Captain. Miss Timkul's already piggybacked on my system."

Brigston leaned back, as he seemed to consider that for a second, then blinked and Cooper and Pivovarova's images joined the channel. Meyers brought Timkul into the conference. Gunfire was a distant chatter over Cooper's connection. He seemed red, and his eyes were nothing more than intense, brown beads deep in the shadow of his brow.

"Colonel." Pivovarova waved and smiled slightly. She wore the same uniform she'd had the first night he'd met her in the hangar: bunny suit and T-shirt, with a dark streak of grease on her cheek. The picture of her from her workspace filled his thoughts and wouldn't go away.

Brigston cleared his throat, a disapproving sound. It was as if he could see what Meyers was thinking. "Chief Pivovarova has an idea, Colonel. To deal with this problem on the mountain."

Pivovarova's face flowed quickly from a pixie amusement to somber. "Is very much like something we saw. In Georgia."

Of course, Meyers thought. Georgia was one of the dozens of dust-ups the Russians engineered over the years to shift borders for "security" or to brazenly claim resources. Meyers remembered how close the Commandos had come to going in right after he'd joined, then things had cooled back down. Pivovarova didn't seem old enough to have been involved in the worst of those engagements.

"Platoon ambushed on mountainside, only a handful of men survive." Pivovarova angled one hand to indicate a mountainside and pointed to a spot near the top. "How to get them out with storm coming in? We rig firebomb for drop on enemy position. Fire because they are dug in.

Shrapnel?" She shook her head, then she wiggled her fingers. "Fire get in tight places, sticks. And smoke." She held up a finger and nodded. "Maybe these people, you smoke them out."

"It's a good idea, Chief," Meyers said. "But we can blow the top off that mountain once we get our people out of there."

Pivovarova's eyes—big and expressive—went even wider. "Yes."

"So, what we need is a rescue plan, not a bombing plan."

She nodded. "The bomb—is for the rescue. Keep the enemy down."

"Colonel." Cooper flinched and ducked as the gunfire intensified. "I don't know that a Dart's going to be any good up here without taking that gun emplacement out. From the sound of it, there's more than one. We've tried to get a look at them, but they've shot the Dart up so much, the camera's dead. What we saw, though." He shook his head. "We don't have the ordnance to scrape the top of the mountain off. Not really. Not without losing this position, and that means we risk losing the valley."

"All right." Meyers didn't like the idea of rigging up a fire bomb, not if it meant slowing down the operation. "How big are we talking?"

Pivovarova smiled her pixie smile. "Half the cargo area. Will be *big* fire."

"How long to rig it?"

"I can walk some of the weapons team through the process," Cooper said. "We'll probably have time. She's going to have to rig a harness and sling to hold everything she's talking about."

Pivovarova nodded enthusiastically. "This I am already working."

"And she'll need to make a few adjustments to pull the wounded up." Cooper's eyes were wider now that he was engaged in working up a solution. "External winch, a basket."

"With straps." Pivovarova placed her hands on her shoulders like a mummy.

"How long?" Meyers was waiting for Timkul to step in, to criticize the lack of organization and planning, to question how the ERF hoped to survive with such haphazard medical and rescue planning. She couldn't possibly understand that what made the ERF successful wasn't just training but resourcefulness and flexibility. What they were discussing was the sort of ad hoc approach necessitated by budget, equipment, and personnel limitations imposed by the United Nations. By *her* type.

"An hour?" Pivovarova shrugged.

Meyers looked to Brigston. "Which Dart? Who's going to pilot it?"

"Two-Seven-Three. Ensign Nunoz will pilot," Brigston said. "I'll want a crew chief helping out, too. Chief Merriman suggested Petty Officer Brinkley."

"Will be tight." Pivovarova smiled, and her eyebrows rose as she spoke. It was a charm offensive, a way of questioning without challenging. She seemed to pick up on Brigston's demeanor pretty well.

"Your operation, Chief," Brigston said. "Brinkley's just there to support you."

"I should—" Pivovarova twisted to reveal a Dart behind her. Tools and straps lay on the hangar floor. She held up one of the straps, pointed it at the cargo bay beyond the Dart's open airlock, and smiled.

Brigston sniffed. "Dismissed, Chief."

Pivovarova's connection cut out, leaving an afterimage that stuck in Meyers's thoughts. Her impish mannerisms and pixie mirth were getting to him. Even worse, she exhibited the same sort of confidence and gumption that had drawn him to Kara. And Camille.

"Colonel Meyers?" Brigston sounded close to another throat clearing.

"Sorry. How..." Meyers looked around, saw the waiting look on their faces. "How long before Ensign Hassan can get down here? I want people on that mountainside ASAP."

Brigston blushed. "She's in the hangar deck now. We had to wake her."

Meyers heard the accusation in Brigston's tone: *She had been promised some bunk time!* "We'll get her out of here as soon as possible. I just need the team starting the ascent."

"Of course. We're willing to support our fellow soldiers all the time." Brigston stared coolly.

"Thanks." Meyers wanted to keep a private channel open to Brigston, to try to reach out to him now that things were heating up but Timkul wouldn't allow that. Brigston didn't seem ready to allow it, either. Meyers disconnected.

Almost immediately, Timkul's stare became even more disapproving.

"Is there something you'd like to talk about, Madam Envoy?" Meyers looked toward the mountain where Cooper and the others were pinned down.

"Frankly, Colonel, it seems to me this is a lot of effort for a handful of personnel."

Something inside Meyers snapped. "The ERF sent two squads into one of the most deadly places known to humans to try to rescue your mother. Was that a lot of effort? Private Starling was one of the soldiers who went in. She could have walked away from service after what she went through but she didn't. We need people like her, and she's up there on that mountaintop."

Timkul crossed her arms over her chest. Even in armor, it made her seem petulant and childish. "Perhaps you should learn from my mother's death, Colonel? How many people died and the outcome was the same as not trying?"

"That's not the way the ERF works." Meyers pointed toward the mountain, all but invisible in the white haze. "You heard that call? You saw the video. We could only manage that because Commander Cooper has the gear running up there. We need that mountaintop as much as we need those people."

"Maybe what we need is to pull up stakes and leave. Now. Before these Lancers arrive and kill us all."

"Is that an order? Is that the Special Security Council speaking?"

"No. It is the voice of reason. It is someone who can see the absolute lack of objectivity and the tragic folly of blind loyalty. You are going to get all these people killed, Colonel Meyers. And you will die with them."

There was a strange sound in Timkul's voice, a concern that Meyers hadn't expected. He wondered if that was part of her diplomatic training. "We're committed to the mission."

He headed for the TOC, feeling her close behind, almost clinging to him. They stomped across the snow without another word, passing between clumps of soldiers hauling weapons around, preparing for the inevitable approach of an overpowering enemy. Shelters shuddered in the freezing wind, and before long Meyers realized that he was walking past the spot where the saboteur had been killed. He wondered if it might be the senseless deaths of the two young women that had gotten to Timkul, if she was dealing with her own sense of mortality. He stopped and glanced back at her. She stopped also, watching him curiously.

And beyond her, the valley was shrouded in wintery white. The enemy was out there. Watching. Moving closer. Bringing death.

11

2 October 2175. Siberia.

MEYERS STOPPED outside the TOC and sank slightly in the snow. He needed to give Timkul a chance to catch up, but he also needed to give himself a moment to think. The cold was getting through his armor, causing his heel to throb where the new skin and muscle had been regrown. Just another wound from the Bellar operation—a physical wound. It was one of the many pains that kept accumulating: the deaths, the uncertainties, and the frayed relationships. He opened his visor to experience the world through human senses—white and gray from the snow and buildings, brilliant and blinding in the LED light banks; sweet, fresh air occasionally tainted by a sharp chemical exhaust or residue that marked the human presence; the muffled crunch of snow from soldiers hustling about their duties.

Timkul struggled up to the TOC, finally coming to a stop not a meter shy of him. She opened her visor and looked around, blinking away the snow flurrying about her. "Is something the matter?"

Her cheeks were flush and tears were forming in her eyes. He could feel the determination that had to be behind everything she was doing. "Just taking it all in."

She nodded, maybe even really understanding, and then she sealed up. "It's cold."

It was. And getting colder. He thought of her eyes, the hint of tears he'd seen there. Was it the cold wind, or was she feeling anger and frustration? He'd been unpleasant to her from the start. Have I been fair, he wondered. He opened the entry flap and waved her in. She hesitated for a heartbeat before entering.

Hecker and Paxton stood in front of the wall of displays, helmets off. The mountainside was spread across the displays in an uninterrupted panorama shot. They turned, barely acknowledging the new entrants, then returned to studying the screens.

"This mountainside they will assault, have you seen it, Colonel?" Hecker asked, one eye squinting, neck craning his head forward.

Meyers looked up from sealing the flap and spotted the area they were focused on. It was the best spot for insertion, one of several narrow ledges but this one with a path up. "I looked at it earlier. It won't be easy."

"Sergeants Klinsmann and Domnikov have been studying it." Hecker's upper incisors pinched his bottom lip. "They are concerned about the drop."

Paxton shot Meyers a look, searching for support. "Might want to have McNutt drop first, Colonel. He'll be the one to gauge whether or not it's something the others can try. What do you think, sir?"

"Sounds reasonable." Meyers caught Hecker's reaction: His lips curled like he'd just been offered up spoiled meat. "Captain?"

"Sergeant Klinsmann knows mountain operations quite well."

Meyers surreptitiously looked toward Timkul, who seemed to be putting on a show of indifference. Meyers wasn't sure what angle she was working, but he was sure she'd let on soon enough. "How's Klinsmann's shoulder holding up?"

"He is good, Colonel." The "good" sounded like "goot" again. Hecker seemed to realize he sounded defensive. He shook his shoulders and bowed his head slightly. "The restoratives have made healing accelerate. The bruise is all that remains, and it is fading."

Meyers looked around the interior, trying to appear relaxed and as indifferent as Timkul. He spotted the devices the saboteur had planted inside the camp and made his way over to them, picking one up to examine it. It seemed to be a different level of work than the devices taken from the woman killed outside the perimeter. "Ensign Hassan's still en route, Captain. You have plenty of time to figure out how to assign your people." It was the illusion of complete autonomy, the sort of thing Rimes would have done to defuse a prickly moment with a testy junior officer. Like me, Meyers thought.

Hecker turned his attention back to the displays. "Perhaps Sergeant McNutt descending first would defuse any problems between Klinsmann and Domnikov."

Meyers turned his back to Hecker, pretended to study the device, and smiled. Rimes had been a natural at command. Meyers envied that ease. He felt the familiar doubt return, the painful questions about his competence as a commander and his desire to lead. Rimes had seen something in their time together, but it was something Meyers couldn't feel. Meyers had always thought command should be something you want, something you sought out. He'd pictured himself working in an off-world design shop by now, making serious money for one of the metacorporations. Battalion commander? He snorted softly.

His earpiece chimed; Pivovarova was requesting a connection. He accepted.

"Colonel, I do not wish to disturb," Pivovarova said.

Meyers straightened. "That's perfectly fine, Chief. What's the status on the prep?"

"The winch is..." Pivovarova made an almost purring sound. "It is done. Oh, and Ensign Hassan, she just departed. Adjustments were necessary. For the winds and a rope drop."

"Adjustments?" Meyers stroked the device absently, admiring the dark, smooth curves and slick surface sliding beneath his gloved fingers. It was a magnificent design. Artful. Timkul shifted in his peripheral view, and he realized she was watching his face. She's on the channel, he thought. "By the way, Miss Timkul is joined to my channel. She's...observing all aspects of the operations."

Pivovarova's pixie smile returned, and she waved enthusiastically. "Miss Special Envoy! I hope it is not too cold down there?"

"These suits keep us warm enough, Irina, thank you." Timkul moved closer.

Meyers had to fight back a frown. He hadn't realized the two women knew each other well enough for Timkul to call Irina—Pivovarova—by her first name. "What sort of adjustments did you make to One-Zero-One, Chief?"

"Minor adjustments. To fans." Pivovarova mimicked the rotor movements with her hands. "And checked ailerons. Better for big blowing."

"I see." Meyers noticed the way Timkul's features had softened, as if talking with Pivovarova were a pleasure and dealing with the men an unpleasant necessity. "And Ensign Hassan was okay with this?"

"Oh, yes, Colonel! She very well understood!"

"Okay. Make sure you let the rest of the folks know. Chief Merriman will probably—"

"Eh, yes. Chief Merriman. He is why I contacted you, Colonel."

"Is there a problem?" Meyers couldn't help picturing Merriman's scrawny body stuffed into the airlock of one of the Darts. He would be no match for Pivovarova.

"His eyes go big!" Pivovarova circled her thumbs and index fingers over her own eyes. "He turned red, like cherry, and stomped. He goes to talk to captain."

Jeremy, Meyers thought. Drama. Challenges to authority. Meyers's palms itched; he rubbed them against his thighs, heard the scrape of armor, and stopped. "All right. I don't think there's much we can do about it for now. How's Two-Seven-Three coming along?"

"Is nearly done, Colonel. Ensign Nunoz is inspecting." Pivovarova's excitement and sincerity shot through the connection like a current.

"That's good. Leave Captain Brigston to me."

"Thank you, Colonel. I am sorry for troublemaking."

Meyers smiled. "The ERF was cooked up by a guy who seemed to thrive on troublemaking. It's what we do." He disconnected just as a connection request came in from Brigston. All the excitement and joy

Pivovarova had gifted Meyers drained away as he accepted Brigston's call. "Jeremy, I—"

"Goddammit!" Brigston was apoplectic—red-faced, blinking, a white stream of spittle stretching between his lips. "You're letting that Russian bitch—"

"Miss Timkul, this discussion might get a little heated. Would you mind if I disconnected you?" Meyers gave Timkul a pleading glance. She didn't need to hear Brigston in his current state.

"Of course," Timkul said.

Meyers broke Timkul's piggyback. "Jeremy, you need to be more careful."

"I don't give one shit about your precious UN envoy, Lonny. They made their decisions, and now they sent you a little present for your cooperation. What I do care about is you undermining my authority. You're putting my people at risk and costing us precious lives and materials! You may not give a damn about the people under your command, but I'll be damned if I let you risk any more lives! You hear me?" Brigston was leaning forward. His eyes bugged out, and his head shook with fury.

"Are you finished?" Meyers tried to keep some level of calm in his voice.

Brigston squinted and leaned back. "Oh, I'm not through yet."

Meyers noticed the way Timkul's eyes had narrowed. She almost seemed concerned. He turned and walked toward the corner of the TOC where the bunk was set up. "Jeremy, listen. Please."

"You're not in command yet, Colonel. I'm not about—"

"Captain Brigston!" Meyers was hissing, quietly shouting, losing his cool. "If you can't stop with this behavior, I'm going to ask you to pass your command on to Commander Muwafi. Is that what you want? Jeremy? Is it?"

Brigston shook. He blinked, and his mouth twisted into a snarl. Finally, he sucked in breath and adjusted his uniform coat. "I will log every single one of my concerns about your decisions, Colonel."

"I know you will." Meyers heard the quaver in his voice. It sounded too loud and obvious. "Don't let that stop you from supporting the mission, please." He disconnected.

Meyers felt everyone's eyes on him.

"I need to step out," he said.

He closed his visor and hurried to the flap, which he fumbled with for an eternity. He lurched into the blinding snow, stopping to seal the flap behind him. With no one watching, it was easier to deal with even the simplest things. It would have been easier without the device in his left hand but he'd let it settle into his palm, and it seemed to act as a comforting talisman at the moment.

Finally alone, he wandered through the camp, stopping to observe the fruits of Hecker's command. Soldiers hauled heavy weapons and ammunition into position, spread out wide across the valley floor. It looked similar to Starling's plan.

Meyers brought up the BAS Command, Control, Communications, Computers, and Intelligence interface. Command and Control was run by Hecker, although Meyers could step in at any time he needed. Intelligence fell to Barlowe, at least until the ERF team was planet-side. Communications and Computers—Systems by most terminology—was run by the Systems Team, a group of corporals under Lieutenant Briles, a skinny hotshot with curly, black hair and a perpetual sneer. He reminded Meyers of his own younger years, a time when he thought his intellect would take him wherever he wanted to go. The Systems Shack was near the communications uplink. Meyers headed that way, finally realizing that he'd meant to stop by after picking the saboteur's device up in the TOC. Too much going on, he grumbled to himself. It was always that way.

As he trudged through the snow, he examined Hecker's munitions deployment. He brought up what Starling had put together and made an overlay, then merged her assessment in with the overlay.

He dictated a message: *Captain Hecker. Excellent deployment. Take a look at this. Starling put it together, and Commander Cooper agrees it could be an optimal use of munitions, especially in conjunction with any orbital support. It seems you had the same idea about placement. Give her idea a look and see what you think.*

Meyers imagined Starling's smile at the recognition. They couldn't lose her. They couldn't lose Cooper. Or Banh and his squad. They'd already lost too much.

He sent the message on to Hecker. Don't see it as meddling, please, Meyers thought.

A Rover slogged quietly past on the north side of camp, disappearing behind a structure to the east. The communications uplink came into view: a gray dish, nearly two meters in diameter, pointed skyward. Gray cables snaked from the white casing, plunging into the snow and disappearing, diving toward the buried generator and batteries. He followed the path to the Systems Shack and stopped outside. It was the same size and appearance as the TOC, but heat glowed yellow on his thermographic overlay as he approached. The shack would have been miserable to work in on Bellar, if they hadn't lost their entire intelligence and systems team to the Arrow crash.

Camille! Meyers pulled his hand back from the flap, momentarily shocked by the intensity of his feelings of loss. Kara, Rimes, Camille...

It's the stress, Meyers told himself. Just the stress.

He turned away from the shack, searching for someplace he could be truly alone. The uplink stood at the eastern edge of the camp, north of the LZ. It would block him from sight and give him a moment to pull himself together. He made sure no one was watching and walked up the raised area leading to the LZ. He stepped over the low ice wall surrounding the LZ and headed to the far side of the uplink, then rested against the casing and slid down into the snow. His breathing was deep and ragged. Heat seemed to be spreading throughout his body. He opened his visor and sucked in the cold air; it was a loud, pathetic sound.

Pull yourself together, he wanted to shout. He didn't. He needed a moment like this, a chance to deal with all the emotions he'd been stuffing down and fighting off.

Too much death, too much responsibility, and now someone he'd counted on had been turned against him. Friendships lost. Meyers couldn't understand the why of it. He'd never wanted to be in a position like this.

"Fuck! Why'd you do this to me, Jack?" Meyers knuckled away tears, not caring that the gloves scraped at his tender skin.

Snow popped nearby, and Meyers snapped his visor shut. He stood, right hand reaching for the CAWS-5 mounted on his back brace. Timkul came around the corner of the uplink, visor raised, hands cupped to shield her eyes.

"Colonel Meyers?" She seemed genuinely unsure.

He stepped back and opened his own visor, doubling over to hide his eyes. "Shit. I could have shot you."

"You disappeared..."

"Yeah." Meyers turned and patted the uplink. "I wanted to check with the Systems Team, but I ended up getting distracted by the uplink." He held up the device he'd taken from the TOC. "These things the saboteurs put down. I just wanted to take one apart, see what makes them tick."

Timkul stared at him.

"They..." He forced a smile. "They just planted three of these things. Doesn't make sense, does it? If you think about it." His nose began to drip; he wiped at it with the back of his hand. "Why not leave bombs behind?"

"Are you all right, Colonel?" Timkul stepped closer. Her head tilted sideways slightly.

"Depends on what you mean by *all right*." He laughed, and it sounded like he imagined a hyena's bark would. "Shit." His heart seemed to go crazy, hammering hard enough to vibrate in his armor. Nausea jabbed at him, and he exhaled hard, doubling over again. "I'm sorry, Madam Envoy."

She was at his side, hand on his back. "The Special Security Council recommended you take leave after Bellar. Why didn't you, Colonel?"

"Leave?" He was gasping, fighting the urge to vomit. It was a panic attack, he was pretty sure. "Too much to do. Too many to bury. Too many to train. Who would replace me?" He shook his head, and the snow swam beneath him; he closed his eyes. "We need to rebuild. We never had the chance after the war. Still...not ready."

She patted his back, something his audio sensors picked up even if he couldn't really feel it through his armor. "There's a good deal of concern for you."

"My mind's fine." He straightened and sucked in more of the cold, sweet air.

"You've refused requests for psychological evaluations."

"No expert system is going to tell me anything I don't already know."

"If you would prefer a human, that can be arranged. It's the council that wants to know about you, Colonel. You've been through..." She winced. "And now this."

"We'll manage." His heartbeat seemed to level off. He squeezed his hands into tight fists. "It looks worse than it is." He laughed at himself and looked down at the device. There weren't many things worse than having an enemy who wasn't supposed to even be aware of you inserting saboteurs before you were even fully prepared. "Well, it shouldn't be as bad as it looks." He jerked his head toward the Systems Shack. "Maybe if I can get a look at what's inside, figure out what these devices were supposed to do, we'll have a better understanding of the situation."

Timkul looked at the device. "I don't think—"

Meyers's earpiece chimed twice in succession. The first chime was a connection request from Barlowe, the second a request from Hassan. Meyers accepted Hassan's request. "Go ahead, Ensign." He reconnected Timkul's piggyback as he spoke.

"One-Zero-One is two minutes out, Colonel. Visibility's going to be a problem."

"The snow, yeah. We'll have the LZ cleared for you."

"I'm more concerned about the drop."

Of course, Meyers thought. "Understood. You're going to need to pick up Sergeant McNutt. He's probably about two klicks out still."

"Understood, Colonel. One-Zero-One out."

Meyers accepted Barlowe's request. "Go ahead, Ladell."

"Lonny, what the hell is wrong with you? McNutt's only good for killing and breaking shit, and now—"

"We need him up on the mountain—"

Meyers gasped as a high-pitched squeal filled the channel. He muted his earpiece and staggered away from the uplink. Timkul had done the same thing. She had her helmet off and was shaking her head. The wind caught her hair and whipped it around.

She was shouting something, but Meyers could barely hear her.

"What?" He pulled his own helmet off, and as she spoke, he heard what she was referring to.

"That hum!" She pointed at the uplink. "What is it?"

Meyers looked around the camp. In the distance, others were staggering around, pulling their helmets off. He glanced down at the device and saw it glowing, felt it vibrating. The uplink's humming built until it was a truly physical sensation, a bass he could feel in his head.

"It's not disabled." He held it out toward Timkul. "It's not disabled!"

He ran for the Systems Shack. There were tools there, hardware that would let him bypass some of the device's security. Someone staggered out of the shack, apparently disoriented, then collapsed in the snow.

And then the lights throughout the camp went out.

12

2 October 2175. Siberia.

HOT AIR SLAMMED into Meyers as he stepped into the Systems Shack. Instead of the bright light of dozens of displays, the interior was a dark gray. Soldiers lay sprawled on the floor and slumped over cargo cases. Dark panels—dead displays—covered the walls except where stacked gear prevented it. The sharp, acrid stench of fried circuits and overheated plastic enclosures was thick in the air.

It smelled toxic.

Meyers looked down at the device in his hand. It was a weapon, he realized, something much more advanced than he'd thought possible. The case was melted; the shape deformed. He tossed it onto the floor.

He felt woozy and realized the fumes were getting to him. He put his helmet back on, then grabbed the nearest of the unconscious soldiers—a young man—and pulled until his upper body was clear of the building. Meyers went back in for another, and Timkul joined him, pulling Lieutenant Briles out. By the time they had the last soldier clear, the one who had stumbled out initially was slowly rising.

Meyers raised his visor and began checking on the other soldiers.

Timkul settled to a knee beside him, visor raised. "What happened?" she asked.

"The devices. They overloaded the systems. Our BAS should reboot soon but that smell.... I think we've lost all our critical hardware. Ah, there!" The BAS display returned, static-laced but functional. Meyers sealed his visor and indicated she should do the same. She sent a request to piggyback on his system again, and he accepted her connection. Her face—wrinkled in concern, mouth open slightly—rested in the upper right corner of his helmet display once more. "I'm running a search to see who else is online. We've got maybe thirty percent of our forces so far."

"Thirty percent total?" Timkul's eyes jerked left and right. She was doing her own research, apparently.

"Thirty percent of what we have down here." One-Zero-One's signal appeared in his feed. "Shit." He opened a channel to Hassan. "Ensign Hassan, are you there?"

"I am, Colonel. I've lost ILS, apparently." Hassan opened her connection to a full video feed. She looked confused more than anything else. "It was there one second, then it just—"

"A bot attack." Meyers retrieved the warped device and activated his armor's helmet lamp. "Something advanced. Something that shouldn't be possible. We've lost everything—can't even reach the *Valdez*." He rummaged through the cases, searching for tools and diagnostic systems.

"Well, I'm about thirty meters up—"

"Wait! Your systems weren't affected, right?"

"No, sir, not that I can see."

"Put me through to the *Valdez*, please." Meyers set the device down on a cargo case and went to work prying away the warped casing that had been so smooth and pleasing before. The circuits inside the device were black and brittle, some crumbling into ash from the rough handling. There was something strange, something not circuitry beneath the layers of ruined electronics. He upended the device and tapped it against the cargo case. With the ruined circuitry removed, the mysterious material was more obvious: explosives. An icy chill ran through his gut. He should be dead.

"Colonel?" Hassan's voice was strained. "I have Captain Brigston."

Meyers remembered how Hassan had been forced to endure one of the previous fights with Brigston. No way to avoid discomfort now, he thought. Meyers grabbed the device and stormed past Timkul, pointing for her to stay in the shack. "Captain Brigston, we've got big problems down here."

"Oh?" Brigston sounded almost amused.

Meyers took a few steps and heaved the device as hard as he could, out past the uplink, then he turned back toward the TOC. "This is serious, Jeremy. Those saboteurs planted devices that took out our systems. All of our systems."

Timkul fell in behind Meyers as he passed the shack. He caught her glancing back toward where he'd thrown the device but she didn't say anything.

"Really? How long before you can get them running again?" Brigston sounded a little more concerned but not as concerned as he should have been.

"My systems team is down. I'm checking on the TOC—"

Black smoke rolled out of the TOC's flap, which fluttered in the wind. Meyers ran forward and peered inside. A form was slumped against the display wall. It looked tall. Hecker. A soldier, small and slender, was inside and to Meyers's left, kneeling over another form. None of the three had their BAS running. Even without the BAS, Meyers knew who the form on the ground was. The armor was damaged, blackened, but not broken. The form was short, deep-chested. Paxton.

"Colonel Meyers?" Brigston sounded almost pleasant.

"The TOC's down. Bomb."

Brigston should have been there to take in the scene, Meyers thought. He slid his visor open and tapped the soldier on the back, signaling to open his visor as well.

And then Meyers saw the knife in the soldier's hand—the blood-slick blade.

Assassin!

The assassin lunged at Meyers, and he fell back, suddenly feeling awkward and stupid. He bumped into Timkul, who kept him up.

"Get out!" He elbowed her back, hoping she understood.

The little man was on Meyers then, knife slashing for the joints in his arms. He knew better than to count on his armor. There was blood on the knife; it was probably something built specifically for the ERF suits.

Like the devices.

Meyers let the assassin swing again, caught the knife arm once it had shot past, and swept the assassin's front leg. The slender form wrestled free but fell, dragging the knife across Meyers's forearm with enough force to slash open armor and skin. The wound burned.

Poison seemed impractical but if it was, there were injectors to counter most things, assuming he survived the engagement.

He straddled the smaller man, pinning his knife arm with a knee but not before the tip of the blade punched through Meyers's leg armor. He grunted at the pain, then he brought a fist down on the assassin's neck, striking the carotid artery. Even with the armor, the blow registered. Meyers struck again and again, aiming for the same joints the smaller man had been striking at. Neck, shoulder, elbow, neck, underarm, elbow...the knife fell from twitching fingers. Meyers struck the sides of the smaller man's helmet, rocking the head with each blow.

The assassin went limp.

Meyers got up and retrieved the knife. As he suspected, it wasn't ERF-issued. He put it into a thigh pouch and tested his wounds. They stung, but he didn't feel any other effects. He kicked the smaller man in the head. Hard.

Timkul was at Meyers's side suddenly. "What happened? Why did he attack?"

"Traitor. Saboteur." He held back from saying what he wanted to: *One of your precious Russians.* But he recognized the armor: new, too polished to have ever seen action.

He knelt beside Paxton's body, dreading what was almost certain to be shown on his external monitor. A tap brought up nothing. The suit was too damaged from the blast, or the BAS hadn't reset. Meyers searched for blood and other obvious signs of injury other than the blast damage. The suit looked intact. He moved to Hecker. Blood leaked across the front of his armor, starting from the throat. Meyers tapped the external monitor.

Hecker still had vitals. Weak, but they were there.

"Hecker's alive!" Meyers searched the BAS network for a medic—and found one. "Corporal Veitch, report to the TOC immediately. Captain Hecker's critically wounded."

"Coming, Colonel!"

Meyers moved back toward the assassin and tapped the external BAS monitor. "Captain Brigston, we've had an assassination attempt down here." The display showed Rhizov, Ilya, Corporal.

"Assassination? The bomb?"

"After the bomb. Someone sent in to finish the work. One of the—" Meyers unsealed the helmet and pulled it off. Long, black hair unfurled from dusky skin. Blood trickled from a wide, strong nose and from the heavy eyebrow over her left eye. "Shit. One of the saboteurs. We missed one."

Timkul leaned over the other woman. "She's just like the other two."

"Yeah." Meyers didn't like mysteries. He didn't like things not connecting logically. "Captain Brigston, could you have whatever spare systems you can scrounge up brought down here ASAP? We're blind right now. My command staff is incapacitated." He looked at Paxton. "Or dead."

An armored form burst through the entry: Veitch. Meyers waved toward Hecker.

"Well..." Brigston cleared his throat. "We're already overextending the ships—"

"Jeremy, are you serious? Don't you see how exposed we are down here?" Meyers's cheeks burned. "This isn't about your career or the changes the UN pushed off on us. Dammit, we've got nearly two hundred of our brothers and sisters down here."

Brigston said nothing.

"We need all hands on deck," Meyers said. He didn't care how pathetic he sounded.

"I'll see if Chief Merriman can put something together. I believe Zero-Eight-Nine is already prepped. Ensign Nunoz can switch over to that and let Ensign Shazier take Two-Seven-Three to the mountaintop."

Meyers didn't feel like challenging the decision. Any progress with

Brigston was too precious to undermine. "Thanks, Jeremy. I'm going to ask Hassan to do a flyover of the valley before she drops the team off on the mountainside, if that's okay with you. The timing of all this...I don't think they'd do this unless they were ready to mobilize."

"Of course. Will there be anything else?" Brigston's voice was as cold as the blowing wind.

"No." Meyers watched the medic for several seconds after Brigston disconnected. Timkul's visor was open and her gloved fingers were pressed against her cheeks. Hecker's helmet was off. Blood covered his throat and jaw. Veitch calmly worked around Hecker's neck. Meyers exhaled softly. "Ensign Hassan, could you connect me to Chief Pivovarova?"

"Yes, Colonel. Um, I can see the team below. BAS shows Sergeant Klinsmann, Sergeant—"

"Can you get low enough for them to board without you landing?"

"I think so."

"Contact them, tell them to load up, then go get McNutt. On your way to pick him up, put me through to Pivovarova. I'll need a flyover of the valley before you take them to the mountaintop. I think the Lancers are out there."

"I can do that, sir." Hassan sounded relieved.

Meyers raised his visor and put their channel on mute before stepping past the saboteur and Paxton's body to stand next to Timkul.

She turned her head enough that he could see tears in the corners of her eyes. "He seemed like a good man," she said.

Meyers didn't know how to respond. Losing Paxton was a greater blow at the moment. "Veitch is still working on him. Maybe..." He shrugged.

There wasn't anything to be gained by watching Veitch, so Meyers looked around the tent for any sign of the devices. Plastic fragments were embedded in the walls and several of the displays. The cargo case the devices had been sitting on was pressed against the wall opposite the entry flap. The explosions had torn off the case top and shredded the foam inside.

Movement caught Meyers's attention, and he turned, ready to simply shoot the saboteur. But it was Paxton who was moving.

"Carl!" Meyers ran to Paxton's side and carefully pulled his helmet off. "Carl?"

Paxton's eyes fluttered open but didn't focus. He muttered something.

"Corporal Veitch, looks like we've got another patient for you over here." Meyers squeezed Paxton's left hand. "Carl, I thought the blast got you."

Paxton seemed to try to focus, then his eyes closed. Meyers brought up the battalion commander interface and manually probed Paxton's BAS until an interface came up. The BAS was registering numerous failed systems, so it had simply shut down to preserve power. Meyers overrode the BAS and brought it back online.

Veitch was there suddenly: sturdy, with a squarish face and a round nose. She blinked a few times as she punched through the external monitor's interface. "Solid vitals, Colonel. Much better than the captain."

Meyers glanced over his shoulder at Hecker's pale face. "Is he going to make it?"

"I have the cut sealed but he lost significant blood." She glanced at the saboteur and sneered. "She is the one who did it?"

"Yeah." Meyers wondered how long he could afford to keep the saboteur as a prisoner. Spies and saboteurs faced summary execution during a lot of conflicts. "We might be able to get some good intelligence from her."

Veitch's sneer didn't go away. "I have summoned assistants to help me move the captain to the infirmary. We will move the master sergeant, too."

"Thank you."

Veitch stood. "Maybe the saboteur should be moved as well, Colonel."

Meyers understood the message: *Not into the infirmary.* "I'll keep her with me."

"Your cuts?" Veitch nodded at his arm. "I can seal those. Armor, too."

He extended his arm and let her spray the cut shut. His channel to Hassan chimed; she was trying to speak to him. "Go ahead, Ensign."

"Your mountain expedition is aboard, Colonel. I can get some altitude and prepare for a flyover."

"Good. Thank you, Genevieve. I know we've pushed you harder than the other pilots."

"We'll all contribute equally. By the way, Corporal Cho was with Sergeant McNutt."

"Cho?" Meyers couldn't recall naming Cho.

"Sergeant McNutt said there were wounded up there. He said he would explain to you." There was a tone in Hassan's voice that said she might have challenged McNutt.

"I'll talk to him in a bit. Thank you."

"Also, as you asked, Chief Pivovarova is ready if you are, Colonel?"

"Thank you. Please patch her through."

Veitch sprayed his armor shut and stood. She mouthed, "All good," then returned to Hecker.

"Corporal, we've got some more folks up at the Systems Shack. Smoke inhalation, mostly, but it smelled pretty toxic."

"We'll swing around to get them," Veitch said. She looked worried.

Meyers sealed his helmet, then grabbed the helmet he'd taken off the saboteur and slid it back over her head, not bothering to stuff her hair back inside. Clumps of hair fell away from the seal. He pulled the woman's body up in a fireman's carry and headed out into the snow. Timkul followed without saying a word.

"Colonel, you asked for me?" Pivovarova appeared on Meyers's display. She was using a camera inside one of the Dart cargo bays, where she was bent over a piece of equipment. The airlock was blocked from sight by tight-packed gear. Pivovarova squeezed herself between the piled-up gear and the equipment. Something caught her T-shirt and pulled it away, exposing a soft, pale hip. She yanked her T-shirt free with a growl and stuck a section of the neckband in her mouth, then shook sweat from her flushed face.

"I just need a status update." Meyers watched the way she shifted. He saw the picture of her again, down by the stream, barely in a bathing suit. She wiped sweat from her face, streaking it with more grease. "We..." He tried to remember why he'd called her. The weight of the saboteur shifted on his shoulder, and he remembered. "We need to bring some more gear down. An emergency. The saboteurs left a bomb."

Pivovarova straightened, spat out the neckband, and brushed a bicep across her forehead, then she blew at a strand of blond hair. "There is only Zero-Eight-Nine ready, Colonel, and it has not been fully modified."

"It's just bringing gear down, not going up the mountain."

Pivovarova puffed out her cheeks. "Better to assume worst, no?"

"Well, it depends. How're you doing on Two-Seven-Three?"

She grabbed at cargo webbing secured to the wall and tugged. "The bomb, it will be secure and safe." The pixie smile returned to her face. "Ensign Nunoz, he said is as good as any bomb net he had seen."

"Well, he's coming down on Zero-Eight-Nine. Captain Brigston's idea."

"Oh." The smile disappeared. "I will give a look."

"And, uh, Chief Merriman's going to be handling the loading of Zero-Eight-Nine."

"Merriman?" Pivovarova's face pinched tight. "Best to stay away from Zero-Eight-Nine. He does not approve."

"All right." Meyers turned into the Systems Shack and set the saboteur down in the left rear corner. He grabbed cabling from one of the cases and tied the woman's wrists and ankles together behind her back. "I just wanted to prevent..."

"A fight?" Pivovarova laughed—a throaty sound. "Thank you, Colonel."

"Thank you." Meyers disconnected and glanced up at Timkul's face. She glared at him, disapproving, head shaking. "What?"

"Nothing." Timkul looked around the shack. She wiped a hand across one of the darkened displays. "What do you plan to do now?"

"Wait. There's not really any other choice, is there?"

Timkul looked toward the saboteur. "No torture or execution?"

He looked at the bound form and wondered if that was what had gotten under Timkul's skin. "Not unless we have to."

Meyers suddenly remembered that the saboteur was wearing Corporal Rhizov's armor. That meant Rhizov was probably dead somewhere. He sent out an alert to the entire network to be on the lookout for Rhizov. After doing that, he settled onto one of the cargo cases and surveyed the ruins of the shack. The saboteurs had hit them hard and had done so with remarkable ease. It certainly seemed like they were receiving inside help, but it also seemed unlikely now that the help had come from the Russians. Pivovarova was working harder than anyone to see the mission succeed, and Rhizov had probably been killed.

So, who does that leave? Meyers wondered.

He sighed. It felt like he might not live to find the answer to that question.

13

2 October 2175. Siberia.

A HUMMING NOISE filled Meyers's BAS as he laid systems out atop the cargo cases the Systems team had been using as furniture. Even after leaving the entry flap open for nearly an hour, the stench of burned circuitry was bothersome. Timkul sat to his right, on a smaller cargo case, staring at the guts of a device he'd popped open earlier. It was as if she'd never seen circuit leaves before. She shivered suddenly, and Meyers got up to seal the entry flap.

Timkul tracked him with her eyes as he returned to the case that had become his seat by default. She frowned and returned to staring at the circuitry, then said, "You didn't have to do that. The space heaters are making a real difference."

Meyers smiled. "I did it for me. It's already too cold to work without gloves on, and that's exactly what I need to do. These leaves require a delicate touch."

"I see." She tapped at one of the near-transparent layers. "What are they?"

"Circuit boards. Or what's left of them." He picked up one of the blackened leaves and tapped it against the case top. A charcoal-like powder slid along the surface and collected in small piles. He flicked one of the powder piles. "Each one of these represents probably five or six microsystems—radios, video controllers, encryption and decryption..." He sighed. "Systems. Components within major systems. But they're just ash now."

She flipped over the leaf she held. "Why is this one clear instead of blackened?"

"That's what I'm hoping to find out. Whatever bots they hit us with were attuned to our systems. Highly attuned. They sent self-destructive commands, sent more power through than these could handle. That shouldn't have been possible." He pulled another leaf from the pile he'd laid out on the case top. It was like the one she held: completely intact. "Something set these apart. There are a couple systems that were barely hit at all."

Timkul glanced over her shoulder at the door. "Can the Systems team salvage anything?"

"Maybe. Once Veitch releases them." Meyers glanced at his BAS time display. "Zero-Eight-Nine should be on approach soon. We're going to be busy replacing things—" The humming became a distorted voice, and then it resolved into Hassan speaking: choppy, but it was clearly her voice. "Ensign Hassan? You've got a lot of distortion on the connection. Can you hear me?" He turned the BAS's auto-dictation conversion on and sent the same message as simple text. A few seconds later, the humming disappeared along with the audio.

"Can you hear me more clearly, Colonel?" Hassan's voice sounded as clear as if she were sitting next to Timkul.

"Perfect now. What's up?"

"I have my cameras working. Agent Barlowe helped me to sync his imagery systems and to use radar and infrared. I am swinging back around for a run over the valley."

Meyers scratched at the ash piles. All the delays were putting them at risk but they didn't really have any choices. Without good imagery, a flyover of the valley wasn't worth it. "No signal from Zero-Eight-Nine yet, so you're clear to make your run. Can you send me a sample image?"

The connection hummed again, and an image slowly built out on his BAS display. He put his helmet on and sealed his visor to get a better look. Wireframes showed the surrounding mountains as a great white skeleton, and the jarring reds and grays of the infrared fleshed everything out. Meyers's earpiece ran quick conversions, turning the imagery into something more acceptable.

"That's good. Sharp." Meyers rubbed the ash from his gloves. "I think we're ready."

"Heading over the valley now, Colonel."

Timkul propped her elbows on the case top. The glow of the space heater turned the side of her face a warm gold. "What if they are out there?"

Meyers muted his connection and lifted his visor. "Not 'if' but 'where.'"

"You think they are approaching?"

"They have to be. They have the advantage now. They wouldn't blow this sort of opportunity. This has all been coordinated. Everything. From the second we departed Plymouth."

Timkul's brow wrinkled. "A trap? You seemed so confident your source was reliable."

"I don't think Captain Taylor was in on it. She was a dupe, same as—" Meyers's earpiece chimed. Zero-Eight-Nine was calling; he accepted. "Ensign Nunoz, this is Colonel Meyers. I assume you can put down without ILS?"

"Roger that, Colonel. I've done instrument landing in worse blizzard conditions, and I've landed blind. It's part of what we train for. These ships can manage."

Meyers chuckled at Nunoz's cockiness. "Good to hear."

"You have people ready to handle unloading, sir? I'd like to get airborne and provide fire support when Two-Seven-Three drops its present."

"We're spread a little thin at the moment but we'll have people there."

"Just over...three minutes out."

Meyers set a timer in his BAS. "How far back was Zero-Eight-Nine?"

"Chief Pivovarova said ten minutes at the outside, and I'm not about to question her."

Me neither, Meyers thought. "All right. We'll get you back in the air pronto." He disconnected and stood. When Timkul looked up, he said, "I'm heading to the landing zone."

Timkul stood uncertainly. "I thought you were sending someone to unload?"

"We don't have anyone to spare. Anyway, I need everything Brigston sent down as badly as we need Nunoz up there supporting Shazier in Two-Seven-Three. I should be able to get everything unloaded quick enough. It's the lugging it into camp and hooking it up that'll be a problem." He smiled but Timkul didn't return it.

They trudged across the snow, which seemed to have grown deeper. Several meters out from the LZ, Meyers spotted a sunken ring in the ice where the instrumentation and lights had superheated. He stopped and looked skyward.

Lights kicked on: blurry, distant but bright against the gray haze.

Meyers waved, even though he knew he wasn't visible to Nunoz. "You're clear, Nunoz."

"Lots of white down there, Colonel," Nunoz said, the slightest hint of nerves in his voice.

"Lock on to my BAS signal. You can set down five meters southeast of that."

"Better than nothing."

The Dart descended with a deafening hum. It kicked up snow and settled with its tail just outside the sunken ring. Meyers stepped down from the ice slope protecting the LZ and ran to the Dart's rear, followed closely by Timkul. When the ramp descended, Meyers ran up it as quickly as his tender heel allowed. Nunoz was already in the cargo bay along with his crew chief, releasing cargo straps. There wasn't as much gear as Meyers had hoped for.

"Just you, sir?" Nunoz grunted as he worked a cam buckle free.

"Doesn't look like I'll need much more."

Nunoz's face twisted in a sour grimace. "It's what the captain could spare, sir."

"I understand. You did great work."

Meyers pulled off the topmost case and staggered at its surprising heft. Timkul was suddenly there, pushing away his left hand, grabbing the handle, and taking the lead to the ramp. He followed, doing what he could to take most of the weight.

At the top of the ramp, he set the case down. "We can slide it from here."

He pushed the case and watched long enough to be sure it was headed down the ramp, then returned to the cargo bay. Nunoz and his crew chief had the last of the straps off. As Meyers grabbed another case, his earpiece chimed. It was Hassan.

"Colonel?" Hassan sounded concerned. "There's definite movement at the northwestern valley entry. I had to pull up. I'm circling back around for a lower altitude run at higher speed, then I'm heading out for the mountainside drop."

Meyers wished he could be at a terminal, analyzing the imagery. "Be careful. We should have some systems running in a few minutes."

"They...they looked like they were moving fast, Colonel. Full speed."

Of course, Meyers thought. Their target was helpless. "We're doing what we can. Could you patch me through to Cooper when you get close enough to him?"

"Yes, sir." There was a wet sound, like Hassan was licking her lips. "Heading in for the low-altitude flyover now."

Meyers sent the second case down the ramp as he listened. On his way back for another case, he had to dodge around Timkul, who was carrying a long, folded sheet of black plastic about twenty centimeters thick. It looked like a carrying sleeve for displays.

"Oh, Colonel!" Hassan's anxious voice caught Meyers's attention. "They're in the valley. Deep! Halfway to the camp. I missed the head of the column on my first pass. They'll be parallel to Agent Barlowe's position before long. Not even an hour!"

"Okay. Give him a warning." Meyers could only imagine Barlowe's response. "Tell him I'm going to get comms running first. We'll coordinate defense for his position."

"Yes, sir. Heading toward the mountain. I'll patch Commander Cooper in soon."

Meyers dragged the last of the larger cases through the airlock and pushed it down the ramp ahead of him. He brought up the manifest for each case, tagging the items he needed most: C4I systems. The first thing he had to have was a replacement for the fried uplink circuitry. That was in the biggest case.

He grabbed a handle and pulled the back of the case from the snow with some effort. "Would you be able to help me with this case again, Miss Timkul?"

"Only if you'll call me Priya." She took the other handle.

"Lonny, then. I guess no one will complain if we lose formality at a time like this."

Nunoz connected again. "Colonel, we've set the rest of the gear out in the snow."

"Thank you, Ensign. Keep connected, please."

Meyers and Timkul hauled the case out to the uplink, both listening in to Hassan and Nunoz's chatter. At the uplink, Meyers pulled the replacement gear out of the case and quickly assembled it. There was a half-size antenna that he quickly secured to the top of the uplink casing after brushing away snow and ice. The case had a tube of powerful adhesive that quickly set as hard as a weld. Next came a device that would manage encryption and decryption along with transmission and reception, then a power-boosting device, and finally a BAS integration device. It took less than ten minutes to get everything put into place and powered on. Twenty seconds later, he could hear Hassan and Nunoz perfectly.

"Ensign Hassan? Ensign Nunoz?" Meyers watched Timkul's face in the corner of his display as he waited for a reply. Her eyes were closed, as if she were praying.

"I hear you, Colonel," Hassan said.

"Clear signal, sir," Nunoz said. "If you can find something to boost the signal, that would be helpful."

Meyers almost laughed. Nunoz had to know what Brigston sent. "We'll see what we can do. Try video feeds, please."

Hassan's belly camera came in over the channel; Meyers shifted it to the top left quarter of his helmet display. Ice and snow raced by, and he thought he recognized a ledge. Nunoz's face showed over his channel. Dark lips stretched ear-to-ear in a grin, brown eyes twinkling, the slightest discoloration above his chin from a scar. He quickly switched to his belly camera. He was following Hassan up the mountainside, trailing her by about one hundred meters.

"I have clear video." Meyers tried to connect to Cooper. "Commander Cooper?"

"Lonny?" Cooper's voice was high-pitched; he was stressed. "Shit—" Gunfire drowned out his voice for a second. "Sorry. I had external audio sensors way up. Brigston said you got hit by a bot attack?"

"Yeah." Meyers closed the case and pointed Timkul back to the LZ. He followed close behind her, dragging the mostly empty case across the snow. "Rescue's on the way. We've got comms up. Can you send video?"

Cooper's channel filled with an image of white. It was a little grainy but otherwise clean; snow covered everything. "We're still pinned down. That gun they've got, it doesn't stop. At least it can't get to us."

Meyers told himself there was at least that. "How're the wounded?"

"In shock. Private Starling's doing what she can. She's been trying to get the control systems working. One of them isn't syncing right."

"At least they weren't down here when the bots hit."

"Yeah. Shit." Cooper sighed. "They would've been. We got lucky."

"So, Cooper, here's what we need to do. Ensign Shazier should be there soon with Two-Seven-Three. They'll drop medical supplies and a litter for the wounded. Ensign Nunoz is bringing Zero-Eight-Nine in for fire support. Ensign Hassan's dropping a squad-plus about two hundred meters down from your position."

"They're gonna try that trail up?" Cooper sounded skeptical.

"Yeah. Can you pull Sergeant Banh in on this connection?"

"Sure." Cooper turned to his right, where a soldier was half-buried in the snow behind a boulder.

Banh's video feed appeared, then his face. "Colonel? It is good to hear you, sir."

Meyers grabbed the case containing command-and-control systems while Timkul dug the display sleeve from the snow. "I'm going to leave it to Commander Cooper to fill you in on the details, Sergeant, but we're about to pull your wounded off the mountaintop. What I'm going to need from you and your squad is to suppress that gun when the time comes."

Banh switched back to his external camera and looked around the boulder. The machine gun fired, chipping off pieces of rock; Banh quickly leaned back behind cover. "The emplacement is tagged, Colonel. At your signal, we will move around and attack the position."

"Don't take any unnecessary risks. We just need that gun quieted some."

"Off to the left, there is another area like this, Colonel. They cannot see it. Off to the right and forward, there is an area where we can fire from cover."

Meyers didn't like the idea of Banh's men moving to the areas, not if there were some sort of advanced imaging on the machine gun. "Okay. We don't need more casualties. Can Private Starling help you?"

"She is dealing with the wounded and trying to get the imagery systems running, Colonel."

"Right. But if she can help you—"

"Yes, Colonel. We will move now."

Meyers started to suggest that Banh should see what Starling might be able to do but stopped. They could work on better overcoming whatever issues Banh had with Starling later, when there was less at stake.

Banh shared his orders to the rest of his squad over the channel. He had already mapped out the entire area in his BAS. There were limited fields of fire for the gun emplacement based on its position. Meyers couldn't challenge Banh's work without seeing the terrain. Banh and Corporal Nguyen's diminished fire team crawled toward the boulder on the left while Corporal Mai's team moved to the right.

The machine gun didn't seem to track them.

Meyers stopped outside the Systems Shack and released the two cases he'd been dragging. He took the display sleeve from Timkul and set it inside, on top of a cargo case, then he dragged the other two cargo cases in.

"Colonel?" It was Nunoz. "Two-Seven-Three's not coming."

"Not coming?"

"I contacted the *Valdez* when I couldn't raise Shazier. Captain Brigston isn't happy with the way Chief Pivovarova has the bomb secured. He won't approve launch until Chief Merriman approves."

"And the *Valdez* didn't bother to tell us this?" Meyers balled his hands into fists. He should have known better than to think Brigston was past his petty games.

Nunoz swallowed hard. "There was, uh, a breakdown in communications, sir. Shazier—"

"We have wounded personnel on that mountaintop."

"Ensign Shazier sounds very upset."

Jeremy, Meyers thought, what the hell is wrong with you? A confrontation seemed inevitable, or at least it seemed to be what Brigston wanted. "We can't delay. If we can suppress that gun, can you hover long enough for an evac?"

"We'll smoke that gun emplacement, Colonel, then we'll pull everyone out."

"All right. Sergeant Banh's squad is in position. They'll lay down suppressing fire, then you come in and take that emplacement out. When it's gone, get our people out of there. Sergeant Banh, are you copying?"

"We are in position, Colonel." Banh sounded calm, ready.

Meyers knew it was a solid plan but couldn't shake off the nagging sense that it wouldn't be enough. They needed Two-Seven-Three.

But there were wounded, and the enemy was rapidly closing.

"Let's take that damned gun out," Meyers said.

Banh brought his squad's video together into a shared network, revealing the mountaintop from a nearly 180-degree view. His people popped from around cover—protected, just as he'd described—and opened fire on the gun Banh had already tagged. Snow and ice flew free of the curved rock protecting the gun, and it returned fire. It was ineffective, unable to wheel far enough to the right to reach Mai's fire team, and limited to blasting away chunks of boulder when firing at Nguyen's fire team.

Zero-Eight-Nine crested the mountaintop, the belly gun already locked on through Banh's BAS tag. Before the machine gun could shift to target the Dart, its belly gun tore out the protecting section of stone. Sparks flashed as rounds shredded the machine gun, which went silent.

Nguyen's fire team advanced, guns raised.

"Scratch one gun empla—" Nunoz's voice was silenced by the roar of a machine gun.

Nguyen's head was torn from his body in a spray of blood. Before he hit the ground, his left arm had been torn loose as well. His fire team dropped. Banh advanced toward them, firing but rounds crashed into the boulder, driving him back.

"Three more guns, Colonel! Three more guns!" The calm was gone from Banh's voice.

The guns shifted to Nunoz's Dart, forcing him to juke and twist. The Dart's engine died just as the belly camera revealed the blur of mountainside passing by before winking out.

"Nunoz!" Meyers twisted his head around, trying to use Banh's interlocked BAS view to get a sense of what had happened, but the video feeds showed nothing but snow.

14

2 October 2175. Siberia.

MEYERS SQUEEZED his eyes shut to reset his world view. Against the black of his sight, the afterimage of snow and Nguyen being torn up by the machine guns burned bright. Meyers heard the machine guns firing still, and he could see them now in an unwanted replay of memory: curved sections of the snow- and ice-covered wall at the base of the peak simply fell onto the snow, revealing weapon barrels that instantly lit up.

They had been lured in. The enemy had held back its true capabilities until needed.

He opened his eyes. His heart thudded, and he heard his breathing, loud and fast. The shack felt hot, smothering, its air noxious. He had underestimated the enemy. He had focused on the large force. He had miscalculated the threat of the mountaintop.

Meyers opened his eyes again. "Ensign Hassan, we lost Zero-Eight-Nine. We need to abort the drop."

"Sir?" Hassan sounded confused. "Sergeant McNutt's already on the ground."

"Get him back in. We can't send anyone else up there. It's too risky."

"Sergeant Klinsmann's at the outer airlock door, Colonel. He's ready to go."

Meyers stood. "Put Klinsmann and McNutt on. Domnikov, too."

A faint chirp sounded on Hassan's channel. "They're on, sir."

McNutt's face showed up first—dark blue eyes squinted in anger. Klinsmann's face appeared next, heavy jaw clenched tight. Finally, Domnikov appeared, gray eyes calm, almost dead, lip curled in a slight sneer. Meyers spread their images across the top half of his visor display area.

"Sergeant McNutt?" Meyers searched through the mountainside video he'd reviewed earlier. "You're on the ascent path?"

"If you wanna call it that, sir, yeah." Wind whistled as McNutt spoke; he probably had his helmet open. "It's not a walk in the park."

Meyers looked the imagery over. Sections of it would be extremely demanding. "Sergeant Klinsmann, Sergeant Domnikov, we took out the gun emplacement above you, but more gun positions were revealed when Sergeant Banh's squad moved in to confirm the kill. We lost Corporal Nguyen. I think it's too dangerous sending you up until we can firebomb that area. It's your call."

"I'm going, Colonel," McNutt said. "Cho, too. We don't care about anyone else."

"I understand." Meyers imagined McNutt would charge a machine gun nest with a knife if it meant saving someone from his squad. "Sergeant Klinsmann?"

"The mission hasn't changed, Colonel, not just because of a few more guns." Klinsmann's dark eyes glanced down, probably watching McNutt below the Dart.

Meyers watched Domnikov for a reaction. The sneer didn't change, really, and if his gray eyes moved, it was too slow to catch. "Sergeant Domnikov?"

"My squad, Colonel Meyers. My mission. We go." Domnikov's voice was deep, his speech as slow as the movement of his features.

"All right. Be aware that we have no idea of the full strength or placement of the enemy force." Meyers brought up an image of the video from just after the new gun emplacements had opened fire on Banh's team. He marked the guns and sent the image to the three sergeants. "Those are the positions we—"

"Colonel?" Hassan sounded excited. "Zero-Eight-Nine just flew past! Ensign Nunoz is waving with his wings. He's alive!"

"Great news." Meyers tried to keep his voice even, but knowing they hadn't lost a second Dart was a huge relief. "See why he went silent."

"He texted that he took a couple hits and needs to set down and reset his systems, Colonel."

"All right. Maybe Two-Seven-Three will be planet-side when he's ready." Meyers turned his attention back to the NCOs. "Sergeants, if you're going to assault that cliff, you better get going. Looks like we still have Dart Zero-Eight-Nine to support future operations."

"We don't need Dart." Domnikov's sneer became more pronounced.

"Yeah, I'll remember you said that," McNutt muttered.

Meyers didn't like the way Domnikov laughed at McNutt's comment. It wasn't just cocky but...malicious. "All right," Meyers said. "I need to check on Sergeant Banh and the rest. Move as quickly as you safely can, and hug that cliff wall."

McNutt glanced up, and his video feed shifted to external cameras as he inspected the path. "Yeah, should be fun."

"Ensign Hassan, see if you can get another flyover of the valley, please." Meyers disconnected from the channel before Hassan could reply. He didn't need to see the strain and fatigue on her face to know he was pushing her too hard. He returned to Cooper's channel. "Coop?"

"I read you. What the hell happened?" There was a quaver in Cooper's voice. His camera showed the open area between his boulder and the machine gun emplacements.

"Listen, we're going to be losing our Dart relay soon. Hassan's going to do a flyover of the valley, and Nunoz is headed back to camp to reset his systems. I don't know what connection quality's going to be like when they're out of the area."

"Shit. I can check Three-Zero-Eight, see if I can use its comms as a relay. Those new guns don't have clean line of sight on it like the first one did."

"What's the status with Banh's team?"

Cooper's image went white, and Meyers nearly panicked. Then he realized Cooper was belly-crawling through the snow.

"They said Nguyen's dead. Banh confirmed—no vitals." Cooper looked up the ice-slick ramp, then he looked back toward the open area. There was no sound of machine gun fire. Private...Vo?"

Meyers flinched. "What about him?"

"I just wanted to be sure I got his name right. He's wounded. Nothing life-threatening. He made his way back to Private Starling, and she's patching him up."

Meyers watched as Cooper belly-crawled up the ramp. He was a big man and not particularly graceful but he managed the ice well enough. His camera revealed the dark shape of Kumar's body. Blood had pooled for a meter around the corpse. Light leaked through gaping holes in the fuselage. Cooper's camera revealed ice crystals at the edge of the blood pool. Suddenly, little artifacts shot through the video, and it began to stretch and freeze.

"Coop, Hassan must be moving away." Meyers searched through the case that had held the communications gear. There was a local booster buried at the bottom, something designed to pump up signal strength within his own network. He plopped that against the wall where the ruined gear had been stacked and powered it on. "Coop?"

Cooper's image was completely frozen.

Brigston's lack of support, Meyers thought. Frustration shot through him, and he brought a leg back to kick one of the empty cases. He froze when he saw Timkul watching. She had her helmet off. Her hair streamed down and over her shoulders. Her narrow mouth was twisted in disapproval.

"I—" Meyers caught movement out of the corner of his eye.

The saboteur. Her head came up and jerked around.

Meyers moved to her side and pulled off her helmet. The left side of her face was slightly discolored where he'd kicked her. Blood had caked in her eyebrow and beneath her nose. "Can you understand me?" He felt Timkul at his back.

The saboteur nodded. The eye on the bruised side of her face fluttered.

"You understand that we could have executed you? You were in our camp in our uniform attempting to assassinate our personnel." When the saboteur nodded, Meyers glanced over his shoulder at Timkul. She had to understand how war worked. Summary executions during conflict were often a necessity for survival.

Timkul's frown said all Meyers needed to know: She was disgusted.

He turned his attention back to the saboteur. "What unit are you with? Who hired you?"

The saboteur looked past Meyers, apparently seeing support or hope in Timkul. "Murad's Star," the saboteur said, her English clear enough. "Three years, I have been Murad's Star."

Meyers hadn't heard of the unit. "Who hired you?"

The saboteur did her best to shrug.

He couldn't tell if she didn't know or wasn't going to give the information up. His earpiece hummed and squeaked. Cooper was back on the channel.

"Coop?" Meyers checked the saboteur's bonds, then moved back to the cargo cases and began unpacking displays from the carrying sleeve.

"Three-Zero-Eight's got a few more hours of battery power," Cooper said. His video showed up—clean, crisp—and revealed the Dart's cockpit. "Might be worth moving the wounded in here. Temperature's about the same but the goddamned wind's not as bad."

Meyers pulled the dead displays from the wall and dropped them to the floor with a crashing thud, then slid two displays into place on the wall and brought them online. "Only if you're sure it's safe."

"Safer. Nothing's safe up here."

"We're going to get you off that mountain." Meyers checked to be sure Timkul wasn't too close to the saboteur before pulling more displays from the sleeve. "I need to check back in with McNutt and Klinsmann."

"McNutt's coming up here? I guess I feel safer."

Meyers snickered. "Keep Starling alive and you'll be fine." He sent a connection request to McNutt.

"Colonel?" McNutt's camera showed the trail up the mountainside.

The video was choppy and full of artifacts, but Meyers could make things out well enough. The Russians were at the front, Domnikov leading, swinging an ice tool wildly, then Klinsmann and Strauss. They all had climbing gear—ropes, harnesses, cams, carabiners, and their boot soles had been modified to crampons. McNutt looked back; Cho was struggling at the rear. "Thought we'd lost connection."

"Commander Cooper's got Three-Zero-Eight's comms running. We've got a few hours of battery. How's the progress?" Meyers didn't like that his strongest climber was at the rear, but there was no choice other than to ask. "Any problems?"

"Domnikov's been telling us how his boys are former mountain infantry, alpine qualified. They climb like a bunch of—"

"I get the idea. How's Klinsmann dealing with it?"

"Yeah, there's not a lot of kisses and hugs between—" McNutt dropped flat as a several-meter-thick sheet of ice came free of the cliff wall farther up and shattered on the path between the trailing Russian soldier and Klinsmann. McNutt spun around and waved Cho down. When Cho was pressed against the cliff wall, McNutt looked up the path again. Klinsmann and Strauss were similarly pressed against the cliff wall. Chunks of ice as big as a human head were still skidding down the path, slamming into soldiers' legs before sliding down or off the narrow ledge.

The Russians were hurriedly scrambling up the path ahead. Domnikov dug into the stone and ice with his ice tool.

"Fucking assholes!" McNutt shoved a chunk of ice off the path. He stood, and Meyers saw an ice tool raise up in McNutt's right hand. "You fucking idiot! You nearly got us killed!"

The Russians stopped, and Domnikov made his way back toward McNutt. When Klinsmann stood to block Domnikov's path, the larger Russian shoved the German aside.

Meyers imagined the tension running through McNutt. He wasn't a patient or tolerant man. "Sergeant McNutt, you need to worry about the people on that mountaintop."

McNutt moved toward the approaching Russian, ice tool jabbing like an accusing finger. "You and your *alpine experts* get to the back of the formation! You don't know the first—"

Domnikov swung his ice tool at McNutt. It wasn't intended as a lethal strike, but it was the sort of thing that would get the Russian giant a reprimand.

And it was exactly the sort of thing that triggered McNutt.

He brought his own ice tool up with an angry grunt. He was shorter than Domnikov but about the same weight, and McNutt had frightening power and speed. He used his ice tool to hook Domnikov's, then yanked it hard and fast toward the open side of the path. Domnikov lost his balance for a second, then let go of his ice tool. McNutt drove a fist into the Russian's exposed ribs, knocking him even more off balance. He windmilled his arms, and McNutt swatted at the nearest hand.

Timkul screamed, "He's killing him!"

Meyers cursed himself for not shutting off her piggyback. But he was in the moment, leaning forward, as if he were on the path, reaching for Domnikov. "Sergeant McNutt, don't you—"

McNutt grabbed Domnikov by the bundle of rope dangling from his hip and hauled him back onto the path. Domnikov crashed onto his back and McNutt was there, knee driven into chest. Then the point of the ice tool head was centimeters away from Domnikov's throat. The Russian's hands went up as McNutt's visor hissed open. "Listen close, you big piece of shit. In the field, people die, and no one says a fucking word about it. You come at me again, you'll be going back to Plymouth in a body bag."

Gun barrels poked into view. Domnikov's squad had Klinsmann and Strauss pinned against the cliff wall, and two of the Russians were just up the path from McNutt. A third Russian stumbled down the path and nearly slid over the edge. His visor popped open.

Repin. His lips were wet and wide with a ridiculous smile. His red eyelashes fluttered, almost invisible. "Eh, Sergeant? McNutt, yes? McNutt, is like slight nut?" Repin laughed. "Please. If you could? Sergei, he was trying to make point. Was misunderstanding." Repin squeezed between the other two Russians and tentatively extended a hand toward Domnikov.

McNutt looked at the two soldiers pointing guns at him. Meyers could sense the calculus, the curiosity about whether the ice tool would be enough to kill them before they could shoot.

Domnikov slowly took Repin's hand.

"Eh, maybe enough?" The skinny Russian's face was red but he laughed. It was a forced sound. "Was just trying to make sure one squad made it to the top, you see? Nothing more."

McNutt stood and backed away.

Repin hauled his sergeant up with a loud grunt, then Domnikov brushed himself off. He raised his visor and stared at McNutt, gray eyes like ice. When Repin clapped Domnikov on the shoulder, he took the smaller man's ice tool and headed back up the trail.

The Russians waited until their leader was back at the front before releasing Klinsmann and Strauss.

Meyers muted his connection to McNutt and rounded on Timkul. "There's a reason I wanted to put those soldiers through training. They're not ready for an operation like this. They haven't been held to the same standards of discipline as the ERF."

Timkul took a step back, as if she thought he was going to attack her. "Your man seemed like he was the one with discipline trouble."

"Domnikov swung at him."

"And what about his threat to kill him?" Timkul crossed her arms. "That seemed real."

It probably was, Meyers realized. "McNutt's an intense soldier."

The entry flap opened, and a short, broad-shouldered, armored form stepped through. It moved stiffly and stopped just beyond the threshold to secure the flap, then it turned around and removed its helmet.

"Carl!" Meyers extended a hand and quickly closed the distance.

Paxton set his helmet on one of the cargo cases, straightened his back, and looked toward the saboteur. His face was red and swollen. "Keeping prisoners, Colonel?"

"I was hoping to get some information from her."

Paxton looked at Timkul, swollen eyes squinted.

Meyers could feel the question Paxton wasn't voicing: *Were you afraid to kill a woman in front of the special envoy?*

Paxton moved closer to the saboteur and squatted at her side. "Did you check her for other gear, Colonel?"

"Shit. No. I've been trying to get our systems back online." Meyers didn't want to ask himself if that was an honest answer. The idea of peeling the saboteur from Rhizov's armor was troubling enough. Doing it in front of Timkul...

"Corporal Veitch can do the strip search." Paxton rummaged through the woman's pouches and pockets. He came away with a palm-sized device and a small knife, which he tossed onto the nearest carrying case. After a few seconds, he pushed himself up from the ground with a grunt and settled onto his butt in front of the cargo case Meyers had been using to tear equipment apart. "Captain Hecker's stable but critical."

"That's good," Meyers said. "I'll have someone collect the prisoner and have Veitch search her."

"Already told her, Colonel." Paxton twisted around with a grunt to look at Timkul and the saboteur. "Just needed to see what was going on for myself."

Meyers pulled some more displays from the carrying sleeve and set them into place on the wall. He had enough of them running to forward his own video to the displays. "We've got vehicles moving into the valley. Shit, they'll be close to Barlowe's position soon." Meyers opened a connection to Hassan as he dug out imagery processors and set them against the wall where he'd placed the booster. "Ensign Hassan, what are you seeing?"

"Thirty vehicles, Colonel. Tracked, skis. Do you have weapons control systems running yet?"

Imagery from One-Zero-One filled Meyers's earpiece display and the displays on the wall: a field of blue snow, wireframes of vehicles filled with orange and red. Barlowe's position was a faint yellow against the blue of the snow.

"Can you connect to Agent Barlowe, Ensign?" Meyers examined the imagery, gauging the distance between the nearest vehicles and Barlowe.

"He knows they're getting close." Hassan's voice cracked.

"We've got soldiers with him," Meyers said, but he knew that wouldn't be enough to keep Barlowe calm.

"Agent Barlowe's been feeding me imagery as well. That's where some of the better data is coming from. You might want to get those heavy weapons ready, sir."

"Good." Meyers knew that keeping Barlowe's mind off how close the vehicles were was best for everyone. They would need his analysis once things got hot. "We'll have system functionality in just a few minutes."

"That's good, Colonel." Hassan's voice evened out. "Ensign Nunoz is ready to head back up."

"All right. I'm going to need you to stay ready. It doesn't look like they're aware you're up there."

"I'm staying high enough that they shouldn't be able to pick me up."

"Good. Maybe they think we're still operating blind. If they stay clumped like they are, the mortars might wrap this quickly. A few strafing runs from you might be enough to break that column if the heavy weapons aren't enough."

"Understood, sir." Hassan's voice betrayed the same skepticism Meyers saw in Paxton's eyes.

Meyers set the concerns aside. They still had time. They still had a chance.

He set the command and control system against the wall and booted it up, then looked back at the wall displays. The vehicles were large. They were armored and they bristled with guns. He thought back to Bellar and the losses suffered there.

Timkul's gaze caught him. She didn't like what she was seeing.

Another debacle, he thought. Just like Timkul had said. It would be the end of the ERF.

15

2 October 2175. Siberia.

THE TOC GLOWED, washed in the white of snow projected from the wall displays Meyers had relocated from the Systems Shack. He knuckled at his already raw nose, but the stench of burned electronics wouldn't go away, even in the TOC. The powdered circuits, the soot— the saboteurs had left a mark that wouldn't be erased. It was a bitter taste. Paxton shifted on a cargo case to Meyers's left, the scrape of armor and grunt of pain combining into a signature sound he had already classified as "Wounded and Pissed-Off Paxton." Somewhere behind Meyers, Timkul stood with crossed arms and a disapproving frown.

Meyers tried to focus on a thin green bar crawling across the bottom of the lowest row of displays. Weapons system control was searching the network, connecting to machine guns, railguns, and mortars. The BAS network was nearly done rebuilding. They were nearly combat ready.

Meyers opened a connection to Barlowe.

Barlowe's face—tight with anger and anxiety—filled the top right wall display. "Lonny? Where the hell have you been? They're almost on top of my position!"

Meyers pressed his hands flat against the carrying case surface. He needed to stay calm. "We've had some problems of our own. We're trying to rebuild things in the TOC. Those vehicles aren't going to see you. They're coming straight toward the camp. That shack gives off a negligible heat signature. Just keep a low profile, and you'll be fine."

"Gerhardt's out in the valley." Barlowe straightened, and his face took on a defiant rigidity.

"What the hell is he doing out there?"

"One of our motion sensors went offline. He's trying to fix it."

Meyers felt anger gnawing at the edges of his mind. A motion sensor was important, but it wasn't worth giving away the forward position. "Pull him back."

"He's already in position. We need to know if someone's getting too close."

"It's a stupid risk, Ladell. Pull him back."

"You assigned his squad to protect my position. This is my call." Barlowe's features—normally almost feminine-soft—were hard.

"All right." Meyers couldn't see a way to win the argument without losing Barlowe's cooperation, same as Brigston. "We need the imagery you're pushing out. Ensign Hassan can't stay over the area forever, and I don't want her giving away her position until we're engaged."

Barlowe let out one of his dramatic sighs. "Then let me run things my way."

"I am. Can you get into their network? Maybe get in some bot attacks of our own?"

"What do you think I've been trying to do, Lonny?"

"All right." Meyers's head throbbed, and his sinuses felt raw from the stench of burned circuitry. "I need to check on the mountaintop team. They're having serious trouble up there. Are you able to hear the machine gun fire at your position?"

"Are you kidding me? We can't hear anything but the wind on this slope."

"Good. I'll keep this channel active."

Meyers flipped to Cooper's channel. His video feed showed Starling crouched over a snow-covered armored form in the forward section of the Dart. Her helmet was off, and her hair was flared out stiffly. She chewed on her bottom lip and blinked rapidly as she moved the armored form's arm. Cooper shifted slightly, and Meyers saw the hint of a bloody stump on the armored form instead of a hand. It was the wounded crew chief, Petty Officer Hollins.

"Coop?" Meyers realized he was almost whispering and felt embarrassed.

Cooper's camera shifted back toward the open airlock door. "Lonny? Shazier's on his way down. Chief Pivo..." The image shifted left to right and back; Cooper was shaking his head. "The Russian crew chief. She came down with it. I don't think she's interested in being Brigston's best friend anymore."

"Probably not." Brigston's list of friends was being whittled down pretty fast. "What's the situation like up there?"

"Banh's got his squad in position to take another whack at the guns. They're quiet for now. If Shazier drops that firebomb from a good enough height, they shouldn't even be able to fire on the Dart."

Meyers frowned. It would be an ideal approach but not realistic. "With the winds blowing the way they are, I don't think that's an option. It's not a guided missile."

"Yeah. Starling said the same thing. She got a look at the bomb and said it's gonna have a lot of wobble to it. It's a big storage container with an impact detonator on it. Pretty simple stuff, but..."

"So, we'll need Banh's team to engage again. Nunoz should be up there soon. I'd like some airborne imagery. We missed something in the initial flyover." As he spoke, Meyers brought the old imagery up. The smooth symmetry of the ripple at the base of the peak was even more obvious now that he knew what he was looking at. "I think that's a bunker, like a continuous series of gun emplacements."

Cooper's view moved closer to the airlock. "On a mountaintop? Why?"

"For the same reason we're up there. It has strategic value."

Cooper poked his head out of the airlock. His camera barely picked up Banh's squad. The destroyed machine gun was a dark scar in the distant white of the mountain. "You don't think we caught these guys by surprise?"

Meyers wrestled with how much to say. "Don't tell Brigston. It would only make things worse. But, no, I think we were lured here. Saboteurs, gun emplacements…"

"Yeah."

"I need to check on McNutt's progress." Meyers switched over to the channel he'd opened with McNutt earlier. McNutt's camera still showed the trail and the soldiers ahead of him. "Sergeant McNutt?"

"Yeah, I saw you hop on. We're moving at the pace of the slowest climber, Colonel. That's the Russians, just in case you didn't know." A bright red outline highlighted one of the Russians. "Repin. The fucking clown. Came back at one point—red faced and breathing like he was squeezin' out a baby—just to say his father tried out for the Olympics. Must be adopted."

"We're going to need everyone when you get up there. Keep that in mind."

"I'm not planning to kill anyone. Unless you're giving the okay to take Domnikov out?" McNutt snorted as the red outline shifted to the towering Russian.

"That's not funny, Sergeant."

"Was to me. The guy's putting the mission at risk."

Meyers watched the video for a moment. There was an undeniable lack of urgency in the way the Russians moved. Klinsmann and Strauss both looked back at McNutt, and even in enclosed armor, their bodies betrayed tension and frustration.

"Your video will go into the record," Meyers said. "Maybe we can train this out of them."

"Looks like it's pretty well already trained into them."

"Noted." Meyers returned his attention to the imagery from the first flyover. Nunoz had recently added imagery from his belly camera, which the system slowly integrated, along with Banh's BAS network imagery. "I think we have a lot more troops dug in up there than we estimated."

"Typic—"

A loud crack drowned McNutt out. His view twisted up and around, and Meyers realized why: A huge sheet of ice had torn free from the cliff face above Klinsmann. The ice plunged toward him. He looked up, saw the threat, and shoved Strauss back against the wall. The ice sheet struck the path centimeters away from Klinsmann's boots and shattered. Blocks of ice exploded outward, some bouncing down the path past Strauss and toward McNutt, who shouted for Cho to drop flat. Klinsmann twisted, struggled for balance, and whacked his ice tool against the wall. It wasn't a clean strike and didn't gain meaningful purchase. He fell back, and the ice tool came free.

And then Klinsmann disappeared over the edge.

McNutt moved forward, hunched down as far as Meyers could see, eyes on the path, kicking white chunks of ice aside as he ascended the path. Strauss was at the edge of the narrow strip of rock, on his belly, looking down. His visor went up. "Down there! On a ledge!"

McNutt looked over the side. Klinsmann was flat on his back on a narrow ledge about fifteen meters down, left shoulder and arm and both feet dangling over open space. But he was alive and moving.

"Fall like that could've killed him," McNutt muttered, his voice shaking slightly. "Armor probably saved his life." He rubbed at his chest.

The polished stone, his father's death, Meyers thought.

McNutt turned to the cliff wall and ran a shaking hand along the ice until he found a spot he must have liked, then he began hacking at it. "Don't know how many tons of ice that was, Colonel. Something caused it to come free."

Barlowe's channel chimed.

"All right. I need to check back in with Barlowe." Meyers glanced at the green bar on the bottom display. It hadn't budged in the time he'd been distracted. He brought up the interface and began running through the message logs. "What's up, Ladell?"

"A vehicle broke off from the column." Barlowe sounded less confident, more anxious. "Smaller than the others—faster."

"A scout. Sure. Not that surprising." Meyers glanced up at the display coming in from Barlowe's position. The vehicle was approaching the low hills below the slope where he, Gerhardt's squad, and the rest of McNutt's soldiers were hidden. The scout was hugging the canyon wall closer than the rest. "It's probably trying to hit the camp with some sort of passive sensor scan before the others advance."

"Yeah, well..." Barlowe's voice caught. "Here."

A green dot appeared on the display, maybe five hundred meters in front of the advancing vehicle. Meyers drilled down until the dot resolved into a human shape. He didn't need to see the ID to know that Gerhardt was stuck out in the valley with the column approaching.

"Why's Gerhardt still out there, Ladell?"

"He was working on the motion sensor. I told you." Barlowe's lips squeezed together. "Someone had damaged the sensor. It wasn't just a fault."

"The saboteurs." Meyers's eyes flicked from the approaching vehicle to the log messages coming from the weapons control console. It was reporting everything fine throughout the network other than the weapons themselves. He could see them, but when he tried to access their interfaces, he got back nothing.

"You're not thinking very clearly, Lonny. The saboteurs were closer to the other side of the valley. They would have been past this point before we got here."

"Right. Yeah. Sorry." Meyers elevated his security privileges, accessing one of the mortars' interface at root level. It was a dense and unfriendly design, offering up options like compensation, orientation, and elevation metrics—things that mattered to indirect fire experts.

"Lonny, are you listening? Do you see what's going on?"

Meyers glanced down at the display again, saw the vehicle approaching Gerhardt's position. "Yeah, I'm seeing it." He glanced back at the interface and finally spotted what he was looking for: weapons control interface. He selected that.

"So what do we do?" Barlowe's voice sounded even more frantic than before.

"What do we—?" Meyers looked back at the display and blinked. The vehicle was almost on top of Gerhardt. "Is that—" Meyers pushed the image in closer. "Shit!"

The vehicle was actually coming right at Gerhardt.

"Why didn't you tell me he was directly in its path?" Meyers drilled in closer. It looked like Gerhardt was lower than the vehicle. The motion sensor enhanced the image, revealing the vehicle's straight path and Gerhardt's stillness. "Where is he? Under the snow?"

Paxton had been leaning forward, probably trying to cope with the pain from his injuries, but now he looked up. "What's going on, Colonel?"

"Gerhardt." Meyers pointed to the display. "He's directly in the path of a scout vehicle."

"Yes," Barlowe said. "He burrowed. That's why it took so long. There's a trough in that area, and the snow doesn't reach the bottom. There's an ice sheet over the top."

"How deep?" Meyers drilled down even closer.

The scout vehicle was nearly on top of Gerhardt.

Barlowe sucked in air sharply. "Almost a meter."

Paxton stood with a grunt and walked up to the display. "Not much of a trough."

Meyers shook his head. Antagonizing Barlowe wasn't the objective. "So, maybe we're—"

The vehicle rolled over Gerhardt.

And came to a stop.

Paxton turned, and his face twisted in pain. "It stopped."

Meyers tried to shift the imagery around. "Ladell, what are you seeing?"

"Hold on." Barlowe looked away, eyes dancing.

The image shifted to a sideways view of the vehicle. A hatch popped open, and a form climbed out, assault rifle pointed down at the spot where Gerhardt was hidden beneath the snow.

Meyers's mouth dropped open. "Ladell, tell Gerhardt to move."

"They can't possibly—"

"Tell him to move. Now!" Meyers deleted the BAS network, dropping all his connections.

Paxton cocked an eyebrow. "Colonel, you mind telling me what the hell—"

"It's my ID. It's compromised." Meyers pounded a fist against the cargo case top. "Those bots, they weren't just meant to take down the system; they were meant to compromise it if it came back up. How could they do that? How could they get that deep into our security?"

Paxton cocked an eyebrow and glanced toward Timkul, who was absorbed in the imagery frozen on the displays. Meyers shook his head but without conviction. He had been skeptical of her and the UN's intrusion from the start. She didn't even have to be aware of her involvement in any betrayal. She could have a compromised BAS identifier, like his. She had been piggybacking him from early on.

Meyers scanned the room. "We have to get the network back online."

"What you got in mind, Colonel?" Paxton set his hands on his hips.

"Miss Timkul, could you stay with Master Sergeant Paxton? He's going to need your help if this works." Meyers grabbed his helmet and headed for the entry flap.

Timkul followed. "Where are you going?"

"I have an idea for how to bring things back online. Just stay here." He undid the flap and ran toward the infirmary, leaving the flap for Paxton or Timkul to secure.

Meyers pulled his helmet on as he ran past structures, once again shrouded in snow beneath the overcast gray. Soldiers stumbled around, helmets off, shouting and waving at each other. Without their BAS network and the critical control systems, they had very few advantages over the enemy. He let himself into the infirmary structure and pulled his helmet off again.

The interior was bright and warm, with two rows of stretchers running four deep. A curtain blocked off the far corner to his right. Space heaters glowed redly in the corners.

Veitch looked up from between two occupied stretchers. "Colonel?"

Meyers scanned the wounded. Hecker lay on the stretcher farthest in from the door. "Where's Captain Hecker's armor?"

Veitch nodded toward Hecker's stretcher. "Under there, sir."

Meyers fished through the armor, brushing away caked blood and ash. He found the panel he was looking for and tapped it. There was still power in the suit. He set it down, worked his right hand free from its glove, then dug a piece of data film from a pouch on his pants. The film easily slid into a slot on the armor. He tapped in his command code, and the suit dumped all its information into the film before draining its batteries.

He poked his head up over the stretchers. "Where's the prisoner?"

Veitch jerked her head at the curtained area.

"Rhizov's armor?"

Veitch indicated the curtained area again. "With his body."

Meyers slipped through the curtain entry. A young, small man he assumed was Rhizov lay inside a partially open plastic bag on the cold floor. Another soldier Meyers didn't recognize was similarly laid out. The prisoner was next to the corpses, held in a sitting position by restraints that were secured to the floor and wall. She was mostly covered by a foil thermal blanket; she looked away when he entered.

He wanted to reassure her he wasn't there to hurt her, but then he looked at Rhizov's corpse. His throat had been cut, just like Hecker's. She didn't really deserve reassurances.

Meyers crouched next to Rhizov's armor, inserted the data film, and tapped the same panel he'd used on Hecker's armor. Rhizov's armor flushed its data to the film and drained battery power. Meyers held the data film up.

"You're in our network," Meyers said. "You don't have to tell me. I already know."

She looked at him with dark eyes. Cleaned up and bandaged, she looked sad rather than intimidating. "We were told they would make this easy, shut you down," she said.

"They almost did. Maybe it's already too late." He waved the data film. "Or not."

He slid the film into his earpiece. It displayed streams of data, far too much for him to make sense of. He immediately brought up a virtual keyboard and typed in several filters. Soon, the data streams began falling into meaningful categories. More filtering, and he had what he was looking for. He ran another query, then he loaded the resulting data into his own suit. As the BAS software reset, he stood. He turned at the curtain entry.

"Do you know who they are?" he asked. "In case none of us make it."

The prisoner shook her head. "Very wealthy is all I know."

"Yeah."

He ran back to the TOC, helmet tucked under his arm. Lights were already kicking on throughout the camp, and soldiers were returning to their positions. The BAS network was rebuilding. As he ran, he redirected messages and reconfigured IDs. At the TOC entry flap, he stopped, waiting for things to complete. His face stung from the cold wind. He stuck his tongue out and caught a snowflake. It was sweet, pure. The thought of anything being pure made him snort.

He entered the TOC and settled in front of the displays. Messages were coming in now. He accepted Barlowe's first.

"Lonny, what..." Barlowe's brow was furrowed; he looked flabbergasted. "The scout vehicle—"

"It moved on, didn't it?" Meyers leaned toward the displays as the video feeds slowly resumed, hoping he was right.

"Yeah."

"Gerhardt?"

"He's on his way back."

Meyers shook out his hands. "Keep your eyes open. That position isn't as safe as it should be."

"We will."

Meyers flipped over to McNutt's channel. "Sergeant McNutt, sorry for the interruption. Looks like you've made progress?"

"Yeah. Nearly done, Colonel." Ice came away in chunks beneath McNutt's strikes, and then his camera revealed the stone of the cliff face. There was a shadow, a wide crack in the rock. He pulled a cam from his belt and shoved it into the crack, adjusting the cam until he couldn't get it to move. He threaded the end of a rope through the eye at the end of the cam. "Don't much care for the rock face or the ice." He glanced up the cliff face. "Don't much care for this whole fucking mountain."

"Me either." Meyers watched McNutt's movements, fascinated by the speed and grace.

Rope floated out over the cliff face before piling lazily on the ledge between Klinsmann's knees. As McNutt backed toward the edge of the path, he looked up. The Russians hadn't moved from their position. In fact, it looked like they might have moved higher up. "Good riddance, you—"

A familiar cracking pop boomed from below, and McNutt fell. He twisted, and his camera revealed the cliff face rushing by and another sheet of ice plunging ahead of him toward Klinsmann.

16

2 October 2175. Siberia.

THE TOC'S display wall showed ice-covered stone. Meyers could make out every dip and bubble in the surface, every bulge and divot. Where the earlier ice fall had scraped everything down to stone, he could see the grain of the almost-black rock. McNutt accelerated toward the ledge where Klinsmann lay; Meyers wasn't sure whether to hope for the fall to end on the ledge or to count on the cam holding. In the end, it was a little of both, as McNutt fell past the ledge but got a hand on it. Although he couldn't keep his grip, it was enough to swing him inward and slow his fall. Four meters down, the rope went taut.

The cam held.

Meyers blinked to break his contact with the images on the displays. He sucked in the foul air. "Sergeant McNutt?"

McNutt gasped. "Yeah, yeah. Give it a minute, will ya?"

Meyers couldn't do anything more than watch as McNutt looked up the mountainside. The rope was the center of his focus, rising up and over the ledge and then disappearing far above. Corporal Cho looked down, then Strauss. They began hauling McNutt up.

"I'm not crippled," McNutt shouted.

The Russians peered over the side. Domnikov's visor lifted, and for the first time Meyers could recall, the smirk was gone. In its place was a serious scowl, a firm resolution.

Domnikov pointed down toward the ledge. "The German, he is alive?"

"Yeah, I'm fine, mate, thanks," McNutt muttered beneath his breath. When he was even with the ledge, he grabbed onto it and hauled himself up. He brushed ice chunks off Klinsmann, then straddled him. "BAS is offline, but I'm getting basic vitals from the external display. He's alive."

Domnikov handed his ice tool to the redheaded Russian clown. A second later, all the Russians but Domnikov disappeared from sight, and ice began raining down.

"We have done rescue like this before," Domnikov said. "He can move?"

McNutt tapped away at the external interface. "How the fuck do these things reboot again, Colonel?"

"Let me in through your system." Meyers waited for the connection, then brought up Klinsmann's external interface. "All right, it looks like it's intact. It just went into power saving mode. He might be seriously injured. Give it a few seconds to restart."

Klinsmann's head moved slightly.

"Looks like he's awake." McNutt patted the side of Klinsmann's helmet and brushed away the small chunks of ice still remaining on his armor. "You hear me, Ernst?"

"*Ja...*" Klinsmann gasped and snorted. "Yes."

The BAS came up, and Meyers poked through the health interface, sluggish over the long distance. "Not good. Looks like the suit took the worst of that ice sheet but it couldn't stop everything. Pretty good odds his hips are crushed—decent odds of internal bleeding. The suit's fighting shock. You're going to need to make the abdomen and hip joint immobile before moving him."

McNutt leaned in close to Klinsmann's helmet. "Hey, Ernst? Don't usually do this sort of thing until the second date, okay? Don't let it go to your head!"

Klinsmann seemed to nod. McNutt rubbed his gloves over the abdominal sections and hip regions of Klinsmann's armor. The armor took on a smoother, more rigid look as the stroking intensified.

"Your...hands, so...smooth." Klinsmann let out a choked laugh.

"Yeah, get that all the time." McNutt looked up in time to see another rope—also red—snaking down toward the ledge. "See that, Colonel?"

"I do." Meyers watched as Domnikov leaned backward over the edge of the path, jerking against the rope his team had anchored into the wall. He waved his team back, then kicked out and began an aggressive descent. "Not sure what to make of it, either."

"Ought to be real cozy here soon." McNutt stood and kicked more ice from the ledge.

"Give him a chance to prove himself. I need to check on Commander Cooper's force."

"We'll be just fine, Colonel. Best of friends."

Meyers took one last look at the towering Russian hastily rappelling down the mountainside, then connected back to Cooper's channel. "Coop?"

"Hey, just got word from Pivo..." Cooper sighed. "Can I call her Pivo?"

"For now."

"My head's not in this. She's on the way down with Two-Seven-Three. She sounded like a babysitter with that bomb. I hope it delivers."

Meyers smiled. "I'm sure they followed your instructions."

"Well, it should be pretty simple: impact, pressure to spray the chemicals into the air for a few seconds, then a detonation. We'll be down in the snow or in the Dart. If it comes close enough to those emplacements, it should fill them with fire. Almost worth risking gunfire to see that. That should mess with anything short of a fully sealed, hardened environment suit. Unless they've got something much better than our armor, they should be dead."

"Depending on the placement," Meyers said.

"Yeah." Cooper was looking around the edge of the outer airlock doorway. "I was talking with Starling."

"About?"

Cooper shared a workspace with Meyers. It was a fairly detailed rendition of the base of the peak using imagery from the flyovers and Banh's BAS network. "What if they've got more emplacements in there, like you said?" Cooper drilled down into the diagram, traveling in through the opening the dead gun had been using. The interior showed a room of stone with a closed door opposite the destroyed machine gun.

"So, not one big ring of carved-out rock?" Meyers moved the view around. Cooper and Starling had detailed out a hallway beyond the door. That hallway circled around to match the symmetrical shape hidden beneath the snow and ice. There were other doors, each opening onto a gun emplacement room. At the far end of the hall, a soiled, blue plastic tarp covered something big. At the top of the semicircle of the hallway, another hallway ran a few meters before ending abruptly. "That's, what, eight emplacements?"

"Yeah. We tried a few sizes. Make the rooms too small, they can't hold ammo and they'd be cramped. Make them too big, it's wasteful."

"What's that other hallway go to? An ammo dump?"

"At least. Probably a sleeping area." Cooper repositioned the view to look into one of the unexposed rooms. "Imagine four or five more guns, all sealed off."

"Firebomb goes off, we run to confirm the kills—"

"Yeah. Same sort of thing as last time." Cooper made a hissing noise. "They could've waited one or two more seconds and they would've gotten all of Nguyen's team."

"How'd you get this imagery, Coop? It's not just built from speculation."

"Well. We had a probe."

"A probe?"

Cooper's face reddened. "Something I'd put together..."

"Uh huh." Meyers couldn't imagine Cooper doing anything that wasn't strictly by the regulations. "And you put this probe on the BAS network?"

"No! It's...it's Starling's spider-bot. Really simple. Some basic optics, safe for the network. We sent it in through the blown-out emplacement opening, snapped some basic imagery, got it into that hallway, then we pulled it out. We didn't compromise the network, I'm sure of it."

"Okay." Meyers played around with the imagery a bit more, smiling at the way Cooper had shifted from a security nut to someone bent on mission success. Starling seemed to have a magic about her like that. "So, what's the proposal? Abort the firebomb?"

"I don't know."

"C'mon, Coop. You're the simulation expert. What do you think they'll do?"

"I test out theories against expert systems. That's not the same as real life. Expert systems wouldn't have made the mistake of opening fire too early."

Meyers drilled down to examine the covers hiding the gun emplacements. They seemed a mixture of real imagery and near-real. "Are these supposed to be airtight? Armored?"

"We don't know. Becky—" Cooper hissed. "Sorry. Starling found a pretty good image from Nguyen's feed just before...we lost it. Based on how it shot out straight from the wall and broke off ice, it looks like the cover was ejected, and the way it fell, it seems pretty heavy."

"Okay, armored and airtight, both. What about having Nunoz take some shots from overhead? He won't be able to wipe out the guns, but he just needs to punch holes in the rock wall for the chemicals to get in."

"I guess."

"Is it a good guess? C'mon. We need more than guesses, Coop. It's nearly go time."

"It's worth a try." Cooper's voice lacked even a hint of conviction.

"What?"

"Well, it's just that there's who knows how many centimeters of ice on top, and probably twice as much stone, and maybe they reinforced it."

Meyers felt pressure building in his chest. "What about grenades then?"

"Not likely. That's pretty thick rock."

"We need *something*. I don't want to pull Two-Seven-Three off. That would give Jeremy everything he wants." Meyers winced at the way that sounded. "You know what I mean. He's fighting against me on every decision."

"I know. I *am* trying. It's just that they're dug in good."

"Nice trap." Not what I want to hear, Meyers thought. His earpiece chimed; Two-Seven-Three was calling. "I'm adding Ensign Shazier."

"Okay." Cooper sounded glum as he closed down the workspace.

Shazier's image appeared next to Cooper's. Cooper's pale, pudgy face was dimpled and his mouth was twisted into a frown. His dark eyes were squinted so tight they were barely visible. Shazier smiled, a bright flash of teeth against dark skin. His broad nose was wrinkled by the smile, which seemed to make his big, dark eyes sparkle.

"Two-Seven-Three en route, Colonel. Finally. Three minutes out." Shazier's eyes danced left and right, probably checking out the console.

"How's the payload?" Meyers asked.

Shazier's smile broadened. "I'll let Chief Pivovarova answer that, sir."

The Dart's ceiling camera feed showed Pivovarova moving slowly between tight-packed rows of piled cargo cases. Rather than being strapped directly to the floor, they were secured to pallets that were connected to anchor points. Between her and the cabin, the webbing that held the firebomb rocked gently, adding to the image Meyers had earlier of the firebomb as Pivovarova's baby.

"Chief?" Shazier's voice—normally full of energy and humor— almost bounced with joy.

Meyers doubted Brigston understood what he was doing to his people, but the strain was there for anyone to see.

Pivovarova looked up at the camera. She wore a flight helmet like Shazier, but with the visor up; her bunny suit was replaced by a gray flight suit. It was lightly armored, about comparable to what Timkul was wearing. Even so, Pivovarova had to squeeze through some of the spaces in the Dart.

"You are talking to me, Ensign Shazier?" Pivovarova waved at the camera and gave the pixie smile that transformed her face into a beacon. Her breath blossomed as she laughed.

"You're online with Colonel Meyers and Commander Cooper."

Pivovarova waved even more enthusiastically, and then she saluted.

"Colonel, the ship has escaped the *Valdez*! And look!" She pointed at the web hammock holding the firebomb. "Is present. For the hiding people!"

Meyers felt the electricity and enthusiasm, but even without looking, he felt Timkul's presence; he fought back a smile. "Chief, we've got a little problem."

"Oh, no! Is tight!" She squeezed between the final row of gear and stretched out to grab the hammock. She tugged, but the bomb didn't move any more than it had before. "Cannot go anywhere until release, Colonel!"

"That's good. The problem is the release. It's going to have to be extremely precise."

The smile left Pivovarova's face. "We can drop straight." She held a bunched glove up to the camera and then made an opening motion, then she fluttered her hand down to the floor while whistling, as if the bomb were falling away.

"Good." Meyers didn't know what else to say. Two-Seven-Three didn't have anything to punch a hole through the rock walls. It could fire from above when Nunoz engaged, but there was only so much even a railgun could do when the target was mostly covered by ice and rock. "Ensign Shazier, I want to bring Ensign Nunoz into the channel. We'll need to coordinate this tightly."

"Please do, Colonel. I don't need him shooting all crazy like he does." Shazier chuckled.

Meyers brought Nunoz onto the channel. "Ensign Nunoz—we have Ensign Shazier, Commander Cooper, and Chief Pivovarova on the channel. Two-Seven-Three is...thirty-one seconds out. We're thinking the Darts should open fire on the enemy positions from overhead, out to whatever angle you feel is safe. We need to punch holes in the rocks wherever possible and optimize the effectiveness of this firebomb. I'm sharing what Commander Cooper and Private Starling think that little compound could look like."

Nunoz made a sound that might have been a "Hm" after Meyers shared out the workspace.

"I see it, Colonel," Shazier said. "You'd want us to fire before or after dropping off the supplies?"

"After." Meyers added an area to the workspace, where he listed out the sequence: supply drop, fire on gun emplacements, clear, firebomb. "If we have agreement on this, I'll bring in Sergeant Banh, and we can get this moving. We're about to have visitors down here in the valley, so time is short."

"I've got it, Colonel." Shazier sounded as ready as anyone could be.

"Got it, Colonel." Nunoz sounded a little less enthusiastic.

"I don't see any alternatives," Cooper finally said.

Meyers hoped his frustration with Cooper wasn't showing as Banh joined the channel. "Sergeant Banh, we're in position for the attack on those guns. Can you see the workspace we're sharing?"

"I see the workspace, Colonel." Banh seemed to almost bow. He squinted as he examined the imagery. "This is new intelligence, Colonel?"

"No." Meyers wished that Cooper had engaged Banh while rendering the structure, but it was too late for that now. "This is based off the data we had before, plus some of the imagery we captured from the earlier engagement."

Banh's face remained passive, immobile. "And the firebomb, Colonel, it will get to these other emplacements?"

"Not if they're sealed off, no. That's why the Darts are going to fire on that structure from above before the firebomb drops. What we need from you is to have your squad as far back as you can safely be and face down in the snow. This will be an air burst—right, Commander Cooper?"

"If it works right, the blast should be concentrated about a meter off the ground." Cooper finally seemed engaged again. "There shouldn't be a whole lot of concussion to it. It's mostly fire. That snow's going to melt, probably all the way up to the Dart. Not too much, though."

"We will fall back, Colonel." Banh tapped a spot that was halfway between his current position and Cooper's.

"All right. Let me check on the progress of rescuing Sergeant Klinsmann, then we'll—"

"Sergeant Klinsmann is hurt, Colonel?" Banh sounded concerned.

"An accident." Meyers hated the way the squads were operating in isolation. Ideally, they would all be on a broader BAS network, aware of positioning and mission objectives. Squad leaders were disciplined enough to keep everyone focused on their own piece of the operation. Whoever was behind the saboteurs' bot attack and explosion had studied ERF operational tactics. "A section of ice gave away. He'll be okay."

Banh's lips screwed up, but he didn't respond other than that.

Meyers switched back to McNutt's channel just in time to see him helping Domnikov pull Klinsmann up onto the path. The Russians had already pulled a litter from their backpacks; Repin and Strauss gently moved Klinsmann to the litter and strapped him down.

"Sergeant McNutt?" Meyers waited for McNutt's camera to shift slightly, the sign he was listening. "We're getting ready to launch the attack above you. How long before you reach the mountaintop?"

"Well..." McNutt looked down at the litter and then up the path. The suit's rangefinder estimated another 120 meters to the mountaintop. "A bit, Colonel."

"If we drop a fire bomb in...ten minutes, would that be all right?"

"Take the top of the mountain off, far as I'm concerned."

"Sergeant—"

"Yeah, yeah. Ten minutes is fine, Colonel. We're fifteen minutes down. That's if things don't get twisted up more."

"Ten minutes from this mark, Sergeant McNutt." Meyers brought up a timer. "Mark."

"Got it. Best of luck to the team up there. Rescuers coming up with wounded. Never a good idea."

"You're doing as well as anyone else, Sergeant." Meyers flipped back to Cooper's channel and shared out the timer. "That's your signal to drop the bomb, Ensign, Chief. Adjust your plan accordingly."

"Looks great, sir." Shazier's head whipped around. "We're ready to drop the pallets now, so keep your people clear of that open area to the south, Commander."

Two-Seven-Three's airlock doors opened, letting in snow and gray light. Lines ran from Pivovarova's suit to eyeholes in the ceiling. She squatted, unlatching the cams pinning the first pallet down, then kicked something on the bottom of the pallet. A large, heavy, black rubber skin expanded over the pallet, forming a balloon. The Dart's angle shifted, and the pallet slid toward the airlock door.

"Is first pallet away," Pivovarova said.

The pallet tipped over the floor of the outer airlock and disappeared. Meyers checked the timer. They had a little over eight minutes before they would drop the bomb. He had air superiority and a weapon that should take out the enemy's mountaintop force, and a rescue team was on the way. The valley's weapons systems were coming back online. They had a chance to end the mission without serious losses.

But all he could think about was the rendering of the gun emplacement and what it said about the enemy. They had been here for weeks. Months. A long time. Waiting. Planning.

What else do they have ready to throw at us?

17

———

2 October 2175. Siberia.

"YOU GOT MORE than that mountaintop to worry about." Paxton's voice was raspy and heated in the confines of the TOC. His face was pale, and the bruises—like everything else in the structure—were washed out by the snowy mountaintop showing on the wall of displays.

Meyers pulled his focus out of the connection to Cooper and glanced around. Timkul and Paxton both looked tense. Meyers realized his hands were shaking, a nervous tremor that remained from the mountaintop situation. That same tension was in his head, taking him back to Bellar Colony. He reminded himself that Siberia couldn't possibly be more different. This was his call, his mess.

He licked his lips, tasted salt, felt the chill. He forced a chuckle and said, "These space heaters just aren't cutting it."

"This armored column is getting close, isn't it, Colonel?" Timkul indicated the displays that still showed the mountaintop. The intent was clear: *Pull your head out.*

Meyers brought up the imagery from the valley. "Yeah."

She leaned in and tilted her head while examining the images. "Are your forces ready?"

"Sergeant Paxton?" Meyers realized that Timkul was back to calling him "colonel."

"All ready except for the heavy weapons." Paxton squinted as he looked from Timkul to Meyers. It was the sort of look the grizzled veteran put on during uniform inspections. "Some people might consider those weapons somewhat important, those being armored vehicles and such."

The weapons control system! Meyers nearly kicked himself. "Shit! I'm sorry. I thought..." He brought up the interface again. The BAS network had rebuilt itself, but the weapons control system still showed the machine guns, railguns, and mortars offline. That made sense for one of the mortars but not the other. "They should be up."

Paxton exhaled loudly. "Might want to get them up soon, Colonel."

"Yeah." Meyers drilled down through the network until he was in one of the weapons. Once again, he was forced to access the system through its root interface and drill down through the crude design. "It's not the weapons control system—it's the weapons themselves. I thought rebooting the network would reboot the weapons but they're still showing offline." He shared the interface visuals on one of the displays. "This is the mortar in the middle of the line. See what it's showing? Ammunition type, sighting, manual compensation for wind and everything, all online."

"I don't see it in the network, and the teams say they can't do anything through their interface." Paxton pulled an image from his own display and threw it onto one of the displays. Three soldiers were hunched over a mortar, one examining the guts via a panel opened at its base, the others checking the weapon tube and nearby antenna assembly.

Meyers ran through the arcane series of menus and command windows until he found one deep in that was red.

"What's that?" Timkul asked.

"I'm not sure." Meyers tapped at the interface, but it wouldn't respond. He backed out and examined the layer above. "That's..."

"Says Operational Check." Paxton stood slowly and approached the display.

"Yeah." Meyers shifted through the interface hierarchy: up, down, sideways. There wasn't much to explain what he was looking at or why it was red. "They don't see any physical damage?"

Paxton waved at the display with the weapons crew. "Corporal Tilly, any sign of physical damage?"

The soldier who had been looking at the open panel at the mortar's base looked up and gave an exaggerated head shake. He tapped the mortar tube and gave an equally exaggerated thumbs-up.

"Thank you." Paxton turned back to Meyers, eyebrows raised.

Meyers sighed. "Have them take it offline. Power it down and back up. I'll work with the other one for now." He was missing something, and they were running out of time. He ran through the interface on one of the railguns. It had the same red Operational Check window. "Deploy the rest of the squads away from the heavy weapons. Use hard cover. Go to AP loads."

"AP loads, Colonel?" Timkul asked.

"Armor-piercing rounds."

"They can pierce those vehicles? Some of them look big."

They all looked too heavily armored to Meyers, but he didn't want to say that. "They have a chance. Closer in."

Paxton bunched his hands into fists and set those against his hips. "They'll get chewed up by the APC guns before they can return fire. What about getting some explosives out into the valley, Colonel? Get Private Starling down here and have her improvise something from mortar shells."

"That'll take too long." Meyers stared at the red Operational Check image. "Maybe Ladell can figure this out." He selected the channel to Barlowe. "Ladell, we've got a problem."

Barlowe was looking down a slope and past a pair of snow-covered boulders, where gray shapes were spreading out across the valley floor. "You seeing this, Lonny?" Barlowe's voice was soft.

"Yeah, I'm seeing it." Meyers pushed deeper into the image. The APCs were breaking from column formation into something that looked like combat-ready formation. The deep, bass hum of motors and the clank of tracks was a distant rhythm over Barlowe's audio. Barlowe's BAS showed the closest APC was eighty-three meters from his position. "They're getting ready to attack, and we can't return fire."

"Why not?"

Meyers forwarded the feed from the mortar to Barlowe. "You ever see this?"

"I don't know mortars. Looks bad."

"Bad enough we can't bring the systems onto the network. We can't even see them." Meyers maneuvered through several layers of the interface for Barlowe to see. "Everything's green but that. No physical damage. All the heavy weapons were on the BAS network before the bot attack."

"Is the network compromised?"

"That's why I reset it. I had to take the entire thing down and rebuild it using Hecker's ID and code, turn them into mine. They had my credentials somehow." Meyers saw the look of surprise on Paxton and Timkul's faces. He couldn't tell them what he'd found when he'd searched Rhizov's system. Not yet. "But everything has been reset. Everything."

"These guys knew a helluva lot about your mission here." There was noticeable tension in Barlowe's voice.

Don't say it, Meyers thought. "We'll revisit operational security when we get back."

"If."

"Ladell, can you give it a look? See if you can figure out what happened? It has to be software. The only damage we took here was the explosion in the TOC."

Paxton cleared his throat. "Might want to ask Captain Hecker about that, sir."

Meyers nodded and mouthed, "I know."

Barlowe sighed. It was one of his more dramatic sighs. "I'll give it a look."

"Thank you." Meyers disconnected.

"You said they're positioning to fire," Timkul said. "How long?"

"Ladell can only see the front ranks from his position, but we have to assume the others are doing the same." Meyers imagined the best-case scenario, with no tracks getting bogged down in the snow, no confusion or system malfunctions. That seemed fair based on what they'd seen so far. "Maybe five minutes?"

Timkul repeated the estimate under her breath; she seemed shaken by that.

"We still have Ensign Hassan and One-Zero-One."

Paxton harrumphed. "Would've been a lot more effective using her when they were bunched tight."

"I'm still hoping to minimize casualties." Meyers couldn't see a way to prevent things escalating anymore. His desire to keep things limited was looking more foolish by the minute. He imagined the APCs spread out in the valley, taking advantage of the space it offered. Even the heavy weapons wouldn't be able to tear the vehicles apart as quickly as they would have when the vehicles had been packed tighter.

"Colonel?" Timkul stepped closer. She was rubbing her hands up and down her arms as if cold. Or anxious. "What about this firebomb?"

"We need that to take out the mountaintop position."

"You have a much larger force here in the valley."

"And we still have a chance to control the situation down here. We can't say that about the mountaintop." Meyers questioned if that was a true statement anymore. He saw Paxton smirk. Maybe the situation in the valley was even worse than it appeared. "Anyway, the firebomb would have been best when the vehicles were still in tight, same as the heavy weapons. The bigger the target area, the less the effectiveness."

"But it could make a difference." Timkul sounded as if she were pleading.

"Those are sealed-up vehicles. I don't think they would be affected."

Timkul bowed her head. "What about the Darts? They could help Ensign Hassan when—"

"They will, Miss Timkul," Meyers snapped. He saw Paxton's head shoot up and realized the response had been too forceful. "I'm sorry. That came out wrong. We'll be bringing every available asset to bear when we get the chance."

Timkul nodded. "I feel I should take a walk."

"Of course." Meyers chastised himself for losing control. He checked the timer for the mountaintop operation: two minutes, fifty-five seconds.

Time was slipping away. He connected back to Cooper. "Coop, is everyone in position?"

"Yeah, as good as it can be." Cooper was still at the back of the Dart, looking out its airlock. A white haze hung over the ground, and the snow seemed to be coming down harder than before. "Visibility's down. Maybe that's to our advantage?"

Meyers scanned the enemy position through that view. He tried to see what they would see. Obviously, the mountaintop was vital, the best position available to watch the valley and connect to the task force above. And it was equally obvious the enemy had a great position for an ambush. But that seemed to assume a lot. What if the flyover hadn't caught the mountaintop? What if it had been deemed not worth the bother? The bunker structure they built would have been useless. They would have had units of their own tied down.

It all seemed too coincidental, too convenient.

"Coop? This place they've built. It doesn't seem…odd to you?"

Cooper's view shifted to focus on the gutted emplacement. "In what way?"

"Positioning, for starters. That's obviously artificially reinforced. Why not build it nearer the ledge? Where they put it, they can't support the valley; they can only prevent us from supporting operations in the valley."

"Doesn't that have the same net result?"

"Sure, but it also presupposes us spotting that area and landing on it or bringing troops up the mountainside." Meyers veered from wondering why Cooper couldn't see the obvious to wondering if the "obvious" was actually outlandish.

"I guess. Did you have something in mind?" Cooper's voice was thick with impatience.

"No. Forget about it. It's time to get this going." Meyers connected to the broader channel—Nunoz and Shazier in their Darts, McNutt on the mountainside. "We're forty-five seconds out. Any concerns?"

"Ready." Nunoz smiled devilishly.

"We're in position and ready, Colonel." Shazier nodded his head.

"Still moving like a bunch of drunk llamas in a skating rink, Colonel,"

McNutt said.

"Uh." Cooper's voice shook. "Banh's squad's in position. The guns are quiet. I guess we're a go, sir."

The counter ticked down to twenty seconds.

Meyers brought everyone onto Banh's BAS network and pushed the display out to the display wall, ignoring Paxton's exasperated grunt. The network combined imagery from Banh and his team's suit cameras with imagery from Two-Seven-Three overhead, and existing imagery to create a lifelike, comprehensive view. "Sergeant Banh, this is Colonel Meyers. Everyone is on your network."

"Understood, Colonel." Banh sounded as unflappable as ever. "I see the new image."

The timer ticked down to zero.

"Let's go," Meyers said. His throat tightened as Nunoz brought Zero-Eight-Nine over the peak at the west end of the mountaintop and Shazier brought Two-Seven-Three in closer from the east end. Meyers could see Two-Seven-Three from Cooper's live camera feed. That wasn't ideal. "Ensign Shazier, you look a little low on your approach."

"Shit!" Shazier sounded anxious. "Gaining altitude. Readouts say I'm seventy-five meters off the deck. Didn't look right to me, but you have to trust the instruments."

Meyers glanced at the entry flap as Timkul let herself back in. When he looked back at the display, Two-Seven-Three seemed to have dropped even lower.

"Shazier, you're too low! Pull up!" Meyers leaned toward the displays.

"I'm trying, Colonel. Something's wrong with the controls. Chief, can you give it a look?"

"Looking!" Pivovarova's voice was energetic and excited, as if caught up in a game.

Does she even realize what's happening? Meyers wondered.

"Colonel, Zero-Eight-Nine's in position to fire," Nunoz said. "There's movement down there."

"Movement?" Meyers scanned the curved bump at the base of the peak.

More guns had appeared.

Meyers squinted. One of the emplacements looked different. "Fire at will, Ensign Nunoz. Watch for Two-Seven-Three."

Snow and ice kicked up along the top of the bunker half-ring but at the same instant, the guns within the emplacements opened fire, tearing away chunks of boulder between the bunker and the downed Dart.

"Cooper, get your people down," Meyers shouted. "They're firing on your Dart!"

Cooper turned to Starling and the wounded. "Lie flat! Down!"

Fresh holes opened in the fuselage, running from where Starling's head had been before she had dropped flat over Petty Officer Hollins to the airlock, where Cooper stood. He looked down, and his camera captured blood bubbling out of a tear in his armor at the hip. He wiped at the dark fluid and brought the blood-slick glove up close to his face, then the Dart floor rushed up.

"Cooper!" Meyers looked from one display to another, but he had no view inside Three-Zero-Eight.

"Colonel?" Shazier sounded even more anxious than before. "My controls aren't responding."

Meyers turned to find Two-Seven-Three. "Drop that bomb and get the hell out of there, Shazier."

"I'll try, Colonel."

Two-Seven-Three spun lazily until its rear was pointed toward the gun emplacements. There was a wobble and sluggishness to its movements that brought back memories of the crash on Bellar, and the altitude drop continued.

"Disregard that order, Two-Seven-Three," Meyers said. "Get the hell out of there. Now."

"Bomb is ready to drop, Colonel," Pivovarova said.

Meyers searched frantically and found her video feed; she was still using the ceiling camera in the cargo area. He could see her in the airlock, wrestling the bomb harness in. It looked close.

"Nearly have present, Colonel. Big fire!" Pivovarova waved at the camera, and her pixie smile seemed to glow.

And then Two-Seven-Three shuddered, wobbled violently, and dropped toward the frozen ground.

18

2 October 2175. Siberia.

MEYERS STEPPED BACK to get a better view of the displays. Pivovarova was barely visible in Two-Seven-Three's airlock, which was mostly filled by the webbing and harnesses that kept the firebomb stable. The back of the cylindrical container was still in the cargo space, and the tip just beyond the external airlock door. Meyers switched his view from Two-Seven-Three's interior to Banh's BAS network view of the mountaintop and then back to the interior of Three-Zero-Eight, where Starling belly-crawled toward Cooper. He was twitching, bleeding heavily. Gunfire again tore into the fuselage, and Starling stopped to throw her hands over her head; the rounds hit only a few centimeters above her.

Timkul turned from the wall of displays and covered her face with a hand. "They're going to be killed."

Chills worked down Meyers's spine. Nunoz's gun was having no visible effect on the gun emplacements. Two-Seven-Three seemed ready to fall out of the sky before the bomb could be dropped.

"Might want to pull folks out of there, Colonel." Paxton stood in front of the wall of displays, studying Two-Seven-Three from an exterior shot.

Meyers tapped a finger against his thigh armor. "We need that mountaintop."

"Need to stop that armored column, too."

"We're close." Meyers switched back to Banh's BAS network view. Two-Seven-Three was still losing altitude, but Pivovarova had gotten the bomb out farther from the airlock.

Paxton looked up from the displays. "Those APCs are going to fire any minute now."

"Colonel…" Timkul looked at him. For a second, her brow was knit in anger, then it was relaxed and eyes opened in sympathy. "They can't be saved."

Cold sweat filmed Meyers's forehead. He switched to McNutt's channel. "Sergeant McNutt, it's going to hell on the mountaintop. Can you get up there?"

"Yeah." McNutt pressed past the two soldiers carrying Klinsmann's litter and accelerated through the Russians ahead of him on the pass, apparently unaffected by the slick, narrow path. The camera spun back around as McNutt looked back down the path; Cho was following more cautiously. In seconds, they were past Domnikov and moving quickly to the top. The last time McNutt looked back down the trail, Domnikov was waving for everyone else to hurry.

"Keep your head down up there." Meyers switched over to Barlowe's channel. "Ladell, anything? We need these weapons."

"I think I've figured it out. Almost." Barlowe's voice was low and neutral; he was deep into something.

"Call me if you get it."

Meyers switched back to Banh's BAS network; Starling was finally on. She fed video from Three-Zero-Eight's interior. Weak light showed through the holes punched in the fuselage by the machine guns. Cooper's blood was far too bright in that light. Every detail of his armor popped out. His hands twitched weakly.

Meyers connected to Starling. "Private Starling? How bad is it?"

"Bad, Colonel. Really bad. One of those rounds went completely through."

There was no way a bullet passed through the width of a lower body and didn't do serious damage. "Do what you can. Cho's on the way up with McNutt."

Starling's helmet bobbed up and down; she'd heard.

Meyers switched back to Two-Seven-Three. "Ensign Shazier, if we can't get that bomb dropped soon, you're going to be too low."

"It's not responding, Colonel." Shazier's camera showed the console display; instruments blinked on and off. "It's like they're in the systems somehow."

"Can you get the nose up so Pivovarova can get that bomb out of the airlock?"

Shazier tapped at one of the instruments. "Nothing's working." He unbuckled from his seat. "I'm going back to help her out."

Meyers stayed with Shazier's video feed as he leaned against the Dart's tilt and headed toward the rear. His camera caught Pivovarova— half out of the airlock, face glistening with sweat—tugging at the harness. She had attached one of her grip cables to the airlock ceiling. Anything more would have probably limited her movement too much.

"Is caught, Ensign," Pivovarova said. She slapped the top of the bomb's webbing hammock, which was hung up on something Meyers finally realized was a wire harness hanging down from the ceiling. She leaned further out of the airlock, planted her boots against the hull, and hauled against it. It didn't budge. "You have knife?"

Shazier turned back toward the cockpit. "Emergency knife on my seat. Not a good one."

Pivovarova blew out a shaky breath. "Any is better than no."

Shazier almost skidded back into the cockpit. He slammed into the still-blinking display console. The snowy ground seemed far too close below the Dart's nose. His camera took in the snow and boulders, then turned to the seat. He tugged the knife from its built-in sheath and headed back up to the airlock. Meyers had seen the emergency—survival —knives before. They had short blades that were somewhat sharp on one side and a fairly smooth tip that could be used as a screwdriver. He wasn't sure they could cut through cargo webbing.

After stumbling and nearly going to the floor, Shazier reached the airlock, knife held high for Pivovarova to see. He grabbed onto the hammock and pulled himself up to get the sharp side of the blade against the problematic strap. It took a few tries before he settled into a sawing and twisting motion.

"That wire bundle harness supposed to be down like that, Chief?" Shazier grunted between every other word.

"No, Ensign Shazier." Pivovarova was already tugging on the front of the bomb again. "It get caught, and now I wonder, you know?"

"Yeah—"

Shazier and Pivovarova squealed as the drone of Two-Seven-Three's engines went silent, and the Dart plunged. Just as quickly, the engines came back online. The abrupt change tossed the two of them and the bomb around.

Meyers gulped. "You two all right?"

Shazier grabbed onto the harness and pulled himself back up. "More problems, Colonel. Once we drop this, I'm going to need to put down somewhere, change out my flight suit."

"I understand. Hurry, please."

As Shazier's camera tracked back to the place where he'd been cutting, Meyers felt a rush of excitement. The cargo webbing was fraying!

"You're making progress, Ensign. Keep—" Meyers's earpiece chimed; it was Barlowe. "Keep at it." He flipped to Barlowe's channel.

"Lonny?" Barlowe's voice had the higher pitch it took on when he was irritated. "That interface you sent me? It's not to the mortar."

"What do you mean?" Meyers closed his eyes and tried to remember the weapons system interface. "I got in through the root access. You can't go any deeper in. That's the interface. The weapons control system won't connect—"

"It's not the mortar's root interface. It's something else. Something fucked up."

Meyers sighed, exasperated. "I don't understand."

"The mortar's interface is gone. That's some sort of...I don't know. I guess it's a dummy. It doesn't even really have anything underneath it. No functionality, no code, really. Nothing functional, at least."

"It looked like—"

"Lonny," Barlowe snapped. "I'm telling you, it's not real. The reason you can't see those weapons from the control system is they don't have that root interface that you think you saw. They don't have *operational code*. This is just a fake front end to make it look normal. I've looked. They're empty."

Meyers shook his head. The interface had looked so real. "Could the bot attack have done that?"

"Yeah. Wipe out the interface code—lay down the fake interface. Sure."

"Can you fix it?"

Barlowe sputtered. "What, you mean restore the old interface and control software? Do we have a backup?"

"Not—" Meyers thought back to the gear Nunoz had brought down. "There's a case of specialized ammo and a mortar back at the LZ. Could you copy the interface from that?"

"For the mortars, sure. Not the guns."

Meyers muted and turned to Paxton. "I need to head to the LZ. Have Hassan do a strafing run on the closest vehicles. Harass them. Draw attention. Buy us time."

Before Paxton could say anything, Meyers was out of the TOC and moving as fast as he could for the landing zone. He saw Timkul following but didn't slow. She could hear what was going on.

"Ladell, I'll have that functional mortar online in a minute." Snow crunched beneath Meyers's boots. "Can you access Hassan's Dart? One-Zero-One. Pull the railgun interface from there and upload that."

"What about the machine guns?"

"The least of our concerns." Meyers saw the landing zone ahead. Snow had already covered the cases in a white sheet. "I need to check progress on the mountaintop. Two-Seven-Three's acting up, like a systems attack."

Barlowe made a soft rumbling noise. "Russians, Lonny."

"I think Miss Timkul would disagree with that assessment if she weren't on mute." Meyers glanced over his shoulder. Timkul was looking at him coldly. He could almost feel Barlowe's glare over the connection. "We get through this, we'll do a thorough investigation."

Meyers jumped over the raised ice wall surrounding the LZ and dropped to the ground. He settled to his knees next to the case that contained the mortar just as a loud droning sound came from overhead. He could almost make out One-Zero-One in the gray haze. A few seconds later, the distant hum of its railgun was immediately followed by the crack of rounds shattering ice and rock. Meyers hastily unlocked the cargo case and pulled out the mortar's base. He powered it on while he set the tube into place. The familiar green of a new weapons system appeared on his BAS. He connected to the mortar and drilled down into its interface. It was similar to what he'd seen on the other weapons systems. Now that he knew what to look for, he could identify the differences.

"Ladell, the mortar's online. Can you see it?" Meyers looked up at Timkul, who was standing a half-meter away.

"I'm accessing it. That looks right." Barlowe's voice became marginally more excited. "I'll start pushing everything out to the weapons systems. It's going to take a little bit."

"I need to check on the mountaintop. I'll get back to you." Meyers set the mortar back on top of the case and closed the lid, then he grabbed the case handle and started hauling the case back to the TOC.

Timkul marched along at his side, arms crossed in front of her. "Your people suspect the Russians are behind all the problems?"

"Some do." Meyers didn't want a big fight if he could avoid it.

"What about the dead one?"

"We'll figure this out later. Whoever's behind this is going to be caught." Meyers wondered how likely that statement was to come true given the way the bots had wiped out so much and left no obvious trail.

"Why can't it be one of the people you already had on the team?" Timkul glared at him from his visor display.

"Anything's possible. We'll see. I need to check the mountaintop sit—"

"Lonny..." Timkul seemed to search his face to see if it was okay for her to still call him by his first name. "Your main force is down here."

"And Master Sergeant Paxton has the defense under control." Meyers felt impatience creeping into his voice. He needed to get back to Banh's network, to Dart Two-Seven-Three.

"The master sergeant is wounded."

"He's fine. Priya, I need to get back." Meyers saw the disapproving glare beneath Timkul's wrinkled brow. He didn't have time to worry about whether or not she was offended. He switched back to Two-Seven-Three.

Shazier's knife was cutting through the last centimeter of the webbing. Pivovarova was once again pulling against the hammock. The snowy field below the Dart seemed far closer than Meyers remembered.

"Nearly got it, Chief," Shazier said. He sawed quicker, desperately.

"It gives." Pivovarova grunted. "I feel it!"

Meyers stopped, realized he'd been so distracted by the video feed that he'd walked past the TOC, and backpedaled as he brought Nunoz into the channel. "Ensign Shazier, your altitude's looking dangerous. Ensign Nunoz, any progress?"

"I'm hitting these things with all I've got, Colonel," Nunoz said.

"We're still above the blast area, Colonel." Shazier hacked at the webbing.

"All right." Meyers looked down from Two-Seven-Three's belly camera. He could see the path leading up to the south face of the mountainside; McNutt and Cho would be coming from there soon. Banh's squad was dug in behind boulders and beneath snow, and Starling was in Three-Zero-Eight's airlock with Cooper. Somewhere to the west, above Two-Seven-Three, Nunoz was raining down fire from his belly gun.

The pieces were in place to clear the mountaintop. They just needed the bomb to drop.

Meyers flipped back into Two-Seven-Three's ceiling camera. Pivovarova was mostly outside the airlock, face contorted and red with exertion. She was shouting in Russian. The front third of the bomb hung out of the airlock and wobbled loosely. Shazier's shoulders and head were blocked from view by the airlock.

Suddenly, Two-Seven-Three's tail dropped so that Meyers could see the snowy ground below. Shazier lost his grip on the webbing and fell into view. Pivovarova came free of the airlock, shifting her grip from the webbing to the line she'd secured to the interior. Her boots kicked at the air.

Two-Seven-Three dropped toward the ground and then abruptly stopped.

"Shazier? Pivovarova?" Meyers drew the cargo case into the TOC and turned to the display wall. "Get that Dart out of there. Abort the mission!"

Shazier hooked a boot into the webbing overhead, preventing him from falling completely out. "Understood, Colonel." Shazier grunted as he stretched toward the airlock exit. "Just need a second."

Meyers adjusted the display wall so that he was looking down on the entire mountaintop from the consolidated view of Banh's BAS network. Nunoz's Dart provided an angled overhead view of Two-Seven-Three, which the BAS corrected into a clearer overhead shot. Meyers dedicated the center display to a merged video feed from Shazier and Two-Seven-Three's cameras.

The sense of impotence was eating at Meyers. He was aware of Timkul at his side and Paxton at the other end of the structure, barking orders to someone.

The merged video feed showed Pivovarova climbing up the safety line, gloved hand extended toward the airlock opening, where Shazier's hand reached toward her. The tips of their gloved fingers touched, then their arms stretched out more, and their fingers intertwined. Shazier somehow stretched out more until he had her wrist in his grip.

"Chief, you need to pull!" Shazier's voice was strained.

"Am pulling!" Pivovarova tugged her way up Shazier's flight suit sleeve with her left hand and her safety line with her right. She wrapped her hand around his elbow just as one of the gun emplacements below opened fire on their Dart, clipping her safety line and Shazier's free upper arm, which went limp. He gasped as rounds rattled against the fuselage and the tip of the bomb. One of the rounds made a zinging sound and Pivovarova let out a deep grunt, as if she'd fallen hard onto her back. Blood misted around her abdomen.

"Chief, hang on," Shazier shouted.

Pivovarova shivered, and then her head slumped forward. Shazier's hand lost its grip, and her damaged safety line snapped with her full weight.

She plunged toward the snowy ground below, trailing red streamers.

The machine gun fired again, and Two-Seven-Three's engines sputtered and then died. The Dart slid forward slightly, and the engines came to life again for a second, jerking the craft around and sending it lurching toward Three-Zero-Eight on the ledge below.

Meyers watched in horror as Two-Seven-Three's belly scraped along the roof of Three-Zero-Eight, bounced, then shot past and slammed into the snowpack, tearing off its right wing and flinging Shazier out like a rag doll. He landed a few meters shy of the edge, just as Two-Seven-Three slid over.

It skidded along the mountain path, straight toward McNutt and Cho, not ten meters below.

Meyers shook his head in disbelief as the wounded Dart sped down the path. McNutt hooked his left arm around Cho and disappeared over the side of the path while the Dart continued on. Meyers was vaguely aware of the bomb's hammock finally coming free of the wiring harness and bouncing out the airlock, but he was mostly focused on the Dart accelerating down, teetering and threatening to fly off and down the mountainside but never actually doing it.

The rest of the alpine team came into view: Domnikov, his Russian squad, Repin, Strauss, and the wounded Klinsmann.

Domnikov spun around and shoved the nearest of his team down, then waved at all those below to drop. The Dart shot forward and its momentum finally carried it off the path, but not before the jagged stump of its right wing clipped Domnikov in the chest, gashing deep into his armor and pulling him after. He staggered at the edge, looking down at the Dart. His head slowly turned to look up the path, and a second later, Meyers realized why: the bomb was bouncing off the path and down, misting the air as it descended with the special concoction Cooper's team had whipped up.

Meyers blinked.

And Two-Seven-Three's camera feed winked out as a fireball blossomed over the mountainside.

19

2 October 2175. Siberia.

"What happened?" The brilliant flash of the firebomb's flame still burned Meyers's eyes. "Sergeant McNutt? Sergeant Banh? Private Starling?"

All he heard from his earpiece was the roar of the machine gun emplacements.

Timkul's hand settled on his shoulder. The air felt hot but a chill ran through his gut. The image on the wall of displays was static and full of artifacts: jagged diagonal lines, black pixel blocks, distorted overlays. He tried to see the mountaintop from a different perspective, but all he could think of was the people he'd sent to their deaths in his quest to take the snow-covered mountain.

"My white whale," he whispered. His earpiece chimed: Ensign Hassan.

"Colonel? I've broken up the second rank of APCs. They're repositioning. One's not moving, and another seems to be damaged. I have their attention, but I could use help."

"Keep—" Meyers glanced back at the opposite wall, where Paxton stood, watching. He tapped his nose, and Meyers nodded in understanding. They needed his head in the situation. "Keep at it, Ensign. Help's on the way."

"Coming back for another run," Hassan said.

Meyers shook himself, hoping the physical act might clear his thoughts as well. He scanned the displays again. "Ensign Nunoz, we need you down in the valley. Can you get some altitude and perform a flyover before you head down?"

"Can do, Colonel."

Banh's video feed changed, with sections clearing and turning from live to static as Nunoz took Zero-Eight-Nine higher. Meyers winced at the bloody patch of snow where Pivovarova had fallen and trained his eyes forward, on Three-Zero-Eight. As Nunoz flew closer, the damage where Two-Seven-Three had struck became more obvious. Another bloody patch of snow revealed Shazier's body. Black smoke climbed up the mountainside, obscuring most of the path.

"Colonel, this is Sergeant Banh. Can you hear me?" Banh's voice was impossibly calm.

Meyers searched through the smoke, hoping he might find something where it thinned. He vaguely realized the gun emplacements had gone silent. "Go ahead, Sergeant Banh."

"We had feedback when Two-Seven-Three crashed, Colonel. It is now clearing."

The wall display came alive, and the last of the artifacts faded. Starling's feed refreshed, showing Three-Zero-Eight's airlock and Cooper's bloody form. She connected to Banh's channel.

"Colonel, this is Private Starling."

Meyers shifted his attention to Starling's video feed. "Go ahead, Private."

"Commander Cooper's bleeding bad, and I can't stop it. I need coagulant spray and a drip. He's slipping into shock."

"Can you get to the supplies, Chief—" Meyers felt his throat constricting. He swallowed. "Chief Pivovarova dropped medical supplies southeast of your position. Can you see the curtain of rock?"

Starling's video feed shifted as she moved to the back of the airlock. She glanced south and then tracked east. "Black balloons?"

"That's them." Meyers could see the black globes through her feed.

"I'll have to crawl through some open spaces, but I can make it."

"There should be some Porcupine ammunition and grenades in those cases, too. Shredders and flash-bangs." Meyers doubted the shredders would be effective against the enemy. They had to be in fairly heavy armor or at least sturdy environment suits in the conditions they were facing. The flash-bangs could be devastating in the small bunkers Starling's spider-bot had revealed.

"I'm on my way, Colonel."

Snow rushed up to Starling as she slid down the ice-slick ramp. At the base, she began a low crawl. All Meyers could see was snow.

"Colonel, I would like to provide cover," Banh said.

Meyers fought the urge to tell Banh not to expose the squad to too much risk. It was the sort of overly cautious comment no one needed to hear. They were soldiers; risk was in the job description. *You keep saying that, so accept it.* "Approved."

Banh's video feed showed the squad belly-crawling toward the boulders and other hard cover positions that gave clear lines of fire.

Nunoz's channel chimed; Meyers activated it. "Colonel? Might want to check this out."

Zero-Eight-Nine's belly camera was locked on the mountainside, where smoke slowly peeled off the icy face and curled out, lured by the Dart's rotors. Through the thinner smoke, Meyers could see two forms slowly climbing using a combination of ice tools and rope. The IDs showed McNutt and Cho.

"There's a team farther down the path, too, Colonel." Nunoz shifted the camera west and down the path, locking onto smoke-obscured forms moving up the path. "Looks like some of them were hit by the fire but some are moving."

Meyers's lips quivered. "Thank you, Ensign Nunoz. I'm passing you on to Master Sergeant Paxton. Ensign Hassan needs you now."

"On my way, sir!" The camera view swung in a dizzying arc as Nunoz dropped out and away from the mountainside.

"Sergeant Banh, Private Starling..." Meyers paused to calm himself. Timkul was turned toward him, visor lifted. She was smiling. "Several members of the team coming up the mountainside survived Two-Seven-Three going over the edge. They should be up in a few minutes."

"That is good, Colonel," Banh said. "We could use more shooters up here."

"Is Sergeant McNutt alive, sir?" Starling's voice shook.

"He's alive."

"Thank you, sir. Almost to the balloons."

Meyers checked Starling's video. She had another ten meters to the wall of rock, most of that without any cover to speak of. "Sergeant Banh, now would be a good time," Meyers said.

The roar of gunfire flooded the channel. The CAWS-5s had clear lock-ons to two of the openings. Meyers hoped for a ricochet or without that at least enough lead in the air to keep the enemy pinned down. One of the emplacements returned fire, then another, then all of them, and Banh's squad ducked back behind cover.

Meyers checked Starling's progress. She had reached the cover of the stone wall and was cutting through the protective balloons.

"Careful with that," he said.

Her camera shifted up and down; she was nodding. "Tough material, sir."

She rose to her knees and popped the cases open. When she found the medical supplies, she moved to the edge of the stone wall closest to the Dart and hurled the packets, which skidded across the snow. She tied the lines from the ammunition cases around her waist and began the long crawl back.

Banh's BAS network shimmered like a heat mirage, and a new section appeared, showing the path on the southern mountainside west and below the ledge where Three-Zero-Eight rested. A chime indicated someone was joining the open channel.

"There's a BAS channel, so someone's still alive up there, yeah?" McNutt sounded winded but otherwise okay.

"Sergeant McNutt, this is Colonel Meyers. Sergeant Banh's squad is mostly intact. Private Starling is moving medical supplies back to Three-

Zero-Eight. The gun emplacements are still operational. What's your status?"

"Well, aside from tighty-whiteys being discolored after dodging several tons of aircraft, we're okay. Can't say the same for Domnikov. Completely lost his signal. Klinsmann's still alive. Repin and Strauss are hauling him up, but we got three badly burned down the path."

Meyers pulled Starling into the channel. "Private Starling, that medical gear include anything for burns?"

"General treatment, sir. Painkillers, coagulants. It'll help anyone for a while."

"Becky, can you spare some stims? My arms're a wreck." McNutt sounded happier than Meyers could ever recall.

Starling chuckled and then said, "Plenty of stims to spare."

Meyers stripped Banh's BAS network down to team signals and locational markers. She was a green shape, not yet completely protected by identified blocks that represented boulders and other cover. "Private Starling, you might want to pick up—"

Timkul glanced up at the change in his voice. "What is it?"

Meyers leaned closer to the displays. He pointed at five red dots slowly moving along the southern edge of the plateau, flanking Banh's position. "Sergeant Banh, check your nine. South flank, five bogeys. Sergeant McNutt, hold position."

"I see nothing, Colonel," Banh said.

"Almost directly south of your position. Fifteen, sixteen meters. Just your side of the ledge."

"Nothing, Colonel."

Meyers blinked. The dots were still there. "Someone's BAS is picking something up—something not us. Signals."

"There is noth—" Banh's voice was drowned out by gunfire. "Taking fire, Colonel!"

"Switch from visual to pure BAS sensor readouts," Meyers said.

"I see them, Colonel." Banh's weapon showed lock-on; the gunfire grew louder. The red forms retreated west and then disappeared. "I-I... Those were direct hits, Colonel. We hit them. Private Lamh and me."

Meyers remembered how hard it had been to kill genies during the

Genie War. The only thing he'd seen that could match that were the proxies used during the Metacorporate War. "See if you can get someone over there to check for blood and see where they came from."

"Sending Corporal Mai and Private Luong, sir."

Meyers scanned the display for any more bogey signals. His eyes locked onto a faint, green trace northwest of Banh's position. "Sergeant Banh, do we have someone out in the open. Northwest of your position?"

"Just Chief Pivovarova's body, Colonel."

Pivovarova! Meyers felt a surge of hope. "I'm seeing a trace of a signal. Can you detect her vitals?" He listened, barely noticing the frown and furrowed brow on Timkul's face. She was obviously concerned as well, he realized.

"There is a pulse coming from her suit, Colonel. I am very sorry for missing it."

"We're all missing things, Sergeant. It's a war zone. It happens. Can you get to her?"

Banh's feed filled with video from just his external camera; he overlaid Pivovarova's vitals over the image. The vitals were weak. He was more than fourteen meters east of her position, which was out in the open. "I would need to tunnel through the snow, Colonel."

"She won't last long enough for that, not with those vitals. Can you get a grip-cable on her?"

"I will try, Colonel."

"Just get her to cover. Private Cho will do the rest." Meyers switched to McNutt's channel. "Sergeant McNutt, if you can get Private Cho to Three-Zero-Eight, we've got some serious casualties in need of attention."

"Yeah, doesn't do anyone any good if we're casualties, too, Colonel. You held us up on this path just before gunfire broke out. What's up there?"

Meyers tried to figure out what he'd seen and what Banh hadn't. "Advanced chameleon suits. That's my guess, at least. Something in our suit sensors picked up enemy movement or, more likely, some signal leak. Banh got a lock-on, but we couldn't get a visual. Whatever they were, they retreated."

"Ain't that sweet." McNutt exhaled heavily. "We're heading up."

Meyers switched back to Bahn's BAS network and watched the signal feed. There were only green symbols now, other than the immobile red boxes that marked where Banh's squad had locked on to the gun emplacement openings. The mountaintop had settled into a stalemate for the moment, but that was the same as victory for the enemy forces. Tying down three enemy squads and downing two aircraft with a handful of heavy weapons...Meyers would take that any day of the week in their position.

We need something to break things our way, he thought. But there was nothing to flip the odds back in their favor. The enemy had superior firepower, cover, even mobility.

Mobility.

Meyers flipped back to the last flyover Nunoz had done. The hump around the base of the peak that marked the gun emplacements ended nearly twenty meters shy of the drop-off to the mountainside. Whoever had come out of that emplacement had disappeared well out from the hump. That meant there was access to the bunker system somewhere near the mountainside.

He flipped back to the signal feed and located McNutt's ID. He was approaching the mountaintop. "McNutt, send Cho on to Three-Zero-Eight, but hold position when you get to the top. I'm sending Starling to meet with you."

"This got something to do with those chameleons?" McNutt grunted.

"And taking out those goddamn guns, yes."

McNutt snorted breathlessly. "I'm in."

Meyers switched over to Starling's channel. She was recording through the airlock camera, which looked down on her and Cooper. Meyers winced at the sight of Cooper's abdomen: pale, blood-covered, bloated, and discolored. Twisted flesh glistened wetly around two black holes on either side above his hips: the entry and exit wounds, covered in coagulant spray. At least his chest seemed to be rising and falling. "Private Starling, how is he?"

"Not good, sir." The surgical gloves covering Starling's hands were gory with clotted blood. She pulled a silver thermal blanket over Cooper's chest and peeled the gloves off. "We need a medic up here, or we're going to lose him."

"Corporal Cho's on his way. I need you for something else. You up for it?"

Starling pulled her helmet off and palmed sweat from a face that seemed paler than its normal milk chocolate tone. She sucked in her full lips. "Honestly, anything's better than this, Colonel."

"Sergeant McNutt's waiting for you where the path comes up to the mountaintop."

Starling glanced toward the airlock outer door as she pulled her suit's gloves on. "What's out there, sir?"

"Invisible enemies and a bunker full of gun emplacements."

"I think I know what we need, sir." She pulled her helmet on and jumped out the back of the airlock. The video feed switched to her suit cameras. She was face down in the snow; she raised her head and glanced around, focusing on a cargo case. She popped the case open and began pulling things out: grenades and CAWS-5 magazines.

Cho came into view, visor raised. He was covered in snow, even his face. He shook his head, revealing a pale face, broad cheekbones, and small eyes that were a brown so dark they could have been black. "We got more wounded?" he asked.

Meyers realized Cho was dragging Shazier. "Is Ensign Shazier alive, Corporal?"

Cho glanced back at the form. "Barely, Colonel."

"See if you can keep him that way."

"I'll do my best, sir." Cho looked back to Starling.

"Three wounded," she said. "Commander Cooper's the worst off. He took a round through his abdomen. His armor has all the relevant data. The other two are stable and resting."

"Got it." Cho started to stand but dropped immediately when Starling waved him down. "Fuck! They can get this far out?"

"If you're high enough." Starling pointed at the chewed-up fuselage and then out to the boulders where Banh's squad had taken cover. "There's a big gap between those rocks. Just keep low."

Cho belly-crawled toward the ramp. "Where're you going?"

She looked down at the snow, and Meyers knew she would have that same shy, embarrassed look on her face that she always wore when she received praise. "Goin' ghost hunting with John."

John. Not Sergeant McNutt. Meyers wondered if there might be a problem he'd have to address with the squad's discipline.

"Okay," Cho said. "Well, stay down. It's wide open about twenty meters back."

Starling's camera showed snow ahead, white and clumped, with areas cast in gray shadow. The sun was obscured again, and it would be growing dark before too long. She followed the trench Cho had dug with his crawling, occasionally shifting around Shazier's blood trail and peering up to get a sense of where she was. Finally, her camera caught movement ahead.

"John?" She sounded relieved.

Meyers felt guilty for still listening in, but he needed to know what was going on.

McNutt waved her forward. When she was beside him, he raised his visor and gave her a stern glare. After a second, he turned in the opposite direction, raised his right hand vertically, pressed thumb tip to nose, and chopped down toward the west. "Looking for an access point somewhere about fifteen to twenty-five meters that way, *Private*." He gave her the glare again.

"U-understood." She turned onto her side, knocked snow from her leg, then dug into a pouch and pulled out some grenades and two CAWS-5 magazines. She handed them to him.

He held up the magazines, now squinting his eyes in confusion.

"Porcupine rounds." She held a fist out and opened it suddenly. "Set them to fragment at a predetermined distance."

McNutt smiled and swapped out a magazine, then stashed everything else in a leg pouch. He sealed his visor and crawled in the direction he'd indicated earlier, and after a few seconds, she followed. Meyers switched to a merged video of their cameras. Before long, McNutt stopped.

"You seeing this, Colonel?" McNutt's head was raised above the snow.

There were clear shallow and wide depressions—snowshoe prints.

The prints headed about eight meters west before disappearing at a shallow depression in the snow.

Meyers flipped back to the signal view. Everything was green. "Looks promising. Proceed with caution."

McNutt crawled forward, Starling in tow. They stopped at the hole, which was about elbow-deep and circular. "I think we got us a hatch, Colonel." McNutt tentatively pushed down on the circle bottom, then he brushed snow and ice clear. "Meter diameter. Hard. Doesn't budge."

"Private Starling, any signals?" Meyers checked the BAS signals feed again. It showed all-clear. "Can you get into any interface they might have?"

Starling fished around for something in a jacket pouch and pulled out the IB ADPAX she'd worn on the *Valdez*. "No signals, sir. I'll see if there's something listening, though."

Meyers licked his lips. They tasted like blood and felt chapped and tender.

"You think that's the way in and out of their position?" Timkul asked. She seemed entranced by the image on the displays.

"It has to be. One of them."

"And if it is, then what?" Timkul cocked an eyebrow at him.

"We see if they're ready to have the fight taken to them."

"Colonel?" Starling sounded excited. "There's a device on the hatch. I can disable it, but it's probably part of a secure network. It's probably better to let a bot hack it, keep the door on the network. They won't know we've come in unless they have a camera watching the hatch."

Meyers considered the options. "Can you see if there's a camera before you open the hatch?"

"I can send a more aggressive bot attack at their network, flood the nearby sensors. That would probably freeze their feeds for a little while. It won't trigger an alarm unless they have something really top of the line."

"Do it."

Time crept by. As he waited, Meyers alternated from watching Timkul to analyzing Paxton, who had his visor down. He'd settled on the edge of the bed in the corner of the room. He was still, apparently absorbed in running the valley operation. In the minute Meyers watched, Paxton only moved a few times while Timkul began pacing. Meyers wanted to know what was going on in the valley, but his gut told him the mountaintop was too important to abandon.

"Colonel, we're in," Starling said.

McNutt's camera revealed a tube with ladder rungs and a grate on a stone floor below. Lights reflected off smooth-cut stone walls. It was a tunnel dug into the mountain. No one was in sight. Starling leaned into the hole and set something on the top ladder rung.

"What's that?" Meyers asked.

Starling pointed down the ladder. "Charlotte."

"What?"

"My spider-bot." She added a new video feed to her own. The spider-bot hopped from rung to rung until it was on the stone floor. "Definitely a tunnel, sir. It tees up ahead. Wet footprints. Those look like the snow-shoes leaning against the wall."

Meyers wished he were on the mountaintop with McNutt and Star-ling. "Proceed. Remember, though, Sergeant Banh put several rounds in one of these guys. They could be genies or proxies or something we've never seen before. Don't underestimate them."

"Understood." McNutt pulled his CAWS-5 from its harness and set a foot on the top rung.

Starling pulled her own weapon and covered him. "Colonel, we might lose contact."

"Keep that hatch open. That should help some."

Meyers scratched at his armored thigh as McNutt dropped to the floor and moved forward at a crouch.

Timkul grabbed Meyers's hand, firm enough that he could feel it through the glove.

"Sorry." Meyers locked his hands together. "I just wish I could be there."

"That's not what a commander does, is it?" Timkul smiled pleasantly. She wasn't teasing. "They need you here."

"I think it helps to have skin in the game," he finally replied.

McNutt and Starling moved down the tunnel in a bounding overwatch, him moving forward three meters while she squatted against the opposite wall to provide cover, then her moving past him while he provided cover. Their video took on a slightly grainy quality but held up.

"We should just drop some mortar rounds in there," Meyers said. "We should've taken some explosives up—"

Paxton's visor shot up, and he shouted, "Down!"

Meyers barely had time to tackle Timkul before bullets punched through the TOC walls. He was suddenly aware of gunfire. It was close, coming from the valley.

Paxton looked up from where he lay prone, wincing from the pain of dropping to the floor. Meyers could see in the older man's eyes, though, what the greater pain was: The enemy in the valley was on them now.

They had run out of time.

20

———————

2 October 2175. Siberia.

GUNFIRE ROARED AGAIN, and bullets tore through the TOC. One of the displays shattered; distorted images continued playing across the ruined surface. A round cracked the top of the space heater nearest the entry flap, and a hum filled the open space. Meyers caught a whiff of burning plastic and remotely powered the heater down. Timkul shouted something to him, but her words were lost in the gunfire.

He muted his audio sensors and shouted. "Seal your visor! Use your microphone!"

Timkul's visor slammed shut. "I thought Ensign Hassan was harassing the vehicles?"

"She's just one Dart. She needs to change things up to avoid getting shot down. What we need right now is those mortars." Meyers connected to Barlowe's channel. "Ladell, we're under—"

"I know." Barlowe's face was pinched tight, and his tone was snippy. "We can see the muzzle flashes."

"We need the mortars, or those guns are going to tear us apart."

"We've got problems here, too. Platoon-sized problems." Barlowe switched to a view of the valley from his position on the southern slope. Red boxes crawled over the snow toward his position. Gerhardt's people were dispersing among the higher hills and behind boulders.

Meyers squinted, but at best he could see distortions inside the red boxes. "Red outlines. We had something like that up on the mountaintop. Chameleon suits?"

"Better than what you'll find with any Lancers outfit I know of."

"Yeah." Meyers was convinced the trap on Siberia was another meta-corporate effort to destroy the ERF; the advanced chameleon suits just sealed the deal. "Banh popped six shots into one of the phantoms on the mountaintop. Lamh got in nearly as many. No kill."

Barlowe chortled. "I think I have something that might change the equation."

"Mortars could definitely be an equation changer."

"Not anytime soon," Barlowe said. "Not without one of the devices that delivered the bot attack."

Meyers glanced toward the LZ through the holes in the TOC walls. "Why?"

"Because the bots scrambled things in the ROM. Without an image of the bot code to tear apart, I'm operating blind. I've got my systems trying to access code combinations now, but it could take days."

"What if I can get you one of the devices?"

"I thought they all detonated?"

Meyers crawled toward the flap, which was smacking against the entry frame. "I had one in my hand when the other two detonated. I shut it down just before it exploded. It's somewhere out beyond the LZ and the uplink."

"Find it, Lonny." Strange symbols formed around one of the red squares on Barlowe's video feed. The symbols jumped to another form, and Barlowe chuckled. "When I'm done with these guys, I'm pretty sure this position will be the next target, so hurry."

Meyers crawled out of the TOC and headed for the LZ. He stayed on his belly until he was at the edge of the LZ, then he got to his feet, jumped down, and low-jogged east, toward the uplink. The dish was a vague, dark gray form in what little sunset light the snow let through. Sparks occasionally lit sections of the rectangular base—damage caused by the gunfire. He ran to the back of the structure and leaned against it, trying to get his bearings. Fresh snow had already partially filled his old footsteps. He worked through what he had done, where he had thrown, and how hard the throw had been. There was nothing but snow as far as he could see.

"You looking for that device?"

He wheeled around, hand already on his CAWS-5 before realizing it was Timkul. He relaxed. "Yeah. You heard Barlowe, right?"

She looked in the direction he'd been looking. "That's a big area to search."

He nodded. "It should've created an obvious hole. That might still be visible." He headed in the direction he thought he'd thrown; she followed.

"Any chance you might think about pulling your people out?" she asked.

Meyers ducked as a round cracked against something behind them. "No."

"When I was an officer in the Thai Defense Force, we were taught about hopeless situations. There is honor in surrender."

"You were in the military? I thought you said you trained for security forces." Meyers tried to imagine Timkul in a full-on uniform. It was a distracting image.

"Our security forces are our military. I was a captain." She glared at him resentfully, then looked away, eyes lowered. The snow crunched loudly beneath their boots. "I was a liaison with the Royal Thai Police. Stationed in Bangkok."

"Is that a prestigious assignment?"

Timkul seemed unable to meet his gaze. "It was mostly...ceremonial."

Meyers let that go. "If we surrendered, out in the middle of nowhere like this, and the intent was to ambush us and destroy us in the first place, what do you think they'd do to us?"

At that, Timkul looked up, eyes wide and mouth formed into an o.

"I still want to give these people a chance to surrender," Meyers said.

"Most of them are innocent Lancers. They probably had no idea what they signed on for. But if I can get the people who put this together, take their representatives alive? That's another step toward breaking the meta-corporations."

For nearly a minute, they searched in silence, eyes scanning the thick snow. It stretched out ahead of them, smooth and white. Meyers switched to a thermographic overlay. His suit flashed a warning that it was below fifty percent capacity; he lowered his internal heating to eleven degrees.

One of the Darts dropped low from the gray sky just as his earpiece chimed. It was Banh. Meyers twisted to watch the Dart climb and bank as it headed out into the valley. "Go ahead, Sergeant."

"Colonel, it is the chief petty officer," Banh said.

"Pivovarova? What about her?" Meyers spotted a dark spot in the snow to the north.

"She is alive, Colonel. Private Lamh is taking her to Private Cho."

Meyers paused mid-step toward the dark spot. "Thank you, Sergeant."

"There is also the Russian, Private Repin?"

Repin was the drunk joker, Meyers recalled. "What about him?"

"He had helped bring up the wounded. Sergeant Klinsmann and the Russians. Now he asks if he can work with Sergeant McNutt. Should I tell him something, Colonel?"

Meyers stopped a few meters short of the dark spot; it wasn't a hole but a depression. He squatted and plunged a hand in the sunken area, just to be sure. It came up with nothing but snow. "What's he know about what McNutt's doing?"

"He knows nothing, Colonel. He is asking where the other NCOs are."

Realization hit Meyers; Repin might have problems with Banh. More cultural nonsense. "How's he behaving?"

"Behaving, Colonel?"

Meyers tried to come up with a way to describe suspicious activity that wouldn't plant seeds in Banh's mind. "What's he doing? You think what happened on the mountainside affected him?"

"Ah!" Banh was silent for a moment.

Another dark spot drew Meyers's attention. It was farther north and too small, but he headed toward it anyway. As he drew closer, he realized the hole was larger than it at first appeared, the nearer side obscured by a raised mound of snow. Up close, it was definitely a hole—big enough and, even with fresh snow piled in, deep enough. He dropped to his knees and probed through the snow cautiously, gritting against the burning sensation in his still-healing heel. He remembered his days in the Commandos and the way the older Commandos had griped that their injuries would get them killed long before they could retire. It often came true.

"I think he is nervous," Banh finally said. "*Anxious* is a better word."

"Not disoriented or anything?" Meyers felt something hard in the snow. He dug glove tips into the hard surface and tugged. The thing didn't budge.

"No, Colonel. He is fine."

"Then send him in. I'll warn McNutt." Meyers tugged again. Something shifted and the thing came free. He pulled it out and examined it: It was about half of the device. The shell was blistered and cracked. Black dust was suspended in ice. Ash, he realized. All that remained of the circuits. His heart sank. He waved the device in front of his camera. "Looks like it's pretty much destroyed, Priya."

He looked around for Timkul, saw her heading his way, and connected to McNutt and Starling. As the BAS established its link, Meyers reached back into the hole. It was easy finding the other piece of the device. He pulled it free.

The chime indicating connection sounded in Meyers's ears. "Sergeant McNutt, status?"

"Colonel? Welcome back. That 'T' at the end of the hall? We took the left turn," McNutt said. "They've got a fuckin' reactor down here. Drilled into the mountainside. A fuckin' reactor." McNutt's feed showed what looked like a pretty typical fusion reactor, about the size of what a smaller spaceship would carry.

Meyers took in what he could from McNutt's ever-moving cameras. "All right. Hold up there. Repin's on his way."

"Pfft! The ginger? No thanks, Colonel."

"He's looking for guidance, Sergeant, and unfortunately it sounds like he doesn't think Sergeant Banh's the type to provide it. We don't want another Gerhardt situation, do we?" Meyers hated to leverage McNutt's hatred of Gerhardt, but it seemed the most likely means to success.

The only sound McNutt made was a hiss, like air escaping. "He fucks up, I'm not saving him. Colonel."

"We're all one team." Meyers remembered the lesson that had been hammered into him when the ERF had been formed. One team; succeed or fail as one. It was something Rimes had believed in when he'd come up with the ERF concept. It was something he'd died believing.

While McNutt and Starling waited for Repin, Meyers examined the other piece of the device. It was in better condition than the first. There was no blistering and no sign of ash in the encasing ice. He knocked ice free from the shell and turned his headlamp on. The light caught the gray of an explosive compound but also reflected gold off circuit leaves. He dug the explosive compound out with his index finger and turned the device around so that Timkul could see. Her face lit up with a smile.

Meyers waved for her to follow and headed back to the camp at a jog, crouched low. "Sergeant McNutt, update me when Repin reaches you."

"Can't wait, Colonel."

Meyers flipped back to Barlowe's channel. "Ladell, I've got the device. Half of it's fried, but the other half has circuit leaves"

The men approaching Barlowe's position were now all red human silhouettes. The symbols circling the silhouettes moved faster than before. "A little busy, Lonny," Barlowe said.

Meyers moved as fast as he could, running in a crouch. Shortly after passing the LZ, he dropped lower. The guns had gone silent, but he knew they could start up again at any time. He settled onto his belly and crawled for the TOC. It was even more torn up than before. Half the displays were out, and one of the others flickered.

Paxton looked up from the floor. He held his CAWS-5 at the ready. When he saw it was a friendly, he went back to whatever he'd been doing. Meyers set the device pieces on the floor and searched around for tools: screwdrivers, pliers, a circuit analysis tool, and tools meant for finer work. He tore the pieces apart with a mix of delicate tools and patient effort, then he finished with frustrated screwdriver strikes. His first focus was on removing the last of the explosive. After that, he extracted the circuit leaves and laid them out to dry. There were only a few that seemed perfectly intact and another with minor burn damage. He took a cleaning cloth from the display carrying sleeve Timkul had hauled in earlier and started dabbing at the moisture.

"Are they usable?" Timkul asked.

Meyers considered the leaves. They *looked* intact. "We'll know shortly."

Machine gun fire began again, and Paxton's visor went up. "More infiltrators. We lost three, but the infiltrators are down."

Meyers's heart raced. "Any devices on them?"

Paxton shook his head. "Demolitions charges. We got lucky. They were seconds away from taking the mortars out."

Meyers set the circuit leaves down and turned his attention back to Barlowe. The silhouettes were filled in 3-D—all red for some but most in gray and white. If the images weren't real, they painted what reality should have been. Meyers whistled. "You hacked their chameleon suits?"

"Crude but yes. We're still seeing an image, but the cameras are showing the suit now instead of the snow beneath them. And that's what we needed before—"

Barlowe's audio sensors picked up gunfire from Gerhardt's team. It was brutal. With the advantage of the chameleon suits nullified, the Lancers were just slow-moving targets. Whatever Banh had fired at on the mountaintop wasn't the same as what was down in the valley. Half the Lancers were dead before the others even realized they'd been spotted. There was a quick exchange of fire, but then the last of the Lancers broke. None of them escaped.

"All right," Barlowe said. "They know we're here. Now *I* need those mortars, or I'm not going to make it out of here."

Meyers pulled off his gloves and grabbed the nearest circuit leaf. "First circuit."

His hands shook in the cold. He laid out a static-free sheet and set the leaf down before connecting the circuit analysis tool to the power input strip. The circuit showed green on the analysis tool display, then smoke rose from the leaf and Meyers smelled burning circuitry. He tried to pull the tool from the power input strip, but the circuit flipped to red before he could.

"I'm not seeing any—" Barlowe howled as machine gun fire erupted close to his position. Something shattered nearby. "They're firing on us, Lonny!"

Meyers grabbed the second circuit leaf and connected it to the analysis tool. He checked to be sure the leaf was dry before powering it on. It came up immediately red. He cursed and disconnected it, tossing it on top of the first. The third circuit showed green, then amber, then green again, and then it showed red and the smell of burned circuitry hit Meyers's nose. All the while, the racket of the gunfire from Barlowe's position filled the channel.

There were only two cards left, neither of them in good shape. He connected to Nunoz's channel. "Ensign Nunoz, there are APCs firing on the northern side of the canyon wall. I'm marking the area. I need you and Ensign Hassan to get those APCs to move. Do not fire on our troops on the slope." Meyers marked several meters beyond the area Gerhardt's squad occupied.

"Coming in for another run now, Colonel," Nunoz said.

As if for emphasis, one of the Darts flew low over the camp, the hum of its fans deafening.

Meyers turned back to the circuit leaves. He wiped them down again for good measure, then he inspected them for any cracks or other damage he could repair before trying to power them on. All they needed was for one of the memory modules to survive the power-on attempt. With that, Barlowe could run quick searches for known bot code blocks. A circuit only needed to be alive for a few minutes to get a good search.

To the naked eye, the circuits looked okay. Meyers set the next leaf down and connected the analysis tool. He powered the circuit up. It wouldn't power on. Not red, not amber. Nothing.

He disconnected the leaf and tossed it aside, then he checked the last one. It flickered to life on the analysis tool, jumping from amber to green.

Stay green, he thought. The circuit stabilized at a sickly green.

Meyers connected back to Barlowe. "Ladell, I've got a live circuit leaf from the device. I'm connected into the analysis tool. Can you see it?"

The machine gun fire sounded as intense as before. "I see it. Shit! They're getting closer!"

"Hassan and Nunoz are doing strafing runs."

"Well they need to do more!" Barlowe's voice seemed ready to crack. "You sure that circuit's operational? I'm seeing the tool but it's not showing anything."

Meyers checked the tool. The display jumped between green and amber. "Shit!"

"What?"

"There's something wrong with the analysis tool's connector." Meyers jiggled the power strip connection. The display jumped to amber and then red. He heard a distinct popping sound, and the display died.

"We've lost the last circuit leaf," Meyers said.

They were going to have to deal with the Lancers without the mortars.

21

2 October 2175. Siberia.

BULLETS CRASHED like thunder against the defense works the ERF soldiers had set up along the valley-facing perimeter. Meyers crawled the last few meters to a boulder and pressed tight against it as more rounds chipped away at the rock. At the first hint of a lull, he advanced south, always seeking cover. With each bullet impact, he had to fight the impulse to cover himself and freeze just to be sure he hadn't been spotted. He looked into the valley, noting that several of the sensors he'd seen earlier were down; they were little more than thin stumps that barely rose above the snow. He crawled behind one of the larger boulders, where two soldiers had hunkered down, dug into their waists. What little was visible of them was snow-covered and camouflaged. Meyers lifted his visor to make identification easier in case they were offline. The soldiers saluted quickly.

One of the soldiers' visors opened, revealing a youthful, round, dark face creased by anxious tension. "Dangerous out here, Colonel." It was spoken with a thick German accent. Corporal Schall, Meyers recalled, another of Hecker's bright stars.

Meyers glanced over his shoulder and spotted Timkul stubbornly crawling along the same path he'd taken. He marveled at her bravery but wondered if there might not be a dangerous level of denial at work for her to move through a combat zone facing such heavy fire.

"Stay under cover, Corporal," Meyers said. "We'll do the same."

Bullets ricocheted off the boulder, and Schall closed his visor.

When Timkul was safely behind the boulder, Meyers signaled for her to open her visor. "The mortar I want is eight meters to the north." He pointed to a sunken area protected by a battered defense wall. Much of the ground between their position and the mortar was unprotected. "Stay here."

Timkul frowned. "Is this more of your 'skin in the game'?"

Meyers considered that. It probably was part of what was driving him. "That mortar went offline before we discovered what the bot attack did. There might be code in the memory Barlowe can use to get through the bot damage. Five minutes, then I'll head back."

"All right." The frown didn't leave her face.

He sealed his visor and waited for the gunfire to die off slightly before crawling out from the boulder. Even with his suit's temperature set so low, he was sweating. His throat was raw from heavy breathing, grunting, and constricting. He tried to think about that instead of just how exposed he was, a gray and white form, hidden behind piled snow. They're firing on fortified positions and the visible structures inside the camp, he told himself. They couldn't possibly care about a single person stupid enough to crawl out from hard cover.

The crawl stretched on in centimeter chunks. Each burst of gunfire, each rain of rock and nano-fiber chunks from the defensive positions tested his resolve.

And then he was at the mortar, once more relatively protected.

He powered the mortar back on and connected. It still showed the bogus interface the bot attack had created. He would know soon enough if the memory image of the bot code had survived the power down.

Meyers reconnected to Barlowe's channel. "Ladell? I've got the mortar online. Can you see it?"

Gunfire filled the channel, but Barlowe said nothing. The feed still showed the video collected from the imagery equipment arrayed along the base of the slope. Except for one vehicle that was leaking smoke, the APCs had moved closer to the camp and Barlowe's position.

"Ladell?" Meyers could see Gerhardt's squad in the feed. They were still alive, but now they were hidden behind cover, just like everyone inside the camp. Barlowe's life signs showed green as well, but he could have suffered a non-lethal injury that left him unconscious. "Ladell?"

"Give me a minute!" The tension in Barlowe's voice was worse than Meyers could ever recall hearing. Barlowe was normally relatively cool.

The roar of gunfire stopped suddenly.

"I'll see if we can get another strafing—" Meyers caught a flare of heat out of the corner of his eye, a contrail dropping from the sky and heading toward the camp. He faced down and covered the back of his head with his hands. A second later, an explosion shook the ground behind him, and he found himself airborne, flying over the defensive wall. He landed on his back. He couldn't see the mortar. Rock and mud rained on him.

He looked around, disoriented. His ears were ringing, and his boots were pointed forward, like normal. A thin trail of smoke floated horizontally off to his left. More smoke drifted from his armor, into the clouds covering the ground. Strange sounds chirped and squealed inside his head.

I've been hit, he thought.

He examined his legs, wondering distractedly if they were still attached. Somewhere beneath him, a small craft flew by, twisting to show its slate-gray belly, trailing fire. Another contrail followed, this one well off the mark. It plunged into the piled snow covering the sky and sent more rock and dirt deep into the ground.

Meyers rolled over, and his legs miraculously moved with him. He thought about touching them, and his gloves appeared in front of him, tracing from hips to thighs to knees. Everything was connected and functional.

The ringing changed to a dull, continuous hum at the same moment he realized he was actually lying flat on the ground. Something slate-gray appeared from the murk of the clouds and dropped low enough that he thought he might be able to stroke its smooth belly. It was another of the sleek aircraft, dipping low, sending lead into the camp.

Concussion, Meyers thought. He needed a stim. There was a packet of them somewhere. In a suit pouch. On the armor. On the chest.

His gloves moved over his chest. Material tore away, still smoldering.

Someone was there, lifting him. He went over a shoulder and smacked into a back, and his sense orientation took another flip. Jostling. Movement. The gray snow rushing past beneath.

His stomach lurched; his visor shot up just in time. Something streamed out behind him, yellow against the snow.

Whoever was carrying him hit the ground, and Meyers groaned.

I can hear myself, he thought.

His rescuer hovered overhead, visor up. Dark skin, paler eyes, youthful. He looked so smart, so clever.

"Colonel? Colonel Meyers?" Corporal Schall and his thick German accent.

Meyers felt the scrape of his glove against his lips. The vomit was a sharp, acidic taste. "Stim."

Schall looked around for a few seconds, then pulled something out of a pouch on his chest. Meyers giggled; it was the same pouch he'd stored his own stim in. He reached for the pill, missed. Schall set it against lips cracked and bruised.

Meyers tried to swallow. His mouth was dry. There was a nozzle to drink from somewhere in his helmet. He searched around, then remembered where. He sipped and swallowed. Schall shouted something over his shoulder, then his face was close to Meyers's again.

"Colonel, they have aircraft, you understand? We must fall back. The APCs advance now." Schall seemed very concerned based off all the wrinkles on such a young face.

"What about the..." Meyers tried to remember what they were, the aircraft he'd brought down. Darts! "The Darts?"

"They are coming back to engage, Colonel, but the numbers favor the enemy." Schall pulled Meyers to his feet. "Hurry, Colonel."

Meyers dropped his visor. He struggled to maintain his balance as they hustled through the snow. The stim was working through his system, starting with a tingling in his fingers and toes. It would take longer to counter the concussion, and that respite wouldn't last for long. Suddenly, it occurred to him that he'd come out to the front to access the offline mortar. He looked back and saw the crumpled tube and twisted bipod. The base plate was shattered in three pieces.

Barlowe, Meyers thought. "Ladell?" The BAS prompted with a bright, painful piece of text: *Do you want to reconnect to Barlowe's channel?*

Meyers accepted.

"Lonny? What the hell happened? I heard an explosion."

"They've got aircraft," Meyers said. His stomach seemed ready to flip again.

"I've seen that. Four of them. Fighters of some sort. I think they're proxies. Ensign Hassan said she's engaging one now."

"Lots of money."

"What?" Barlowe's line hissed, and then the gunfire resumed. "Shit. I guess that was what was keeping the APCs from firing."

"Hm?" Meyers couldn't remember the guns not firing, and then he remembered the silence. "Just before the missiles. Yeah."

"You okay?"

Meyers dropped to his knees behind the boulders. Timkul was there, visor raised. Even with her face wrinkled like a prune, she was so much prettier than Meyers remembered. She said something to him, and he realized he needed to up the volume in his earpiece. "What?" She said something again, but it was lost in all the line noise. He shook his head and opened his own visor.

"I asked if you're okay," Barlowe shouted; it was painful with the volume so high.

Meyers squeezed his eyes shut and cranked down the volume.

"Lonny?" The voice was softer, more pleasant. Timkul. "Can you hear me?"

Meyers opened his eyes. "Just a concussion. I'm stimmed. I'll be okay."

Timkul grabbed his arm and threw it over her shoulder—so slender, Meyers thought—and headed back along the path they'd crawled down so recently. He struggled to keep his weight off her and it struck him as funny they could move so easily with aircraft overhead and machine guns firing. He looked up and saw the fire of the slate-gray hawks through the cloud cover. They were twisting and climbing so fast. The Darts weren't really meant for air engagement but Hassan and Nunoz were good. Not Kara good. She should have been up there, he thought.

"We really need Kara," Meyers told Timkul. She made the sort of face people made when they didn't get the reference or didn't understand the terminology. "We were going to get married. Maybe. She didn't like the way I wouldn't commit. Just like Camille. Both good pilots. I bet you'd be a good pilot. You like to argue, like them."

She pulled him along, and her expression changed. He thought it became...troubled.

"I mean because you're right." Meyers squeezed his eyes shut against a humming noise starting somewhere in the back of his head. "Or you think you are. Doesn't matter. You're strong."

The next he knew, he was in the TOC. It was more battered than he remembered. The displays were dead. Paxton had a bloody bandage around his right shoulder. He raised his visor as Timkul settled Meyers to the floor. "Down to seventy-five percent strength, Colonel. Won't get better anytime soon." His eyes were watery, but before Meyers could guess the cause—the injury or the casualties—Paxton looked away.

Twenty-five percent strength loss. Frazzled as Meyers was, he knew that was terrible.

There were tools and burned-out circuit leaves spread around. Snow fell in clumps through holes in the roof and settled on his armor. He listened as Paxton and Timkul chatted, acting as if they couldn't be heard. The humming in Meyers's head became a deep buzzing sound, then it began to fade, and things took on a surprising clarity. After a few minutes, Meyers felt more like himself, but before he could say anything, Paxton sealed his helmet and crawled out of the TOC.

"He'll be back," Timkul said. She smiled, but it didn't hide her worry. "Were you finished talking to Barlowe?"

Barlowe! Meyers had forgotten. *The heavy weapons!*

He reconnected to Barlowe. "Ladell, you there?"

The machine gun fire was a deafening chatter through the connection. "For a little longer. They've got more infantry coming at us. Those APCs can't get up here, but they've got us pinned down. We're dead."

"The mortar? Did you get into the mortar?"

"I think so, but my ADPAX is in the shack. What's left of it." Barlowe sighed, long and dramatic. "I can't get a connection to the ADPAX, so it may be gone."

"We lost one of the mortars anyway." Meyers looked around the TOC. There'd been something earlier...

"You're going to have to call down fire from the *Valdez*, Lonny. We're all fucked otherwise."

"They're so close in now. That's risky." Plus, Meyers realized, it would mean having to turn to Brigston for help. Like admitting to the old man that university was too expensive. Turning to Brigston would mean acknowledging the mission was a bust. Meyers spotted a tube and recalled the mortar that had been in the resupply. "Ladell, those APCs are bunched in on you, right? If we can just get one mortar run—"

"I told you—I can't get to my ADPAX."

Meyers pulled the tube to him and searched for the case it had been in. "I have all we need. Well, except for rounds. Let me connect to Schall."

"Who?"

Heat flashed through Meyers's face, bringing with it a bit more clarity. "One of the soldiers serving with you, Ladell."

"Whatever. I'm not a soldier anymore. You keep forgetting that."

Meyers disconnected. Barlowe's disdain for the military might be rooted in his bad experiences, but that didn't excuse his continued coolness toward those who protected him.

Timkul crawled closer through the snow. "Is that safe, having an IB liaison who doesn't support the mission?"

"Agent Barlowe supports the mission," Meyers said. "He just doesn't support the idea of risking himself."

"You keep saying risk is part of the job." She smiled.

"It is. And I need to ask someone to risk their life right now. Excuse me." He closed his visor and sent a connection request to Schall.

Schall's face, still tight with tension, appeared on Meyers's visor. "Colonel?"

"Corporal Schall. Thank you for saving my life. Now I need to ask you for something else."

"Of course, Colonel."

"I need a case of mortar rounds, assuming any survived that missile strike."

"Some did, Colonel. We will retrieve a case and bring it to you." For some reason, it stood out that Schall's speech had *v* sounds for *w*s.

"I'll be at the LZ," Meyers said.

Schall disconnected.

Meyers raised his visor again. The cool air felt refreshing. He reminded himself to wash his face. After gathering up the rest of the mortar components and setting them in the cargo case, he recorded a message for Paxton: "Carl, we're setting a mortar up at the LZ. If it works, we'll try to get the APCs off Barlowe's position, then we'll open up on the center of the valley. I'll warn Hassan and Nunoz when I'm ready to launch."

Timkul took one handle of the carrying case and crawled toward the tattered flap; Meyers followed. Shortly after leaving the TOC, they got up into a low crouch and pulled the case behind them. It was painfully slow and awkward, but they eventually reached the LZ. Meyers took a moment to rub snow across his face, then he scooped more snow from the main landing area while Timkul lay flat. Before long, he had about a half-meter-deep circle dug, revealing a fairly flat piece of stone that was big enough for the mortar base. There was plenty of room for the case when it arrived. He carried the mortar into the center of the hole and set the plate down. While he assembled the mortar, he tried to hold off the mother of all headaches.

"I need more stims," he muttered under his breath.

As he waited for news from Schall, Meyers glanced to the south, imagining the great, white mountain where the rest of his forces were fighting.

He connected to McNutt and Starling. "Sergeant McNutt, Private Starling..." Meyers tried to remember what he'd been hoping to find out from them. The merged video feed showed Starling's face, which was lit up with excitement. Repin was behind her, guarding a door.

"Colonel?" Starling looked into her camera.

"Um..." Meyers squeezed the armor covering his thighs and tried to concentrate. "Status?"

"Repin's here." McNutt didn't bother to hide the disdain in his voice. "Reactor's been searched. Private Starling can give her thoughts on that. There's an access hatch." McNutt's camera spun around to the wall opposite the door Repin was guarding. The hatch looked out of place—crude, flimsy. "Looks like it's purely physical, off their Grid. Feels to me like it should open right up against the mountainside. Gotta be close to it already."

Meyers couldn't imagine the value of having a physical, unsecured door so close to the outside. Then again, he was having a hard time understanding the sort of preparation and costs involved in putting the mountaintop complex and the ambush together. If they could connect the metacorporations to the whole thing, there would be no way to hide behind claims of innocence or ignorance. The operation had been planned for a long time, and tens of millions had been spent on it.

Suddenly, he remembered the data film he'd taken from Rhizov's armor. Meyers looked down, and his chin sank against his chest. His pouches were gone, destroyed by the blast. The data was gone. They'd lost the evidence. They'd lost everything.

With a sigh, Meyers said, "Private Starling, your thoughts?"

"I think this is a fairly advanced reactor, sir." Starling sounded excited like she was in her element: dealing with technology and making a mess of it. "I'm in their Grid, and I could probably get it to shut down, but I don't see any way to do anything more than that. With some explosives, I could blow out the coolant and launch radioactive steam into the air, but —" She looked toward the hatch. "I think that hatch would give under the slightest pressure, and the steam would just exit that way. Don't have any explosives on me, anyway."

We need a miracle, Meyers realized. "What about the rest of the complex?"

"I sent my spider-bot down the other way." Starling pointed to the door behind Repin. "It's airtight. We're going to have to go in."

Meyers saw someone coming toward the LZ, hunched low, dragging a case.

"One moment." Meyers ran to help the soldier, then realized it wasn't Schall. "Where's Corporal Schall?"

The other soldier shook his head and looked away.

Dammit! Meyers took the case and waved the other soldier back to the front. "Private Starling, can you see what's beyond that other door?"

"No cameras, Colonel," Starling said. "None I can see."

"We need that complex shut down." As Meyers examined the mortar rounds, he tried to remember why the mountaintop mattered so much. The only thing he could think of was that it had mattered to the enemy, so it must have been valuable. "See what you can do."

McNutt moved to the door, nearly pushing Repin aside. "Heading in now, Colonel."

Meyers watched the door open, saw nothing but darkness beyond, then turned his attention back to the mortar. At least it gave them a chance. Timkul settled to her knees at his side.

"These are mostly automated," he explained, sharing the interface with her. "We've got decent targeting data, better..." He tried to get a refresh on the imagery from the Darts or from Barlowe's position.

Timkul laid a hand on his arm. "What is it?"

Meyers hurriedly checked his BAS. It was functioning fine. He could still see the video feed from McNutt and Starling, but he couldn't connect to the targeting data he'd been counting on.

"Something's wrong. I can't get targeting information," he said. "Without that, the mortar's useless, and without the mortar, we can't break this attack."

22

———

2 October 2175. Siberia.

THE GRAY SKY overhead shifted suddenly from a tempestuous boiling of low clouds to a fog-like calm. Despite his armor, Meyers felt the winds die down as much as he heard it. Snow fell, slower now, dropping straight to the trampled gray carpet. Faint slivers of sunlight snuck through the cloud cover. He glanced to the south, where the giant mountain was little more than a distant base of ice-caked stone that faded into uncertainty. After a second, he caught the scent of plastic and synthetic cloth burning —the residue of the missile strikes, no longer torn away by the winds.

He glanced down at the case of mortar rounds. Useless now, he realized. The weapons were automated, simplified, meant to make operations possible by nearly anyone. Other than for clubbing someone over the head, the mortar shells served no meaningful purpose.

Timkul stared skyward. "What now?"

"I don't know." His head ached, and his heel throbbed, but the relative silence troubled him more. "It sounds like they quit firing into the camp."

"A chance to surrender?"

"Why bother? They can slaughter us in battle and not be troubled by their conscience." Meyers thought about contacting Brigston, calling down missile strikes to cleanse the valley. Things were bad, but admitting defeat seemed a step too far. The mountain drew Meyers's eyes again. That seemed to be the solution, if only he could figure out how.

He connected to McNutt and Starling. "Private Starling, we've lost targeting capability, and I can't connect to Barlowe. Could they be running another bot attack against us?"

"Another bot attack, Colonel?" Starling stood in a broad, stone hall lit by yellow LED strips. McNutt and Repin squatted in front of a sturdy-looking door a meter behind her.

Meyers remembered Starling had been off the main BAS network; she had no idea about the bot attack. "We got hit by a bot attack earlier. Saboteurs got past our perimeter sensors and planted devices: bombs and bot carriers. They had my credentials."

Starling gasped. "How could they have those?"

"We'll worry about the why later. Let's focus on that complex up there. It's a great question, though. I don't think a battalion of Lancers in APCs makes sense as the source of the attacks, do you?"

"No, sir."

"An underground bunker with a reactor seem a little more likely to you?"

A smile spread across her face. "It does, Colonel."

"They might have battery backups, or I'd just say shut that reactor down."

"Whatever they've got, we'll find it, sir."

"I'll watch." Meyers looked at Timkul. "There's nothing else we can do."

Starling nodded, and McNutt opened the door. The hallway continued on, also bathed in the yellow light. Cable troughs and pipes ran along the walls, just below the ceiling. What really caught Meyers's eyes, though, was a doorway on the right maybe two meters into the hallway. Through the opening, he could see a body slumped against a wall. Bulky snow camouflage and a helmet covered the body. Everything about it—arms, torso, head—said the person was dead. Another few meters beyond the doorway and corpse was another door, also on the right side. The hallway continued on from that door another few meters, ending at another door.

"Colonel..." McNutt held a hand up to stop Repin from entering the hall.

"I see it." Meyers shifted his head around to get a better view, a pointless exercise. "Do we have any dead missing?"

"No one's reported it if we do." McNutt moved to the right side of the doorway and trained his weapon down the hall. "Looks clear, Colonel."

"Then let's get a look at that corpse."

McNutt waved Repin forward.

Repin moved into the hallway in a low crouch. He chuckled, but it sounded forced, nervous. "Checking bodies, that is the easier thing," he whispered. "Being a body, not so fun."

"Yeah, keep up the chatter, and we'll see about that." McNutt adjusted his grip on his CAWS-5. "Just clear the fucking room."

Starling moved to the hinged side of the doorframe, opposite McNutt, and pressed tight into the corner for cover. Her camera provided a better view than McNutt's. Her weapon was pointed down, ready to be brought up at any moment. Repin stopped at the doorway, squatted even lower, and took a breath. He glanced back before lowering his visor, then he popped his head around the corner.

He turned to McNutt again, visor raised. "Is six," Repin hissed. "Just sitting on floor."

McNutt's camera didn't budge. "Room? Passage?"

"Eh, room." Repin nodded, as if convincing himself. "Two, two and a half meters by three. No other way out. Like storage."

"Check them," McNutt said.

"Check?" Repin laughed, but the humor quickly drained from his face. "Is corpse, right?"

"Check them."

Repin wiped at his big, watery eyes. He seemed ready to challenge the order, then he shrugged and moved through the doorway. "Sergei, he liked to check bodies himself. Find nice things, sometimes. Me? I prefer living. More fun you can have, right? Party?"

McNutt's camera turned to Starling, and Meyers caught a quick head shake in the camera's movement.

"One team," Meyers whispered. *We survive or die as one.*

The wind began blowing again, and Meyers heard jets booming overhead. Enemy aircraft skimmed just inside the clouds, visible for a moment, trailing fire, then disappearing into the gray. Meyers thought he might have heard railguns, but there was no sign of the Darts. Distracting Hassan and Nunoz with a call was out of the question. The lack of missile fire on the camp told Meyers all he needed to know: the engagement was still ongoing.

"Something is wrong," Repin said. He sounded confused and close to panic.

McNutt snorted. "Yeah, they're dead."

"No, no." Repin's head poked out of the doorway. "Two have bullet holes but there is no blood."

McNutt sighed. "Armor. Ever heard of it?"

Meyers scanned the swirling clouds. The hum of railguns was real—he was sure of it. Just above the gauzy soup, he thought he could make out the flash of the Dart's bulkier bodies, spinning and climbing, trailing the fighter craft. He wondered what the enemy had brought with them. Had they gone cheap, like the metacorporations had during the war? Had they counted on numbers and treachery to win the day, or did they bring top-flight aircraft to ensure victory?

A growl brought Meyers's attention back to the situation up in the mountain.

"Just fuckin' check them," McNutt said. "You've seen corpses before."

Repin looked back into the room. "Is like my grandfather, dead in his chair. I found him, sitting in his office. I thought, he is sleeping and made him coffee and vodka. These are the same. But they are different."

Meyers looked around, imagining himself in the hallway and the room. "Sergeant McNutt, are they ours? Have him share his video."

"Repin, Colonel wants to see what you see," McNutt said. "Hop on the feed."

Repin's camera feed—showing his face in high detail—merged with McNutt's private BAS network. After a second, Repin must have realized he was on his helmet's internal camera and switched to his suit's cameras. The room came alive in greater detail. It was rough-cut from the mountain, same as the hallway. The six bodies were spread out three to a side along the longer walls. Meyers spotted bullet holes in three, not two. But there was no blood, and if armor had stopped the bullets, that didn't explain the bodies.

"Private Repin, can you hear me?" Meyers asked.

Repin's right hand shot up to his helmet. "I can hear, Colonel."

"Lift the right arm of the one nearest the doorway. Yes, that one. Was there any stiffness to it?"

"No, Colonel. Like spaghetti noodle."

"Can you tilt the head up for me to see the face?" Meyers leaned in, unable to shake off the sensation of being there, where Repin was.

Repin cupped the body's chin and lifted it up. Dead, silvery eyes stared at the camera. The skin that wasn't covered by the helmet was smooth and flawless, almost rubbery. There was a generic, everyman plainness to the underlying bone structure.

"Proxies," Meyers muttered.

"What's that, Colonel?" McNutt's camera shifted slightly.

"Those are proxies. I'm not familiar with the model, but the way they—"

A loud clank echoed from one of the doors beyond the room full of proxies, and a second later, the door on the right opened into the hallway. Starling brought her CAWS-5 up, but McNutt waved her back and slid up against the wall opposite her.

"Repin, stay low," McNutt said.

Meyers was still able to see the hallway. It took a second for him to remember that they were riding the facility's internal Grid. There were cameras in the hallway. Two men and a woman stepped through the doorway. They were tall and thick, with athletic frames beneath bulky clothing that Meyers realized matched the uniforms of the proxies Repin had found. There was an almost Nordic look to the people in the hall, with pale skin and fair hair. Something about their mannerisms and movement reminded Meyers of Sahara and the proxies they'd encountered there.

"Proxies," he whispered. "Three of them, moving down to that far door..."

The female stopped and looked back to the open door hiding McNutt and Starling. It tilted its head, an act that seemed forced, artificial, as if it were simulating a natural response.

Maybe they're new to their bodies, Meyers thought.

The largest of the three continued on toward the far door.

"McNutt, Starling, they know the door's open." Meyers held his breath. "The female is moving toward you." He wasn't sure they were seeing the same thing; it all depended on what they had running inside their visors.

"Is someone on patrol?" It was the female. Its voice was...off. It sounded like an Irish person attempting a bad German accent.

The shorter of the two men turned and said, "No."

"Second one moving toward you," Meyers said. "The third one stopped at the door."

McNutt lowered his left hand toward his knife; Starling did the same.

Meyers shook his head. "These are proxies. They're probably on a scale with genies."

"Never fought a genie," McNutt said.

"You can't take them. Not with a knife." Meyers remembered the Metacorporate War, the way the proxies had killed with their bare hands. Only Rimes could stand against them, and he had turned out to be... "Use your guns. Get out of there."

The two proxies moved closer, the smaller male drifting back slightly. The third one, the tallest, just watched, hand still outstretched toward the far door.

The woman froze. "Who went out on the raid? Gundersen?"

"*Ja*," the shorter proxy said. It laughed; it seemed the sort of sound a robot might make trying to emulate a human. "He is horrible with the doors."

The taller proxy snorted and opened the far door. "Gundersen!"

The female proxy's lips quirked up in a smile. "Then he can close the door." It turned and reached a hand out toward the shorter male proxy, then stopped suddenly and looked toward the room full of inert proxies.

The shorter male proxy seemed to tense.

Meyers looked around, but from the hall cameras, he couldn't see what she was seeing. "Private Repin, they see something. The woman's looking into the room."

McNutt hissed what sounded like a partially formed "fuck."

"She's looking into the room," Meyers said. He couldn't see her from Repin's feed.

Repin made a blubbering, whimpering sound.

"Matilda?" The shorter male proxy stepped toward her.

"It's the proxy you were looking at. She's just...staring at it." Meyers glanced toward Timkul, saw the way she was rigid with tension. He wanted to tell her it was going to be all right, but he doubted that would reassure her. He doubted it was true.

The female proxy bent lower, and the gold hair braided high on its head disappeared into the room and showed up on Repin's video. He was pressed against the wall opposite the direction the proxy was looking. The female proxy's body blocked the proxy Repin had been examining from the hallway camera. Repin's knife came into view, held just centimeters below the female proxy. His left hand slowly reached toward the golden braids.

Don't, Meyers thought.

Repin screamed, and he grabbed the braids, yanking the female proxy into the room and pulling it to the floor. He bore it to the ground and went after its throat and the back of its neck with the knife. Wet, meaty *thunks* came over his audio channel between his sustained screaming.

"Go!" McNutt charged from around the corner, running straight at the confused, smaller male proxy. The CAWS-5 swung up one-handed and then arced down; the proxy easily backed away and blocked the swing. McNutt used the inertia of his charge to get past the proxy and turned, back to the far proxy, knife raised.

The smaller proxy recovered, knocking the CAWS-5 aside and closing. In the background, the larger male proxy seemed to realize things were amiss. It stepped back into the hallway and froze for a second. The smaller proxy moved toward McNutt, swatting away his knife thrusts and pinning him against the wall.

And then Starling was in the hallway, knife already shifted into her right hand. She kicked the smaller proxy in the back of the knee, and when it staggered back slightly, she locked her arm beneath its chin. She plunged her knife into its eyes with frightening quickness and certainty. The proxy released McNutt and fell onto Starling. She locked her legs around the smaller proxy's waist and continued stabbing and slashing at its face.

McNutt raised his visor and turned to face the larger proxy. Meyers could only see a little of McNutt's face, but the reaction of the larger proxy—a cocky smile replaced by a surprised cock of an eyebrow—told Meyers what he feared. McNutt seemed to be smiling, as if he sincerely believed he could take the larger proxy.

The big machine closed, exhibiting the same sort of speed and power of the models Meyers had seen. McNutt let the charge come to him. Instead of striking with the blade, he rammed the palm of his left hand into the proxy's throat, drawing a slight gasp. The proxy grabbed the striking hand in a powerful grip that produced a popping sound, and McNutt began a series of fast, deep thrusts into the proxy's gut. The proxy growled and fell back, wiping at its gut. Its hand came away bloody.

McNutt shook out his left hand; it was apparently still functional. He looked down, and the video registered the buckled armor across the back of the hand. And then the proxy charged. Once again, its speed was more than anything McNutt could have been ready for. It shoved McNutt back and pinned his knife arm against the wall.

Meyers connected to Banh's channel. "Sergeant Banh, we've got a situation in the bunker complex."

"Yes, Colonel?"

"The team stumbled into trouble. We need a distraction."

"We will distract, Colonel."

Gunfire erupted, and the gun emplacements returned fire.

Meyers switched his focus back to the hallway. The proxy had a powerful hand around McNutt's throat. McNutt's face was turning red. He struck at the proxy with his left hand, but none of the blows seemed to register.

It was the same scene Meyers had watched too many times before. He closed his eyes and looked down, then he opened them, certain he'd seen a flicker of movement.

Starling. She was on the larger proxy, gory knife striking up into the base of its skull and beneath its jaw, drawing gouts of black blood. The proxy released McNutt and turned on her, but McNutt tangled his legs into the proxy's, and they all three went down together. McNutt and Starling took turns fending off the proxy's blows and hacking and slashing. Blood gushed from every part of its body, and it finally fell limp.

Starling got to her feet and returned to the smaller male proxy, which was still thrashing weakly. She pinned its head to the ground with a boot and drove her knife up into the base of its skull, twisting until the proxy quit moving.

McNutt was at her side, his own knife held up a little shakily. They turned toward the room with the inert proxies and took a step.

Repin stepped through the doorway, pale, shaking, and covered in blood. "Is like I said..." He gulped and shook his head. "Being a body, not so fun."

And then he smiled.

Meyers looked toward the open door at the end of the hallway and waited for the inevitable rush of proxies.

23

2 October 2175. Siberia.

THUNDER CRACKED, and fire rolled through the clouds, a giant orange tongue visible through the gray murk. Meyers immediately knew the source of the fire: a missile had exploded. A smaller fiery trail arced down, twisting and at the last moment tumbling; Meyers saw the distinct shape of a missile plunging toward them.

He threw himself on top of Timkul, covering her face with his own, trying to create a crude seal with his helmet. She gasped, her breath sweet in comparison to his own.

And then they were shaken by a deafening boom. Water, mud, and stone rained down on them, bouncing off him. Heat and bright fire touched their armor, but only for an instant. The shockwave didn't even nudge them.

Meyers pushed himself off of her and looked around. The mortar and the carrying case with the shells were still intact.

He got to his feet, his headache more pronounced than it had been since taking the stim.

Timkul picked herself up and brushed away snow. "Was that a missile?"

Meyers pointed to a spot about fifty meters beyond the uplink. "I think it was meant for the uplink." He considered the mortar. "Or us. Something knocked it off course."

They stared skyward for a second, watching the ghostly forms of aircraft streaking through the ethereal cover. To Meyers, it felt like watching giants or gods battle.

Timkul looked at him. "You said they couldn't kill those proxies."

"They shouldn't have been able to." Meyers checked the connection to McNutt's shared channel; it was gone. A reconnect attempt failed. "Maybe that missile took the uplink down after all."

He hurried back to the uplink as quickly as his shaky legs would carry him. Timkul was there, her hand on his back. Although she was just trying to help him, it seemed an affectionate gesture. He glanced back at her, meaning to tell her he was fine, but he bit back his words at her smile. Overhead, the giants clashed, occasionally spitting out fire and metal.

As they drew closer to the uplink, Meyers saw perforations in the outer panels that hadn't been there before. Smoke rose from inside. His heart jumped, but then he realized none of the holes were higher than a meter and a half. The replacement equipment was still safe, above the main structure.

He opened the panels and poked around inside. "We've been seeing problems with the network. I'm wondering if there's something remaining from that bot attack."

Timkul glanced inside the panel beside him. "Like what?"

"A circuit that survived and carries the bot code, something the saboteurs slipped in—" He shrugged. "Something I missed."

"Something that waited until now to shut things down." She shivered.

"I know. It seems convenient and complicated, but we're dealing with a very determined enemy, and they seem to prefer convoluted approaches to overwhelming force."

Timkul smirked. "Tell me you remember what's going on, Lonny?"

"It could be worse." Meyers turned his attention to the replacement devices. The main amplification unit showed offline intermittently. "Shit." He connected to the device's interface, saw the same sort of bizarre behavior he'd seen in the mortars: jittering signals and flashing indicators. He told the device to power down. "They got into the amplification unit somehow. I don't get it. The bots don't have anywhere to attack from."

"I thought the weapons were still corrupted."

Meyers closed his eyes and tried to concentrate. Barlowe had said the systems were clean except for the fake interface. "The bots are gone. Like you said, why wait to take the system down now?"

Timkul moved closer and looked around. "Another saboteur?"

"Or they attacked the system with another device, something we missed." He looked toward the front line. The armored vehicles were silent, vague gray hulks hiding in the snow fog. "And they aren't firing at us." He connected to Paxton. It was a weak connection but functional. "Carl, something's wrong."

"You just gettin' to that point of the problem, sir?" Paxton sounded angry.

"I'm at the uplink. The network's down because the primary amplification device was misbehaving."

"Goddamn saboteurs," Paxton muttered.

"No. These devices came down after the saboteurs. They weren't in place until after the bots were expended." Meyers tried to gauge the distance to the smoke rising from the missile's impact point. It seemed more likely the missile had been intended for the uplink than the mortar, but that made no sense if the uplink had been compromised by the bot attack. He turned back to the perimeter and the silent APCs beyond. "Why aren't they firing at us?"

"I don't know, sir. Maybe they're reloading." Paxton was laying down the sarcasm hard.

"Think about it. Put yourself in their position." Meyers broke it down for his own understanding: overwhelming firepower, superior numbers, compromised infrastructure. "Text everyone to move back to secondary positions. Low profile. Keep the perimeter under observation."

"Move back from the defensive barriers?" Paxton's tone was close to a challenge.

"Hurry." Meyers powered the amplification device back on.

"What's going on?" Timkul leaned around the side of the uplink structure. "Are they attacking?"

"I think so."

She ducked back behind the structure. "Then why give up cover? Won't those guns tear your people apart if they're out in the open?"

Meyers poked through the device's interface after it powered on. It seemed normal. The network came back up. He connected to McNutt and Starling. They were in the proxy room. The three Nordic proxies were stuffed in a corner, out of sight. Everything was covered with blood. Meyers realized McNutt and Starling were hacking at the six inactive proxies. Starling stopped what had looked like a furious eye-stabbing exercise and began cutting the proxy's head off.

Meyers cleared his throat. "Sergeant McNutt, status?"

"And it was so peaceful for a bit there." McNutt shook his head. "Preventive work, Colonel. These ain't flesh-and-blood proxies like the others. More like the old-school combat and construction models: mechanical. Tougher to take down. Repin's watching the hall. Sounds like the guns are going crazy out there." McNutt stomped on the hands of the proxy he'd been stabbing.

Banh! Meyers winced. "I asked Sergeant Banh to cause a distraction when you got into trouble. I need to check on him."

"You do that," McNutt said. "Starling's going to rig these boys to detonate if they move."

Starling pulled a grenade out of a pouch and set it in the lap of the proxy next to the one she had mostly beheaded. "We're going hunting for the command systems, Colonel. Take that offline, this whole mountain should shut down. Assuming they're all proxies."

Meyer hoped the whole operation would collapse. "Hurry."

He flipped over to Banh's consolidated BAS network. He was pressed tight and low against a boulder, watching the nearest soldier, who was doing the same thing behind another boulder. Bullets thumped into the snow and cracked against the stone, sending pieces of rock flying around them.

"Sergeant Banh, you can stop the distraction," Meyers said.

Banh flinched as a sustained rain of rock rattled off his armor. "We have not been able to fire for a while, Colonel."

"They've just been firing at you? High like that?"

"They have, Colonel. Just now. We cannot risk returning fire."

The high shots didn't really make sense. Meyers pulled the view back, trying to see what cameras on Banh's network still showed the mountain-top. Mostly, it was Banh and his soldiers, all of them behind cover. Cho's cameras showed the interior of Three-Zero-Eight. The Dart's batteries were drained, so even operational cameras would be inaccessible. Without the other Darts in the air, there was no view of the gun emplacements.

"Sergeant Banh, did we recover all of our dead?" Meyers asked.

"No, Colonel. We could not get to Corporal Nguyen."

"I'm not seeing his camera feeds." Meyers reached out through Banh's interface. Nguyen's suit still showed active. "Looks like his suit went into standby mode. Probably low battery."

"All our batteries are low, Colonel. We are sharing power over the network."

"Drop your suit temperature to eleven. Conserve power." Meyers tapped into Nguyen's suit and told it to display video. Half the cameras showed snow or darkness; he immediately powered those down. The other half showed snow and mostly worthless angles.

Paxton requested to join the channel. "The teams have moved back, Colonel. Seems like this would be a great time to fire on the APCs, don't you think?"

Meyers let out a frustrated growl as he stared at Banh's video feed. "I think this is a time to do something unexpected, Master Sergeant. I think..." Meyers suddenly realized Nguyen's main camera—his helmet camera—wasn't in the list of options. He poked around, saw the helmet was still functional but even lower on power. "Sergeant Banh, could you redirect some of your power to Corporal Nguyen's helmet?"

Banh didn't respond at first. "But Corporal Nguyen is dead, Colonel."

"I understand. I just need a little power. Just enough to test the camera."

"Yes, Colonel."

The helmet's battery indicator nudged up from blackish-red into a less deep red.

"Perfect. That should be enough." Meyers probed the helmet camera, and it flickered to life. The lens was damaged, but the image was good enough. The helmet caught the top of the mountain peak, angled a little too far up and to the west to pick up the emplacements. "A little more juice, Sergeant." Meyers opened the lens and shifted it, managing a fisheye effect that captured a horribly distorted view of the tops of the central emplacements. He could barely make out the emplacement Nunoz had destroyed.

"You were saying something about doing something unexpected, Colonel," Paxton said.

"Yeah, sorry." Meyers tried to push the camera around some more, but he had it as far as it could go. "One second, Master Sergeant. Sergeant Banh, I hate to ask this of you, but do any of you have a shot at the helmet?"

"Colonel?" Banh sounded mortified.

"Can one of you get off a shot at Corporal Nguyen's helmet? Based on what I'm seeing, even a grazing shot along the...top would knock it around to face the gun emplacements."

"Corporal Nguyen's...head is still in the helmet, Colonel."

Meyers groaned inwardly. It was another of the religious limits of Banh's squad, the idea of protecting the dead from desecration. With the sort of weapons that were commonplace, it seemed a hopeless notion for a soldier. Meyers already felt bad about the way he'd had to turn down Banh's request for a chaplain but asking him to shoot the head of one of his soldiers...

"Just grazing the top of the helmet would be okay, right?" Meyers asked.

"I-I will see, Colonel." Banh's hesitation and uncertainty removed any doubt about how the request affected him. He was normally unflappable. After a few seconds, his video feed showed him glancing out toward

Nguyen's corpse, then tracking over to his helmet. "I will take a shot, Colonel. I see mostly helmet."

"I know this is asking a lot of you, Sergeant Banh." Meyers bowed his head. He couldn't meet Timkul's gaze. She probably had no idea what the request meant, both in potential intelligence value and the toll it was taking on Banh.

Banh's shot was louder than the machine gun fire, but Meyers imagined he heard a grunt just beneath the crack of the weapon. He checked the camera. It had shifted enough to get a better view of the black hole that had once contained the first gun emplacement, but now the optics were useless, and the battery was running low.

"A little more power for the battery, Sergeant Banh. Master Sergeant Paxton, I haven't forgotten about you."

"I'm not going anywhere," Paxton said.

Nguyen's battery indicator turned a slightly brighter red; Meyers shifted the lens around. "Perfect, Sergeant Banh!"

The camera showed the snow-draped near-semicircle of gun emplacements. Meyers spotted the black hole that had been the first emplacement and the other two emplacements nearest it. Muzzle flash was bright and constant in the near-dusk.

And sections of the snow between Banh's position and the machine guns flickered slightly. Then the camera shut down.

"More power, Sergeant Banh."

"But we are running low—"

"Now. Hurry." As soon as the camera was available again, Meyers switched to just a high-contrast monochrome image. The flickering images became a little more clear: human forms. "Sergeant Banh, you've got three, maybe more enemies crawling toward you! Twelve meters out! Proxies!"

Explosions overwhelmed the channel, and Meyers instinctively ducked as he looked skyward. It wasn't the aircraft. There were no flames or falling debris nearby.

"What was that?" Meyers couldn't see any sign of explosives in Banh's feed.

"Son of a bitch," Paxton shouted. "Perimeter's under attack, Colonel.

Grenades, rocket launchers. They're hitting the cover. Must be more of that chameleon skin shit."

Meyers thought back to the attack on the mountaintop, where the proxies had snuck out earlier to attack Barlowe and Banh's positions. Now they were moving in while Banh was pinned down. "It's coordinated. Sergeant Banh, they'll be on you anytime. When the machine guns stop firing, they'll charge."

"I understand, Colonel." Banh's voice was once again calm.

"These are proxies. Work in teams. Be ready to go to knives. Master Sergeant Paxton, hold fire until we can see the Lancers."

Paxton made a sound halfway between a snort and a gasp. "Let 'em in the perimeter, Colonel?"

"Yes. Stay under cover. Let them think they've got us. Tell everyone to rely on BAS signal view. You won't be able to see them with our optics, so watch for red indicators of enemy signals. Their gear's good but it leaks signals, maybe comms. If that doesn't work, use naked eyes."

Paxton grunted. "Understood."

Meyers waved for Timkul to follow and headed for the TOC. He kept one eye on the camp, another on Banh's BAS network feed.

Timkul kept up easily. "Where are we going?"

"The TOC." Meyers muted the connections and gritted his teeth; it was about to get ugly. "For you, at least. I need to get to the perimeter."

"Then we should both go to the perimeter." She made a face he was coming to recognize as her stubborn, ready-to-fight face: clenched jaw, eyebrows bunched together.

"Master Sergeant Paxton's going to need your help."

She grabbed Meyers's wrist. "You're barely able to walk."

"I'll be fine." Meyers wasn't about to let on how stiff his heel was, or how his entire left side felt like one big bruise, or how his head felt like it was in a vice. "I need to be out there."

Just as they reached the TOC, the sound of machine gun fire died off from Banh's feed. At that same moment, the explosions from the perimeter stopped. Meyers gently pushed Timkul in through the tattered flap, which had lost its rigidity and whipped around in the wind. Before she could protest, he moved as fast as he could toward the perimeter. Gunfire cracked, a distant layer of sound from his external pickups. Closer in, the audio was of the desperate, more brutal and visceral struggle between Banh's squad and the proxies. Meyers split his attention between the gray snow trail running between the camp's broken structures and the slightly brighter white mountaintop snow. Banh's BAS struggled to keep up with the input from his squad's video feeds; the figures moved jerkily, making it nearly impossible to figure out the flow of battle, but it seemed the brute strength and hardiness of the proxies was too much for Banh's diminished squad and the surviving rescuers.

And then a round caught Meyers in the ribs, and his attention was drawn back to the camp. His armor absorbed the worst of the impact but it still stung. Ahead, vague forms shifted around a small clump of ERF soldiers. Meyers dropped flat and switched to the BAS's signal feed; the forms became red outlines. Ten red outlines.

It was enough for targeting. He locked onto the nearest figure, center mass, and fired a burst.

The target dropped.

Meyers shifted to the next-closest target and fired again. That target dropped. He switched to a third and dropped it. The enemy forces realized what was up and returned fire. Meyers stayed focused, dropping a fourth.

A round cracked against his left shoulder, producing more than the sort of dull pain it should have. It had penetrated. Another round smashed into his CAWS-5.

Meyers dropped a fifth Lancer, and the last few broke.

He checked his weapon as he rolled onto his side to dig out a fresh magazine and remembered that his external pouches were gone. The CAWS-5 was damaged. He checked his shoulder; his glove tips came away with blood. Rolling the shoulder told him it was still functional but tender as hell and weak.

Gunfire came from off to his left. He got up, checked the clump of ERF soldiers. Two were dead, the third too wounded to be of further use in battle.

Meyers opened a channel to the soldier—Mönch, from one of Hecker's squads. "Stay down. I've sent a general signal marking your location and condition."

Mönch nodded weakly.

After taking Mönch's CAWS-5 and clearing it to accept any ERF connection, Meyers helped himself to a weapons belt and stuffed it with spare magazines and grenades from the dead before heading toward the gunfire. Four green signals were surrounded by twelve red. Two of the green signals were showing diminished vitals. The gunfire had died off significantly by the time Meyers came up on the closest pack of red signals: three squatting behind pieces of cover hauled from the broken perimeter defenses. The cover protected them from the ERF soldiers' fire. Meyers gauged the distance and cover would be enough to ensure the ERF soldiers were protected from a grenade, so he threw one just about dead center of the trio of Lancers. One of them turned toward the hole in the snow, but it was too late.

The explosion took all three of them out. As Meyers moved toward the position, he searched for more enemies clumped together. The best he could find was a pair deeper in the camp. He lobbed a grenade toward them and, when one got up to move away, fired a burst. The explosion finished both Lancers off.

Bullets laid down a steady beat against the cover Meyers was using. The Lancers had good battlefield awareness. He had a decent angle on two more Lancers, but they were prone, almost impossible to hit. They were also too far away from each other for a grenade to get them both. He waited for a lull in the fire on his position, then lobbed a grenade at the closest of the two targets. When the grenade detonated, he belly-crawled wide of the other Lancer, moving into the valley beyond the perimeter. The APCs couldn't fire at him without risking hitting their own.

With all the soreness in his body and the pounding in his head, the crawling seemed to take forever. He opened a channel to the four ERF soldiers; only three accepted. "This is Colonel Meyers."

"Corporal Schweinsteiger, Colonel. We're pinned down."

"Hold your position and keep under cover. I show six Lancers still active, four of them on your northern side. I should be flanking them soon. I'll clear the easternmost momentarily."

"I see you, Colonel. Be aware that the two deepest into the camp are maneuvering back toward you."

Meyers paused to check his signal feed. The red signals began to disappear. "Something's wrong. I've lost all their signals." He glanced past the broken defensive position he had been using for cover. The Lancer he'd been moving to flank was invisible.

The line was silent for a few seconds, then Schweinsteiger said, "Same thing to the north, Colonel."

"Okay, whatever they were doing that our network was picking up, they've stopped." Meyers crawled forward and raised his visor. His armor had chameleon capabilities of its own. He was going to have to use it and risk the battery drain. Without the signals leak, his eyesight was the only way to find the Lancers.

He stopped against the base of the defensive wall that had been broken by the Lancers' explosives. The only red Lancer signals he was picking up were coming off the corpses. That was enough for crude targeting. He scanned from the one he'd just killed with the grenade until he spotted a ghostly silhouette. The Lancer he'd been moving to flank, now two meters southwest of the old position, was watching the position Meyers had abandoned. Even the Lancer's gun was largely obscured by the chameleon effect. Meyers sighted center mass and fired. The Lancer slumped, twisted, and brought up its weapon.

Meyers fired again, and the Lancer fell back.

After counting to three, Meyers crawled forward, watching for any more hints of movement. He stopped just as he was ready to cross the raised wall of snow the Lancers had been using for cover. Something had caught his eye, and he didn't know what. He looked closer and spotted it: a fine line.

"Corporal Schweinsteiger?"

Gunfire filled the channel, then Schweinsteiger said, "Yes, Colonel?"

"They've mined the eastern approach. I'm going to try to clear it." Meyers backed out to the cover and threw his last grenade just over the line. The detonation became two detonations. "All right; I think we're clear. Any movement?"

"I am sure there is, Colonel, but I have seen only one."

Meyers crawled between the two Lancer corpses. Their armor and outer garments were damaged and blood-covered to the point he could make them out clear enough.

"Schweinsteiger, anything?" Meyers asked.

"My audio pickup is at peak sensitivity, Colonel," Schweinsteiger whispered. "I hear snow crunching, but nothing is out there."

Meyers listened. The wind had died down again, so he could hear the gunfire from the groups engaged to the north clearly. Smoke had settled in the area, but it was barely visible against the churned snow in the limited light. The attack's timing was perfect, with the sunset and the downed systems. Even if they drove the Lancers out of the camp, they had already done more damage than could be recovered from. He was going to have to call down support from the *Valdez* and hope they could manage a retreat.

His earpiece chimed. It was Barlowe. "Go ahead, Ladell."

"You...have that mortar...online?" Barlowe's breathing was labored, and his speech was broken by gasps.

"Yeah, but the network's a mess. I couldn't access targeting data."

"Try now."

Meyers heard snow crunch ahead and to the right. He twisted around, but he couldn't see anything. "A little busy with an invisible assault team."

"Hold on." Barlowe grunted. "What about now?"

"No change—" Meyers blinked. About five meters away from him, a Lancer in a low crouch, gun raised, became largely visible. Meyers fired, for a second feeling bad about killing someone who had been failed by technology. "Schweinsteiger—"

More gunfire sounded throughout the camp.

"I see, Colonel," Schweinsteiger said. "We see!"

Meyers laughed. "Ladell, you may have just saved the mission!"

Paxton issued an open channel request, pulling all existing channels in. "Hold fire! This is Master Sergeant Paxton. I repeat, hold fire. Enemy forces are in retreat. Get to cover where possible and expect those APCs to start firing again soon. See what you can do about the wounded, people. I need status, pronto."

Meyers crawled beneath the remaining cover and swapped in a fresh magazine. The railgun that had been protected by the cover was a wreck. He checked the nearest corpse, and beneath all the garments and armor found a patch that seemed vaguely familiar.

"Colonel? Colonel Meyers?"

Meyers looked up. A fair-skinned young man was looking at the corpses with wide blue eyes. "Schweinsteiger?"

The young man nodded and wiped snot from a long nose with the back plate of his glove. "We have lost three guns."

Meyers tore the Lancer's patch free. "See what we can get running."

Schweinsteiger looked past the broken defensive barrier. "Is it worth it, Colonel?"

Meyers considered that. Even with the mountaintop still in contention and air superiority unknown, they were broken. The initial casualty numbers being reported to Paxton were staggering.

"Don't give up just yet," Meyers said. He squeezed the patch tight in his fist, and then he began the long crawl back to the mortar, knowing from the look in Schweinsteiger's eyes that he had already given up.

24

2 October 2175. Siberia.

THUNDER BOOMED IN THE VALLEY, the sound of the APCs' sustained machine gun fire. Meyers could barely manage any distance at all in the shallow groove he'd dug with his frequent trips from the TOC to the LZ. He smelled burned plastic and circuits and looked up; he was just outside the Systems Shack. Suddenly, bullets crashed into the structure. He flattened himself as deep into the snow as he could. He shivered and watched in quiet amazement as the top third of the shack was torn away, exposing the Rover he'd seen earlier. It was still partly hidden by what remained of the shack.

Like the shack, the ERF was being torn apart. He brought up Banh's shared BAS network, fearing the worst.

The video feed was less choppy than before, although there were dead spots where there were no functional cameras. Only Banh and Lamh still stood, Banh with one arm hanging low, Lamh squeezing his thigh. They were back-to-back, gory knives raised. Three proxies surrounded the two of them. The chameleon cover was no longer working or had been turned off. The proxies seemed to be enjoying the moment.

One of them leapt in and punched Banh's limp arm, eliciting a muffled groan; the proxy easily swatted Banh's knife away, and another of the proxies closed.

Gunfire sounded, and the closing proxy staggered. All three proxies turned toward the sound, which came from the Dart.

Cho, Meyers realized.

The gun fired again, and the wounded proxy fell. The one farthest away from Banh and Lamh charged toward the Dart. Meyers could clearly see Cho now, squatting in the snow, CAWS-5 raised, aiming. He fired again: two bursts close together. The proxy stumbled and then fell facedown.

The last proxy ran.

Lamh dropped to the snow and dug, coming up with a CAWS-5. He examined it, tossed it aside, and crawled to one of the downed ERF soldiers. That soldier's CAWS-5 seemed to satisfy Lamh, who crawled up to a boulder and fired. Three bursts—the last one emptying the magazine —dropped the proxy.

At that, the machine gun emplacements opened fire again. Meyers watched long enough to see Cho crawling toward the wounded, then switched his attention back to the camp. When his body protested, he shouted at himself, "We're going to make it!"

Barlowe requested a channel again. "Lonny?"

"Almost there," Meyers said. "We're taking lots of fi—" His words disappeared in the roar of machine guns from across the feed. "Never mind."

"Yeah, same here." Barlowe wheezed for a couple seconds. "Another group ready to charge, too. This time..."

Meyers pushed forward, ignoring the frequent thunk and hiss of machine gun rounds disappearing in the snow nearby. The LZ was just ahead, the drop-off easy to roll down. He shivered as the wind gusted again, and then he saw a ball of fire overhead, blossoming orange. Something fell toward him, crashing several meters west of the ruined Systems

Shack. It was a twisted hunk of metal, sizzling and hissing in the snow. He looked skyward again, caught the arc of the fireball, and saw whatever it was crash into the northern valley wall a few kilometers to the west.

It could be one of the Lancers' aircraft, he reminded himself. Could be.

He crossed the last several meters in a low crouch. It didn't take too long to get the mortar up and running again. Targeting data slowly filtered into the interface.

"Ladell?" Meyers selected a spot on the outer edge of the general APC cluster, then he turned to dig a round out of the case. He recognized a green-tipped round: sensor disbursement. He dropped that into the tube, ducked back to let it fire, then dug out a conventional round.

"You seeing—" Barlowe coughed.

"Yes, I'm getting targeting data. I just put a sensor disbursement round near your position. First conventional round is ready to go. Are we clear?"

"Clear." Barlowe's voice dropped off. "Fire...on target."

Meyers held the shell at the top of the tube and waited for the mortar system to confirm targeting based off the incoming data. The motors whirred, and the barrel shifted, but they never seemed to lock. The readout flashed several changing values—Deflection, Charge, Timing— and the red outlines of the APCs flickered. A message popped up in Meyers's display warning that targeting data was unreliable. It would take a few seconds for the sensors to rain down over the valley and build out their own three-dimensional data network. Over Barlowe's audio, the machine guns started to taper off.

There wasn't time to wait for better data; the infantry assault against Barlowe's position was imminent.

Meyers ordered the system to override the mortar's reliability threshold, set the interval to ten seconds, and manually selected the position he'd indicated. After taking a calming breath, he dropped the round down the barrel, then he ducked back and covered his head. The mortar round launched with a deep thump he felt through his armor.

"Incoming, Ladell," Meyers shouted.

He brought up another round, shifted the targeting a little east of the first, and launched when the counter hit zero.

The third round went farther west and slightly north, closer to Barlowe's position.

Meyers listened close to Barlowe's audio. An explosion—distant—seemed to vibrate through the channel. "Ladell, talk to me. What are you seeing?"

"Too low...to ground to see." Barlowe wheezed and groaned. "Closer!"

Meyers adjusted the mortar to the northern edge of the APCs and walked three rounds from what he hoped was the eastern top of the infantry position to the western bottom.

The explosions were almost deafening over Barlowe's feed. Meyers shook, almost too afraid to ask. "Barlowe, what's happening?"

The last explosion boomed, and Barlowe screamed. Static flooded the connection, then Meyers realized it wasn't static but rocks and debris falling. "Barlowe!"

"Too close!" Barlowe gasped. "Five meters."

Meyers stared at the targeting display. Five meters. There wasn't that level of granularity. He searched the interface, found a way to grid out distance, and set it to meters. Barlowe was guessing about the distance, but Meyers didn't want to drift too far; he went for eight meters and repeated the launch sequence, walking down east to west.

"That's it," Barlowe shouted over explosions. "Right...in the middle!"

"I'm running low." Meyers counted only three remaining rounds. "I'm going to put the last ones in the middle of the APCs."

Once again, Meyers manually shifted the targeting. The data coming in was clearer, painting the APCs in detail. He dropped the rounds right in the heart of the shapes of the APCs, bunching the targets about three meters apart. The explosions came in fairly clear over Barlowe's channel, but there was gunfire now, too.

"Running," Barlowe said.

"They're running?" Meyers pulled the view out. Sure enough, the APCs were breaking up and moving back into the valley. "I'll get more rounds back here. Can you hold out?"

"Good..." Barlowe groaned.

"What happened?"

"Bullet fragments. Next..." Barlowe hissed. "Next time, heavy armor."

Meyers brought up a channel with Schweinsteiger. "Corporal, what's the status on the guns down there?"

"There is one mortar still functional, Colonel, but we must change out the barrel from another. One railgun is also functional, but the defensive barrier is ruined. We are moving the gun and rounds to another position."

It was worse than Meyers had hoped for. "Ammunition?"

"The railgun has quite a lot. It will run out of power before ammunition. We lost two cases of mortar rounds." Schweinsteiger paused for a second. "Was that our mortar firing earlier?"

"Yes. If you can get a team up here at the LZ, the system is functional, but I'm out of rounds." Meyers turned when he saw movement out of the corner of his eye. Timkul raised a hand, and he waved her forward.

"We don't have many left to spare, Colonel. I will bring someone back with me when someone gets back from the triage."

One of the enemy aircraft dropped from the cloud cover and sped low over the camp. The roar of its engines followed, a part of the clouds seemingly trailing from the aircraft's wings. Meyers waited for the machine gun to fire, but the aircraft instead performed a barrel roll and climbed back out of the valley. He searched the cloud cover and thought he might have caught another hint of fire.

There was no sign of either Dart.

Meyers checked the network, but neither vessel nor pilots showed up. He assured himself they were just out of range. If not, he reasoned, the aircraft would be destroying the camp.

Timkul crawled up to the mortar. "It sounded like you fired this?"

It took a second for him to remember that she was still piggybacked on his system. He nervously patted the tube. "It bought Barlowe some time. I think."

"And Sergeant Banh?" She frowned.

"It looked bad, but Corporal Cho's there. Any survivors, he'll pull them through." Meyers realized he had time to connect to McNutt and Starling. "I need to see what's going on in that mountaintop compound."

Timkul nodded.

Meyers sent a connection request to McNutt and Starling; he didn't receive a reply. He tried again, this time only sending to Starling.

Nothing.

"What's the matter?" Timkul asked.

"I don't know. Maybe the network?" Meyers tested the feed from Banh. It was fine. He tried connecting only to McNutt.

Once again, nothing.

"They could've lost the local Grid connection," Meyers said.

"Sure." Timkul's eyes said she believed that as much as Meyers did.

A text message appeared in Meyers's communications queue. Starling's signature, he saw. He opened it.

Hiding in what looks like a proxy control room, Colonel. People in some sort of reclining couches. Proxy drivers, I think. Alarm went off. Way too many people running around. Must be thirty up here. On alert or something.

"You seeing that?" Meyers cocked an eyebrow at Timkul.

"Yes." Timkul's brow creased. "Can she break the proxy...what are they, systems?"

"I have a better idea."

Meyers dictated a quick reply: *Are they proxies or humans? Can you kill them? Can you disable the proxy network?*

Timkul shook her head. "If you kill them, what happens?"

He shrugged. "Hopefully, it breaks the force up there."

"And then?"

"And then we focus on the valley. We rescue the team up on the mountaintop. Maybe we bring those machine guns down here where they can help us." Meyers took a deep breath. "Anything's better than having our people pinned down—"

Starling's reply showed up: *They look pretty close to humans, sir, but I think they're proxies. This can't be all of the drivers. If we kill them, will probably alert the others, and we don't have a way out of here. Trying to get into the proxy network instead. Just shooting it up's not enough; redundancies are likely. Need to find control console.*

Meyers replied: *Shut it down, if possible. Kill them all, if possible.*

"That seems cold-blooded," Timkul said. "No opportunity to surrender?"

"Did you see any of our people get an opportunity to surrender?" Meyers felt the pressure of all the dead and wounded pressing on him. The pain of his injuries stripped away his patience. "We're in combat. I'm concerned about minimizing further casualties for my people right now."

Timkul crossed her arms. "Then call in support from Captain Brigston. Master Sergeant Paxton said they could drop missiles into the valley that would destroy those vehicles."

"And kill Lancers who would probably surrender once their employers die."

"You're not thinking this through." Timkul moved closer and wagged a finger at him. "You've turned this into a personal vendetta or—" She shook her head. "Something."

Meyers wondered whether he was losing his objectivity. "I think I'm still being objective," he finally said. "We want to break this force, but with as few Lancer casualties as possible."

"But it's okay to murder those proxies?"

"Yes. We can find out who they were later." Meyers brought up a connection to Paxton and forwarded the Starling text exchange. "Master Sergeant Paxton, I'm sharing an update from Starling with you. Banh's squad took a beating, but he broke the enemy. I think we're close to securing the mountaintop."

"Good to hear, Colonel, 'cause we damn sure don't have enough to help them out from down here." The heat in Paxton's voice was withering.

"We've got a mortar and railgun operational on the perimeter. I've got another running back here at the LZ."

"Mm-hm." Paxton still sounded furious. "What about Agent Barlowe, Colonel?"

Meyers saw two soldiers crawling toward the LZ from his left, each pulling a case. "He's alive. He helped me drive off a ground assault on his position."

"Two mortars and a railgun and we're down to twenty-three percent operational strength." Paxton cleared his throat. "Colonel, isn't it time we made the call to request orbital support and extraction? We don't have the numbers to stand up to another assault."

Meyers waved the closest of the soldiers forward and pointed to the space where the empty ammunition case sat. "We have enough to pull this off." Meyers leaned out to push the empty case away and make room.

The soldier stood to haul the ammunition case over the snow wall just as machine gun fire punched through the battered structure hiding the mortar from the valley. A round caught the soldier in the back, knocking him onto the case. Blood sprayed from the wound onto Timkul. She threw herself flat with a scream.

Meyers checked the soldier's vitals: low but steady. He waved Schweinsteiger forward and shouted, "Get him to triage!"

Schweinsteiger crawled to the wounded soldier, attached a grip cable to his armor, then began the crawl back toward the perimeter. Meyers helped until they were past the ammunition case, then he crawled back and pulled the case the rest of the way back to the mortar. Timkul glared at him while cleaning her face with snow.

Meyers tried to ignore her. He scanned the sky again and searched for either of the Darts on the network. He felt exposed without air superiority. A missile would wipe him and the mortar out.

He looked at Timkul. "Priya, this isn't going to be safe. Once I start dropping rounds into the valley, they're going to call for those aircraft to take me out."

Timkul rubbed snow against her bloodstained armor. "Nothing down here is safe."

His cheeks burned. He began searching for targets. The front rank of APCs firing on the camp seemed his only real option.

I'm doing the right thing, he told himself. It wasn't about him.

"When I fire, you need to curl up and cover," he said, then he showed her how.

Once she nodded, he dropped a round down the barrel and turned away. With a deep thump, the mortar launched the round. Meyers pulled the next round from the case, shifted the target selection, and waited for the timer to count down. He dropped the round into the barrel and leaned back. He fell into a rhythm of launch, adjust targeting, reload. The sound of the first round exploding barely reached him, but he heard it.

Something roared in the clouds overhead, or maybe it was just the second mortar round exploding. Whichever, Meyers forced himself not to look up. He needed to break up the APCs. He needed to stop the assault. It was only a matter of time before the Lancers' aircraft found him.

25

———

2 October 2175. Siberia.

PRESSURE from the mortar launch hit Meyers at the same time he heard the bass *whump*. It was like a friendly slap on the back, but his back was tender from the explosion that had launched him airborne earlier. He took in a shallow breath, held it, and closed his eyes to gather himself. The firing charge left a pungent chemical smell in the air that was bitter and sharp on the tongue. The air warmed just enough that he could feel it on his face, especially with his armor's internal temperature reduced. He blew out the held breath and got back to the routine: adjust targeting, position the round over the barrel, watch the countdown, drop the round, and turn away.

Five rounds launched, and there was still no roar of the enemy aircraft, no fiery bloom from a missile strike. In the valley, the APCs fell back, leaving behind the broken and dead. Meyers dropped another round in the path of the retreat and stopped. He thought he heard the hum of a railgun from the perimeter and the distant hoots of celebration.

The BAS's signal feed showed only red silhouettes: three unmoving vehicles, two moving slowly, and several human shapes.

No reason to feel mercy for them, he told himself but he did.

He glanced up at the approach of a green silhouette, tagged with Paxton's ID. The movement was jerky and too fast to be someone belly-crawling. That wasn't Paxton's way. Bullets veered away from him, or at least he seemed to think so. He rounded the corner, visor raised, steam pluming from a snarling mouth.

Meyers got to his feet and offered a hand to Timkul. She declined and got up on her own. He looked back at Paxton, saw the anger in his eyes, and focused on hauling the ordnance cases farther behind the mortar.

"You think you might have time to go over your force composition, Colonel?" Paxton put enough of an inflection on the rank to get through the fog in Meyers's head.

He straightened.

Paxton was leaning against what remained of the shack that had shielded their position from view. Smoke and steam curled around his feet and the base of the structure. Soot blackened his armor and the outer wall. Snow clung to them for a moment, then melted.

Meyers brought up the report and scanned the summary for the essential data. Seventy-one percent casualty rate, nineteen percent fatalities, expected to nearly double. The command structure in the camp was down to him, Paxton, and two corporals. The BAS network was listed as amber, and overall C4I capabilities were listed as red.

"We might still have air superiority." Meyers considered the dark clouds long enough to realize how absurd that sounded. The air battle had left the valley.

Paxton pushed off from the building, which shivered. "Call down the thunder from the goddamned task force, Colonel. Turn this valley into a furnace."

"I can't." Meyers wouldn't meet Paxton's bloodshot glare.

"This ain't about you and your father. You can't let your soldiers die to show Brigston he's an ass!" Paxton's swollen cheeks puffed out as he yelled.

"It's not just about pride, Carl." Meyers glanced at Timkul. "We have a mission—"

"Fuck the mission, sir!"

The words stung. "What do we do then?" Meyers clenched his right hand into a fist that he pinned against his hip. "Kill everyone? Forget about trying to save some folks who are just doing their jobs like us? Give up trying to find a solution because things aren't going our way?"

Paxton seemed to take the fist-clenching as a challenge. He moved closer, jaw jutting out, his own hands balled into fists. "If it means saving your soldiers' lives, it's what you're obligated to do!"

Timkul glared at Meyers, wide-eyed, as if to say, *Cool it down!*

Meyers opened his hands and held them up slowly, palms out. "It's not just about our lives. It's about doing what's right and what we're obligated to do."

Paxton stood rigid, but his cheeks shook, and his eyes watered.

"I'm not saying our lives don't matter, Carl." Meyers searched for the right words, the magic message that would calm Paxton without sacrificing the greater truth that valuing all innocent lives mattered, not just those of the ERF. "Those Lancers are being exploited. The enemy is whoever's behind all of this."

The snarl returned to Paxton's lips. He held up a hand and swiped, pushing a data packet to Meyers's BAS. "You tell the survivors of those soldiers about what matters, Colonel. Look those names over. Study those faces. I can't see anyone mattering more than them."

Meyers slumped as Paxton stormed away. There was no winning the argument.

Meyers's earpiece chimed. Of course, he thought. He checked; it was Banh. "What is it, Sergeant?"

"Colonel, we are having problems now," Banh said. He could have been reporting a slight increase in the snowfall or discovery of a nuclear bomb, and he would have sounded the same. "The proxies are gone, and the guns are quiet, but we have used up all of our power getting the wounded stabilized. We will lose our heat and the network in less than fifteen minutes."

Meyers imagined Paxton's reaction to losing people to something as trivial as power for their armor. Someone should have thought to have more power systems and batteries brought down with the medical supplies. "Drop your network down to basic communications. You don't need the...fallen feeding you video anymore. I'm going to check with Private Starling to see if she has any ideas."

"Yes, Colonel." Squeals and hisses—audio artifacts—flooded the line as Banh disconnected.

Meyers dictated a text message for Starling: *Team at shuttle running dangerously low on power. Any chance you could push power out over that Grid to them?*

He paced as he waited for the reply.

"Do you think Carl is right?" Timkul asked. She was far enough away, and it was dark enough that Meyers couldn't be sure of her expression. "About ERF lives being the most important."

Meyers came to a stop and looked around. The wind had picked up to full again, knocking around the broken structures and tossing snow up into the air. They were fast-heading to twilight, and when night settled in, the temperatures would drop even more. It would be miserable. Already, his once frostbitten toes and recovering heel were a constant ache. "Look around you. Breathe in this air. You feel the way it burns your throat? Not just the cold, but the smoke and who knows what chemicals. You're shivering." He pointed to her chest plate. "Now think back to that young soldier who bled on you. Think about Genevieve flying around up there, trying to contend with aircraft armed with missiles. Faster aircraft. Smaller. Unmanned. Aircraft meant for engagements like this. How many people do you know who could handle five minutes doing what we're doing?"

Timkul crossed her arms over her chest; he didn't need to see her expression. "I'm not talking about the living conditions."

"I'm not, either. I'm talking about the people. They make sacrifices. They give up their lives. They train constantly. Objectively speaking, yes, their lives matter more."

"More than those they serve?"

Meyers shivered. The way she'd worded the question was wrong, too open, almost like a trap. "When your mother went down in Widowmaker, we sent in sixteen of our people to rescue her. Six came out. You tell me whether my ERF soldiers value themselves over the people they protect.”

She walked past him, arms still crossed over her chest, and stared at the giant gray haze of the mountain. “Is that what makes them special? Sergeant McNutt and Private Starling. The fact that they survived?”

Meyers followed her gaze. It took a special sort of person to survive what those two had been through, and surviving changed people. “They’re special.”

Starling’s reply caused a small flash of light in his display: *Won’t be fast, but pushing a low power signal out, Colonel. They’ll need to keep their network up.*

Meyers replied: *Network is running at minimum power, but it’s up. What’s your status?*

Timkul turned as he dictated. “She said there were thirty of them up there.”

Meyers nodded. “If anyone can figure a way out of a tight place, it’s them.”

“It must be a big complex.”

And I didn’t see it, Meyers thought. None of us did. “We should have caught it. That symmetrical fold at the base of the peak...it’s not natural. They did a good job hiding it, but—” He shrugged.

Timkul shivered and lowered her visor.

Starling replied: *Seeding bots, sir. Can’t find the main console, but if I can get enough bots onto their Grid and gain elevated privileges, I can overwhelm the network. No network, no proxies. Would be nice to find that console and shut this all down directly.*

Meyers replied: *Keep at it.*

After a few seconds, he connected back to Banh. “Sergeant Banh, keep the network running, and you’ll get a low power signal.”

“We are seeing it already, Colonel,” Banh said, sounding excited, Meyers thought. “There is enough power coming in. Private Lamh and me, we would like to test the gun emplacements.”

“Test the gun emplacements?”

“Yes, Colonel. They have still stayed silent.”

Meyers wondered if the alert inside the complex had pulled the gun crews away from their positions. "Do you think you can manage to move closer without getting too much exposure?"

"Oh, yes, Colonel. There is a path we can take to another set of high rocks. Where...we lost Nguyen. That path."

Meyers could see the value in knowing the guns' disposition. Even just getting close enough to take out one of the emplacements with flash-bangs might mean getting more people into the complex. That might be all McNutt and Starling needed to get out. Then again, just two more soldiers wouldn't be enough to change the odds. If anything, it could just mean sending two more people to die.

"No," he muttered. The pressure from everyone was getting to him. He had to take some chances. "Sergeant Banh, if you think you two have a good chance of getting in closer, if you think you can take out those guns, do it."

"We will see what we can do, Colonel."

"I'll check back soon." Meyers disconnected and scanned the feed coming from the valley. The APCs had already fallen back several kilometers and had spread out even more. They were regrouping, planning for another attack, probably once evening had settled. That's when he would do it.

Meyers connected to Barlowe. "Ladell, you there?"

"Wish I wasn't," Barlowe replied, still struggling to speak.

"What's your situation? Gerhardt and McNutt's men?"

"Alive." Barlowe groaned. "Mostly." He coughed. "Running low...battery."

"Same on the mountaintop. Starling and McNutt found a complex up there, burrowed down in the mountain. Proxies. And they have some very powerful combat proxies. She's tapped into their systems, siphoning off energy from their Grid for the wounded."

Barlowe seemed to process that for several seconds. "We don't have idiots down here." He caught his breath. "No easy Grid to hack."

Meyers chuckled. "Didn't think we would be so lucky. If we could get one of the Darts down here, we could recharge quick enough." He paused to listen, but the dogfight was somewhere beyond his audio sensors. "So,

Paxton's in a mood. He wants to have Brigston turn the canyon into a big channel of fire."

"You gonna?" A barely audible hum of static settled on the connection.

"You think you could make it back to camp before they counterattack? Just to be safe."

"No." Barlowe sounded resigned, then he snorted. "I'm probably the best off."

"That bad?" Meyers looked at the Systems Shack and saw the Rover; it was still connected to the now-ruined structure. Without sustained sunlight, the vehicle would quickly burn through its power reserve struggling through the snow. "We've got a Rover here. We could squeeze everyone on and make a run for it."

There was nothing but the hum for a while. "I'll get Gerhardt."

Meyers wiped snow from his armor distractedly. He watched the APCs—big red shapes on his display—and stared at the dark sky. The whole time, he did his best to ignore Timkul's watchful eyes staring at him from the top right corner of his display. Finally, there was a pop and a hiss on the connection: Gerhardt. Meyers let out a quiet, relieved sigh.

"Sergeant Gerhardt, did Agent Barlowe tell you what we're thinking of doing?" Meyers pulled away a piece of charred cloth that had somehow stuck to his armor throughout everything.

"I'm having a hard time with all his gasping and wheezing, Colonel," Gerhardt said. "I think it's best if we just stay here a bit, let him catch his breath."

Meyers squinted. He wanted to see Gerhardt's face to be sure, but it sounded like he was being sincere rather than making fun of Barlowe. "Are you saying you think you should hold that position?"

"No one else can do it. We'll stim up when they come at us again. There's lots of cover up here."

"You realize once they attack again, you'll be cut off. I'm not sure we'll have another chance." Meyers didn't want to challenge Gerhardt, but the situation called for absolute certainty. "The next attack…"

"Colonel, you need the imagery we're providing. We all know that." Gerhardt's voice was even.

"Get into the best defensive positions you can," Meyers finally said.

"We've got a few picked out. I better crawl back to mine."

There was another pop, and then the worst of the hissing disappeared from the channel.

"Ladell?" Meyers realized he was choking up.

"That Rover can't make—" Barlowe coughed. "Too far."

Meyers gritted his teeth and turned off Timkul's piggyback. "You were never the hero type. Don't start now."

"I'm making it out." It sounded like Barlowe might have laughed. "Got plans."

"We all do." Meyers disconnected and resumed Timkul's piggyback.

"What was that about?" she asked.

"I'm not really sure." Meyers started toward the Rover. "We need to get this vehicle closer to the perimeter, though. Maybe it can help with repairs, moving supplies around. It can definitely speed movement along. That I'm sure of. And it's doing no good back here."

He climbed into the driver's seat and checked the battery charge: forty-two percent. Without siphoning from other sources, the vehicle wasn't going to go far at anything more than a crawl. When Timkul settled into the other seat, he pointed to the belts and let her strap in, then he drove toward the perimeter, rocking as the Rover's tires fought for a grip in the slick snow. It would be hardening to ice soon enough.

That's when the Lancers would attack.

26

2 October 2175. Siberia.

Someone had rigged a strip of LEDs across the front of the Rover. The light painted the snow a ghostly blue. Meyers focused on the crunch of freezing snow beneath the vehicle's wheels, seizing on the solidity of the sound and the vehicle's bouncing and lurching as a refuge from the hopelessness of the moment. None of the camp's structure remained intact, and some were completely obliterated. Gray forms moved from place to place, carrying broken gear, weapons, and bodies. There was a feeling of purpose to it all, a directing intellect that had to be Paxton, but Meyers felt like someone out of step, a living person among the dead.

He parked the Rover a few meters back from the main path that ran behind what remained of the perimeter defenses. Signatures from the earlier battle still hung in the air: the sharp smell of explosives and gunpowder, the faint scent of blood that darkened the snow, and the foul odor of ruptured guts.

Timkul unbuckled and climbed out of the vehicle, wandering toward a boulder where a trio of soldiers seemed to be trying to reassemble a mortar. One of the soldiers put a foot on the base and pulled the barrel free, then took a hammer to a dented area.

Meyers gingerly set a foot onto the snow. He ached, but he could support his weight. Another team of soldiers seemed to be tearing a machine gun apart. He made his way to them. As he got closer, he saw their visors were up. Steam plumed up as they spoke, cursing and grunting and shivering. A dark blanket was laid out on the snow, with parts spread on the surface. The parts were lit by a lamp secured to a rock that looked like it had taken the brunt of an explosion.

The soldiers were caught up in their work and oblivious to his presence. They were quickly identifying components that were functional, repairable, and unusable. It didn't take Meyers long to realize the two machine guns were coming down to a single possible operational weapon.

He shuffled on, barely aware that Timkul was tailing him.

"They look so worn out," she said as they approached another team, this one trying to repair one of the broken defensive barriers.

"Fighting takes a lot out of you. It's pure adrenaline while you're in it, then nerves afterward, and after that..." He looked at her, wondering how she could have been so close to the fighting and not have felt it. It dawned on him that she hadn't really experienced the sense of imminent death that brought all the emotions and chemicals into play. "They'll be okay. They've just got their suit heating down low. When the Lancers come again—"

"How can you be so sure they'll come?"

He nearly sputtered. "Because they have to kill us now."

"Why?" She sounded like she was pleading for the answer to change.

"It's what they were hired to do, and we've shown them that they can." Meyers ran over to help a couple soldiers holding up the barrier while a third applied adhesive. When they were done, Meyers walked away before they had a chance to realize who he was. When he returned to Timkul's side, he found Paxton standing there.

"Colonel." Paxton saluted and nodded along the path they'd been on.

Meyers proceeded and tried to match Paxton's stride. After several steps, Meyers said, "Looks like they might get one of the machine guns operational."

"Could break at any time." Paxton breathed in loudly through his nose. "But any little bit improves the odds."

"I think they can get a couple of the barriers back to where they were." Meyers looked back the way they'd come. "It's not perfect, but it's an improvement over what we had last attack."

Paxton glanced skyward. "We need air superiority to have a chance, sir."

Meyers stopped and considered the cloud cover, charcoal gray and quickly drifting. There had to be a way to contact the Darts, even if Hassan and Nunoz had drawn the enemy aircraft away from the valley as Meyers suspected. Three-Zero-Eight's radio was probably still functional, but its batteries were dead. He wasn't sure how much power it would use up from what Starling was pushing. It seemed worth a try. He opened a channel to Corporal Cho, audio only to save power.

"Corporal Cho, how are the wounded?"

"Better now with the power coming to us, sir. Petty Officer Hollins was pretty bad until I got his temperature back up. He's stable." Cho didn't sound stressed.

"Is the power enough to allow you to recharge?"

"Yes, sir. We're all coming out of the red, almost."

Meyers relaxed a little. "Good. If you think everyone's in a good enough state, I could use your help."

"Uh, sure, Colonel."

"Can you direct some power to the Dart and try to connect to the radio—see if you can bring it into our channel?"

Cho didn't say anything for a bit. The channel picked up a strange buzzing sound that grew louder with each second.

"I think I have the radio on with us," Cho said. "It's taking a lot of power."

Meyers tried to connect to the radio through the channel. There was an interface, but there was a delay when he accessed it. He coaxed a little patience from the small remaining reservoir he had and worked through the front end until he had a remote control system functioning, then he programmed in Zero-Eight-Nine and One-Zero-One.

"Ensign Hassan, Ensign Nunoz, this is Meyers, do you copy?"

The buzz grew louder and then dropped off to background noise.

Meyers licked his lips and reminded himself to get balm from the water nozzle. Later. "Ensign Hassan, Ensign Nunoz, this is Meyers, do you copy?"

Nothing but buzz.

Meyers saw the worried look on Timkul's face and the resigned look on Paxton's. They were thinking what was gnawing at his own gut. Meyers cleared his throat. "Corporal, is it possible the radio's damaged?"

"I don't think—"

"This is Zero-Eight-Nine, Colonel." Nunoz's voice was nearly lost in the buzzing noise. "We're engaging enemy aircraft. Fifty klicks—" The buzzing drowned out his voice.

Meyers smiled at Timkul. "They're still up there."

Paxton grunted. "Need 'em down here, sir."

"I know," Meyers said.

Paxton straightened. "And we need to pull Agent Barlowe and Sergeant Gerhardt's team back."

Meyers looked back toward the Rover. "I already talked to them. They...don't want to come back."

"Don't recall that being their decision to make, Colonel." Paxton looked down at the ground. "Unless you'd rather take over running the operation down here?"

"No." Meyers had passed the tasking to Paxton for a reason. He was the most qualified.

Paxton grunted, satisfied. Somewhat.

Meyers headed toward the last of the heavy weapons positions. Timkul and Paxton followed. Timkul's eyes were wide, and she was biting her upper lip, as if she feared things were about to get ugly again. It felt close.

Meyers decided to try to defuse things one more time. "Carl, they're shot up. Ladell knows that imagery they're sending us is giving us the only edge we have right now, and Gerhardt's volunteering to protect that position."

"I'm not accepting suicide, Colonel."

Meyers slowed to examine the work being done on the final defensive position, then he picked up the pace again, moving nearly as fast as he would on a normal walk. He turned back to see Paxton's expression. The faint lights of his helmet interior revealed bruises, puffiness, and the leathery skin of someone who'd seen more war than Meyers was likely to ever know. There was a set to Paxton's face, a defiance that said he would fight the decision. Meyers wished there were some way for Paxton to see what the decision meant for Barlowe and Gerhardt, the growth they had managed by accepting that they might die.

"I want them out of there, too," Meyers finally said. He looked to where the giant mountain rose from the valley, invisible now, but no less real. "I want us all out of here. I want those bastards up there dead and the rest of us—and the Lancers—warm and secure on our ships."

Paxton came to a stop. "Then get them back here to camp."

Timkul put a hand on Meyers's arm. "You could use Agent Barlowe's systems expertise here. He has broken their chameleon systems already. If he were here, he could do more."

Meyers sighed. "I'll take the Rover out there. I'll—"

The buzzing intensified.

"Colonel Meyers? This is One-Zero-One."

Hassan! "I read you, Ensign." Meyers searched the sky. The signal sounded more powerful, closer.

"We are bringing the engagement back to the valley, Colonel. We think that most of the missiles have been expended. Getting them down in the canyon gives us an advantage if they can't fire on you."

"Thank you, Ensign." Meyers pointed skyward and smirked. "Looks like we're about to get our air superiority back. Ensign Hassan says those aircraft may be out of missiles. They're bringing the dogfight back here. That might be enough to delay the next attack."

Paxton scowled. "Seems like a good time to make that run out to get our people back."

Meyers looked away, taking in the ruined camp. "It does."

He headed back toward the Rover, noting the way Timkul now walked closer to his side. Was she trying to keep the distance between him and Paxton to prevent another flare-up, Meyers wondered.

A chime indicated a connection request; Meyers accepted.

It was McNutt. "Colonel, slight bit of a problem." His video swung around a room full of reclining couches, gray-green in the subdued, green-tinted light coming from strips mounted to the wall about hip high. Bodies lay on top of the couches, wearing only undergarments, their skin similarly sickly green. A white sheet separated the bodies from the couch surface. Starling was barely visible behind one of the couches, Repin behind another.

"What is it?" Meyers asked.

"Someone poked his head in the door a second ago," McNutt said. The video swung around to capture a door; he was against the wall, next to the hinges. "Didn't see us, but said over his radio he was checking another room before coming back."

Meyers considered that. He had no idea what the complex looked like, but Starling said they were stuck in a one-exit room. It didn't look like an ideal layout for a sustained firefight. A grenade would get them all. "Was he alone?"

"The proxy? Yeah. Sounds like most of them're checking another corridor."

"Can you kill him before he can get an alarm off?"

"Yeah, that's the problem, see," McNutt said. His camera panned around the room again, then it froze on the door. "Tight spaces, only a couple good places to hide. I'll have to take him by myself for a few sec—"

Light showed beneath the door, and McNutt's camera shifted, as if he'd pressed tighter against the wall. The door opened, and McNutt's left hand went up, touching the door. His knife came into view as a flashlight beam ran across the opposite wall. A man—tall, muscular, Nordic-looking—stepped into the room, assault rifle at the ready. He seemed to be looking toward Repin's hiding place.

McNutt moved, knife flashing back and out of sight, almost certainly going for a strike at the base of the skull. A whisper-scrape broke the silence, and the Nordic man turned. McNutt struck, but the blade caught the man in the muscles of the neck.

The assault rifle fired, deafening over the BAS connection.

McNutt's left fist crashed against the man's nose and cheek. The knife clattered to the floor, and they wrestled for control of the assault rifle. Starling rushed from cover, and a second later, Repin followed. The proxy released his grip on the assault rifle's stock and landed a quick strike somewhere below McNutt's face. He staggered back and slammed into the wall, then he slid down. The proxy quickly spun around, re-gripping the weapon. Starling came at it with her knife, catching it in the forearm as it fired a short burst point blank at Repin.

Repin grunted and collapsed, knife dropping from his hand.

Starling was on the proxy then, pushing the assault rifle up by the barrel and slashing at the proxy's face and neck. It released its grip on the assault rifle and punched both hands into Starling's solar plexus, driving her back and knocking the wind out of her. It sighted in on her, but McNutt was on it again. This time, his knife found the target, and the blade disappeared in the neck. Blood exploded from the wound, and the proxy staggered. It got off another burst, but the rounds went wide and cracked ineffectively off the floor. McNutt drove the blade in deeper and twisted it until he was almost supporting the proxy's weight by the knife blade alone.

The proxy's head slumped forward, and its assault rifle clattered to the floor.

McNutt wiped his blade on the proxy's shirt, then stomped on its neck until it cracked. "Let's go!"

Starling got up and they moved toward the door, then McNutt looked back. Repin was still struggling to his feet. He was having a hard time just grabbing his knife.

"Fuck, you hit?" McNutt asked.

"Is just a little wound." Repin laughed, but when McNutt looked down, blood could clearly be seen leaking down the front of Repin's armor.

Starling hooked Repin's arm over her shoulders, and they moved into a hallway.

"Looking for a new hiding place," McNutt said. "Nice if it came with a big, red shutdown button. Any ideas, this is the time to share them." His camera scanned the hallway. The lighting wasn't very bright, but it was enough to reveal several other doors on either side and another at the far end, that one open.

"Open door," Starling said. She helped Repin down the hall toward the open door.

McNutt spun around to watch the opposite end of the hall, where there was just an open doorway. It sounded like booted feet were approaching, but no one was there yet. He looked down. Little drops of blood glistened on the floor. "Yeah, well, that's fucked up."

He ran back into the room, tore a sheet from beneath one of the reclining forms, and ran back into the hallway, desperately wiping the blood as he backed down toward the open door at the end. The door slowly shut after he backed into the room. His camera captured forms—people—entering the hallway at the far end.

"Did they see you?" Meyers asked.

"That would be a big bag of fucked up, now, wouldn't it?" McNutt sheathed his knife and a moment later had his CAWS-5 ready. His view panned over to Starling, who was spraying coagulant on Repin's leg. "Hey, he gonna make it?"

"I think so." Starling had her gloves off. Her fingers pushed into the crease of Repin's armor where hip and thigh came together. "Sorry. I need to be sure the coagulant gets in past the armor."

Repin's head pushed back against a wall. His face twisted in a grimace. "Is fine, fine. Normally, I pay for such things." He hissed. "You are so gentle, though. Like...what is it, buffalo in doll shop?"

"I think I got it," she said. She pointed to two holes in the joint armor and matching deformities in the thicker thigh plate below. "A few millimeters lower, and you probably would've been fine."

Repin blinked away tears. "I would not miss your loving caress."

McNutt chuckled. "Yeah, well, stay sharp. You've been a lot more helpful than Domnikov ever was."

Repin shook his head. "Sergei, he was not so bad."

"A fucking bully."

"But for bully, not so bad." Repin smiled. "It was all the life he knew, you see? He was big boy, and then his parents die, and he was raised by big man, eh, what do you say? Uncle? And he said, 'You are big and stupid, so you must push people around.' In Russia, that makes you successful. In military, it get you promoted."

McNutt snorted. "It gets you killed is what it gets you." He looked at the door, and his hand crept toward the knob. "Wonder what they're doin'."

Meyers shook his head. "Don't. Aren't there cameras out there?"

Starling stared off into space for a second, then she shook her head. "Offline, sir."

"Do you still have your spider?"

McNutt looked at Starling, who produced the little robot.

"Right here, Colonel." She skidded the spider-bot across the floor, and it disappeared under the door. She looked up for a moment. "Should have the video...now."

The video was grainy, uneven, and distorted, possibly from damage. It captured most of the hallway but not the far end. The spider-bot shifted, catching first the door to the room they'd just left, then the end of the hallway.

Which was full of advancing proxies.

27

2 October 2175. Siberia.

JETS SHRIEKED in the sky above, shattering the quiet in the valley and yanking Meyers back to his own problems. Orange fire clung to the tail of two of the sleek, gray shapes, both skimming low enough in the clouds that he could see the exhaust flames reflecting from their underbellies. Somewhere above the clouds, the Darts twisted and climbed, their green outlines moving across the earpiece's projected display. The aircraft disappeared, climbing in pursuit.

"That was the Lancers' aircraft." Timkul's statement bordered on a question.

"Hassan and Nunoz are up higher." Meyers selected the Darts' signals so she could see them on her piggyback view. "They need the right opportunity for a strafing run."

McNutt snorted. "What about getting them to squeeze into the compound to give us air support?"

Meyers flipped the display output back to McNutt and Starling's feed. The spider-bot still showed the proxies advancing down the hallway, but they were in low crouches and moving slowly. "Any other exit out of that room?"

McNutt's video feed showed him scanning the room. Starling was squatting to the left of the door, CAWS-5 readied. Repin sat just behind her, leaning against the wall. He was blinking rapidly and sweating. Meyers knew the look too well: the struggle to deal with immense pain. The wall extended beyond their position another meter or more. The room was at least three meters deep and slightly wider. Crates, cargo cases, and plastic-wrapped gear were piled from floor to ceiling, narrowing the room. Another door, this one on the right-hand wall, was partially hidden by the stacked crates.

"Possible exit," McNutt said. He waved Starling over to check the door and covered her.

Meyers first sensed and then saw Paxton staring impatiently. "McNutt?" Meyers bowed his head slightly. "Let me know what you find."

"Yeah, probably an invitation to their master control console."

Meyers killed the connection.

"Good enough time to pull Barlowe and Gephardt back now, Colonel." Paxton looked toward the north valley wall, a pale white ghost in the dusk.

Meyers thought about trying to work out a deal or to reason with Paxton, but the look in his eyes said it all. He wanted everyone back in the camp, and he wasn't going to budge. "On my way."

Paxton stomped away, already adding Barlowe and Gerhardt to the existing channel. "Agent Barlowe, Sergeant Gerhardt, this is Master Sergeant Paxton. Do you copy?"

"I copy, Master Sergeant," Gerhardt said. "Agent Barlowe's a little busy right now."

Paxton glanced over his shoulder at Meyers. "Get him un-busy, Sergeant."

Meyers noticed that the team repairing the nearby defensive position had stopped working and were staring into the valley. He stepped closer and closed his visor to improve the BAS video quality. Red forms moved in the valley, coming closer; some of the vehicles were pulling far ahead of the others. One of the soldiers cursed, and the others checked their weapons.

"APCs are moving back in," Meyers said.

Paxton turned to look out into the valley. "Sergeant Gerhardt, get our people out of there. Immediately."

"We're too banged up to move—"

"Move it, soldier!" Paxton dropped from the channel and went to a knee. He dug into the snow, finally coming away with a clump of muddy dirt. He squeezed it in his hand and sniffed at it, then threw it beyond the barriers. He stood and stomped away, barking orders at the defenders taking up positions behind the repaired defense works.

Timkul took a step, then she stopped and turned back to Meyers. "What about the Rover?"

Meyers shook his head. "Too slow. There's no way we could get out there and back. We'd be easy targets. There's a group of APCs moving back in at full speed."

"But they're slower on foot, aren't they?"

"He just wants them to try, I think. I don't know."

On his visor, the red forms of the APCs closed. The other vehicles followed but at nowhere near the speed. The lead contingent had to be brave, fearless, disciplined. He recalled the patch from the earlier battle, taken from the dead Lancer, now. He'd stuffed the piece of cloth into an armor compartment earlier. He opened the compartment, took the patch out, and turned on his headlamp. Safe behind cover, he examined the vaguely familiar image.

The material was dark, made up of muted colors—browns, blacks, and gold—that formed a cartoonish animal hurling lightning bolts. There was black lettering but it was too dark to read. He scanned the patch with his BAS and had it process the image, then he opened the channel to Corporal Cho.

"Corporal, we've got another engagement imminent down here." Meyers studied the red forms of the APCs speeding toward them. "I may be unavailable for a while."

"Understood, Colonel. Sir?" Cho's voice cracked a little.

Meyers tensed, ready for terrible news. "Yes?"

"We lost Petty Officer Hollins. He went into shock, and combined with everything else, I…"

Meyers realized he had been worried it would be Cooper. It left a dirty feeling. Friend or not, they were all his comrades. "It happens, Corporal."

Something boomed overhead as Meyers disconnected. He glanced up at the sky, dark and gray, hoping the Darts might have felled another of the aircraft. If Hassan or Nunoz could break off for a strafing run, they had a good chance to break the APC charge. Something that might have been jet exhaust flashed between two clouds but was quickly gone.

Meyers raised his visor and looked toward Barlowe's position. Where the valley wall curved in and sloped up, black shapes that could be low hills or large boulders hid everything. The snow between the camp and those hills was a deep gray-blue. The ERF positions along the perimeter were black with green outlines squatting and lying flat.

They were in as good a position as they could be. McNutt and Starling sent a connection request.

"What's up, Sergeant McNutt?" Meyers switched the video feed to his visor.

McNutt was descending a spiral staircase of black, press-formed plastic that seemed to have been glued to the stone wall. His boots echoed hollowly. "Those proxies? They're searching the room with all the sleeping beauties. Should've rigged some grenades for them. Bastards."

Meyers craned his neck left and right, as if that would let him see what McNutt's cameras weren't showing. "Those stairs come off that other door?"

"Yeah. Looks like there's another room down here."

"Can you see anything through their Grid?" Meyers thought he could make out light ahead when McNutt turned around the spiral.

"Nah, Beck—Private Starling says nothing's showing up, like it's a separate Grid or doesn't have Grid connections." McNutt froze. The light below was clear, coming from beneath another door, revealing a small room. He slowed.

"Your signal's still strong," Meyers said. "Maybe they've got a connection in there after all?"

"Maybe, Colonel." McNutt stepped off the stairs and edged toward the door. "We'll know in a second."

A white flash indicated Meyers had received a text. From Barlowe. Meyers opened it.

Lonny, we can't make this. We're too banged up.

Meyers muted his connection to Timkul and McNutt, then he dictated: *It's not my call. Paxton and Hecker were supposed to be running the valley operation—now it's Paxton. He's technically running the operation. If I take over, it won't go over well. We've lost so many of our people, he's not handling it.*

Barlowe replied: *I've broken their chameleon systems. I'll get their comms hacked with a little more time. You don't physically need me there. You do need the data we're capturing.*

Meyers sighed. He didn't need to have Paxton any more upset than he already was but Barlowe was right: Pulling them back to camp was pointless. At best, they would get pinned between the APCs and the camp.

He dictated: *I'll talk to him. Just head back for now.*

Shapes suddenly plunged from the sky: two of the aircraft and a Dart. The lead aircraft pulled up once clear of the clouds, as did the Dart and then the trailing aircraft. They all banked and headed toward the approaching APCs. The Dart's railgun hummed, and the lead aircraft went into a barrel roll, then started to spin. The spinning turned into an end-over-end dance followed by a slow disintegration. The Dart turned back toward the camp just as a fiery trail leapt from the pursuing aircraft.

A missile!

Meyers watched helplessly as the missile closed. The Dart spun and started to climb but in the valley, there was little room for maneuvering. The missile detonated below and behind the reactor, for an instant lighting the sky.

And then the Dart plunged toward the ground, powerless.

Meyers un-muted his connection to McNutt and Starling. They were standing in the small room at the base of the stairs with Repin. "Sergeant McNutt, we've got a Dart down here in the valley. I need to go."

McNutt's camera bobbed as he nodded. "Understood, Colonel."

Meyers ran for the Rover; Timkul followed.

"Where are you going?" she asked, even as she turned to watch the Dart plow into the snow. It scraped out a long trench before coming to a stop.

"That pilot could be alive." Meyers checked over his shoulder to be sure the Dart had come to a stop. Flying in the valley, performing maneuvers...the Dart hadn't been going full speed before the crash. He had to hold out hope. He checked the Dart's signal: emergency transponder, aircraft number One-Zero-One. Hassan.

Ahead of him, Paxton turned. "Which one was that, Colonel?"

"Hassan." Meyers shot past, and a minute later had the Rover moving in front of the defensive perimeter. He stopped to let Timkul run past a barrier and climb in, then they were off again.

"You muted earlier," she said. "Did you know she was coming down into the valley?"

"What?" Meyers remembered the texting with Barlowe. "No. It was something else."

Timkul might have nodded at that. With her visor down, he could only rely on the small image of her face in the corner of his display, so it was hard to read her. The Rover bounced and lurched across the broken snow.

Meyers glanced west, past Timkul's small form, ignoring the way she wrestled with the belt. The red shapes of the APCs were closing. "You should have stayed at camp."

She buckled in and turned to her right. "The APCs? Will they approach a downed aircraft?"

"Probably. A small detachment." To be sure the pilot's dead, he thought.

"And this can't go any faster?" She looked down at the floor.

"It's not a performance vehicle. The harder you push it, the more juice it uses up. It's just meant to get people and cargo around. No armor, no weapons." He shivered and wished they had something like the Crawlers they'd faced on Bellar. He pushed the accelerator a little harder, and he thought he could see the power level drop.

A white light flashed: another text. Meyers confirmed it was from Barlowe, then opened it.

About ninety meters from our position, halfway down the slope. Another infiltration unit. Maybe twenty. Crawling instead of relying on chameleon suits. Can't make it back. Tell Paxton to watch that flank.

Meyers muttered into the voice converter: *Get back to your position. Be careful.* Then he connected to Paxton. "Carl, you've got an infiltration coming in on the southern end of the perimeter. Barlowe just spotted them. As many as twenty."

"Well, fuck," Paxton said. "Nice of him to report that to you."

"I told him you're running operations. He probably figures you're a bit busy with the armor coming in."

Paxton made a sound that could have meant anything.

"I can see One-Zero-One ahead." Meyers scanned the length of the vehicle. Smoke curled skyward, and no light showed along the surface or from the inside. "It's upside down. The fuselage looks intact, a little crumpled near the reactor compartment."

"Cockpit?" It sounded like Paxton was muting and un-muting.

"Buried." Meyers slowed and turned, then he backed the Rover toward the rear of the Dart. "I need to check the airlock."

He leapt out and moved toward the Dart. It had dug a trench in the hard snow for as far east as Meyers could see. Climbing over the piled snow on the nearest side of the trench was tricky, but he managed to keep his footing. Someone was taking a hammer to his skull, and nausea seemed like it might double him over at any moment.

When Timkul seemed ready to try the descent, he waved her back. "If I can't get this airlock open, no need for you to be down here."

He tried to connect to Hassan, but she didn't respond. He tried connecting to One-Zero-One's interface; it was powered down to basic operations. Of course, he realized. Without the reactor, it would go to conserving battery power. He ordered the airlock open and stepped back in case the ramp malfunctioned. The airlock hissed, the door slid aside, and the ramp popped out and up.

Meyers climbed over the airlock top and switched on his headlamp. The Dart's interior seemed to be intact, too. It was quiet except for his clumsy booted steps.

"Lonny?" Timkul sounded anxious. "There are red forms coming toward us."

He froze. "The APCs?"

"No, those are still moving toward the camp, and they're firing now. These are people."

Meyers hurried forward. "How many?"

"Six? No. Wait. Eight."

The cockpit was dark except for the glow of a couple console elements, and those were faint: a red pulse indicating the emergency beacon was activated and a pale green battery power indicator. Hassan's arms hung down toward the ceiling. Her head dangled loosely below the harness securing her to the seat; she was completely unconscious.

"How far out are the Lancers? The ones coming toward us?" Meyers pulled a glove off, bent slightly, and checked her throat for a pulse. He couldn't feel one.

"Ninety-two meters." Timkul's voice shook.

Meyers straightened suddenly and winced at the headache that produced. "Move the Rover to the front of the Dart, then climb down into the trench. Hurry!"

He freed Hassan from the harness and gently slid her to the floor. Her face looked pale and waxy. He reached for a stim, then he remembered he didn't have any external pouches. The only thing he could do was crude CPR, which might kill her if she wasn't already dead. Her neck could be broken or any number of other things could be wrong.

His earpiece chimed: Banh.

Meyers accepted the connection. "Sergeant Banh—"

"Colonel!" Banh was shouting, but he could barely be heard over the deafening noise of a machine gun. "They have the machine guns again. Firing. We are pinned, and there are more, moving behind us."

"More. The big combat proxies?" Meyers struggled to breathe. Everything was moving too fast, falling apart. He'd been counting on Banh to draw attention from McNutt's team.

"These are people," Banh shouted. "They are big, but they are not proxies."

He doesn't know about the big proxies McNutt's team destroyed, Meyers realized. "Can Cho help?"

"Corporal Cho? He is in the Dart."

"I know." Meyers realized he might not be loud enough with the machine gun making so much noise; he raised his voice. "Can you get him to help?"

"I will try, Colonel. They are moving into position to shoot us!"

Meyers glanced down at Hassan's still form, then he disconnected and reconnected to Cho. "Corporal Cho, those machine gun emplacements are firing again."

"I hear them, Colonel." Cho's video feed showed him moving toward the airlock.

"There're some proxies flanking Banh and Lamh. Can you provide cover fire?"

Cho stopped at the outer airlock door. "I'll do what I can."

Meyers disconnected and exhaled raggedly, then he pulled off his other glove and undid Hassan's torso armor. Timkul was climbing in through the airlock by the time he had the flight suit open. He waved her forward; she settled on her knees at his side.

"You know first aid? CPR?" he asked.

"What I learned in the security forces." She was staring at Hassan's waxy face.

"I don't have any stims, and we need to get her heart going again. Can you help me?" He took Timkul's hands and placed them over where he estimated Hassan's sternum would be. It seemed about the right placement. "We're going to compress and breathe for her together." He pushed down against Timkul's hands. "Like that. Okay?"

Timkul nodded. He ran his hand along Hassan's neck and felt nothing strange. He tilted her head back and hoped he wasn't killing her. He scooped three fingers into her mouth to be sure her airway was clear, then he breathed as he remembered the training, signaling for Timkul to compress in time with him. The sequence and duration weren't perfectly clear to him, so he searched his BAS and adjusted once he had the official process. On their third cycle, Hassan began to breathe on her own.

Meyers realized he was shaking from the fear that he might have injured her or worse. He pulled his gloves back on. "Okay, I need to check on those Lancers. Help me get her to the airlock."

With Timkul's help, he managed to get Hassan to the airlock without any trouble. They settled her onto the ceiling, and he waved for the envoy to wait. Crawling out of the trench was tougher than he'd expected it would be but he made it to the top. He popped his head up slowly and scanned the dark, snowy valley floor.

It only took a second to spot the Lancers—red outlines, twenty to twenty-three meters out, spread in a semicircle, and crouched low.

There was no way to make it to the Rover, even without Hassan. In the distance, the APCs' machine guns chattered, drowning out the fire from the ERF camp. The ERF mortars returned fire but against a small number of moving APCs, Meyers knew it wasn't enough. They needed help, or the camp would fall.

McNutt pinged Meyers's earpiece; he accepted the request.

The video feed showed a large room of bare stone. Starling stood in front of systems displays, visor raised. Her breath misted. Repin stood by what Meyers assumed was the door they'd come in through. Lining the wall to either side of the door were racks of gear, fuel cells, and batteries.

"Looky looky," McNutt said.

Starling's mouth dropped open slightly as her head slowly turned to take everything in. "It's a lot of systems power, Colonel. A lot."

Meyers could almost feel her wonder and awe through the connection. If it wasn't as nice as what they were still building out at HQ on Plymouth, it was close. "Is it the master control center?"

"Must be, sir. I was expecting the main proxy driving room. Still don't know where they're at. Where do you hide thirty people?" Starling's hands brushed across millimeter-thick chrome modules: systems processors. When she spoke, she whispered as if she were in a holy shrine. She shook the dazed expression off her face and began swiping at invisible controls. "I need to get the bots seeded, get elevated priv—"

The door burst open, and one of the Nordic proxies leapt in. It spotted Repin and butt-stroked him in the visor, knocking him back, then another proxy came through the door, assault rifle roaring.

And the connection to McNutt and Starling went dead.

28

2 October 2175. Siberia.

When the video feed dropped, Meyers instinctively ducked his head and slapped the side of his helmet, assuming a system failure on his end. That saved his life. The Lancers opened fire on him at that exact moment, blasting packed snow from the edge of the trench onto the back of his armor. He was so surprised that he lost his balance and tumbled down the snowbank, face-planting onto the trench bottom. Timkul jumped out of the airlock; he waved her back. He got to his feet and looked up at the trench top. The Lancers would be coming, half firing to cover the advance of the others.

He fell back to the airlock and climbed inside, CAWS-5 aimed at the spot he imagined they'd appear. Red forms advanced, as expected, but none of them came into view.

Timkul's hand rested on his shoulder. "They're coming?"

It was dark but they had spotted him, he realized. He shoved her back and threw himself on top of her just as grenades tumbled down the snowbank. Even though it was meters from the airlock, the force of the explosion hammered Meyers's suit and rattled his teeth. No shrapnel pelted the airlock. Meyers's foggy brain slowly put together the clues: concussion grenades. The ERF armor handled that better than most.

He got up, unsteady, and tried to find the enemy. Something thudded against the belly of the Dart halfway toward the front. He saw two faint, red dots. Two more slid down the snowbank. Meyers brought the CAWS-5 up and...

His hands were empty, and he couldn't remember dropping the weapon.

The Lancers came around the edge of the airlock, guns raised. Meyers realized he was dead. And then the guns fired.

No. A gun fired. *His* gun. In Timkul's hands.

The Lancers staggered and then dropped. And then the CAWS-5 clattered against the ceiling.

Meyers looked down at Timkul's quivering face. Her lips moved, but he couldn't hear anything she said. After a second, he realized he was hearing the booted feet of the Lancers on the Dart's belly, so he wasn't deaf. Timkul was just in shock.

He picked the weapon up and edged toward the outer airlock door. His thoughts were still a jumbled mess, but they weren't so bad that he couldn't recognize the disadvantage he had if he wanted to clear the Lancers from overhead. They had cover, and they'd be able to see him before he could see them. They could easily lob a couple more grenades down, this time into the Dart.

Seal the airlock, he thought. Plenty of battery power still. Fully charged.

The Dart's interface filled his display. He selected the airlock controls, then he hesitated. He backed out to the main interface. The weapons systems showed green. The missile had hit aft of the reactor; the gun was operational.

He brought the railgun interface up and connected his BAS targeting to the fire controls. The gun tried to lock on but wasn't able to.

Meyers looked up, tried to remember what the Dart's belly looked like. The railgun would be raised above the reactor, almost centered. The thunk of the boots above had been toward the rear of the craft, probably aft of the reactor. He couldn't hear the Lancers moving anymore, as if they were belly-crawling or moving slow and cautious, maybe in a squat. The railgun couldn't bring the barrels up that close to the bottom of the craft. It couldn't fire through the reactor by design. He needed the Lancers standing for the railgun to lock on.

He brought the CAWS-5 up and fired where he imagined the Lancers might be. The gunfire was like an explosion, but the bullets embedded in the reinforced metal-and-composites floor. That was fine; he just needed the noise to startle the Lancers, to get them to stand up enough—

The railgun hummed, and several meaty thunks thudded against the Dart's belly.

Meyers targeted the remaining Lancers and the railgun hummed again; the Lancers' signals flickered out.

He waited a few heartbeats, then he reached out for Timkul to take his hand. She did but she was shaking. Her visor was down but he knew she was crying. It was never easy killing someone.

"Listen to me," he said. "We need to get Hassan back to the camp. It's going to be tough. We don't have a litter, so I'm going to have to rigid her armor up the rest of the way and drag her out of the trench. It's clear out there, but they're going to realize what we've done. They'll send more, so we have to hurry. Can you do this?"

Timkul nodded.

He helped her back to Hassan and crouched beside her.

"All right, put your hands on her right ankle and start rubbing like I'm doing on her left, you see?" Meyers worked his way from Hassan's heel to her ankle, rubbing and repeating the motion enough for Timkul to pick it up. "Good. When you feel the armor hardening, move up. Work one segment at a time—ankle, knee, hip, abdomen, shoulders, neck. There you go. When it's done, she'll be immobile, and we can safely move her. All right? Excellent."

While they worked on the armor, Meyers reconnected to Cho's channel. He was still alive, and crawling through the snow toward the boulders. Meyers realized it wasn't the boulders closest to the Three-Zero-Eight but the set closer to the gun emplacements.

Meyers waited until Cho had reached cover, then said, "Corporal Cho, how's it going?"

"I've got them—"

Gunfire drowned Cho's words out, and it appeared he doubled up.

"Repeat, Corporal."

Cho straightened out and brought his CAWS-5 up. "I was saying I got one of them, and now I've got their attention. I think Sergeant Banh's got cover from the machine gun. Hold on."

Banh's feed joined onto Cho's. He and Lamh were pressed against the icy stone of the bunker semi-circle. A machine gun fired from somewhere outside Banh's camera range.

"Colonel, can you see this?" Banh looked around, and Meyers saw the boulder Cho was hiding behind, then the area where the proxies were firing from. "We have a clear path to an emplacement." He held up a flash-bang. "I need to try this first." He leaned out slightly and the view took in the curve of the wall. Meyers could make out the opening where the machine gun was firing from.

"That's a tough angle for them," Meyers said. "Not an easy throw, though."

"We will throw together." Banh's camera caught Lamh, flash-bang in hand. "We just do not want to leave Corporal Cho alone. We were going to move back along the wall and—"

"Negative," Meyers said. "Corporal Cho can handle it. He just needs to keep those proxies pinned down."

"I got it, guys," Cho said.

"But the wounded, Corporal Cho." Banh's camera shifted toward Cho's position.

"There's nothing more I can do about them. We need to get them up to the *Valdez*."

"Sergeant Banh, I've lost contact with the team inside." Meyers felt lightheaded for a second and had to brace against Hassan's rigid armor. "They need your help. They may already be dead. But everything—all of us down here in the valley—need that complex taken out. You understand?"

"Okay, yes, I understand, Colonel."

"Wait. Do you have any of that Porcupine ammo? The explosive fragmentation rounds?"

"I do, Colonel." Banh set his flash-bang down, then he dug around in a leg pouch. He pulled out a magazine with a thin yellow stripe along the bottom.

"You've got a range to that opening, right?"

Banh brought his CAWS-5 up and leaned out enough to sight in on the opening. "Range is seven meters, 231 millimeters, Colonel."

"Set the ammo to detonate five centimeters short of that, and you should be able to fill that room with lead fragments. Probably won't kill anyone, but it should knock them off the gun long enough for you to get a clean throw."

"Yes, Colonel." Banh hesitated a moment, then he brought the CAWS-5 up again and fired three rounds. Small explosions followed each shot.

The machine gun stopped firing.

Banh set the CAWS-5 down, fetched up his flash-bang, stood, and his grenade disappeared from view. Lamh stood and brought his grenade back. They stepped out together and threw their grenades. One of the flash-bangs bounced off the ice short of the opening, but the other caught the lip of the opening and disappeared inside. A couple seconds later, a loud ringing rolled over the snow.

"We go!" Banh charged from cover in a crouch, CAWS-5 raised, moving with cautious speed.

They reached the opening quickly, and Banh's camera captured the interior. The gun was fine, the room empty. He moved to the second, the one they had targeted. Two forms were inside, staggering around as if drunk. Lamh dropped them with short bursts, then Banh pushed the machine gun barrel up, and Lamh crawled into the bunker. As Banh climbed in, Lamh finished the gun crew off.

"We are in, Colonel." Banh switched back to his normal magazine as he moved to one side of the door and waved Lamh to the opposite side.

Meyers signaled for Timkul to take Hassan's ankles, then he hooked his hands beneath her armpits and lifted. They moved her into the airlock and waited while he listened. There were still no red signals. He climbed out of the airlock and with Timkul's help set Hassan at the bottom of the slope.

"Sergeant Banh, I'm going to put what we know about the interior of that complex into a single map." As Meyers spoke, he had the BAS begin the process of assembling everything. "It'll upload to you when it's done. This will include last known location of McNutt's team."

"We will wait until I have the image, Colonel."

"Can you still access their Grid?" Meyers pulled the silicone hands of his armor's cable grip from the front of his suit and examined them. They'd been damaged by the explosion that had burned away the fabric elements covering his armor, but the gripping surface still seemed functional. He attached a hand to each side of Hassan's armor, just below and inside of the shoulders, then he unlocked the cable line and began his climb up the snow.

"I can see it, Colonel. We are on through Private Starling's connection."

"Cameras? Sensors? Anything..." Meyers clenched his jaw against a groan. His head throbbed, and his heel burned to the point he was sure his leg was going to fail him. "Anything you can use to see outside your location?"

"I—" Banh made a frustrated grunting noise. "Not that I can see, Colonel."

Meyers resumed his climb. "Wait for the map, then."

The snow seemed harder to climb, both slicker and less yielding. He had to kick hard, each strike sending thick needles of pain through his toes. At the top of the trench, he paused, wondering if the Lancers had realized they were giving off signals he could target, like the ones inside the perimeter had. Would they have had the time to power off their comms? Could they be waiting for him to pop his head up again?

He waved a hand instead—a quick chopping motion.

Nothing.

He sucked in a breath and glanced over the snowbank.

Once again, nothing. There was no movement.

He pulled himself out of the trench and crawled about a meter away from the edge, then he locked the cables. Grimacing, he kicked the foot with the tender heel down into the snow. He did it again and again, until he had the leg about shin-deep into the hard pack. He repeated the process with his other foot, finishing just as his suit flashed an amber warning about his suit's battery power: twenty-two percent.

After catching his breath, Meyers leaned back to test the cables. They were secured to Hassan's dead weight.

"Priya, could you give Ensign Hassan a push up the snowbank?" Meyers shifted around, and when he felt slack in the cables, he leaned back. "Excellent. I'm going to start pulling her up now."

He locked his knees and ordered the cables to retract. Almost immediately, his back began to ache. The weight pulled him forward, and his abdominal muscles cramped. Every part of his body shook, and his head felt ready to explode. The explosion had done more than concuss him. He felt fragile and useless. Any sense of orientation evaporated, and he thought for sure someone had punched him in the gut. He folded at the waist, and his arms plunged into the snow with a hollow *thump*. It seemed like he might be uprooted from where he'd planted himself.

And then Hassan's helmet cleared the top of the trench. He squeezed at the snow, crushing it in his hands, scraping at the ice deep beneath the surface.

Hassan's torso cleared the top of the trench.

He slid forward, his bad foot rising halfway up out of the hole and his gloves sliding over the ice. His knees felt ready to snap, and a scream rose up and threatened to escape.

Hassan's hips cleared the top of the trench, and then she fell flat against the snow. She started sliding toward him.

"She's up," he gasped. "Come up. I'll help if you need it."

"Are you all right?" Timkul sounded genuinely concerned.

"How bad do I sound?" He snorted, embarrassed. "I'm fine."

He muted and blew out a deep breath and then sucked in another. Once he was sure he wasn't going to break, he un-muted. He locked the cables, pulled his legs clear, and crawled toward Hassan. He searched for the Rover's signal and found it maybe fifteen meters away. He widened the base of his boots again and began dragging Hassan toward the vehicle, leaning hard into the effort. Timkul reached the top of the trench as he came to a stop. She jogged toward him, and together they put Hassan onto the flatbed. They were both shaking from the exertion. Meyers strapped Hassan down, then he looked toward the camp.

Fireflies danced around the APCs—muzzle flash as they fired onto the camp. Red, human forms rushed forward, using the machine gun fire to cover their advance. From the camp, the ERF returned fire. It wasn't enough to break the advance. Whoever was at the head of the assaulting force was more than just another Lancer. The soldiers were too good, too determined. Too many. They would break the camp and kill his soldiers.

They would destroy the ERF.

My fault, Meyers thought. He remembered the way Ramawat had sacrificed himself on Bellar after realizing how badly he'd screwed up. Rimes had sacrificed himself after what he'd done during the Metacorporate War. They were leaders, willing to pay the ultimate price.

Meyers glanced back at the Dart. The railgun was still good, at least for a short while. It would be enough to get off a few shots. Important shots. No one had reacted to the Lancers' deaths yet.

"Priya." Meyers opened his visor and handed her his CAWS-5. "Listen to me."

Her visor opened. Her brow was creased in uncertainty. "What?"

"I need you to take the Rover, hug the slope over there to the south, and follow it east. Our people won't fire on you. Get into the camp. Get to the rear. Search for some batteries. There's a lot of destroyed equipment. Charge the Rover. You understand? Can you do that?" He handed her another full magazine for the CAWS-5, which she just stared at. He placed the magazine next to Hassan.

"Why? What are you—"

He held a hand up to stop her. "If you see things are falling apart, drive as slow as you can but get the Rover out of the valley. Just keep it moving. Maybe see if you can make it up to the Operations Center. You have to try."

"Lonny, you're being crazy. Just call in a missile strike from the *Valdez*."

"It's too late. They're in too close." Meyers's heart ached at the look in her eyes. He might have gotten her killed, too. He hoped not. He glanced up at the towering mountain, so close and still unconquered. "You were right. I made the wrong call." He gently nudged her toward the Rover.

"No! I'm not leaving you! You need to come back—"

Gunfire sounded, and a round cracked off the front of the Rover. Another round struck Meyers in the back, knocking the wind from him. He dropped and pulled Timkul down with him. He looked out toward the valley. More forms were advancing on him, supported by two APCs.

"Stay down," he said, and then he crawled away from the Rover. He connected back to the Dart's systems and brought up the main interface. More gunfire, all of it the Lancers' assault rifles but then the APCs joined in. Snow popped up into the air all around him. He hastily connected his own targeting information to the railgun and ordered it to fire.

Nothing happened. No hum from the railgun or sound of the turret mechanism. He spun, searching the Dart for any sign of problems. The railgun seemed fine. It showed green on the display.

What is it, then? If the gun is working, and there's still power in the batteries, what else is there? Just targeting—

Meyers flipped back to his main display and cursed. The targeting data was gone again.

29

2 October 2175. Siberia.

CLUMPS of frozen snow popped into the air around Meyers, then rattled off his armor. He felt rather than heard it. He couldn't hear anything except the sustained gunfire, but pieces of ice slowly tracked down his visor like frozen tears. The rounds were getting closer, cracking against stone and ice just a few meters beneath him. Three of the Lancers ran toward him, bright red forms against the black and gray of the night. They had their assault rifles raised. Meyers turned to look at the railgun again. The targeting system had just been working...

Gunfire from close behind and to his right brought his head back around. Timkul was a green shape half-hidden by the Rover. She had the CAWS-5 braced. Another burst of fire, and Meyers realized only one of the charging Lancers was still up.

Meyers fast-crawled just high enough to offer a tantalizing target. That seemed to confuse the Lancer, who froze and swiveled from Meyers to Timkul.

Timkul fired again, and the Lancer dropped.

In response, machine gun fire drifted across the ground toward the Rover. The APCs had picked up her gunfire.

Meyers changed direction, getting to his feet and running in a crouch toward the closest of the dead enemy. They had assault rifles, and maybe they had grenades. More importantly, he would be the greater threat again.

The other Lancers intensified their fire. A round cracked off his thigh, nearly taking it out from under him, and then another round glanced off his chest. He fell but continued forward. His leg ached. It was as if someone had hit it with a sledgehammer. His chest didn't feel much better but he could breathe. His armor was a mess, though, and he was still bleeding from the shoulder wound, which made movement awkward.

Something dark obscured the snow ahead. He crawled as fast as he could toward what looked like a corpse. Rounds cracked off whatever it was. It occurred to him the cover just might be enough to make a difference. He dropped even lower and edged forward, stopping when he saw it was, in fact, a dead Lancer. The corpse had been torn in two by the railgun, the torso closer to him, arms outstretched, assault rifle still clutched tight.

Meyers pried the weapon from the corpse's cold, dead fingers and checked the magazine. Half-full. That was good enough for the moment. The weapon itself seemed intact and was of a solid design. It was heavy enough that it probably had systems integration. He hoped it didn't have biometric keying.

He braced the weapon against the gory torso and sighted in on the closest of the red forms—still moving, still exposed. More rounds cracked against the corpse and into the snow. Meyers fired and missed. The gun had more kick to it than he'd expected, and he couldn't integrate BAS targeting. Concussion, shoulder wound, bullets flying all around him…he scolded himself and forced the distractions away. Behind him, the APC machine guns had found the Rover, and it sounded like the guns were tearing it apart.

"Concentrate," he muttered.

He fired again, this time taking the Lancer's legs out and knocking the form face-down into the snow.

Bullets cracked against the torso, and it sounded like the APC machine guns stopped firing. Meyers nearly panicked. He fired a quick burst at the next advancing Lancer, then began searching the corpse for another magazine. A glance back at the Rover told him what he needed to know: Timkul was still up. He turned his attention back to the corpse. There were no magazines or obvious pouches on the torso, so he stretched out enough to grab the nearest part of the lower half. The snow was slick with freezing blood, making it easy to pull the legs closer. He patted a leg down and felt a bulge on the thigh; it was a pouch integrated into the armor. He fumbled around for an opening, flinching with each round that cracked against the corpse. After a few tries, he tugged the pouch open and fished a magazine out, then he reloaded.

The Lancers moved closer, and the machine guns spoke again, tearing up the snow as they tracked back toward him. Meyers realized the machine gun rounds would tear through the corpse's armor, and it would be all over for him.

He brought up the targeting interface again and tried to connect it to the Dart's railgun.

Nothing.

"Priya, you've got to get that Rover out of here," he shouted.

"It's ruined." She sounded as if she were gasping.

"Are you wounded?" The Rover wouldn't have provided any cover at all. If she was hit...

"No." Timkul paused. "I don't think so."

"Hassan? Is she hit?"

"No. They tore up the rear tires and the underside, though."

Meyers shook his head in disbelief. All he'd wanted was for the two of them to escape, and now—

The machine guns had tracked back to him. Chunks of the corpse's legs flew into the air and bounced off his armor, smearing his visor with clumps of dark blood. Two more Lancers charged toward him from the left, away from the machine gun fire. He was pinned down, dead. Timkul and Hassan would be next. Even his attempts at self-sacrifice were flawed.

Something crashed into the snow maybe twenty meters in front of him. He felt the burst, saw the light, and he heard the explosion before it overwhelmed his sensors.

He stared skyward, half-expecting to see one of the aircraft tearing through the night sky, trailing fire, but there was just the coil and whip of fast-moving clouds.

It dawned on him that his targeting system showed the railgun firing. He couldn't hear its hum but could almost feel the rounds whistling by overhead, burning white-hot in the frigid air.

Something flashed on his helmet display. A text from Barlowe.

Radio inop? Are you seeing the mortar fire?

Meyers laughed. Barlowe had the guns online. Meyers replied: *Mortar round took out audio. My ears are ringing again. Can't hear anything. Everything working?* The earpiece corrected his speech as he dictated, driving home just how bad his hearing was.

Barlowe replied: *Yes, devastating array of weaponry now online. Two mortars, two railguns, and a failing machine gun. Won't make much of a difference.*

It saved our lives, Meyers thought.

He risked a glance over the chewed-up corpse. The Lancers on foot were gone, and one of the APCs was falling back slowly, shooting sparks from fist-sized holes in its hull. The other APC was a twisted mess, its weapons dangling from tangled metal. The interior was exposed and lit by dying LEDs, revealing blood-spattered walls and armored body parts.

Meyers slung the assault rifle over his shoulder and crawled back to the Rover. Mortar fire lit the valley closer by, and he heard and felt the explosion. His audio receptors were back online, and his hearing was coming back.

Timkul ran out from cover to meet him, and he let her help him up. He wanted to yell at her for not fleeing when she could have and for leaving cover, but it felt too good to see her moving and uninjured. He stopped at the Rover long enough to confirm it was ruined. There were gashes torn in the front, and the back left quarter was gone, the destruction ending millimeters from Hassan's boot. Her vitals still showed solid. He unstrapped her with shaking hands.

He dictated a text to Timkul as he pulled Hassan off the flatbed by her arms: *Good shooting. We need to get her back to the camp.*

Timkul nodded, settled the CAWS-5 over Hassan's legs, and lifted her ankles; Meyers turned and adjusted his grip so that he could actually see where he was going, then he headed to camp at the best pace he could manage. His heel was on fire, and his thigh had numbed up. The wounded shoulder and his sore ribs left him weak. He considered switching to his cable grips, but that seemed like it might send a bad signal. His hearing came back to him slowly, every sound distant and muddy, as if he had a pillow pressed against his ears.

McNutt sent a connection request, and Meyers nearly lost his grip on Hassan. He accepted.

"Colonel?" McNutt sounded muffled. His video feed showed what looked like the same room he'd been in before, but now he appeared to be behind some of the stacked cases. Off to his right, Starling leaned against an equipment rack. Her CAWS-5 was propped against the stone wall. She held a bloody can of coagulant spray in a hand that was slick with blood.

"Sergeant McNutt, what happened?"

"We're alive—" Gunfire filled the channel; McNutt's words were lost.

"Say again."

"I said we're alive. I thought you disconnected when the gunfight started."

Meyers thought back. "No. The connection just died."

"Wasn't us, and shouting don't help."

Meyers closed his eyes against the pounding headache and his aching body. "Sorry. Mortar round went off too close. My head's a mess."

"Must be nice. Wouldn't mind a bit more firepower up here. We're pinned in. Starling's got a wicked bleeding wound in the joint between her abdominal and pectoral armor segments. Helluva time trying to get coagulant spray up in there but she's working on it. Repin's brains are scrambled but he can still fire. Wasn't really using them. Just hope he remembers who the bad guys are."

"Is Starling going to be okay?"

"I'm fine, Colonel." Starling waved the coagulant can at him unsteadily.

Meyers grunted. The guilt he'd shaken off when he saw Timkul was unharmed returned. "What about those two proxies?"

"Dead. But they brought friends. Party time at the mountain complex." McNutt's video showed him sneaking a peek around the cases. The door to the room was still open, almost directly opposite McNutt's position. In the small room beyond, two proxies were barely visible. Two more were pressed tight into cover on either side of the door, one of them maybe a meter from Repin, who was pressed tight against the opposite side of the case stack that the nearer proxy was using for cover.

"Banh and Lamh are in the complex. I want to connect them in." Meyers sent a connection request to Banh, who accepted. "Sergeant Banh, Sergeant McNutt's team is in the complex, still alive but they're pinned in, and Starling and Repin are wounded. Can you track their signals?"

"Yes, Colonel," Banh said. His video feed showed a half-closed door, stone walls that were cut into a slowly curving, meter-wide hallway. "We are moving in now."

"Now?" Meyers fought back anger. "I thought you were moving in before."

"Colonel, yes, but we had to wait for the map." Banh didn't sound defensive or upset. His voice said it all: He was just explaining the facts. "While we waited, we found a gun emplacement that could fire on the proxies shooting at Corporal Cho. We eliminated them, and now we have disabled all of the guns."

Meyers blushed. Banh had done the right thing. "I'm sorry, Sergeant. Good work. Can you integrate the map into this connection?"

Banh went silent for several seconds, and then the map became an overlay revealing his position. It was an inexact layout, showing McNutt and his team embedded in solid stone. Banh's BAS slowly corrected the image, updating with data from McNutt's feed.

"There is a corridor ahead," Banh said. He was looking through the half-open door. Another half-open door was visible at the end of a corridor.

Meyers recognized the spot on the map. "That's where McNutt's team took out three proxies. Through that far door, there's a room to the left with combat proxies and the three dead proxies in it. There's a door that opens into another corridor. That's the way to the reactor and the ladder up."

"Yes, I understand, Colonel." Banh hurried down the hall and poked his head out. The floor of the room was dark with blood from the earlier engagement. The other doors were all open. "It is clear."

McNutt traced the route they'd taken to get to where they were. "Shouldn't be much between you and this point right here." He tapped the room full of proxy drivers where they'd ambushed the searching proxy, then he tapped the small room where the others were firing from. "Sort of drew all their attention."

"I think the fact they haven't thrown grenades into that room proves you've found the heart of the complex," Meyers said.

"Yeah, but where's the main driving room?" McNutt's camera tracked along the walls. "Gotta be something somewhere. Thirty humans, driving couches...you don't just hide something like that with an ugly quilt."

Meyers looked the complex's map over. There were plenty of places that could hold a big room, but all of them would have been easily accessed once the facility was breached. The best place to keep vulnerable targets would be where McNutt's squad was: underground, reachable only by a single entry.

"I think you're near." Meyers couldn't see anything else resembling a door or hatch in McNutt's video. "Just hang on. Corporal Starling, how are the bots doing?"

"Replicating," Starling said. There was a trembling to her voice that betrayed the pain she was feeling. "It's slow for some reason. It looks like something's killing them off almost as fast as they generate but I can't see what it is."

"How long?"

"Maybe another five minutes, then they'll launch."

Five minutes. Meyers gritted his teeth. "Get that wound sealed up."

"I think I did, sir. I-I'll take a stim."

"I could use one myself." He scanned the way ahead. He was

following the same course he'd told Timkul to take, hugging the slope. It would be a while but it was the safest bet.

Something dropped from the clouds, a gray shape revealed by blinking running lights. He heard the roar, saw the orange fire tail.

The Lancer aircraft was making a strafing run at the camp.

Suddenly, another shape dropped from the clouds: larger, slower, not as sleek. Nunoz's Dart. The Lancer aircraft broke off and turned but it was too late. Flames bloomed along the back of the fuselage, then expanded out and up, engulfing the entire aircraft. The flames shot out, and the aircraft crumpled, tossing its wings away, and then the whole burning ruin tumbled into the valley like a blazing comet.

Nunoz opened a channel to Meyers; he muted the call to the mountaintop team and accepted. "That's the last of them, Colonel."

Meyers's heart jumped. "How's your bird?"

"I can keep her going for a bit." Nunoz spoke quickly, and his voice was raised.

"See if you can get some strafing runs in. Mind the mortar fire."

"Coming around for that now, sir."

Meyers smiled. Mortars still flew out from the camp, and he could see the muzzle flash of ERF weapons. They weren't out of it yet. They still had a chance. He picked up the pace, and Timkul matched it.

He came off mute. "Sergeant McNutt, Sergeant Banh, don't give up. We've got air superiority again. We've got a chance."

McNutt snorted. "Glad to hear you've turned things around, Colonel, but it's a bit of a mess—"

The connection died again.

Meyers looked up. The mountain loomed overhead, almost sneering at him, unconquered, defiant. He felt its cold heart beating, telling him that he wouldn't escape.

He would never escape.

30

———

2 October 2175. Siberia.

ALL ALONG THE front line of the camp, red forms advanced. They used cover, advancing patiently, maintaining remarkable discipline. Some stopped to lay down fire that kept the small number of ERF soldiers pinned down while the rest advanced. Meyers admired the Lancers' skill. With such superior numbers, they represented a very real threat. If they got in close enough, they could flank the defensive positions, and it would be all over.

He glanced back at Timkul. Despite having her suit's heat turned down, he could see in the video feed that her face was flush, and her hair clung to her forehead. He opened his visor and sucked in the smell of gunpowder hanging on the crisp air. It was a cold slap against his skin, just what he needed to dampen the pounding headache. His arms and back ached, and he imagined hers must, too.

"Priya, open your visor. Cool down."

Her visor flipped up, and she gasped. "How much longer?"

Meyers looked toward the battlefront. "Ten minutes. Can you maintain this pace?"

Timkul continued on in silence, then she shook her head. "I'm sorry."

"Set her down." Meyers squatted and rested Hassan on the snow. "Catch your breath."

He dropped to his butt on the ice, heard it crack beneath his weight. His face quickly grew cold and tight, and he realized his sweat was freezing. He watched the battle with his own eyes for a few more seconds, imagining that he could better appreciate the horrors of it without the suit filtering everything, turning humans into solid red and green images that it wasn't as troublesome to see fall.

Timkul settled at his side, blinking against the wind and shivering. "Are they still advancing?"

"Yes." Meyers guessed there were two platoons in the crawling group. They greatly outnumbered the ERF soldiers. He remembered the patch he'd taken off one of the Lancers and brought up the image in his BAS. The system had identified the patch: a Wolverine. It hit him then, the memory of Terry Lewis and the patrol in Yemen, the Wolverine vehicle that had chewed up an innocent family. Meyers tried to recall what Taylor had said, something about veterans, Rangers who had told her what was going on. Terry Lewis's unit was out there, still alive, probably leading the charge.

APCs advanced from the rear. Their machine guns provided more than enough cover fire to allow the Lancers to move forward as a unit, and they did so by widening out their approach.

Meyers connected to Barlowe. "Ladell. Ladell?"

"Yeah," Ladell wheezed.

"There's a force advancing on the camp. They've got everyone pinned down, and now they're moving to flank."

"Okay. And?"

"They'll cut the front line down. They'll be in the camp." Meyers shook his head at Barlowe's reaction. "They fall, we're all dead."

"There's not much I can do," Barlowe gasped. He sent an image over the connection: they were down to a railgun and the two mortars. "Dart battery's drained."

"Drop a mortar round in the middle of each of those wings of crawling Lancers. Break up the advance." Meyers hated the idea of killing decent soldiers but it was the Lancers or his own people.

"Too dispersed," Barlowe said. "Ineffective."

"What about the APCs providing cover fire?"

"Same problem."

Shit! Meyers connected to Nunoz. "Ensign Nunoz, we've got problems along the front line. There are three APCs providing cover fire for advancing Lancer infantry."

"I understand, Colonel. Master Sergeant Paxton asked me to break up this knot of armor at the back of the valley. They're getting too close to the mortars with their guns."

Meyers closed his visor and scanned the valley. It was flooded with moving red objects. None of them should have been able to get clean shots at the mortars but they were. Losing the mortars would result in the same problem as losing the front line. "All right, do what you can."

Snow crunched as Timkul shifted at his side. "Maybe if we headed back?"

"Sure." Meyers didn't even want to know what Timkul thought they could do.

Almost immediately after lifting Hassan from the snow, Meyers's arms began to shake. Tremors shot through his lower back. He tried to let the sound of gunfire distract him. After several steps, he decided to try to connect to McNutt and Starling again. If Banh was still connected to them, Meyers hoped they might have something positive to update him with. He was surprised to connect with Banh.

"Sergeant Banh?" Meyers almost stopped in his tracks. Banh's video feed was cut through by strange patterns, artifacts Meyers couldn't recall seeing before.

"Colonel? I did not know you were connected."

"I was trying to reconnect to the channel I had to Sergeant McNutt and Private Starling. Are you still connected to them?" Meyers had seen some strange Grid behavior before, but connections still registering to someone not on the channel was worrisome. It would require spoofing an active ID, something that even Barlowe had a hard time pulling off.

"I am still connected, Colonel." Banh's audio became choppy, and the video artifacts became more noticeable.

Meyers scanned the area Banh was moving through. "Close the channel and fall back."

"Colonel?"

"Do it. Now. I'll connect to you direct." Meyers disconnected and opened a new channel to Banh. The video artifacts were gone, and the audio came through clean. Banh was moving backward through a corridor Meyers hadn't seen before. "Sergeant Banh, I need you and Private Lamh to find some cover."

Banh's video showed that he was searching the corridor. There was a darkened doorway a few meters back. He signaled Lamh to move to the doorway and then followed. The video darkened, then brightened again as Banh spun back toward the hallway. "We are in a room, Colonel."

"Stay low." Meyers was so focused on the video feed that Timkul's voice made him jump. "What? I wasn't listening. Could you repeat that?"

"Someone's coming toward us." Timkul sent a pointer to his helmet display. Three of the Lancers had broken off from the nearest group and were now moving toward them in a low crouch.

"Banh, stay sharp." Meyers muted his connection to Banh, then lowered Hassan to the snow and dropped flat. Timkul crawled up next to him. "Hold here." He crab-crawled to their left until he was sure they couldn't be taken out by a single grenade. He smiled at the realization that Timkul had the CAWS-5 up and was sighting in on the advancing Lancers.

"I've got the one on the right," she said.

He brought the assault rifle up and targeted the Lancer on the left. The Lancers slowed and seemed ready to drop. "They see we're targeting them. Take them down."

Timkul fired a second before he did; her target staggered and dropped. Meyers fired, but his target had already dropped prone. The Lancers returned fire. Their bullets cracked against the ice. Meyers cursed how reliant he'd become on the BAS for something as simple as targeting. He took a calming breath, targeted the shoulder and chest of the Lancer he'd fired at before, and squeezed the trigger. The Lancer slumped.

"Keep that last one down," Meyers called to Timkul.

He edged to his left another couple meters, then got to his feet and charged forward. The Lancer realized what was happening, but there was no way to get a shot off without risking getting hit by Timkul. As Meyers brought the assault rifle up, the Lancer took the risk and raised up to fire at Meyers.

Meyers heard the familiar bark of the CAWS-5, and the Lancer slumped. Meyers crossed the last few meters and kicked the assault rifle from the Lancer's hands. The Lancer moved slowly; Meyers kicked the Lancer in the head until the movement stopped. A quick search of the bodies produced three more magazines and several grenades. Meyers checked for vitals. As far as he could tell, two were still alive.

Movement in the corner of the display grabbed his attention. It was Banh's video feed. Meyers un-muted the channel. "Sergeant—"

"I see them, Colonel," Banh whispered. "Three proxies. They are searching."

"They have a systems expert. A good one. Good enough to spoof active IDs." Meyers jogged back to Timkul. "I think that's how they keep breaking my connection to McNutt and Starling."

"So they know we are inside the complex, Private Lamh and me?"

"Looks like it. I think they were hacking your BAS through McNutt's connection." Meyers tossed the assault rifle over his shoulder and squatted to pick up Hassan. The adrenaline that had gotten him through the firefight was fading. His arms and legs shook and felt weak. He had to wait for dizziness to pass before lifting. He heard gunfire, and it took a second to realize it was coming over the connection. Banh crept from the room and checked the downed proxies. One shifted, and Banh fired into it point blank.

"Three down, Colonel." Banh waved Lamh from cover.

Meyers blew out a breath and straightened. "There could be more. Let me see if I can reach Starling." He sent a connection request to Starling, saw her accept it, and killed the connection. He tried again; she accepted. "Private Starling?"

"Colonel? Why'd you kill the connection, sir?" Starling's voice was raised over gunfire.

"I wanted to be sure it was really you," Meyers said, his voice raised as well. "I just told Banh I believe they've got a systems expert. I think you're being hacked. It looks like McNutt's ID's been spoofed."

Starling sighed. "So that's why. He can't get his comms to work anymore, sir. We thought it was the round his armor took."

"I don't think so. Banh was still on the connection we had earlier, and when I reconnected, that connection showed McNutt's ID. There was something going on, and my guess is it was an attack on Banh's BAS. The proxies were waiting for him."

"What do we do, sir?"

"Hold on. That's all we can do. How are the bots doing?"

"Just launched them a second ago. You think this systems expert is what's destroying them?"

"Makes sense." A systems expert attacking the BAS actually made a lot of sense. It could be what was behind the problems they had encountered so far, including everything the saboteurs had managed to do. "How long for the bots to get in?"

"They..." Starling's voice trailed off. "They've got elevated privileges now, sir. They're scraping the system. I should have access to all the major sub-systems soon."

Bullets cracked nearby, and Starling leaned out to return fire.

"If you see anything like a command and control system, flood it with bad data, shut it down. Do whatever you can do. We've got Lancers thirty meters out from the front line and closing." Meyers slowed to catch his breath. He glanced back at Timkul, but she didn't seem to have any problems with the new pace.

"I've got access to the complex infrastructure interface so far. Hm."

"What?"

"Well, Colonel, unless we walked past it on our way down here, there's no driver room." Starling's voice had a distracted, almost floating quality to it. "And there's..."

"Yes? Private Starling?"

"There's another room in here, sir," Starling said. "Maybe a storage area. Like a vault. Right beneath me."

"Vault? How big are we talking?" Meyers couldn't think of anything more valuable than the human drivers, and it didn't sound like Starling was talking about a full room.

"Three meters on all sides, maybe a little less. Not big, sir. But I don't see a hatch or panel or—" Starling gasped. "There. Right beneath this tarp. Looks like a hidden hatch. No physical knobs or handles, either."

"Can you switch the bots to attack the security for it?"

"Yes, sir." Starling's video captured a barely visible crease in the floor just beneath her boots. "It's failing. Shouldn't be long."

Meyers brought Banh into the connection. "Sergeant Banh, how are you doing?"

Banh's video feed showed the room full of reclining proxies. The dead proxy soldier was sprawled on the floor, face down in dark blood. "Colonel, we are just down the hall from the room where the proxies are. The proxies in here, they are asleep still. Are they drivers?"

"No. We don't know what they are." Meyers would worry about the improbability of proxies driving proxies later. He marked the room where McNutt's team had discovered the way down. "The enemy is spread around in here and some of them are down below. Can you clear that room?"

"We have grenades, Colonel." Banh poked his head out the doorway, revealing the open door at the end of the hall.

Meyers smiled. "Don't be afraid to use them."

Gunfire erupted, and Banh pulled back into the driver room. "They know we are here, Colonel."

"Okay. Keep them occupied but be ready with those grenades." Meyers sighed. If it were McNutt, the right call would be to toss the grenades down the hall and charge. Banh didn't handle fast-moving situations as well.

"Colonel?" Starling's voice was raised in excitement. "I've got that command and control system you were looking for."

Meyers turned his attention to Starling's video feed. She was looking at an interface not too different from the one he was familiar with. After running a finger over the options, she tapped at a button labeled Objectives. The valley opened up in front of her: APCs, infantry...even the downed aircraft were still accounted for. Starling selected the units along the front line and dragged them back to the APCs. When a command override warning popped up, she accepted it.

Meyers scanned the front line. The red forms had stopped moving. He picked up the pace again. "They stopped advancing. Keep it up. Confused and slowed is better than moving forward."

A white light flashed on his display. It was Barlowe, texting again. The message read: *Robotic kill devices moving into our area in front of more soldiers. Can't crack their security. Imagery systems won't last long. We've cut signals to a minimum.*

"Okay, Private Starling, new objective." Meyers scanned the interface. "See if you can find robotic drones. North canyon wall, west of camp. They've sent something after Barlowe's imagery group. Sounds like they're close, too."

"I-I..." Starling's voice shook. "There's nothing about drones, sir."

"All right, flood their network with noise. Do something. We can't lose that team."

Paxton sent a connection request. Meyers accepted and created a joint channel. "Master Sergeant Paxton, we've got Private Starling on with us and Miss Timkul is listening in as well. Agent Barlowe just reported more infantry moving on his position, backed up by some sort of drones. He called them 'kill devices.'"

"Kill devices, Colonel?" Starling sounded less uncertain. "Hold on." She swiped through the interface, and a second later, the canyon wall where Barlowe and Gerhardt were hidden came into view. "Not drones, sir. Simple robotic devices modified to deliver explosive and electronic payloads. They must be getting desperate. I see them now." She brought up other interfaces—

several individual ones—and began running through them. "I'll have them detonate—"

The interface blanked out.

Meyers leaned forward. "Private Starling, what happened?"

Starling was back at a basic front end. "My privileges. They're all gone. Most…" She swiped and tapped at something he couldn't see. "Most of my bots are gone."

"Colonel, if I could have a moment?" Paxton sounded irritated.

"Go ahead." Meyers couldn't take his eyes from Starling's interface. *How could bots overwhelm a system and then get obliterated? What kind of expert could act so fast?*

"I just want you to know we've repelled the Lancers. They're falling back. We're concentrating everything we can on the rear ranks at the moment, trying to break up their supporting fire if they come again." Paxton's voice became stronger with each word.

"That's excellent." Meyers could at least find some comfort in that. "We'll be back in camp in a few more minutes. Ensign Hassan is alive but unconscious."

Paxton coughed. "I'll have some folks out to you shortly, sir."

"We're good. Protect the camp." Meyers shifted his grip on Hassan. "Private Starling, how long to spawn more bots?"

"A few minutes, sir. Maybe less. I just don't—"

"It's that systems expert."

Starling shifted back suddenly; the panel in the floor beneath her opened. The room below glowed from a few strips of light. Meyers could see racks of equipment—redundant gear, mostly—and more rack components leaning against the wall, unassembled. But what caught his eyes was what was attached to the rails of the racks.

"Private Starling, is that what it looks like?"

"I think so, Colonel." Starling blew out a breath, long and slow. "I'm guessing that's around two hundred kilos of explosives, and I think it's primed to blow."

31

2 October 2175. Siberia.

Snow popped with each booted step Meyers took. He watched the darkness, certain there were still Lancers out in the valley that could hide from the BAS and Barlowe's systems wizardry. As weak as Meyers felt, he wouldn't be able to stop a determined attacker. He scolded himself that even living through the debacle took away any rights he had to complain. Timkul was behind him, Hassan was breathing, and they'd bought a respite for the ERF. Gratitude was all he should feel.

Hassan's armor slipped in his grip, and he nearly lost her.

He threw a hasty "Sorry!" over his shoulder to Timkul, then he realized she was probably still sealed against the freezing night air like him, simultaneously sweating and shivering. He popped his visor and inhaled. His teeth ached from the cold, but it gripped him and reminded him he was still alive. Tears and sweat almost immediately started to freeze, raining fine, salty flakes on his cracked lips. He sealed his visor and pulled more energy from deep inside.

Starling's video feed shifted on Meyers's visor display. McNutt leaned out from cover, fired, and pulled back. Starling fired a short burst as well, then she said, "Colonel, I think they know we got into this vault. They've become more aggressive."

Meyers considered the explosives in the room below Starling, easily enough to destroy the room and the one Starling was in. Probably enough to take out the room above and the corridor beyond. "Maybe they want to disarm the bomb."

"Maybe, sir. I know I do. The bots are doing what they can. We need more time."

It seemed to Meyers that they were always up against time. "Most of that gear looks pretty standard. Why bother to blast it into dust?"

Starling looked down into the room. "Sensitive data, sir?"

"You could destroy everything in both rooms with a third as much explosive."

Her camera drilled down on one of the shelves. A thicker systems module was secured there. Chrome, shiny, but...different. "That's not a normal systems module, Colonel."

"I'll take your word for it. Different enough to warrant all the explosives?"

"Only one way to find out, sir."

Meyers nodded. "If those bots stop that detonator—"

"I'll get them after that module, sir. And if they don't, I guess we'll never know what it was."

"I trust you, Private. We all do."

Starling's camera feed shifted again, and Meyers knew she was looking away, blushing.

"I'll check back in," he said.

"Yes, sir." Starling suspended the connection.

The guilt returned, gnawing at his guts. Starling should have been with Barlowe, not up on the mountain. It was another of the many pointless, bad decisions made from the start. Meyers slumped and felt the energy he'd dug so hard for slipping away. He told himself that Starling being up on the mountaintop had saved lives, and maybe it had.

"We seem really close," Timkul said. Her breath was short and choppy.

Meyers straightened and scanned the defensive positions then looked west, into the valley. "A couple more minutes." There was still so much red out there and so little green ahead.

He dictated a message to Barlowe: *Starling found something in the bunker complex up on the mountaintop. We're nearly back to camp. The defensive positions held. We have a little mortar ammunition left. It's going to be down to our railgun soon. Your imagery and systems feeds saved our lives. How are you doing?*

Eight strides later, Barlowe finally replied: *Kill bots detonated early. Defective. Thought it would save our lives.*

Meyers felt a surge of relief. Starling had gotten the command through after all.

Another text came from Barlowe: *Infantry still here. I got caught in part of a blast, covered by last pieces of shack. I can see Lancers. Crawling right by. Heading for Gerhardt and the others.*

Meyers replied: *How many?* He wanted to look to the north where Barlowe and the others were hiding, even though there was no way to change the situation. If the Lancers were moving around Barlowe, no ERF weapon was selective enough to help.

Barlowe replied: *Twelve, I think. Hard to be sure. These guys are wearing advanced cham suits. Moving so slow, almost invisible.*

Meyers shook his head. *Advanced cham suits.* Chameleons. Better than what his people had. The ERF was supposed to have the best gear.

He texted: *Gerhardt's plan?*

Barlowe sent the image of a red light. *No signal footprint. Power conservation. No idea they're here.*

Meyers blinked. His own suit was below five percent power, and he was burning through the reserves with his constant communications. Even if he wanted to stay hidden from the enemy, he couldn't see shutting down communications. He replied: *Flare? Gunshot? Throw a rock? You need to let him know.*

Why? Barlowe didn't send exclamation points but they sure seemed implied. *They don't know I'm here, Lonny. I can survive this. The imaging system can survive.*

Meyers broke the connection off from Timkul; she didn't need to see what was going on. *Those soldiers saved your life, Ladell.*

And I'm not throwing it away. I respect what they did. I owe it to them to survive.

Meyers was thankful that the text didn't capture the anger in his voice as he dictated: *Then do the right thing. Shoot one of these Lancers, throw a grenade. Whatever it takes. Let Gerhardt and the others know.*

They're nearly past me. Be up to the boulders with Gerhardt in minutes.

Meyers shook with impotent rage. He tried connecting to Gerhardt and the others; they were offline, like Barlowe had said. *Goddammit, Ladell! You used to be a Commando! Find the strength to do something!*

Meyers's earpiece chimed; it was Banh, requesting another connection. Meyers signaled a priority hold, and almost immediately saw a white flash on his display.

Banh had sent a text. Meyers opened it. *Colonel, Corporal Cho has problems.*

"Dammit!" Meyers saw two green forms step from behind cover and run toward him. He set Hassan down, reconnected to Timkul, and then accepted Banh's connection. "What is it, Sergeant?"

"Sorry for troubling you, Colonel, but it is the Grid here," Banh said. He was peeking around the corner at the room the proxies held, the only thing separating him and Lamh from McNutt, Starling, and Repin. "They have done something, Colonel. We are no longer receiving power."

Meyers groaned as he jogged past the defense works. The proxies' systems expert had found that little background process and shut it down. "Can you still function?"

"Oh, yes, Colonel. The problem is at Three-Zero-Eight. The Dart. Corporal Cho says without the power, there will be complications for Chief Pivovarova and Commander Cooper. It will not take long before they die."

"Can you get to that room? Can you hook up with McNutt's team?"

Gunfire roared in the hallway, and bullets cracked against the doorframe. Banh must have seen something, because he pulled back just in time. "We can charge the room, Colonel. Will that restore the power transfer?"

"Not directly." Meyers tried to recall if there were someplace ideal in the complex for a systems expert to hack from. "Okay, hold up. Change of plans."

"Yes, Colonel?"

"There are other rooms off that hallway. They weren't all checked."

"You want us to check the rooms, Colonel?"

"Someone's fighting everything Private Starling is doing. They've managed to wipe out most of her bots, and that was *after* she got into security." Meyers listened for a reaction but Banh said nothing. The enormity of the situation wasn't sinking in. He's not a techie, Meyers reminded himself. "That's who shut off the power feed. Find that systems expert, shut him or her down, and Private Starling should be able to restore the power feed."

"Oh, yes, okay." The camera went up and down as Banh's head bobbed. "Thank you, Colonel."

"This expert could be in that room at the end of the hall," Meyers said. "You may still need to charge it."

Banh held up a flash-bang. "We will save grenades for that."

"No unnecessary risks, Sergeant."

"Of course, Colonel."

Meyers connected to Cho.

Immediately, Cho's face filled the connection display. His eyes were wide, and everything about him was animated. "Colonel, things are going to shit—"

"I heard, Corporal. What about sharing power among the wounded?"

"I've set them up as a single battery pool, sir. But they're still burning through it too fast." Cho flipped his feed to his external camera. He was leaning over Cooper, who was wrapped in an insulation blanket. His helmet had been placed back on his head and was wired into the blanket. "Commander Cooper's the worst for long-term. Infection is becoming a real risk." He moved to Pivovarova and seemed to freeze. The light armor covering her torso was almost black from blood, which seemed to originate from a gash in her abdomen. "I think the chief's got a nicked blood vessel. I mean, she's losing blood—"

Meyers lowered his head. "Do what you can for them, Corporal. We're trying to get power back on."

"I am, sir." Cho stiffened, and Meyers realized what was happening even before Cho said, "They're flatlining, Colonel!"

"I'll leave you to it." Meyers disconnected and reconnected to Starling. She was already talking to someone. Repin, Meyers realized. "Private Starling?"

"Colonel!" Starling was speaking fast, and her voice was raised. Her video feed included Repin's, providing more detail of the room. "Pyotr was just telling me what he saw, what these guys are doing. There's four in the room with us now, two more in the ladder room. I think they're getting ready to rush us."

"They charged in, you see?" Repin's voice was more even than Meyers could recall. "But now they are packed in very tight. Like sardines, yes? Is perfect for grenade."

"I can't get a shot on any of them," Starling said. "I don't think John can, either. Sergeant McNutt, I mean. Sorry, sir."

Meyers had almost missed the way she had referred to McNutt and Repin by their first names. It was becoming a pattern. He stored that away. "Can you get a grenade out? Sounds like if you put one in the right spot, you could take them all down."

"It'd be a blind throw, sir." Uncertainty replaced the excitement in Starling's voice.

"Is one of the few things I was good at," Repin said. "Shooting, not so good. Throwing? My father, he was always, 'Pyotr, you should be throwing. Is something even you can do.' And it is! But there is no way to throw, not with so many."

"All right. Sit tight. I just wanted to let you know that they've shut off the power transfer you had set up to the Dart, Private Starling. Commander Cooper and Chief Pivovarova are flatlining without the power."

Repin said, "Irina? No, no, Colonel! Flatlining? How—"

"Her injuries." Meyers tried to impose some calm. "Without the power to keep her stabilized—"

"No." Repin choked up; the video feed shifted wildly as he shook his head. "Irina is light, you understand, Colonel? From heaven! She cannot go out! Is all I have!"

"Corporal Cho is doing what he can." Meyers felt the same frustration he heard in Repin's voice.

"Colonel, I have to go, to help!"

"You're already doing what you—" Meyers felt a chill in his gut. Repin's video feed was now just him staring at his hand, which held a flash-bang grenade. "Private Repin, what do you think—"

"They will charge and kill us all, Colonel. And Irina will die." Repin hooked his thumb through the grenade's pin.

"No, Pyotr!" Starling shouted. She looked at McNutt, who was curled beneath a carrying case that was so shot up, it seemed ready to collapse in on itself. "The bots are in! I can shut this place down!"

Pyotr shook his head. "She is too precious, my Irina."

He pulled the pin and leapt from cover. Almost immediately, the proxies turned on him and opened fire, but the flash-bang was already in the air. At such close range, the bullets pierced the soft spots in his armor. He fell back, blood spurting from numerous wounds.

But his camera tracked the flash-bang as he fell; it hit almost dead center of the group of proxies.

The audio flooded Starling's connection but Meyers didn't need to hear. What he saw was enough: Starling rose from cover and opened fire on the stunned proxies, and a second later, McNutt did the same. They both ran forward and sprayed bursts into anyone that still seemed functional, then they continued until the proxies were utterly destroyed. The last bit of gunfire came over the channel.

As McNutt reloaded and kicked the proxies' guns away, Starling ran over to Repin. Blood gushed from his armor and spread across the floor. She popped the panel on his shoulder to check his vitals; Meyers already knew what she would see.

He cleared his throat. "Private Starling?"

"Yes, sir?"

"I'm sorry to have to ask—"

"The bots are in, Colonel. I'm setting up the power transfer now." She glanced back at McNutt.

"Got my ID back." The corner of McNutt's mouth ticked up but his voice sounded raw. "That's something."

Starling walked back toward the underground room with the mysterious system module. "Give me a minute. I want to get these explosives, leave a little present for them before we go."

"Yeah, sure." McNutt had his gun trained on the ladder. "Clear for now."

Meyers waited a moment, then said, "Sergeant McNutt, see if you can connect with Sergeant Banh, let him know your status. He'll need to help clear your exit."

"Connecting now, Colonel."

Meyers connected back to Cho. "Corporal, you should have that power feed."

"Got it, sir. The commander's stabilizing. I'm still working on the chief." Cho's video was disturbing. He was doing compressions. That could only mean more conventional methods hadn't worked.

Meyers disconnected and sent a channel request to Nunoz, who immediately accepted. "Ensign Nunoz, the mountaintop gun emplacements are down, and we have two wounded in bad condition. Can you get up to the mountaintop and let Corporal Cho transfer them to Zero-Eight-Nine?"

"You want me up on the mountaintop, Colonel?" Nunoz's voice hinted at challenge. "What about my support down here, sir?"

"I—" Meyers's suit flashed a warning that he was at one percent power remaining. "Carry on, Ensign. I'm sorry."

Meyers changed course and came to a stop outside the ruins of the infirmary. Broken bodies were piled around the structure's foundation. He saw the infiltrator, still tied to what remained of the support strut. Without armor, her death had probably been inevitable once the defensive positions fell. He squatted next to the nearest ERF corpse and began the ghoulish process of searching for battery power to transfer. As his suit probed those of the dead, he thought back to Barlowe's situation. Once again, a matter of self-sacrifice had come up, and Meyers marveled at how easily he had seen himself accepting that fate.

The red of his suit's battery alarm brightened slightly as it crept past three percent and headed toward four. Timkul settled onto the snow next to him. Her face was strained, and for the first time, he saw how red and puffy her eyes were.

"Your battery must be low." He waved a hand above the corpses. "Your suit can search for battery power and transfer it."

Timkul winced, but she seemed to turn her attention to her BAS.

Meyers felt sick for a second. It was the sort of empathy that was dangerous on the battlefield. It left him vulnerable to dangerous feelings. "I know that sounds terrible, but it's just one of the ways we use the dead to keep the living going."

She shook her head. "How do you live like this? Irina, Pyotr, all these..."

"What's the alternative?"

Tears ran down her face. "To turn your back on war."

Meyers wasn't sure how to react to her words. He felt slightly insulted by the possibility she thought war would go away if the ERF went away, but he also thought she might have been talking about humanity in general. He tossed those two possibilities around for a bit, then decided it would be best to assume nothing. "I think most of us would prefer peace, but there's a real problem with that."

Timkul placed a hand on the chest of one of the corpses. The armor was punctured and gory with frozen blood. "What sort of problem would there be with wanting peace?" Her voice was soft and distant, as if her mind were far away.

"*Everyone* has to want peace, or no one can really have it." Meyers checked his suit's battery. It was sitting at twelve percent full. That was going to have to do.

He stood and turned back toward the defense works, then he connected to Paxton. "Master Sergeant, we're back in the camp."

"On my way to your position, Colonel."

Meyers chuckled. He knew better than to assume he was a step ahead. "What's your plan?"

"Depends on the Lancers' next move." Paxton came around the corner of the infirmary foundation and stopped. He seemed wobbly until he spread his legs a little wider. "A few recharging stations are still available, sir."

Meyers offered Timkul a hand. "Lead the way."

They followed Paxton back toward the Systems Shack. Meyers appreciated the slower pace Paxton had forced on them. After the long walk carrying Hassan and squatting to transfer power, Meyers's legs were shaky, and his back spasms seemed on the verge of returning. His shoulder and torso were already stiffening now that he'd gone several minutes without carrying anything.

"Figure they've got us outnumbered pretty significantly still," Paxton said. "Sounds like Ensign Nunoz can at least keep them from massing."

Meyers wondered if Nunoz had passed along the near-redirect to the mountaintop. "We have a shot breaking them."

Paxton stopped and turned. "Your mountaintop?" He shook his head.

"Somewhere in the vicinity of thirty proxies, including six combat chassis. There's something important up there. Starling found explosives in a sealed chamber. Enough to crack that place in half."

"This is what matters, Colonel." Paxton jabbed a finger at the ground. "We lose this, we lose everything."

"I know." Meyers rubbed at the blood coating his armor.

Paxton took a step closer. "They're backed up in the middle of the valley, sir. The *Valdez* could wipe them out and we'd be safe."

Not Barlowe and Gerhardt's squad, Meyers thought. "We can break them without that."

Paxton spun on his heel, sharp as a drill sergeant despite his injuries, and led them to the Systems Shack. He pointed to a device resting in the corner straight back from where the flap had been. "Should be enough to get you to half. Maybe more. If you think you'll need it, sir." He sighed softly, then trudged toward the TOC.

Meyers clenched and relaxed his hands. There were a lot of relationships to repair, if he lived long enough.

32

2 October 2175. Siberia.

MEYERS KNELT in the ruins of the Systems Shack. Snow had collected on the floor and hardened so that it scraped like fine glass particles when he moved. Wind shook the fabric and slammed the flimsy materials into the ground. Without power, the structures were fragile, their integrity unreliable. Too little remained of the interior to fill in the gaps in Meyers's memory. How many displays had been on the wall? Who had been working? What had they discovered before the infiltrators' devices had destroyed the gear stacked inside? Everything was a charred, shredded mess.

Like the mission.

He stared down at the recharging device, lost in thought. Toward the end of the first minute of waiting for the armor's batteries to hit the halfway mark, the shakes settled in, forcing him to bump his suit's heating up two degrees. Timkul had it worse, teeth chattering and lips quivering visibly on his display.

"Turn your environment setting up," he said. "Two, three degrees. We've got power."

Her eyes darted around as she worked through the BAS interface. "What happened with Agent Barlowe? You disconnected me from the piggyback."

Meyers tried to hide his anger. "I guess I need to check." But he didn't want to know. He couldn't believe Barlowe would let others die to save his own life. He had certainly sounded like he would.

Meyers sent a connection request. When Barlowe didn't answer at first, Meyers wondered if Barlowe might have found the courage to stand up and fight after all.

Then Barlowe accepted. His video feed was on, an overlay showing that his suit's battery was at three percent. He wasn't buried beneath a ruined shack. Instead, he seemed to be crawling up a snowy slope toward distant boulders. It took Meyers a second to realize there was something moving just ahead of Barlowe's camera: another human form, crawling, leaving only the slightest impression on the hard-packed snow. Meyers could barely hear the sound of the icy snow cracking over Barlowe's breathing.

Barlowe stopped moving and brought a CAWS-5 up. "Fuck you, Lonny," he gasped. "For guilting me into this."

He sighted on the crawling form and fired.

The gun cracked, loud as a thunderclap. Barlowe's overlay showed the switch to burst fire, and then he changed targets, firing at a form that became more visible when it twisted back suddenly. The form twitched and fell back. Barlowe pulled a pin on a grenade and lobbed it up the slope. Even before the detonation, he was rolling down the slope, screaming and cursing. Gunfire boomed from above, and bullets whacked all around, ricocheting off rock and shattering ice.

And then the grenade exploded—a softer blast than Meyers had expected—and Barlowe came to a stop.

He looked back upslope.

The chameleon suits were still working but not as well. Sections flickered into view, and the overall effect was more like what Meyers would expect from typical commercially available gear. The Lancers continued firing down at Barlowe.

More gunfire joined theirs.

Barlowe stayed pressed low, but his helmet camera caught the engagement. Gerhardt's squad and the soldiers McNutt had left behind took advantage of cover and their own form of chameleon suits: the lack of signal. They were revealed by muzzle flash, but they didn't show up as even green outlines.

The Lancers broke, the survivors dispersing and running downhill. A few disappeared, almost certainly using what remained of their chameleon suits and mundane training to hide. The rest, though...

Meyers disconnected. The situation made it hard to surrender. They had been seconds away from sneaking up and killing people unawares.

"Thank you," Timkul said. She was shivering still, but he wasn't so sure it was from the cold. She rubbed her arms with her gloves, which scraped against the armor; she stopped, probably realizing how futile it was. She looked up at Meyers suddenly. "What did he mean about you guilting him?"

"He wanted to take the easy way out." Meyers shrugged. "He's a former Commando. I told him to get in close."

Timkul cocked an eyebrow and hugged herself. "Agent Barlowe's a strange man."

Meyers's suit registered halfway charged. "What Ladell did there saved our imagery feed. It could be the difference between victory and failure." He killed the transfer and headed for the TOC; Timkul fell in next to him.

"You think they'll make another assault on the camp?"

He looked out into the valley. It was too dark to see anything but the red forms were there, so distant they were clumps. "They have to. It's what they were paid to do."

"All this killing!" She groaned and shook herself, then she bumped into him and she threw her arms out for balance. "Sorry. I'm just... I can't understand how they could continue on. Or how we can, I guess. I mean, I know it's life or death for us but they could stop, just walk away."

Meyers started to respond. It didn't seem possible Timkul still couldn't understand the desperation of the Lancers' situation. He let it go. "I need to check on the—" He stopped and looked toward the mountaintop. A sardonic smile drew up the corners of his mouth. "My white whale."

He connected to Cho first. "Corporal, any updates?"

Cho's video feed moved forward and back over Pivovarova. "Everyone's stable again, Colonel, even the chief and the commander."

Meyers blew out slow and long. "Good to hear. We're close."

"Sergeant Banh said they've got the proxies boxed in and are about to hit the room." Cho stopped rocking and headed back to the airlock. His feed showed distant green dots in the darkness. "I wish I could help them."

"You're doing important work, Corporal." Meyers disconnected and opened a channel with Banh. McNutt and Starling were already connected. "Sergeant Banh, Sergeant McNutt, Corporal Cho said you're getting ready to hit that room with the proxies in it."

"Yeah, Colonel." McNutt snorted and held up a finger-sized brick of the explosives from the vault. There was a detonator attached. The spider-bot was latched to the detonator. "Private Starling's got a little improvised housewarming gift."

"We will wait for the signal, Colonel, then we will throw flash-bangs into the room and charge." Banh held up a flash-bang for Meyers to see.

"What's the holdup?" Meyers asked.

"She's setting a couple charges down here." McNutt turned, quickly looking past Repin's corpse and stopping where Starling knelt in front of the rack of system processors. "Wants to take this place apart thoroughly, Colonel."

Meyers felt the same hatred for the mountaintop complex, but they needed to know who was behind the operation. Only evidence could compensate for all the death. "Private Starling, I'd like to be able to go through their systems when everything's decided here."

Starling tapped the ADPAX strapped to the back of her glove. "Bots are still pulling it down, Colonel, but it shouldn't be long. It's mostly the compression that takes time." She looked at McNutt and said, "We'll need to really discuss everything when I'm done, Colonel."

The words sounded odd coming from Starling, but there was something even odder in her voice. She sounded stressed or anxious, and not from her shyness.

"Of course." Meyers took in the room through the feed. The proxies had fought desperately for whatever secrets were hidden there. He hoped that meant it really was as important as he thought.

Starling joined McNutt at the base of the ladder and took the explosives from him. She pulled the spider-bot from the detonator and sent the little thing skittering up the ladder. She looked up, head cocked in such a way that Meyers knew she was watching the spider-bot's video feed. Suddenly, that feed was laid over her own, showing the room above. The proxies were frozen, like statues, waiting.

She sent the spider-bot to cover and said, "Sergeant Banh, are you ready?"

"We are." Banh shifted his grip on the flash-bang grenade.

Starling glanced at McNutt, who nodded, then she slowly climbed the ladder. She held the explosives in her right hand, arm extended away from her body, as if that small distance might matter should it detonate. Below her, McNutt trained his weapon on the opening overhead. The proxies didn't move in the spider-bot's camera, seemingly fixated on the door to the hallway, where Banh and Lamh would come from. When Starling was half a meter below the opening, she sent the spider-bot into the corner farthest from the clumped proxies.

"Ready to throw the explosive charge," she said.

Banh triggered his flash-bang and tossed it into the hall. "Flash-bangs away!"

The grenades skidded down the hallway with a raspy clatter then detonated with a deafening boom. Starling counted to three before lobbing the explosives through the hole. From cover, the spider-bot's video only caught the feet of the back row of proxies. Those feet disappeared in the explosion, which shook the room with a deafening crack. The spider-bot was tossed into the air. It scrambled to find something to cling to, but everything seemed to collapse around it. Chunks of rock bounced off the walls and floor, and streamers of dust whipped up to the ceiling. The spider-bot plunged back to the ground, and its video feed died.

Banh ran forward, weapon raised, stopping at the edge of the dust cloud rolling out from the doorway. Behind him, Lamh kept his CAWS-5 trained on the room full of reclining proxies. Neither room showed red symbols. "I cannot see but I think they are down."

Meyers couldn't see anything through Banh or Starling's camera feed. "Give it a few seconds to settle, then proceed. I'm keeping this feed open but I'll be on mute."

He hurried toward the TOC, aware of Timkul watching him the whole time but not reacting.

"Was that it?" she finally asked. "That last clump, just squatting there?"

He felt the same way. It didn't *seem* right. "I know."

They stepped into the TOC, or what remained of it. Paxton sat on a cargo case that had suffered just a few tears and cracks. He twisted as they walked through what had been the entryway, then he went back to staring at whatever had his attention before.

"Twenty-one able soldiers," Paxton got to his feet and said. "Twelve HE rounds for the mortars, about four hundred rounds for the railgun, and we'll run out of power before we get that off. Ensign Nunoz puts their numbers at about three hundred, plus fifteen functional APCs and six that can still be a threat."

Meyers dug through the cracked displays that had lined the wall. They were down to the equipment he'd configured at the uplink and what Barlowe had set up in the valley. It was enough to keep a crude BAS network together but that seemed underpowered, even if the defensive barriers held.

"Maybe they don't attack." Meyers tossed a piece of display to the ground. His head throbbed, and his body felt ready to just stop. "I need a stim."

Paxton dug a stim out of a pouch as he shuffled up to Meyers. "We can't take another assault."

Meyers washed the stim down with a swig of water. "We might have cleared that mountaintop complex."

Paxton turned to consider the valley. "Why wait to find out, Colonel?"

"I told you."

Paxton opened his visor and snorted. "You can't make this about proving everyone wrong, sir."

Meyers blushed.

Timkul's visor popped open. "Carl, they caught the last of the proxies in a room." She pointed toward the mountaintop. "There's nothing left of them."

"And there's damn near nothing left of us. Ma'am." Paxton turned to them. His face was battered, bruised, and just plain worn out. His eyes were bloodshot and swollen, and his skin was purple. His cheeks twitched.

Meyers stepped between the two of them. "What if they're ready to surrender?"

"They don't deserve the chance!" Paxton's jaw trembled.

"They're Lancers, Carl. Except for a few lucky breaks, they're us. You take away our opportunity with the ERF, and we're out there, taking orders from whoever pays." Meyers lowered his head. "I can't just order their execution."

Paxton glared for a heartbeat. "If you'll excuse me, Colonel, I need to check on my wounded." He sealed his visor and pushed past Meyers, quickly fading from sight in the darkness.

Timkul settled on the abandoned seat. "He's certainly passionate."

"I'd be disappointed if he wasn't."

Meyers turned his attention to the feed from the mountaintop complex. Banh was in the room where the proxies had made their final stand. The small brick of explosives had wrecked the place. Sections of wall and ceiling had been blown loose, and those now mercifully provided some concealment for proxy body parts. None of them were a threat anymore.

Starling was placing a larger brick of explosives on the wall that faced out into the hallway. Behind her, McNutt slowly climbed out of the hole to the lower room, holding Repin's corpse in a fireman's carry. McNutt gently set the corpse on the floor and climbed the rest of the way out.

Something began to gnaw at the back of Meyers's mind. He came off mute. "Sergeant Banh, when did those proxies on the beds go offline?"

Banh straightened. "I do not recall, Colonel." He spun around and slowly made his way from the room, carefully leaping from one stable spot to another. Once clear of the mess, he jogged to Lamh's position and squeezed past.

The room looked the same as before, with the dead proxy on the floor and the other proxies in quiet repose, but there was no red signal coming off them, no transmissions.

Banh set a hand on one of the bodies and shook it. "They are inactive, Colonel."

Meyers clasped his hands in front of his abdomen and began distractedly rolling one thumb over the other. "But what were they driving before? Private Starling?"

Starling paused in her placement of explosives. "Yes, sir?"

"Were there any other rooms on the map you saw? Any other oddities that could have been a room?" Meyers tried to recall the map. "Strange spaces? Anything?"

"Just the couple rooms we didn't check in this hallway, sir." Starling looked back at McNutt, who nodded. "Everything else checked out like you'd expect: a kitchen, a day room, an armory..." She paused and cocked her head. "No human bodies, though."

McNutt walked past her, bowing beneath the weight of Repin's corpse and all they'd suffered. "What say let's play sleuth once we're back on the *Valdez*—" He came to an abrupt halt as the hall lights went out, plunging everything into darkness. The red lights from Starling's activated detonators glowed like warning beacons.

Helmet lamps came to life, and narrow beams of light crisscrossed in the hallway.

"Think they took out the reactor?" McNutt's voice was a whisper.

"I think I want you four out of there," Meyers said. "Now."

Something heavy scraped and whirred at the far end of the hallway, and dull, sapphire lights reflected off the walls. A clattering, scratching sound echoed somewhere in the distance, and then strange, twisted shadows became visible.

Meyers gritted his teeth. Something was blocking the team's only exit.

33

───────

2 October 2175. Siberia.

MEYERS SHIFTED to get a better look at the blue light source, forgetting for just a heartbeat that he was seeing the BAS feed from the mountaintop team. He blew out a tense breath, tasted the bitterness of the stim still present in his foul-smelling saliva.

"Lamps and lights off; spread out," McNutt muttered.

The ERF team's headlamps powered down. The only light remaining was the red glow from the detonators behind them and the washed-out sapphire of whatever was scraping and clanging toward the hallway. There was a subtle change in the video feed as McNutt and the rest adjusted position. They were splitting up, each taking cover inside the doorway of a room. Starling was in the room with the reclining proxy bodies; she slapped a brick of explosives on the wall. A faint, red light kicked on: the detonator.

A slight weight settled on Meyers's forearm, and he broke from the augmented reality to glance down. It was Timkul. Her eyes sparkled in the display. "What is it?" she asked. "The thing coming to them."

Meyers shook his head. The clanking and scraping grew louder, the glow—now like a flashlight being shown through a cracked sapphire—filled the end of the hallway. He caught the familiar rasp of gloved hands wrapping around the material of CAWS-5s straps and the soft clack of buttstocks being braced against armored shoulders.

The faint red glow of the detonators suddenly brightened.

Starling let out a startled "Shit!"

"What?" McNutt shouted back.

The sapphire-filtered glow was now a direct light, shining into the hallway. Something large shambled forward, a silhouette washed in soft blue.

"The detonators!" Now Starling sounded frantic. "The timer kicked off! Something overrode control of my ADPAX. This place is going to blow in fifty-five seconds!"

"Get out of there," Meyers said, trying to maintain calm.

"Wish I'd thought of that one, Colonel." McNutt fired on the silhouetted form as he stepped out of cover. His bullets rattled off whatever he was hitting.

More gunfire came from the hallway as Banh, Lamh, and Starling moved from cover. Their headlamps lit up again, revealing a towering mining proxy. It was caked in brown mud and dusted in fine, gray sand. There was only the skeletal appearance of a bipedal, human form, with the joints and longest parts of the limbs covered by armored plates. One arm ended in a rotary saw blade that extended at least a decimeter beyond the axis, the other in a tube-like protrusion. Instead of feet, the proxy had two forward-stretching clamp mechanisms that were at about a sixty-degree angle from each other. Meyers had seen a similar model proxy used for construction back on Plymouth and assumed there would be a third, rear-projecting clamp on the feet for balance. The light came from a shoulder-mounted set of work lamps.

"Your bullets aren't going to do anything against that," Meyers said.

Starling pulled something from her carrying satchel: the rest of the explosives. She pinched off a ball that could fit in her palm and squeezed the spider-bot into the top. "Get him, Charlotte! Everyone, get back to cover!"

The proxy brought the tubular arm up, and a brilliant, blue beam flickered. The beam crawled along the floor, cutting into the surface, then tracked over to Lamh, neatly slicing him from the left hip to right shoulder.

"Laser," McNutt shouted as he fell back into a room.

The spider-bot's camera reactivated through Starling's video—blurry and full of random distortions and jagged black lines. Starling stepped back into the driver room and waited for the proxy to take a lumbering step into the hallway. It brought the laser up and aimed at her; she rolled the explosive toward the far corner, to the proxy's right, and then she fell back. The laser cut a gash in the wall over her head.

Meyers stupidly locked on to the spider-bot's video feed. He nearly lost his balance from the sensation caused by the floor-ceiling-floor-ceiling tumble. He closed his eyes just before the sound of the explosion turned the BAS feed into a thrumming bass roar. There was still enough sensitivity to pick up bits and pieces of debris rattling around in the hallway.

"Let's go!" McNutt hurried into the hallway, with Repin's corpse pinned between arm and shoulder. Dust swirled in the big Kiwi's wake.

Meyers felt woozy. Timkul was at his side, taking his weight. "Sorry," he said. It came out raspy due to his dry throat.

He took a swig of water and tried to concentrate. McNutt was at the front, waving the others forward with his weapon arm. In the corner where the explosive had detonated, the wall and floor were shattered, exposing the stone beneath. The doorframe to the hallway beyond was warped, the overhead beam sagging thirty or more centimeters. Chunks of stone had broken free from the tunnel and were pressed down against the beam. The proxy was prone a few meters from where it had been standing. The work lights were dead, and one of its legs was bent forward on a deformed joint. The other leg was completely twisted and had lost its foot clamp mechanism. Neither arm seemed to have suffered significant damage beyond the warping of the armored plates.

Banh paused at Lamh's corpse for a second, then placed the CAWS-5 in its brace and picked up the two halves. After pausing for a second,

Banh moved around the proxy, ducked through the doorway, and checked the intersecting hallway beyond. "Clear!"

Starling moved up, stopping long enough to slap the last of the explosives onto the proxy. The detonator light glowed red. "Parting gift for you assholes."

"Hurry it up!" Meyers licked his cracked lips and wished he were there. They didn't seem to sense the urgency of the situation.

McNutt nudged Starling through the doorway, then ducked to get Repin's body through. Meyers caught the faintest flash of a sapphire glow, heard the slightest hint of heavy machinery straining, and then saw the proxy's torso twist. The rotary saw blade spun to life, and the proxy whipped its arm around, cutting through Repin's ribs and tearing into McNutt's chest armor.

McNutt screamed and tumbled back into the intersecting hallway. Blood gushed from his armor. His CAWS-5 clattered to the ground, and his right arm went limp. Starling was at his side immediately, quickly guiding him down the hallway, away from the doorframe. Meyers tried to keep up with the turns and doorways as the team rushed to the exit, but it felt like a hopelessly intricate maze to him, and the seconds seemed to speed by. They burst into one of the gun emplacement bunkers and slammed the door shut just as the connection died.

Timkul flinched. "What—?"

"The explosives." Meyers wondered how much of the complex would survive the blast. It seemed unlikely the reactor would have been shut down, but it was possible with all the twists and turns that the room with the hidden vault shared a common wall.

"They made it out, right?" Timkul's voice shook.

"Sure." He didn't think a little lie would be a problem. More importantly, he had no idea about demolitions and what Starling had been trying for with her placement of the explosives. "They were just riding on the Grid, and it's gone now."

He looked around, still disoriented by being thrown back into the real world so abruptly. His brain felt like a swollen, festering wound. He settled onto Paxton's carrying case.

Meyers's earpiece chimed; it was Paxton.

"Colonel, that question about what the Lancers will do next? We got the answer." Paxton's video feed showed the valley. What had been red blobs were now wireframes: the APCs and soldiers were advancing.

Meyers sighed. "How long do we have?"

"Ten minutes if they keep this speed. They won't. I'm guessing they accelerate soon, so let's call it five."

Meyers studied the advancing figures. It took several seconds for the significance of the wireframes to sink in. On some of the closest and largest objects, he could make out details—moving tracks and the basic shape of the vehicle—that seemed computer-generated. Everything else was just darkness. He drilled down on one of the APCs that showed detail; there was no doubt it was being computer-generated.

"What happened to the BAS signal silhouette?" he asked.

Paxton growled. "Shit. Something wiped out our network?"

Meyers scanned the images again. There were other APCs almost as close as the ones he could see in computer-generated detail, but he couldn't make out any detail on them at all. "No. That detail is coming from our network. That's our system doing the enhancement but..." It dawned on him then. "That's coming from the north valley wall, from Barlowe's position. That's his imagery system!"

Meyers dictated a text to Barlowe: *We're receiving enhanced imagery from your systems now instead of signal silhouettes. Is that real? Have you been hacked?*

Real, Barlowe replied. *Their system attacks stopped.*

"Of course." Meyers felt like an idiot for not thinking of it.

"Mind sharing with the rest of us, Colonel?" Paxton said.

"The mountaintop. The Grid they were running up there, it's down. The systems expert they had must have been killed. The whole thing must have been hooked in to the Lancers' network. That's where all the advanced signals attacks were coming from." Meyers shook his head in disbelief. "They have no idea their employers are dead."

Paxton made a harrumphing sound. "Or they don't care."

Timkul stared toward the valley. "We have to tell them." She turned back to Meyers. "If they come at us, people will die for nothing."

"I know." Meyers got to his feet and tried to walk a bit. His body felt battered and broken. He just wanted to sleep and heal. "We need to break into their network, send a warning to them." It was the sort of thing Barlowe could do, maybe Starling if she was alive. Neither one was available to pull off such a major systems hack.

Meyers sent a text to both anyway: *Can you hack their system, tell them their employers are dead?*

Seconds passed. Finally, Barlowe replied: *ADPAX is a mess, overheating just keeping imagery systems running, battery low, close to powering down.*

After a few seconds without a reply from Starling, Meyers said, "We're not going to be able to stop that charge." His guts twisted at the thought of unnecessary slaughter. "Master Sergeant Paxton, have your soldiers take up their positions. Let's take advantage of having a functional network."

"Roger that, Colonel." Paxton switched to a broad channel and called out orders. The mortars and railgun came online, along with more robust targeting options.

Meyers headed toward the front line, bending into the wind that was blowing out of the west. He wondered if Terry Lewis might still be out there and if he might realize the pointlessness of the attack. Timkul stuck by Meyers's side. She swapped a fresh magazine into the CAWS-5, and he did the same with the assault rifle. They came up behind Paxton, who stood in the gap between two barriers, hands resting on armored hips. He saw the assault rifle, marched over to a stack of CAWS-5s, and dug one out.

"Full of AP rounds, sir. Just like you ordered."

Meyers tested the weapon's feel and connected into it. The familiar targeting system brought a smile to his face. He searched the length of the defensive line. Eight of the defenders were behind the battered structures, which didn't shield heavy weapons. Meyers saw movement behind and to his left and turned. The triage team was carrying the wounded deeper into the camp, closer to the LZ.

Meyers looked at Paxton. "Where do you want us?"

Paxton's visor opened, and he scowled. Muscles twitched beneath the wrinkled contours of his bruised flesh. Meyers imagined he could see frustration and rage warring with protocol and respect.

Finally, Paxton twisted and pointed to the defensive position to the north, where a machine gun had once stood. "That flank's our weakest point, sir."

Meyers led Timkul to the designated fortification. The barrier should have stood three meters high and been angled back about fifteen degrees. Instead, it bowed forward at the midpoint so that only a little more than a meter above the ground was shielded, but there were still solid wall segments at the base.

Timkul dropped to her knees at the far end and looked the CAWS-5 over. "Will they flank again?" she asked, voice quivering.

"They'll try." Meyers settled onto his stomach and stared into the valley, watching the APCs advance. He sighted on the closest vehicle, then he lowered the weapon to the snow. "They're accelerating. Won't be long now."

Barlowe sent another text: *They've sent another group at us. Just me and Gerhardt standing. Others are too wounded. What a fucking mess.*

For some reason, Meyers chuckled.

Timkul turned to consider him. "What do you find funny?"

Meyers looked back into the valley. "All of this, I guess. The way they laid a trap, the way I fell for it, the way we'll end up dead or killing a bunch of soldiers I wanted to save. All this suffering and death and no one wins. Well, I guess the metacorporations win but for how long? This is so self-destructive and short-sighted."

Timkul turned her attention back to the approaching forces. "You think someone will find out what happened here?"

"Maybe. Unless they have one hell of a fleet hidden somewhere, we own the sky. At some point, Brigston figures out we're dead and he turns this into a fiery lake. Maybe he sends someone down to retrieve our bodies and whatever data survives, maybe he just reports all hands lost and sails away. Who can figure with him?"

"Were you two friends before...?"

Meyers nodded. "I'd like to think so. I really can't understand how he's made this so personal."

Flares arced into the night sky, revealing the lead APCs.

"Listen up!" Paxton's voice was a gravelly hiss over the broad channel.

"Hold your fire until they send the infantry out. Weapons teams, ready to load. Let the guns follow the targeting priorities I've placed."

Meyers sighted on the closest vehicle. He couldn't help wondering about the Lancers inside: Where were they from? What were they like? Had they trained with an army, or had they simply been forced into a life of violence by a world that offered so little else?

The APC slowed and then stopped, and its machine guns opened fire, chewing up snow all along the front. More machine guns joined in as Lancers burst out from the rear and rushed forward. They quickly spread wide and hunched low, reducing their profiles.

"Ready!" Paxton's voice boomed over the machine gun roar.

"I-I'm glad I had a chance to see—to experience this," Timkul said.

Meyers nodded. "I wish we'd met under different circumstances, Priya."

Timkul glanced at him, then she looked back at her weapon.

The Lancers were at full speed now, closing, heading for the outer flanks.

"Fire!"

Meyers heard the hollow cough of a distant mortar launch, and then gunfire erupted down the length of the defensive line. He sighted on the best target he could make out and squeezed off a shot, missing.

The APCs lumbered forward again and laid down supporting fire. Bullets rattled against the wall, rocking it; it held for the moment.

One of the APCs twisted and shot out a ball of sparks, a victim of the railgun. Lancers began to fall but not fast enough. More and more of them charged forward. Meyers fired again, finally hitting someone. The Lancer staggered and then fell, and Meyers tracked across to another target.

A pocket of Lancers raced forward, firing at the barrier, driving Meyers and Timkul behind cover. Meyers could hear the Lancers over the gunfire, snow crunching beneath boots, close. He waved Timkul to press in tight beneath the base of the barrier. They locked eyes through their piggybacked BAS connection, then she flipped to her external camera.

"Stay hidden as long as you can," he said, then he got to his feet and waited for the final rush and engagement.

34

2 October 2175. Siberia.

Two Lancers rushed around the barrier, guns at the ready. Meyers stepped inside the assault rifle of the nearest one and drove his weapon's buttstock into the weaker armor of the Lancer's throat. The Lancer staggered and clutched at its neck. Meyers could see the Lancer on the opposite side through Timkul's video feed—waiting, unsure about firing with an ally at risk. Meyers spun and fired. Another Lancer—big, broad—shoved aside its choking ally and took Meyers to the ground, pinning his arms to his side as they fell. They skidded across the hard snow. Meyers heard gunfire and saw another Lancer fall; Timkul had given away her position.

Meyers growled and slammed his visor against the face shield of the big Lancer's helmet. The visor splintered, the face shield cracked, and the Lancer's grip loosened for just an instant. Meyers took the opportunity to smash his fists against the Lancer's back. It was an awkward strike against armor but it targeted the kidneys.

It wasn't enough.

The Lancer released its grip and pulled its right arm free to draw a knife. It was black in the dark, but Meyers got a sense of the basic shape: long, broad, and serrated. Meyers worked his right arm free and struck at the Lancer's shoulder, then again at the forearm, but the blows didn't seem to get through. The Lancer stabbed at Meyers, and he barely managed to block the strike. Even so, the knife slowly descended. He wrapped his legs around the Lancer and tried to squeeze, but the armor was too thick and rigid to do any meaningful harm. The knife came closer, and then it crashed down and into Meyers's chest, at first scraping across the armor, then finding the weaker shoulder joint and driving through. The blade cut into flesh and muscle. Meyers howled as blood spilled from the wound. The Lancer pulled the knife free and raised up for another strike, and Meyers couldn't do anything to stop it.

Gunfire roared from his left, and the Lancer slumped. Dark blood spurted onto Meyers's visor. He twisted his hips, tossing the Lancer aside. More gunfire came from his left, and Meyers had enough time to recognize Paxton's ID on the flickering visor display, then battle called.

Meyers grabbed the dead man's knife, got to his feet, and dove at the nearest Lancer, who was mercifully smaller. Meyers knocked aside the smaller person's assault rifle, which had been aimed at Timkul. The Lancer shouldered Meyers, but the size difference favored him this time. He maintained his grip on the assault rifle and kicked at the Lancer's ankles and shin, finally knocking the smaller person off balance. That was all Meyers needed; he flipped the Lancer to the ground and followed up with heel strikes to the head and chest until the form went limp. Meyers stuck the knife into his belt and looked around.

"Get to cover, Colonel," Paxton shouted. He was on a knee, reloading. "More coming in!"

Meyers took the Lancer's assault rifle and returned to the barrier. Timkul was already rolling out from beneath. She tried to shove a body out of the way, gave up, and simply braced against it.

Eight more Lancers were charging toward them, firing. Paxton grunted, but with the three of them firing, they were able to hold off the charge.

Meyers turned around to thank Paxton only to see him collapse to the snowy ground.

"Carl!" Meyers turned, then he stopped.

There was no time to check on his friend, not with the enemy still advancing. The APCs shifted fire toward their barrier, which shuddered from the impact. The top section finally gave way and crashed down. Meyers pulled back behind the remaining cover and brought up the heavy weapons fire control system. The railgun was dead, and the mortars were down to one round each. He scanned the battlefield for the best placement, then adjusted targeting priorities to drop the rounds between three APCs that had gotten too close to each other. When the fire control system registered the launch, he connected to Nunoz.

"Ensign, we're getting overwhelmed down here." Meyers poked his head around cover and then immediately pulled back. An instant later, machine gun fire pounded the wall again. He realized the one upside to being the focus of the APCs was that there weren't infantry charges to deal with.

"I've been strafing the rear, Colonel," Nunoz said. "They're breaking up now, but I've only got enough ammo for one more run."

"Make it count." Meyers drew a line across the middle space of the valley, where two APCs were laying down the worst of the suppressing fire. "Hammer these two, you give us some breathing space."

"On my way!"

Meyers popped his malfunctioning visor and watched the sky, tracing the movement of blood-red clouds against the black. Snow settled against his face, cold on his raw flesh. Time seemed to drag on, and then he finally saw the flash of movement above the clouds, the way they parted just before the Dart dove toward the valley, the hawk plunging toward its prey. Meyers watched the Dart's dark form as long as he could, then he switched to the BAS feed. One of the red outlines winked out, and the constant pounding of bullets tapered off. Joy and hope surged through him.

He twisted around. More infantry were charging forward. Was that why the machine guns quit firing, he wondered, or was it desperation?

"Six Lancers, coming at us," he shouted to Timkul.

"I see them." She fired, and one of the Lancers fell.

Meyers dropped his visor and targeted another of the Lancers through the BAS. They were brave, disciplined. They were the sort of soldiers he would have wanted in the ERF. He fired, and another fell. The others continued forward. He cursed at them in silence.

Drop, you fucking idiots! Surrender! Don't make me kill you!

He fired, dropping another. Bullets cracked against his armor, and one of them penetrated. His chest burned, and his arm went limp. Timkul fired and then fired again. The last of the Lancers fell.

Meyers twisted and rolled onto his back, gasping. His chest was on fire in one spot but felt numb everywhere else.

"Ensign Nunoz?" It took an impossible effort just to get the words out. Breathing was a struggle.

"I'm all out, Colonel, and I don't know how long I can stay airborne."

"Mountaintop," Meyers gasped. "Wounded. Hurry."

The world became blurry and distant. He felt someone at his side. Timkul, he realized. Her gloved hands ran over his chest and came away glistening and dark in the flare light. Blood, he realized. Lots of it.

"Paxton?" Meyers thought a small building might have collapsed against his chest. Each breath demanded so much from him.

Timkul's visor popped open. Tears ran down her face. She crawled away, and he closed his eyes. It was so peaceful doing that, so easy to stop breathing. Pain shot through him, and his eyes opened again. Timkul was there, hunched over him, shouting.

"Huh?" Meyers couldn't be sure he'd actually made the sound.

"—alive!" Timkul brushed freezing tears from her face. She waved at someone or something, and Meyers sensed another presence nearby. She looked down at him again, then she sealed her visor.

Someone settled beside him, and a burst of cold washed over him. He was vaguely aware of his armor being popped open. A sharp pain hit him, like a thin knife between the ribs. He struggled again to breathe, remembering that Timkul had yelled for him to do that at some point. After a couple breaths, it suddenly became easier. There was another lance of pain through his chest, followed not long after by warmth that quickly spread outward. He tingled all over, and the strange haze that had settled over his mind began to fade.

The dark form leaned in, and he recognized the beautiful, wondrous, plain face of Corporal Veitch. "You've got a collapsed lung, Colonel. A bullet shattered your clavicle and pierced your lung. You understand?"

Meyers wheezed. It may have been a yes. He hoped it was.

"*Gut.*" It sounded like she had slipped back into German. "I've given you stims and painkillers. The lung will hold for now. The clavicle is glued, so it's stable. Do not test it. Colonel? You understand? You are with me?"

"Yes." Meyers wanted to smile at managing to get that out.

Veitch looked away. "The master sergeant is worse. We must move him now." She looked back down at Meyers. "You will not exert yourself?"

"The battle..."

Veitch got to her feet. "I know, sir. We are all dead."

Meyers tried to sit up. His chest armor lay open, on the ground. The insulated shirt he wore beneath had been crudely sealed, he guessed using surgical adhesive. His stomach churned, and if he'd had anything in it, he was sure it would have come up at that point. As it was, he tasted bile. Timkul gently wrapped an arm around his ribs and helped him to his knees, then pulled him to the crumpled wall. The chemicals Veitch had injected started working, clearing out the worst of the dizziness and nausea.

The battlefield was a strange wasteland of red outlines and forms. Someone had launched more flares, washing everything in shades of scarlet. An APC rumbled toward them, flanked by Lancers that were smart enough to use it for cover. Deeper in the valley, the same was happening, with Lancers falling back to hook up with the remaining vehicles. There was nothing to stop the armor now. They were doomed.

"Colonel?" It was Nunoz. "I've got a request coming in from Sergeant McNutt. He wants to talk to you."

McNutt. Alive.

"Please," Meyers said. He shook the cobwebs from between his ears.

Bullets glanced off the advancing APC's armor; Meyers wasn't sure who was firing. The APC didn't bother to return fire. Nothing was going to stop it.

"Colonel? We took it down," McNutt's voice was raspy. He coughed. "The whole thing. There's smoke pouring from everywhere. I don't think we'll find much after we wrap up."

"Starling? Banh?"

"Yeah, all good." McNutt grunted. "Well, maybe not so good. Alive, though. And Cho's using our suits to keep the wounded going. What about the valley?"

Meyers stared at the advancing APC. "Death."

"Still fighting? What for?" McNutt sounded confused. "This had to be their HQ, right?"

Meyers nodded. "Yeah. The message..." He wheezed. "They don't know."

"Shit. Hold on." McNutt brought Starling onto the channel.

"Good to see you, sir," Starling said. Her armor was caked in soot and blood, but she still managed a bleary-eyed smile.

McNutt grunted. "Sort of. They got a mess down there. Fucking Lancers don't know the whole thing's over."

"Sir, is that true?" Starling's voice held some welcome urgency.

"APC coming right at us," Meyers said. He realized he wasn't sending his helmet camera video feed. It didn't seem to be working. He switched to Timkul's.

"I see it, Colonel. Uh, Ensign Nunoz?" The urgency in Starling's voice intensified.

"Go ahead, Private Starling."

"I'm going to need to control your comms for a minute, sir." Starling looked off into the distance. "Without the systems they had in the complex, their security's pretty modest, Colonel. I have all the bots I was spawning for the attack. It shouldn't take—"

The APC stopped abruptly.

"—long. Wow." Meyers could almost hear the smile in Starling's tone. "Okay, so it was weaker than I thought. I've shut down their weapons systems, too."

Meyers smiled at that welcome reversal.

A Lancer staggered from the back of the APC, assault rifle raised. He was tall and lean, even in armor.

"Tell them it's over," Meyers said.

"I don't see their comms—" Starling sounded irritated. "They've got redundant systems for some reason. Give me a second, Colonel."

More Lancers fell in behind the first. There were still twenty or thirty of them, and there were many more farther back. Meyers couldn't imagine there were enough of his people to stand against a force of that size, APCs or not. He glanced at Timkul, who was swapping in a fresh magazine. He realized that her armor had a few deformities where rounds had glanced off.

"Battle-tested," he said.

She smiled and then turned back to the advancing Lancers.

"All right, Colonel. Found it." Starling cleared her throat. "Lancer force, be advised—" Her voice boomed through the valley.

The Lancers came to a stop.

"Your employers have been neutralized," Starling said. "The ERF has control of your systems. Stand down."

The APC rumbled forward and then stopped again. Its machine guns pivoted around, one locking on the Lancers in front, the other pointed to the clouds above. The raised machine gun fired, and then it targeted the Lancers as well.

"You have ten seconds to surrender."

Meyers shivered and leaned against the barrier, careful of the jagged edges where bullets had cut through. The lead Lancer looked from the APC to Meyers's position, as if considering the odds of a charge.

"Don't be stupid," Meyers whispered.

"Don't be stupid," Starling repeated, emphasizing the last word and bringing the machine guns to bear on the tall man.

He dropped his assault rifle, and a few seconds later the others did the same.

35

4 October 2175. Siberia.

Snow gave beneath Meyers's boots with a hollow, popping sound. He leaned hard against Timkul and tried not to let the world see that his skull was about to burst open. His stomach was still unsettled, and he could barely control the shaking brought on by the nausea and cold. He pulled the thermal blanket tight against him, unconcerned that it had just been plucked from a corpse and was still covered by frozen gore. It seemed appropriate, since they had all died a little in the valley. Ahead of them, the Lancers stood in ranks, separated into companies. Meyers chuckled grimly; he was maybe looking at a hundred forms. He returned the salute of the tall, slender man who had been leading the final assault. The Lancer's arm froze halfway back to his side.

"Lonny?"

Meyers thought maybe the wind was playing tricks on him. He stopped and inspected the Lancer's armor, quickly spotting the same patch he'd taken from one of the dead earlier: a cartoonish wolverine. "Terry?"

The Lancer unsealed his face shield. Terry Lewis stared out from the helmet, a little older than Meyers might have expected and a little more worn but the same man who'd served in the Rangers. His dark eyes were puffy and bloodshot, and his cheeks seemed sunken. Gray tipped the black stubble on his cheeks and around his full lips. "Captain Terry Lewis, Fighting Wolverines Company."

"Shit." Meyers held out a hand and shook with Lewis. "What a mess."

Lewis looked toward the mountaintop. "They didn't tell us this would be you."

Meyers looked down the Wolverines' ranks. They were haggard, broken. "How many did you lose?"

Lewis straightened proudly. "Depends on who pulls through."

"How many?"

"Fifty percent." Lewis slumped and glanced at what remained. A second later, he cast his eyes down. "I lost my nephew on that last assault. I thought sure he'd make it."

"I'm sorry."

Lewis pointed at the knife sticking out from Meyers's belt. "Mind if I...?"

Meyers pulled the knife free and handed it to Lewis, who winced. "Keep it."

Lewis slid the knife between his belt and armor.

"Who were they, Terry?" Meyers glanced toward the mountain.

"You took them down. Why don't you tell me? We never dealt with anything but proxies."

Meyers considered that then nodded. "That's what Cassidy told us."

Lewis's head tilted. "Cassidy Taylor?"

"Yeah. Whoever hired you used her to draw us here. They were counting on her loyalty to Earth."

"Son of a bitch." Lewis shook his head. "I recommended her. I thought sure she'd stayed on. They wouldn't talk to me when she disappeared."

Meyers turned at the sound of snow crunching. Several of his own ERF soldiers walked past and began moving through the Lancers' ranks, collecting weapons. There was no sign of resentment or simmering hostility, but Lewis watched and wiped away what might have been a tear.

"You were used. All of you." Meyers nodded toward the other groups. "What about the others? Who can you vouch for?"

"Nettleman, Yoshika, Karim...they're all solid. Professionals."

Meyers glanced at Timkul as he asked, "Were those infiltrators Karim's?"

"Yeah. I think they were what got his unit hired. Tough ladies. They picked up how to use the tech we were given really fast."

A shiver ran through Meyers for several seconds. "What did they tell you?"

"The proxies?" Lewis snorted. "Earth was going to send a force here and we were going to destroy it. That was it. Other than the battle plans. Awfully detailed, like they were orchestrating the whole thing."

Meyers considered Lewis from beneath squinted eyebrows. "That didn't bother you?"

"Attacking a force from Earth? Of course it did. You know what didn't bother me, though? Getting paid better than twice market value for what we were going to do. For all we knew, you were one of those stuffed-shirt Chinese units that thinks marching around in a sharp uniform is how you win wars. Didn't matter. We're talking about money, Lonny. You know, the shit we were promised before the UN got rid of our jobs? The shit we need to rent an apartment and buy food for our families?"

Timkul squeezed Meyers's ribs. "Excuse me," she said. She blinked away tears that had almost certainly been caused by the biting wind. "Captain Lewis? The UN made cuts to everyone's military. It's what you do when there's peace."

"Yeah?" Lewis pointed to the Lancers arrayed behind him. "Well, take a look. This is what you get when you just kick five million soldiers out into the world with no jobs and no training. There's a whole lot of pissed-off Lancers out there right now, people who were doing okay, laying their lives on the line for governments that fucked 'em pretty hard when they figured it was safe to do so." He turned back to Meyers. "I'm telling you, Lonny, that's why no one backed out when we found out this was ERF. You might want to reconsider hooking up with the UN. I don't think they have a goddamn clue about what they're doing. Everyone's looking to get by, and we're all competing for the same piddly slice of shit."

Meyers held up a hand. "We all know that. I've made the same argument."

Lewis blew out a misty sigh. "It's not just an argument. Someone's got to start thinking this shit through. Private armies, mercenary forces? You can't stop it. Kicking everyone out without opportunities...? Hell, if you're UN, lady, you *created* this. You guaranteed the people with the most money get the most protection."

Meyers glanced at Timkul. Her jaw quivered, but he couldn't know what was in her head, whether she was even affected by Lewis's words. Meyers squeezed against her gently. "We need to get to the infirmary."

"What about us? We were supposed to have our ships summoned once this was resolved. It's more than fifty klicks to either of our camps. You just leaving us out here?" He straightened and crossed his arms over his chest. "Or is this one of those summary execution situations, keep everything quiet?"

"Hell, Terry." Meyers glared at his old friend. "You signed a contract. It was legal at the time. You didn't do anything wrong. If I'd wanted you dead, we would have dropped missiles on you from orbit."

Lewis seemed to relax. "You're damned right we didn't do anything wrong."

Meyers shook his head when he saw that Timkul might say something about the size of the Lancer force. "We'll get you to your camp to the south. You can summon your ships from there. You have food and water? Power?"

"We're good."

Meyers extended a fist. Instead of bumping it, Lewis leaned forward and hugged Meyers, then whispered in his ear, "You watch what you're getting into, Lonny. I mean it."

Lewis straightened and glared at Meyers until he nodded—quick, just enough for Lewis to see.

Meyers guided Timkul back to camp, only once glancing back at the ERF team still dealing with the Lancers. It struck him how remarkably similar their situation was to what faced the ERF overall: a small force, surrounded, outnumbered, on the edge of obliteration.

"He is an ass," Timkul said. She rubbed at her nose with the back of her glove, then she lowered her visor.

Meyers lowered his own visor. "You don't know him."

"I don't have to know him to know he is an ass."

They crunched through the snow in silence for a while, slowing once in a while to look at the shattered defense works or the destroyed structures. Starling had driven one of the Lancer APCs out to retrieve Barlowe and the wounded ERF soldiers from the slope. She'd brought another to the middle of the front line and used its bright lights to reveal most of the camp. Meyers didn't need the clarity brought on by the lights. Blood stained the snow, sometimes forming dark, frozen pools. The dead lay abandoned for the moment, some of them staring skyward, their faces snow-lined and literally frozen.

Climbing the gentle rise leading to the LZ winded Meyers and intensified the headache that refused to leave. Timkul seemed to sense the problem; she took on more of his weight without complaint and they struggled through the trampled gray mush together.

Veitch had set the infirmary up in the lee of the uplink. Someone had dragged three of the shattered structures to the area and surrounded the wounded with the material from the low walls.

Meyers moved from body to body, stopping to check on each. Some soldiers had merely suffered concussions that were too severe for stims; others had suffered more serious wounds. He talked with one German soldier who had lost his left arm below the elbow. Meyers marveled at the young man's spirit and the talk of getting a cybernetic replacement so he could quickly return to duty.

A couple ERF soldiers hauled a litter past and set it down. Barlowe sat up after they ran back toward the front. He slouched toward the uplink and leaned against it, then he slid to a seated position.

Meyers made his way over to the IB agent. He was bloody and shaking. Gerhardt was on a litter next to the one Barlowe had just abandoned, curled up in a thermal blanket.

When Barlowe looked up, Meyers knelt and said, "You did a brave thing."

"Fuck you, Lonny." Barlowe looked around at all the wounded. "This should never have happened. None of it."

"I know."

Barlowe leaned in close and whispered, "You best find out who was behind this."

Meyers nodded. "I will."

Timkul kept her distance, looking over the wounded. She seemed close to shock. Meyers returned to her side, and they made their way to the crude operating room Veitch had set up. It was a ring of gurneys, a carrying case with headlamps secured to the lid, and a tray full of gory surgical instruments. Paxton was on one of the gurneys, stripped out of his chest armor and partially covered by a foil thermal blanket like the one wrapped around Meyers. Veitch was hunched over Paxton's body, shivering and barking orders to two soldiers holding heat lamps. Every now and then, Veitch would look up at her raised visor. Meyers assumed the visor had the vitals displayed on it.

"How long have you known him?" Timkul whispered, even though they were on a private channel.

"Carl? A few years. He was one of the first sergeants Rimes brought into the ERF. Rimes said Paxton was rare, one of the old dogs you could teach new tricks. There's this culture Rimes wanted to break, this idea that every soldier needs someone to wipe his ass and hold his hand and kick his teeth in every step of the way. He said it was old-school thinking and dangerous. When you treat someone like an idiot, they learn to act like an idiot. Paxton bought into the change enough to get him a platoon sergeant billet. Not bad for someone raised in the old culture."

"And what about you?" Timkul bumped against Meyers playfully and smiled at him. "Can you learn new tricks?"

He thought about Kara and Camille and their feisty, independent natures and of the fights those personalities brought on with his. It was the same sort of nature he'd seen in Timkul in their short time together. He pursed his lips and said, "We'll have to see."

~

DAYLIGHT BROKE through the cloud cover, which had been torn apart by gale-force winds in the early hours. Meyers leaned into the remnants of that wind as he strode across the mountaintop toward the bunker complex. Starling and Banh stayed close by. Behind them, Lewis marched between four ERF soldiers. Meyers led them along the semicircle, staring into each bunker as if to assure himself the enemy was really broken. At the last opening, he climbed in with assistance from Banh and Starling. They waited for the others, then they headed in. Something caught Meyers's eye: a charred bunch of material. He remembered the large, tarp-covered thing in the hallway from the imagery the spider-bot had gathered. The material had been the tarp.

He pointed to the blackened heap. "I think this is where that construction proxy came from."

No one said anything. They moved on.

Meyers's boots echoed strangely as he walked the hallway. He attributed the noise to the stone and curvature of the hallway. He checked each of the doors, wiping soot from the handles that faced the complex interior, searching for boot prints, testing the stone for any sign another hidden room might be waiting for them to discover.

The passage into the main hallway was also soot covered, and there were cracks in the wall covering the stone tunnel. Meyers checked his suit for any sign of radiation; they were still mostly green.

He opened his visor and turned to Lewis, eyebrow cocked. "Well?"

Lewis pulled aside his face shield. "Nope. Never went in this deep."

They checked the combat proxy room off the main tunnel first. Parts of the machines were seriously burned but they had largely survived. The three proxies McNutt's team had killed were burned down to the bone.

Meyers held up two fingers to the ERF soldiers guarding Lewis and pointed toward the reactor. "Watch your radiation readout and stay in contact. Check the exits. I want to know if anyone got out of here."

The two closest soldiers moved out with pace. Meyers waved for Banh to take the lead, even though studying the video and maps had given Meyers a good sense of the layout.

When they reached the construction proxy, Meyers stopped to examine the pieces the explosives had scattered in all directions. The passageway beyond had collapsed, and the long hallway where the proxy had attacked his soldiers was a mess. They only moved into the long hallway after pulling debris out and testing the ceiling and walls. The six proxies that had been lying on couches were nothing more than skeletons, same as the three that had been tossed in with the combat proxies.

Lewis seemed intrigued by the bones. He shifted a femur around on one of the skeletons and glanced at Meyers. "These look an awful lot like human bones."

"Probably denser and tougher," Meyers said. He waved one of the ERF soldiers over, who collected three of the skeletons into a body bag.

They went deeper, checking each room, Meyers stomping the floor, shining his headlamp around. Banh tried to squeeze into the final room, but the explosion had wrecked the doorway.

Meyers un-muted from the soldiers checking out the reactor room. "Any sign someone might have escaped out that mountainside passage?"

"No, sir. Ours are the first tracks in the soot."

"What about that door in the reactor room?"

"It buckled, sir. Looks like the hinges are ruined."

Meyers thought about it for a moment: Where had that door led? What was its purpose? "All right, fall back to our position. Stay sharp."

Starling poked her head through the ruined doorway, then pulled back. She walked past him a few meters and turned around; he followed. She opened her visor but kept her back turned to the others. "Wasn't the explosives, sir. All this fire, some of the damage. They had something else rigged in here, something we missed."

"So, we lost everything?"

Starling glanced over her shoulder at the others, then she shook her head slightly and leaned in closer. "I pulled a lot out of here, and—" She looked down, the same sort of thing she did when embarrassed by a compliment.

"What?"

She looked up at the sound of booted steps coming closer. "We need to talk, Colonel. Somewhere private." She looked around. "Somewhere *safe*."

Meyers considered that for a moment, then he turned to the others. "All right, time we got back to the *Valdez*. Let's move out."

He retraced his steps to the bunker Banh had led McNutt and Starling out through, testing the door to the room and glancing back down the hall. The hinges groaned, and the door was slightly deformed but it had done its job, blocking out the worst of the blast. Something was bugging him, but he couldn't figure out what.

He let Starling and Banh help him out of the window and scraped his gloves and boots against the snow until they were clear of soot. They piled into the Dart, and a few minutes later, they were on their way to the *Valdez*.

During the entire flight up, Meyers tried not to stare at Starling and she seemed to be trying to do the same with him.

What does she know, he wondered. There were answers about the mysterious bunker complex, and he was sure she had some.

36

18 October 2175. En route to Plymouth. CFN *Valdez*.

DARKNESS WAS a canvas that Meyers painted with flashes of inspiration and deep contemplation. It was different in the conference room than what he could manage in his cabin. Something about the open space and the fact that he wasn't sitting at his desk or lying on his bed made it easier to just think. Sound had a different quality to it, maybe because of the materials lining the walls, or maybe because of the simple shape of the place. Or perhaps it was the air—cooler and less lived-in. So deep down and close to the void of space, any vibrations that shuddered through the hull felt more real. When there were no vibrations, there was an artificial quiet.

Meyers wondered about that. The tabletop rested upon a thick base, and together they were a fully redundant set of systems images for the *Valdez*. There should be noises—beeps and chimes, maybe the whirr of fans. *Something.* It didn't seem right for humans to live so loudly and clumsily and for so much computerized processing power to be so quiet.

The conference room hatch chimed, and the lights flickered to life.

Meyers sent an unlock signal, and the hatch swung open. Timkul entered, followed by Agent Barlowe and Private Starling. They exchanged curious looks before settling at the table, Timkul to Meyers's right, Barlowe, and Starling to the left. Meyers tried not to be distracted by Timkul's flowery perfume. He had missed it on Siberia. He had missed her impractical and expensive outfits even more. Now, she seemed determined to dress in bland, pseudo-uniforms printed out by the ship's uniform shop.

Starling and Barlowe exchanged whispers and tapped at what Meyers imagined was a workspace shared through their earpieces. They both had an ADPAX attached to the back of their hands, and a new spider-bot rested on Starling's shoulder. No one was going to challenge them now, not after the role those systems had played on Siberia.

Timkul powered on the displays over the conference room table and loaded up presentations. The pages were framed with UNSSC banners. It was the first time she had openly advertised her connection to the Special Security Council.

"Do you want to run this?" Meyers asked. He was surprised by the neutrality in his own voice. His injuries had taken a certain level of energy from him.

Timkul looked at the open hatch. "I thought we would have Captain Brigston lead."

"Sounds good." Meyers didn't think it would matter if everyone deferred to Brigston. Siberia had been the final straw for him.

No, Meyers realized. The final straw had probably come before Siberia.

The crisp click-clack of Brigston's hard-soled dress shoes echoed in the hall. Late. Casual. The captain's prerogative, Meyers thought. Brigston strolled through the hatch, decked out in his formal whites, and took his position at the end of the table. He seemed upbeat, almost pleasant.

"I swung by the infirmary to check on Commander Cooper," Brigston said. He smiled—businesslike, insincere. "He doesn't have the strength to attend the meeting."

Meyers felt a flash of irritation but hid it. An hour before, Cooper had said he would attend via a secure connection from the infirmary, same as

Paxton. There was no surprise in Cooper folding under pressure; he avoided conflict more than most.

Meyers returned the smile but tried his best to make his sincere. "I think that's understandable. Master Sergeant Paxton will connect in, but I doubt he'll be on long."

"Of course." Brigston nodded.

"I'll connect him now, if that's all right?"

Brigston waved a hand at the displays overhead. "We have plenty of space to dedicate to him."

Meyers connected to Paxton and allocated the top left twenty percent of each display to the feed. Paxton's face was pale and his cheeks were hollow but his eyes were active. He had shaved, revealing a few last discolored spots where the bruises and scrapes had dug in stubbornly.

"Thank you, Colonel. Captain Brigston." Paxton inclined his head at each.

Timkul clasped her hands in front of her and beamed at Brigston. "The Special Security Council and Intelligence Bureau liaisons are ready when you are, Captain."

Brigston's eyebrows arched, and the left corner of his mouth ticked up. "Very well. Let's convene the meeting then. Log date and time, please, as well as attendees based on IDs in Conference Room Three and via the secure channel."

All the details scrolled down the display as Brigston droned on and on about the agenda, expectations, and process that would be followed. Meyers sighed at the formality and inefficiency of the approach. It was an After Action Report review, a Lessons Learned discussion. All data was automatically captured unless the systems were told not to do so. He had never seen Brigston relish the role of the bureaucratic obstructionist. It seemed horribly out of character.

Finally, he finished with the unnecessary delays.

"Colonel Meyers, would you like to start?" Brigston's smile was a poke in the eye.

"Of course. Thank you." Meyers straightened and tried to stretch slightly as his AAR filled the displays. "I believe you've all had the chance to review and provide input on the report. I appreciate all the corrections and suggestions, and I've tried to incorporate everything. There's a list in the appendix of outstanding items. Miss Timkul and I will work through a final review before this goes off to the UN, of course."

Paxton's face took on a sour scowl. "We expecting to see our requests for weapons and systems upgrades approved following this report, ma'am?"

Timkul blushed. "The Special Security Council is well aware of the backlog of requests for hardware and personnel, Master Sergeant Paxton. I don't know that the action on Siberia or this report will change anything."

Paxton snorted. "Might want to consider that when we think about how much time we spend on this meeting, sirs."

Meyers fought back a smile. "Thank you, Master Sergeant Paxton. So, to that point, I think we can focus on the executive summary and action items?" Meyers looked at Brigston, caught a hint of annoyance before the slightest wave of a hand. "Very well. The executive summary observes first that the ERF had to move quickly on a tip about an illegal Lancer operation. Rather than explicitly mention the possibility of Waverley, we'll focus on concerns about the sort of funding necessary to field a battalion or more. That should imply metacorporate involvement without irritating anyone at the UN by making 'unsupported claims.'" Meyers watched Timkul for a reaction; her shapely lips curled in a slight smile. "We'll make mention of the limited choices we had for gear and personnel, once again without antagonizing anyone at the UN."

Barlowe leaned forward. "Uh-uh. Nope. You can only go so far without tilting dangerously close to a cover-up, Lonny."

Brigston set an elbow on the armrest of his chair and rested his chin against the palm of his hand. "Cover-up, Agent Barlowe? Are you referring to the gross negligence behind the mission planning?"

Meyers started to say something but stopped when Timkul shook her head slightly.

There was no one to stop Barlowe, though. "No, I'm not talking about gross negligence, Captain. I think we can put that whole notion to rest, actually. We have enough evidence right now to tell the Special Security

Council with complete confidence that Colonel Meyers made the right call putting this mission together. And I have no doubt we'll be opening an investigation into security procedures once we return to Plymouth. The problem wasn't negligence; it was bad security. Compromised security."

"I see." Brigston glanced at the display. "You agree with this assessment, Master Sergeant Paxton?"

"I do, Captain," Paxton said.

"And we'll consult with Captain Hecker, should he recover, I'm assuming?" Brigston looked at Meyers.

"Of course." Meyers tried not to let his irritation show.

"Then I think we've done our due diligence on this point." Brigston looked off in the distance. "I need to do an inspection of the hangar deck soon, so if you'd like to skip forward?"

Meyers wanted to call Brigston out on his ridiculous behavior, just have it out right then and there. It would be a spectacular explosion, a chance to air things out.

And it wouldn't accomplish a damned thing.

"Of course," Meyers said. Dots and flashes appeared in his vision, so he closed his eyes. "Action items coming out of this include the security assessment Agent Barlowe mentioned, tactics and armaments review that will be overseen by Captain Singh, and final intelligence analysis managed by Agent Barlowe and Private Starling."

Brigston nodded and said "hm" a few times, then he stood and stared down at the tabletop. "Well, it sounds like you've managed to put together a thorough analysis, Colonel, all without any blowback. That's commendable. I'll be filing my own supplemental report, of course. Conclude meeting; log attendees and time. Carry on."

And as quick as that, Brigston was gone, his shoes click-clacking in the corridor until he reached the lift.

Meyers ordered the hatch closed and locked through his earpiece. He looked up at the display. "Carl, thank you for your restraint. If you want to get some rest, I understand completely."

"Thank you, Colonel." Paxton grimaced. "Off the record, sir?"

Meyers looked around the room. No one moved. "Go ahead."

"The captain's behavior and positions are misguided, but that doesn't change what happened down on that planet."

"My refusal to call the *Valdez* for fire support?"

"It cost us lives, sir."

"It did," Meyers acknowledged. "And it saved lives. It's an ugly exchange, but it's one we have to be prepared to make."

The sour look returned to Paxton's face. "I will always fight for my soldiers' lives, sir."

"I'll fire you if you don't."

Paxton glared for a moment, then he tapped the end of his nose with a bandaged finger and disconnected.

Timkul stared at the displays, blinking. "What was that?"

Meyers chuckled. "That was Carl reminding me that I have the most valuable asset I could ask for: the fiercest advocate alive for my soldiers."

Her brow furrowed and she pushed back from the table. "Well, I feel as if I wasted my time preparing my presentation. It hasn't even had a good review, which I think it needs before I give it to the SSC."

"I'd be glad to listen to it," Meyers said. He unlocked and opened the hatch.

"Let me give it another pass. Would you be available tonight? Perhaps after dinner?"

A tingling sensation ran down Meyers's spine. "I'll clear my schedule."

Timkul bowed slightly, nodded at Barlowe and Starling, then left. Meyers watched the way the loose uniform moved on Timkul's body without hugging it. It wasn't such a bad design, he decided.

Barlowe stood next. He was still slow and awkward; he swore as much from the aggravated back injury as the injuries sustained on Siberia. He pushed his chair in and leaned against the back for support, looking much older than his age. After a few seconds, he seemed to relax slightly and said, "Brigston's going to resign his commission before I can nail him."

"Nail him for what?" Meyers was pretty sure being petty and disagreeable weren't crimes.

"Undermining the mission from the second we got to Siberia. He was out to make you fail." Barlowe shook his head. "I'm fine with you officers having your little territorial squabbles, but the second you put my life at risk, it's over. He damn near got me killed."

"And me? You think I put your life at risk unnecessarily?"

Barlowe stared at his reflection in the overhead displays. "No. You did what you had to do." He looked down at Starling. "You ready to go?"

Starling glanced at Meyers, then she looked down at the tabletop. "I need to talk with the colonel. ERF stuff."

"Swing by when you're done. I want to go through some of the coding you showed me. I can't tell if it's sloppy or brilliant. Probably sloppy." Barlowe pushed off from the chair and made his way out through the hatch.

Starling smiled and watched the hatch until the echoes of Barlowe's uneven shuffle couldn't be heard, then she looked up at Meyers and the smile disappeared.

"Private Starling, what is it?" Meyers caught the glance she gave toward the hatch; he closed and locked it again.

She stood and swiped at her ADPAX, circling the room and studying the walls and table before returning to her seat. Seconds crawled by as she stared at something in her earpiece display that Meyers couldn't even guess at. Finally, she met his eyes for a moment. "I told you we had to talk in private, sir."

"And you think this conference room is secure?"

"We've got about ten minutes."

"I see." Meyers wondered what sort of bots she was using to block the room's devices with so much confidence. "This is about Siberia? The bunker complex?"

"Uh-huh." Her mouth dropped open, and she held a hand up. "Sir. I'm sorry."

Meyers chuckled. "That's fine, Private. This is just us. Off the record."

She seemed to relax. "I didn't feel comfortable sharing this with anyone else, not even Ladell. Um, Agent Barlowe. Not yet. I think he's too angry right now."

"I think we're all upset. We lost a lot of soldiers. A lot of people suffered."

"I understand, sir. The thing is, what we went through, it was all a dead end. The people who funded it, they didn't even know who was behind it."

"The people who funded—" Meyers drummed his fingers on the table. "You mean the metacorporations?"

"No, sir. The people we killed in that complex. Well, the things we killed."

"But those were metacorporate proxies."

"No, sir, they weren't."

Meyers shifted in his chair. The headache seemed to be returning. "If the metacorporations didn't fund this, then—"

"They may have, sir. We're probably never going to know, though. But the things we destroyed down there, they weren't metacorporate proxies. I don't even think they were proxies, not like we're used to thinking of." Starling glanced up at one of the displays, and images appeared: the oversized chrome processor from the hidden room, pictures of the reclining proxies, and video of the compound interior. She froze the video and highlighted some of the gear. "I've been analyzing some of the data I captured. It's going to be a while tearing it apart. But this equipment? It's part of a dedicated network. They had a Grid within a Grid down there. It was running through that processor, and it used wiring and a non-standard frequency. Good encryption, too. Really good. I may have to get Ladell to help me crack it."

She focused on one of the reclining proxies. "But I don't need to get in deep to know that these weren't proxies. I mean, they were. Sort of. But not..." She sucked in a breath and let it out slowly.

"What?"

"Okay. Every proxy driver has an ID, almost always their Grid ID. Even the metacorporations give their people Grid IDs. Even the genies had them. So that's logged, right? Inside the proxies, it's logged. In case something goes wrong. That's the law, and it's built into proxy systems. You can always track back who was in control of the proxy at any time."

Meyers drew a circle on the tabletop with his index finger. "People can get around that. Any system can be broken."

"I know. Sir. But these proxies had the logs. I checked. I have copies.

And I may not have the data traffic through that Grid-within-a-Grid, but I have the end traffic."

"The logs?"

Starling nodded. "And those logs say a lot. These things knew we were coming. Down to the minute when you would land to set up that Operations Center."

"Of course they knew. They built a trap and laid out bait."

"No, sir. Someone was feeding them data, data that could only come from someone inside the ERF or the UN." She lowered her head. "Or the Intelligence Bureau."

Meyers's fingers froze in mid-drumming. "That's a big accusation."

"That's why I didn't want to make it in front of anyone else, sir." Starling seemed to struggle to meet his eyes. "You're the only person I feel I can trust with this right now."

The headache pounded against Meyers's skull. He was still struggling with the aftereffects of the concussion, and he felt ashamed asking for medical attention with the infirmaries full of seriously wounded. "You keep calling the people behind this 'things.' Why?"

"Because I don't know what else to call them. They're not human."

"Not human? What's that mean?"

Starling seemed to study the conference room table for a few seconds, then the image of the oversized processor appeared on the display. "Those IDs? The people who ran all those proxies?" She pointed at the chrome system processor on the display. "They're in here, Colonel. They're some sort of AI."

THE END

ACKNOWLEDGMENTS

Thank you for reading *Valley of Death*. I hope you found it a worthy follow-up to *Turning Point*. As you might have guessed, the story of the Elite Response Force continues, with the next few books constituting a pretty significant trilogy, starting with *Jungle Dark*.

This book draws from the events of Operation Anaconda, which was an important battle early in the Afghanistan conflict. I was retired by the time 9/11 happened, but I followed the war in Afghanistan closely. It was heartbreaking reading about some of the engagements, but I took heart from the acts of brave service members.

If you enjoyed *Valley of Death*, I hope you'll consider posting a review and letting friends know about the book. Reviews can make or break a book.

For updates on new releases and news on other series, please visit my website and sign up for my mailing list at:

http://www.p-r-adams.com

ABOUT THE AUTHOR

I was born and raised in Tampa, Florida. I joined the Air Force, and my career took me from coast to coast before depositing me in the St. Louis, Missouri area for several years. After a tour in Korea and a short return to the St. Louis area, I retired and moved to the greater Denver, Colorado metropolitan area.

I write speculative fiction, mostly science fiction and fantasy. My favorite writers over the years have been Robert E. Howard, Philip K. Dick, Roger Zelazny, and Michael Crichton.

Social Media:
www.p-r-adams.com
pradams_author@comcast.net